R

P9-CQN-340

COPYCaT

Also by ERICA SPINDLER

KILLER TAKES ALL
SEE JANE DIE
IN SILENCE
DEAD RUN
BONE COLD
ALL FALL DOWN
CAUSE FOR ALARM
SHOCKING PINK
FORTUNE
FORBIDDEN FRUIT
RED

ERICA SPINDLER

COPYCAT

PAPL
DISCARDED

MIRA®

ISBN 0-7783-2312-9

COPYCAT

Copyright © 2006 by Erica Spindler.

All rights reserved. Except for use in any review, the reproduction or utilization of this work in whole or in part in any form by any electronic, mechanical or other means, now known or hereafter invented, including xerography, photocopying and recording, or in any information storage or retrieval system, is forbidden without the written permission of the publisher, MIRA Books, 225 Duncan Mill Road, Don Mills, Ontario, Canada M3B 3K9.

All characters in this book have no existence outside the imagination of the author and have no relation whatsoever to anyone bearing the same name or names. They are not even distantly inspired by any individual known or unknown to the author, and all incidents are pure invention.

MIRA and the Star Colophon are trademarks used under license and registered in Australia, New Zealand, Philippines, United States Patent and Trademark Office and in other countries.

Printed in U.S.A.

First Printing: June 2006
10 9 8 7 6 5 4 3 2 1

For Rita J. Spindler
mother, mentor, best friend

AUTHOR'S NOTE

When I decided to set *Copycat* in my childhood hometown of Rockford, Illinois, I didn't fully realize what a great setting Rockford would prove to be, or how much I'd enjoy making that "trip home." Nor would I have been able to guess that I would actually finish this novel while living in Rockford, displaced by a she-devil named Katrina.

I discovered that much about Rockford has changed in the years I've lived away—but much has not. It's still a close-knit community of hardworking folks who don't put on airs. Families come first, people are welcoming and really good pizza can be found on almost every block. With all that in mind, I offer an apology: sorry, but in this type of novel people have to die, neighborhoods must be singled out for murders to occur in and yes, somebody has to be a really twisted bad guy—even in a breadbasket community like this one.

Everyone I spoke with at the Rockford Police Department was welcoming, and they were consummate professionals. Special thanks to Deputy Chief of Detectives Dominic Iasparro, Officer Carla Redd and Identification Bureau Detective Gene Koelker.

Huge thanks to my sister-in-law Pam Schupbach, the most bighearted woman I know. Not only did she act as hotelier, tour guide and chauffeur while I refamiliarized myself with Rockford, but she housed me again after hurricane Katrina, even taking on the role of babysitter so I could finish this novel.

On the home front, thanks to Mariea Sweitzer, former St. Tammany sheriff's deputy, for the information on phone trace technology—great help for a technology-challenged writer.

Finally, appreciation to the people who provide day-to-day professional support: my agent Evan Marshall, editor Dianne Moggy and assistant Kari Williams. And as always, last but first, thanks to my family for the love and my God for the blessings.

part  one

Rockford, Illinois
Tuesday, March 5, 2001
1:00 a.m.

The girl's hair looked silky. He longed to feel it against his fingers and cursed the latex gloves, the necessity that he wear them. The strands were the color of corn silk. Unusual in a child of ten. Too often, as the years passed, the blond darkened until settling on a murky, dishwater color that only bleach could resuscitate.

He cocked his head, pleased with his choice. She was even more beautiful than the last girl. More perfect.

He bent closer, stroked her hair. Her blue eyes gazed lifelessly up at him. Breathing deeply, he let her sweet, little-girl scent fill his head.

Careful...careful...

Mustn't leave anything for them.

The Other One insisted on perfection. Always pushing him. Demanding more. And more.

Always watching. Every time he looked over his shoulder, the Other One was there.

He felt himself frown and worked to smooth the telltale emotion from his face.

My pretty baby. Most beautiful creation.

Sleeping Angel.

The woman detective, Kitt Lundgren, had coined the name Sleeping Angel Killer. The media had jumped on it.

The name pleased him.

But not the Other One. Nothing, it seemed, pleased him.

Quickly, he finished arranging the scene. Her hair. The nightgown he had chosen just for her, with its pink satin bows. Everything had to be just so.

Perfect.

And now for the finishing touch. He took the tube of pale pink lip gloss from his pocket. Using the wand, he applied a coat of the gloss to the girl's lips. Carefully, smoothing, making certain the color was even.

That done, he smiled at his handiwork.

Good night, my little angel. Sleep tight.

Violent Crimes Bureau detective Kitt Lundgren stood in the doorway to the child's bedroom, a queasy sensation in the pit of her stomach. Another girl was dead. Murdered in her own bed while her parents slept just down the hall.

Every parent's worst nightmare.

But for these parents, this family, a nightmarish reality.

The sounds of a scene being processed swirled around her. The click of a camera shutter, a detective on his cell phone, a muttered expletive, conversations.

Familiar sounds. Ones she had become accustomed to along with losing her squeamishness years ago.

But this was a child, the second victim in six weeks. Another ten-year-old girl.

The same age as her Sadie.

At the thought of her daughter, her chest tightened. Kitt fought the sensation, fought to keep focused on this child. On nailing the monster who had killed her.

He'd left the first scene eerily clean. Now they had another chance. Maybe this time the bastard had screwed up.

Kitt entered the bedroom. She moved her gaze over it, taking in the girlish interior. Walls painted a delicate blush pink. White provincial furniture, a canopy bed. Ruffled white eyelet curtains that matched the canopy. A shelf of American Girl dolls. She recognized Felicity; Sadie owned the same one.

In fact, the room was a near replica of Sadie's. Move the bed from the right side of the room to the left, add a desk in the corner and change the paint color from pink to peach.

Focus, Kitt. This isn't about Sadie. Do the job.

She glanced to her right. Her partner, Brian Spillare, had already arrived. He stood with Detective Scott Snowe, one of the Identification Bureau detectives. There were nine detectives and a supervisor in the ID Bureau. Unlike most big, urban PDs, crime scene techs in the Rockford Police Department were sworn officers, highly trained in all areas of evidence collection. ID processed the scene for fingerprints and trace evidence, collected blood and analyzed blood splatter and spray, retrieved bullets and casings, and ran ballistic checks. They had also been known to collect insects and larvae from corpses, whose life cycles aided in the determination of time of death. In addition, the ID guys were responsible for diagramming and photographing every scene and attending every autopsy, which they also photographed.

The fun never stopped for those guys.

After recovering the evidence, they shipped it to the state crime lab, located just down the street from the Public Safety Building, or PSB, as they called the structure that housed not only the Rockford PD, but the sheriff's department, city jail and the coroner's office as well.

The deputy chief of detectives had sent the entire ID Bureau to the scene. Kitt wasn't surprised. Two dead children in six weeks was a very big deal in this family-first industrial town that averaged only fifteen murders in an entire calendar year—none of those typically blond, blue-eyed girls safely tucked into their beds.

Kitt caught her partner's eye and pointed toward the bed. He held up a finger, indicating she wait. She did; he concluded his conversation with the other detective and crossed to her.

"This guy is really starting to piss me off," he said.

Brian was a big guy. One of those easygoing, teddy-bear types. In his case, a teddy bear with freckles and red hair. His cuddly good looks masked a damn impressive temper. If a bad guy crossed Brian, he invariably wished he hadn't.

She would love for Brian to get his hands on this bastard.

"You been here long?" she asked.

"Maybe fifteen minutes." He glanced toward the victim, then back at her. "You think he'll go for three?"

"I hope to hell not," she said. "He certainly won't if we catch his ass."

He nodded, then touched her arm, leaned toward her. "How's Sadie?"

Dying. Her daughter, her only child. Kitt's throat closed as emotion swamped her. Five years ago, Sadie had been diagnosed with acute lymphatic leukemia. She had rallied so many times in the past, from chemo and radiation treatments, from the bone marrow transplant that hadn't been successful, but Kitt sensed she had given up. That she simply didn't have the reserves to hold on much longer.

Kitt couldn't speak and shook her head. Brian squeezed her arm, understanding. "How about you?" he asked. "You hanging in there?"

More like hanging on, by her fingernails. "Yeah," she managed to say, the catch in her voice giving her away. "As best I can."

To his credit, Brian didn't call her on it. He, more than anyone other than her husband, Joe, knew what she was going through.

Brian gave her arm another gentle squeeze, then released it. They crossed to the victim. Kitt pushed all expectations of what she would see from her mind. Yes, it appeared the same unknown subject, or UNSUB, had killed both these children, but she needed to come to this scene, this murder, fresh. A good investigator always let the scene and its evidence tell the story. The minute a detective started doing the talking instead of the listening, objectivity—and credibility—went out the window.

The first look at the dead girl hit her hard.

Like the last one, she'd been pretty. Blond. Blue-eyed. Save for the gruesome indications of death—lividity, petechiae (blood vessels broken in the eyes and lips) and the advancing rigor mortis—she appeared to be sleeping.

A sleeping angel.

Just like the last one.

Her blond hair fanned out around her head on the pillow, like a halo. Obviously, the killer had brushed and arranged it. Kitt leaned closer. The killer had applied lip color to her mouth, a sheer pink gloss.

"Looks like she was suffocated," Brian offered. "Just like the last one."

The absence of outward signs of violence and the petechiae supported suffocation, and Kitt nodded. "Which means the killer applied the lip gloss postmortem." She glanced at her partner. "What about the gown?"

"Same as the last. Mother says it's not hers."

Kitt frowned. It was a beautiful gown, white with ruffles and tiny pink satin bows. "And her father?"

"Nothing new. Neither of them touched the body. Mother came in to wake the girl up for school, took one look at her and screamed. Father came running. Called 911."

She would have found the fact they hadn't touched their child weird, but with all the press about the previous murder, the mother would have only needed one look to know her daughter had been a victim of the same monster.

"We have to check them out," he said.

Kitt nodded. Overwhelmingly, fewer children were murdered by strangers than by their own family, a statistic that seemed impossible to most but was a grim reality for cops.

However, this time they both knew the chances of this being a domestic incident were slim. They had a serial child killer on their hands.

"Like last time, it appears he came in through the window," Brian said.

Kitt glanced at her partner. "It was unlocked?"

"Must have been. Glass is intact, no marks on the casing. Snowe says they're going to take the entire window."

"Footprints on the other side?" Kitt asked, though since it hadn't rained in a week, the earth below the window would be rock hard.

"Nope. Screen was cut, nice and neat."

She brought a hand to the back of her neck. "What does it mean, Brian? What's he telling us?"

"That he's a sick prick who deserves to be skinned alive?"

"Besides that? Why the lip gloss? The fancy nightgowns? Why the little girls?"

From the other room came a sudden, rending wail of grief. The sound struck Kitt way too close to home and she shuddered.

How would she go on without Sadie?

Brian looked at her, face tight with anger. "I have daughters. I could go to bed one night and the next morning find—" He flexed his fingers. "We need to nail this bastard."

"We will," Kitt muttered fiercely. "If it's the last thing I ever do, I'm bringing this son of a bitch down."

part  two

3

Rockford, Illinois
Tuesday, March 7, 2006
8:10 a.m.

The shrill scream of the phone awakened Kitt from a deep, phar-maceutically induced sleep. She fumbled for the phone, nearly dropping it twice before she got it to her ear. "H'lo."

"Kitt. It's Brian. Get your ass up."

She cracked open her eyes. The sunlight streaming through the blinds stung. She shifted her gaze to the clock, saw the time and dragged herself to a sitting position.

She must have killed the alarm.

She glanced at Joe's side of the bed, wondering why he hadn't awakened her, then caught herself. Even after three years, she ex-pected him to be there.

No husband. No child.

All alone now.

Kitt coughed and sat up, working to shake out the cobwebs. "Calling so early, Lieutenant Spillare? Must be something pretty damn earth-shattering."

"The bastard's back. Shattering enough?"

She knew instinctively "the bastard" he referred to—the Sleeping Angel Killer. The case she never solved, though her obsession with it nearly destroyed both her life and career.

"How—"

"A dead little girl. I'm at the scene now."

Her worst nightmare.

After a five-year hiatus, the SAK had killed again.

"Who's working it?"

"Riggio and White."

"Where?"

He gave a west Rockford address, a blue-collar neighborhood that had seen better days.

"Kitt?"

She was already out of the bed, scrambling for clothes. "Yeah?"

"Tread carefully. Riggio's—"

"A little intense."

"Territorial."

"Noted, my friend. And...thanks."

4

Tuesday, March 7, 2006
8:25 a.m.

Detective Mary Catherine Riggio, M.C. to everyone but her mother, turned and nodded to Lieutenant Spillare as he reentered the murder scene. None of their fellow officers who witnessed the exchange would guess that the two of them had a personal history—an ill-conceived affair during the time he had been separated from his wife.

The affair had ended. He had gone back to his wife, and she to her senses. She had been considerably younger, new to the force and starstruck. Brian Spillare, then a decorated detective with the Violent Crimes Bureau, had been larger than life, on his way up the RPD ladder. His on-the-job war stories had affected her like an aphrodisiac. Where most women reacted to "sweet nothings" whispered in their ears, stories about bullets, blood and busting the bad guys revved M.C.'s engine.

No one had ever accused her of being a typical girl.

She had come away from the affair, heart intact and an important lesson learned: playing hide-the-salami with a superior was not the way to be taken seriously. She'd vowed to never put herself in that position again.

M.C. crossed to the lieutenant and was immediately joined by her partner, Detective Tom White. Tom was a thirtysomething African-American, tall and slim with elegant features. He and his wife had just had their third child, and the nights of interrupted sleep showed on his face. All in all, Tom was a damn fine detective and a good man, and though their partnership was new, it was solid. He respected both her skills and instincts without any of that annoying "Me Tarzan, You Jane" crap.

During her year in the Violent Crimes Bureau, M.C. had gone through a number of partners. She was, admittedly, intense and ambitious. She recognized that about herself. She recognized that a little softening around the edges would endear her to her fellow officers, but she just couldn't bring herself to change. If she felt she was right, she fought for it—no matter who thought otherwise. Even a superior, like Brian Spillare.

Warm and fuzzy was for baby ducks and bunnies.

"This looks familiar, doesn't it?" she said.

The lieutenant nodded. "Unfortunately, very familiar."

Five years ago, a series of three murders had sent the city, a town located ninety miles west of Chicago on the edge of corn country, into a panic. The nature of the crimes and the fact that the victims were all blond-haired, blue-eyed girls, murdered in their own bedrooms while family members slept nearby, had struck the very heart of the community's sense of safety. M.C. had been working patrol at the time; they'd gotten calls for every bump in the night.

Then the killings stopped. And after a time, life had returned to normal.

Now it appeared he might be back.

She narrowed her eyes on Brian. He no longer worked in the Detective Bureau, but had been promoted and was supervisor of the Central Reporting Unit, or CRU for short. The CRU took all calls to the RPD, was responsible for all accident reports and registered all sex offenders.

But she understood his interest in this murder. He had been one of the lead detectives assigned to the original case. The other had been Kitt Lundgren.

M.C. struggled to recall the details of the case, of Detective Lundgren's part in it. Solving the Sleeping Angel murders had been the department's biggest priority; Lundgren's leadership had been the talk of the RPD. The detective had become obsessed with catching the perpetrator. She'd let other cases slide, had defied her supervisor and was rumored to have let the killer slip through her fingers. M.C. recalled stories of bungled crime scenes, alcohol abuse and ultimately, forced leave.

A leave Lundgren had only recently returned from. One that had included a stint in rehab.

M.C. frowned. "Lundgren's a head case."

"True," Brian said. "But with what she's been through, she's earned it. Cut her some slack."

Tom White stepped in. "Pathologist's here."

The coroner's office employed two full-time forensic pathologists. They went to the scene of every death, made the official pronouncement of death, examined and photographed the body and brought it to the morgue for autopsy.

This one, Frances Roselli, the older of the two, was a small, neat man of Italian descent.

"Frances," Brian said, crossing to him. "It's been a while."

"Lieutenant. Not long enough, no offense."

"None taken. You know Detectives Riggio and White."

He nodded in their direction. "Detectives. What've we got?"

"Dead child," M.C. said. "Ten years old. She appears to have been suffocated."

He looked to Brian, as if for confirmation. "Sounds like the Sleeping Angel Killer's MO."

"Unfortunately, that's what it looks like."

The pathologist sighed. "I could have lived the rest of my life without another one of those cases."

"Tell me about it." Brian shook his head. "Press is going to be all over us."

M.C. looked at her partner. "Let's get the door-to-door of the neighborhood started. See if anybody saw or heard anything unusual last night."

Tom agreed. "I'll get a couple uniforms on it."

"The house is for sale. I want a list of every Realtor and every prospective buyer who's been through."

"Looks like it's been freshly painted, as well," Tom said. "Let's get the names of painters and handymen who've been within a hundred feet of the place."

M.C. nodded, then turned to the pathologist. "When will you have a report?"

"As early as tonight."

"Good," she said. "Expect a call."

Kitt double-parked her Ford Taurus in front of the modest home. To keep the curious away and provide parking for official vehicles, the first officers had cordoned off the street a hundred feet in both directions. She saw the coroner's Suburban, the crime-scene van, a half-dozen patrol units and an equal number of unmarked squad cars.

She swept her gaze over the home—a small blue box, probably not even a thousand square feet of living space. Outsourcing and downsizing had hit Rockford hard. Industries like Rockwell International and U.S. Filter, once major area employers, were gone. Other, smaller outfits continued to limp along, but the forecast looked bleak. Last total she heard, the area had lost thirty thousand manufacturing jobs. A drive through town supported that figure—there was one empty factory after another.

Kitt had lived in Rockford, a meat-and-potatoes kind of community with a large Italian and Swedish population, all of her forty-eight years. In truth, she'd never even toyed with the idea of leaving, even after Sadie died and her marriage ended. Rockford was her home. She liked living here. Folks didn't put on airs, fabulous pizza could be found every second block, and if she craved a bit of glitz and glamour, Chicago was just over an hour away.

Frankly, she rarely craved the glitz and glamour. She was one of those people who found comfort in middle-class familiarity.

She climbed out of her vehicle, and the gray, chilly day enveloped her. She shivered and hunched deeper into her jacket. In northern Illinois, winters were hard, springs slow to come and summers too short. But the falls were glorious. She figured the residents deserved it for sticking out the rest of the year's weather.

She crossed to the crime-scene tape and ducked under it, then headed directly for the first officer. She signed the scene log, ignoring the curious glances of her fellow officers. She didn't blame them for their interest; she had only returned from forced leave eight weeks ago and had been assigned nothing but no-brainer assault-and-battery cases.

Until this morning, uncertain of her own emotional strength, she had been fine with that. Grateful Sal Minelli, the deputy chief of detectives, had allowed her back. She'd melted down on the job, big-time. She'd jeopardized cases, endangered her fellow officers and the department's reputation.

Sal had championed her, as had Brian. She would be forever in their debt. What would she have done otherwise? She was a cop. It was all she had ever been.

No, she thought. Once upon a time, she had been a wife. And a mom.

She shook the thought off. The memories that came with it. The ache.

Kitt stepped into the house. It was warm inside. The child's parents huddled on the couch. Kitt didn't make eye contact. She swept her gaze over the interior. Pin neat, cheap furnishings. Sculptured carpeting that had obviously seen its day; walls painted a handsome sage color.

She followed the sound of voices to the girl's bedroom. *Too many people in this small room. Detective Riggio should be doing a better job controlling traffic.*

She wasn't surprised to see Brian, though he was no longer part of the detective unit. As if getting wind of her presence, Mary Catherine Riggio turned and stared at her. In the eighteen months she had been away, a handful of officers had made rank of detective; of them one, Mary Catherine Riggio, had joined the VCB. From what she'd heard, the woman was smart, ambitious and uncompromising. All to a fault.

Kitt met her eyes, nodded slightly in acknowledgment, then continued toward the bed.

One look at the victim told her it was true: he *was* back.

Kitt swallowed hard against the guilt that rushed up, threatening to drown her. Guilt at not having nailed the son of a bitch five years ago, about allowing him to kill again.

She wanted to look away but couldn't. Despair overwhelmed her. Her daughter's image filled her head, memories of her last days.

A cry crept up from the depths of her being. She held it in. Her daughter's death and the Sleeping Angel murders had become weirdly, irrevocably intertwined in her mind.

She knew why. She and her shrink had discussed this one ad nauseam: the first Sleeping Angel murder had occurred as Sadie was slipping away. Her fight to keep her daughter alive had mirrored her fight to stop the SAK, to keep the other girls alive.

God help her, she'd lost both battles.

Kitt suddenly realized that this victim's hands were positioned differently than the others had been. In the original killings, each victim's hands had been folded primly on her chest. This one's were posed strangely, the fingers curled, one seeming to point to her own chest, the other out, as if at another.

It might mean nothing. A variation in the killer's ritual. After all, five years had passed since the last known victim.

She didn't think so. The SAK she had hunted had been precise, his scenes had never varied and he had never left the police anything to work with.

Excited, she turned and called Brian over. Riggio and White came with him.

The other woman didn't give her a chance to speak. "Hello, Detective Lundgren."

"Detective Riggio."

"I appreciate you coming out to offer your perspective."

"Thank you, Detective," Kitt said, though Mary Catherine Riggio looked anything *but* appreciative. Kitt shifted her attention to her former partner. "The hands are different."

Brian nodded, expression admiring. "I'd forgotten." He looked at M.C. "In all the previous murders, the hands were positioned the same way. Folded on the chest, near the heart."

Roselli looked over his shoulder at them. "Actually, the hands present a very interesting scenario."

M.C. frowned. "Why?"

"Clearly, the positioning is unnatural. In which case, the killer posed them postmortem."

"No surprise there. What's so—"

"Interesting? How long he waited to do it after the death."

"I don't understand," Kitt said. "He had to act fast, before rigor mortis set in."

The pathologist shook his head. "Wrong, Detective. He had to wait until *after* rigor mortis set in."

For several seconds, no one spoke. M.C. broke the silence first. "What kind of window are we talking about?"

"A small one. Depending on temperature, rigor mortis sets in two to six hours after death. Since the furnace is running and the house is relatively warm, my guess is it took three to four hours."

Kitt couldn't believe what she was hearing. "Are you saying he sat here and *waited* for her to get stiff?"

"That's exactly what I'm saying. And for his patience to pay off, the body had to be discovered before rigor mortis broke at ten to twelve hours after death."

Brian whistled. He looked at Kitt. "The hand position is extremely important to him."

"He's making a bold statement. An arrogant one."

"Most killers get in and out, as quickly as possible."

"Most *smart* ones," Kitt corrected. "And the original SAK was damn intelligent."

"So, what does the positioning mean?"

"Me and you," White offered.

Kitt nodded. "Us and them. In and out."

"Or nothing," M.C. said, sounding irritated.

"Doubtful. Considering the risk he took to pose them." Brian glanced at Kitt. "Anything else jump out at you as different?"

She shook her head. "Not that I've noticed—yet." She shifted her gaze to Detective Riggio. "Is anything missing from the scene?"

"Excuse me?"

"The original SAK didn't take a trophy from his victim. Which, of course, doesn't fit the typical profile of a serial killer."

M.C. and White exchanged glances. "We'll need the girl's parents to carefully inventory her things," she said.

White nodded and made a note in his spiral.

"You mind if I study the scene a bit more?" In an effort to earn the other woman's good will, Kitt directed the question Riggio's way, though asking Brian would have yielded an easy yes and, as the superior officer of the group, his decision would have been unarguable.

But Detective Riggio was lead on the case and, Kitt could tell, hungry to prove herself. She was one of those "ballbuster" women cops, a type Kitt had seen too often. Police work was still a boys' club—women had to fight to be taken seriously. Until they were, they were relegated to second-class citizens. So, many contorted themselves into humorless hard-asses with a severe case of testosterone envy. In other words, a woman acting like a man. Hell, she'd done a turn as one herself.

She knew better now. She had learned what made a female cop an asset was the very fact she *wasn't* a man. Her instincts, the way she responded and interacted—all were shaped by her gender.

"Go for it," she said. "Let me know if anything jumps out."

Nothing did, and forty minutes later, Kitt left the scene. It felt wrong to be leaving without questioning the parents, lining up the neighborhood canvas and other interviews.

Dammit, this should be her case! She'd worked her ass off to solve it five years ago, every nuance of this killer's MO was burned onto her brain.

She'd also blown it. And it had been ugly.

"Lundgren!"

Kitt stopped and turned. Mary Catherine Riggio strode toward her, expression set. "I wanted a word with you before you left."

No surprise there. She folded her arms across her chest. "Floor's yours."

"Look, I know your history. I know how important the SAK case was to you, and how it must feel to be shut out now."

"Shut out? Is that what I am?"

"Don't play games with me, Lundgren. It's my case, and I'm asking you to put aside your personal feelings and respect that."

"In other words, butt out."

"Yes."

Kitt cocked an eyebrow at the other woman's arrogance. "May I remind you, Detective, I know every detail of the original SAK killings. Should this one prove to be a fourth, that knowledge would be invaluable to you."

"May I remind you, Detective, that each and every one of those case details are already available to me."

"But my instincts—"

"Are shot. And you know it."

Kitt fought the urge to become defensive. Riggio would perceive it as weak emotionalism. "I know this guy," she said instead. "He's smart. Cautious. He plans his crimes down to the tiniest detail. He prides himself on his intellect, the fact that he keeps emotion out of his crimes.

"He stalks the children, learns their routines. Bedtimes. Location of their bedrooms. Spots the ones who are vulnerable."

"What makes them vulnerable?"

"Different things. The parents' situations. Socioeconomics."

"How are you so certain?"

"Because for the past five years, I ate, drank and shit this son of a bitch. Catching him is nearly all I've thought about."

"Then why haven't you?"

Kitt couldn't answer. The one time she'd gotten close, she had blown it.

Riggio leaned toward her. "Look, Lundgren, I have nothing against you. I've been a cop long enough to know how the job can get to you. How a case can get to you. But that's not my problem. This is my case. Stand back and let me nail this guy."

"I was so arrogant, once upon a time."

Riggio turned to go. "Whatever."

Kitt caught her arm. "Wouldn't working together be a benefit? Wouldn't my experience with the SAK be a benefit? If you spoke to Sal—"

"That's not going to happen. I'm sorry."

Kitt doubted that. She dropped her hand and stepped back. "You know, Riggio, it's not about you. It's about catching this guy, no matter what it takes."

The other woman narrowed her eyes. "I'm well aware of what this is about, Detective Lundgren. I suggest you ask yourself if you are."

"I'll go to the deputy chief myself."

"Have a ball. We both know what he's going to say."

Kitt watched the other detective walk away, then climbed into her car. Problem was, she suspected she *did* know what he would say. But that wasn't going to stop her from trying.

Deputy Chief of Detectives Salvador Minelli listened quietly as Kitt presented her case. A strikingly handsome man, with silvering hair and at fifty-one, a nearly unlined face, he dressed with panache and walked with the barest hint of a swagger. These days, Sal—as almost every-one in the department called him—was as much a politician as a cop. In fact, most of those in the know felt he was the front-runner for the chief of police's job when he retired in a couple of years.

Sal had been a very good friend to her. He had been her supe-rior five years ago and had been as supportive as a man in his posi-tion could be, maybe more. He'd certainly gone to bat for her, facing the displeasure of the chief himself.

Perhaps it had been because he was the father of five. Perhaps because he came from a family that valued familial bonds above all else. He had seemed to understand how deeply painful the loss of Sadie had been.

"I know this guy," Kitt argued. "I know the SAK case better than anyone, you know that. Give Detective Riggio the lead spot, no problem. Let me assist."

He was quiet for long moments after she finished. He steepled his fingers. "Why are you doing this, Kitt?"

"Because I want this guy. I want him behind bars. Because I'd be an asset to the investigation."

"I suspect Detective Riggio would disagree on the last."

"Detective Riggio's young and overconfident. She needs me."

"You had your shot, Kitt. He slipped through your grasp."

"This time he won't."

He went on as if she hadn't spoken. "You know how important a fresh pair of eyes can be to a case."

"Yes, but—"

He held up a hand, stopping her. "Detective Riggio's good. Damn good."

There was a time, she knew, he had said the same about her. She doubted that would be the case again.

To a certain degree, she *had* become a liability.

"She's headstrong," Kitt countered. "Too ambitious."

He smiled. "White's a good ballast for that."

"How can I prove to you that I can handle it?"

"I'm sorry, Kitt. You're too close. Still too fragile."

"With all due respect, Sal, don't you think *I* should be the one to make that determination?"

"No," he said simply. He leaned forward. "Have you considered that working this case might overwhelm you and send you running back to the bottle?"

"It won't." She met his gaze unflinchingly. "I'm sober. I have been for nearly a year. I intend to stay that way."

He lowered his voice. "I can't protect you again, Kitt. You know what I'm talking about."

She'd let the SAK slip through her fingers.

Sal had covered for her. Because he had felt partly responsible.

And because of Sadie.

"I'll ask Riggio and White to keep you in the loop. Bounce things off you. It's the best I can do."

She stood, shocked to realize her hands were shaking. More shocked to realize that she longed for a drink to still them.

The urge she could never give into again.

"Thank you," she said, then crossed to the door.

He stopped her when she reached it. She turned back.

"How's Joe?" he asked.

Her ex-husband. High school sweetheart. Former best friend. "We don't talk much."

"You know how I feel about that."

She did. Hell, she felt the same way.

"If you see him, tell him I said hello."

She told him she would and walked away, with Joe suddenly very much on her mind.

7

Tuesday, March 7, 2006
5:30 p.m.

"Hello, Joe."

Her ex-husband looked up from the house plans on the desk in front of him. Although his blond hair had silvered over the years, his eyes were as blue as the day she had married him. Tonight, the expression in them was wary.

She supposed she didn't blame him. These days, she never just "popped in."

"Hello, Kitt," he said. "This is a surprise."

"Flo already left," she said, referring to the woman who served as both his secretary and office manager. "So I came on in. How's business?"

"Picking up. Thank God spring's here."

Joe owned his own home-construction business, Lundgren Homes. Northern Illinois winters were tough on builders. Home starts simply didn't happen. The goal was to have several jobs closed in and ready for interior work by the time severe weather hit. Some winters, it had been pretty lean going.

"You look tired," she said.

"I guess I am." He passed a hand across his face. "Judging by the bulge, you're back on the job."

Her shoulder holster. Joe had never really gotten used to her wearing it. "Sal sends a hello."

He held her gaze. "And the drinking, how's—"

"Still sober. Eleven months and counting. I plan to stay that way."

"I'm glad to hear that, Kitt."

He meant it, she knew. He had seen the alcohol almost destroy her. And though they'd divorced, he still cared for her. As she did him.

She cleared her throat. "Something's happened. The Sleeping Angel Killer…it looks like he's back."

He didn't speak. Didn't move. She saw several different emotions chase across his face. "A little girl named Julie Entzel," she continued. "They found her this morning."

"I'm sorry." He shifted his gaze to the plans laid out in front of him. "Sal has you working the case?"

"No, he thinks I'm too close. Too…vulnerable."

He looked back up at her. "But you don't agree?"

His tone had taken on an edge. She stiffened slightly, defensive. "I see you do."

He made a sound, part frustration, part anger. "You chose that case over our marriage. Over me. I'd call that 'too close.'"

"Let's not start this, Joe."

He stood. She saw that his hands were clenched. "Even after the killings stopped, you couldn't let it go. Even after Sal closed the case."

That was true. It had consumed her. Fueled her drinking, her defiance of direct orders. But she had not chosen it over him. She told him so.

He laughed, the sound bitter. "That case became the focus of your life. *I* should have been your focus. Our marriage. This family."

"What family?" She regretted the words the moment they passed her lips. She saw how much they hurt him.

She started to say so; he cut her off. "Why are you here?"

"I thought you'd want to know. About the little girl."

"Why?"

She frowned. "I don't understand."

"Julie Entzel wasn't our daughter, Kitt. None of those girls were. I'd never met even one of them. And that's the part you never got."

"Oh, I got that, Joe. But I feel a sense of responsibility that you, obviously, don't. I feel a need to help. To do...something."

"Don't you think my heart breaks for that little girl, her folks? I know what it's like to lose a child. That some monster could do such a thing sickens me." He cleared his throat. "But she wasn't Sadie. She wasn't ours. You've got to move on with your life."

"The way you have?" she shot back.

"Actually, yes." He paused for a long moment. When he spoke again, his tone was flat. "I'm getting remarried, Kitt."

For several seconds, she simply gazed at him, certain she had misheard. She must have. Her Joe, getting remarried?

"You don't know her," he went on, before she could ask. "Her name's Valerie."

Kitt's mouth had gone dry. She felt light-headed. What? Had she expected him to pine for her forever?

Yes.

She struggled to keep her turmoil from showing. "I didn't know you were seeing anyone so seriously."

"No reason you should have."

No reason? She had a lifetime worth of reasons. "How long have you been dating?"

"Four months."

"Four months? Not very long. Are you certain—"

"Yes."

"When's the big day?" Her voice sounded strained even to her own ears.

"We haven't set one yet. Fairly soon. It'll be a small service. Just a few family members and close friends."

"I see."

He looked frustrated. "Is that all you have to say?"

"No." She stood, blinded by tears she would never allow him to see. "I hope you'll be very happy together."

8

Kitt sat at her desk, brown-bag lunch untouched, thumbing through the original Sleeping Angel case files. The information was available electronically, but she preferred to review hard copies.

She slipped out the scene photos of the first victim. Mary Polaski. It hurt to look at her. She had let this little victim down. She had let her family down.

Kitt forced such thoughts from her mind and studied the photos, comparing them to those of Julie Entzel. Why had he positioned the hands this way? Why take the chance of remaining at the scene for hours? What had been so important to him?

Her phone rang; Kitt reached for it without taking her gaze from the photos. "Detective Lundgren, Violent Crimes Bureau."

"The Detective Lundgren who was in charge of the Sleeping Angel case five years ago?"

"Yes. Can I help you?"

"Actually, I think I can help *you*."

The call didn't surprise her; the morning newspaper headline had read: Sleeping Angel Killer Returns. What surprised her was the fact she hadn't received one before now. "Always happy to have help. Your name?"

"I'm someone you've wanted to meet for a very long time."

The sly amusement in his tone grated. She didn't have time for wackos. Or for games. She told him so.

"I'm the Sleeping Angel Killer."

For the space of a heartbeat she wondered if it could be true. Could it be this easy?

Of course it couldn't.

"You're the Sleeping Angel Killer," she repeated. "And you want to help me?"

"I didn't kill that little girl. The one in the paper today."

"Julie Entzel."

"Yeah, her." She heard a hissing sound, as if he were taking a drag on a cigarette. She made a note. "Someone ripped me off."

"Ripped you off?"

"Copied me. And I don't like it."

Kitt glanced around her. Everyone, it seemed, was either out on a call or at lunch. She stood and waved her free arm, hoping to catch the attention of someone walking by. She needed to initiate a trace.

"I want you to catch this asshole and stop him."

"I want to help you," she said. "But I've got another call coming in. Can you hold a moment?"

"Now who's playing games?" She heard him exhale. "Here are the rules. I won't talk to anyone but you, Kitt. May I call you Kitt?"

"Sure. What should I call you?"

He ignored her question. "Nice name. Kitty. Kitten. Feminine.

Sexy. Doesn't fit a cop, though." Another pause, another deep in-hale. "Of course, everybody calls you Detective. Or Lundgren. Isn't that right?"

"That's right," she said. "But here's the thing, I'm not working the Entzel murder. I'll transfer you to the team who is."

He ignored her. "Rule number two. Don't expect anything for free. And don't expect it to be easy. Everything costs. I determine payment."

His voice was deep. Relatively youthful. The smoking hadn't yet altered that. She would place his age between twenty-five and thirty-five. "Is there a rule number three?"

"There may be. I haven't decided yet."

"And if I don't want to play by your rules?"

He laughed. "You will. Or more little girls will die."

Shit. Where the hell was everyone? "All right. Just give me a reason to believe you're anything more than a crank. Something to take to my chief—"

"Goodbye, Kitten."

He hung up. She swore and dialed the Central Reporting Unit. Because all the department calls were routed through a switch-board, a trace had to be manually initiated on a per call basis. How-ever, the number of each call that came into the RPD switchboard was automatically trapped.

"This is Lundgren in Violent Crimes. I just received a call to my desk. I need the number, ASAP."

She hung up and two minutes later CRU called her back. It was Brian himself. "It was a cell number, Kitt. What's up?"

A cell number. Unlike a call made from a landline, which could be trapped in ten seconds of continuous connection, one from a cell took five minutes. If the guy was smart, he also knew that all new cellular phones included a GPS chip that allowed a call's location to be pinpointed within ten minutes. Older models, without the new technology, would take hours.

COPYCAT   45

She glanced at her watch. She would guess the call had lasted no more than three minutes. Which meant this guy understood trace technology.

"Guy claimed he was the SAK," she said. "The original SAK. Said Julie Entzel's murder isn't his."

Brian whistled. "Obviously, you want a name and address to go along with that number?"

"ASAP." She glanced toward her sergeant's office and saw he was still out. "Call me back on my cell."

She hung up, collected her notes and headed for Sal's office. She paused as she saw Riggio and White entering the squad room. She pointed toward Sal's office. "You'll be interested in this."

She reached the deputy chief's, the other two detectives right behind her. She tapped on his open door.

He looked up, waved them in. Kitt didn't waste time on a preamble. "I just received a call from someone claiming to be the SAK." Seeing she had everyone's attention, she continued, "He also claimed he did not kill Julie Entzel."

"Why was he calling you?"

This came from Riggio, and Kitt met her gaze. "He wants me to find this copycat and stop him."

"You?"

"Yes."

"Why?"

"I don't know."

Sal frowned. "What else did you get from him?"

"I'm pretty sure he's a smoker. I guess his age to be between twenty-five and thirty-five. He told me—" She glanced at her notes. "'Someone ripped me off. Copied me. And I don't like it.'"

"Did you initiate a trace?"

"Everyone was at lunch or out on call. When I tried to put him on hold, he told me to stop playing games."

"You called CRU—"

"The minute he hung up. Call came from a cell phone. I'm waiting to hear back on the owner's name."

"The caller, did he say anything else?"

"He gave me two rules. Said if I didn't follow them, more little girls would die."

White stepped in before she could finish. "But he claims he didn't kill Julie Entzel? How's he so certain more girls will die?"

"He didn't tell me, so I can only suppose."

"Maybe he knows who the copycat is?" White offered.

"Maybe," Riggio agreed. "*If* we can believe anything he said."

Kitt cocked an eyebrow, growing annoyed with the other woman. "Would you like to hear the rest of what he said?"

Riggio nodded tersely, and Kitt went on. "He gave me two rules. The first—he won't talk to anyone but me."

"Please."

That came from Riggio. Kitt ignored her.

"And the second?" Sal asked.

"That nothing will be free. Or easy. The cost will be determined by him."

"He wants money?" That came from White.

Kitt looked at him. "I don't think that's the kind of 'cost' he was referring to. But he didn't ask for anything."

"Sure he did." Sal moved his gaze between the three. "He asked that you work the case." He picked up the phone and rang Nan Baker, the VCB secretary. "Nan, is Sergeant Haas back from lunch?" He paused. "Good. Get him in here."

Every bureau in the RPD had a senior officer. Sergeant Jonathan Haas was Violent Crime's. He had been Brian's partner before being promoted and was known around the bureau for being a solid cop.

The tall, fair-haired sergeant arrived. He smelled of the burger and fries he must have had for lunch. It looked as if he had dribbled "secret sauce" on his tie. Though the differences between the two men's personal styles was dramatic, Sal and Haas had a good relationship. In fact, early in both their careers, they had also been partners.

As Sal began filling him in, Kitt's cell rang. "Lundgren here."

"Kitt, Brian. Bad news. The number belongs to a prepaid cell phone. I have the name of the outlet that sold it."

Smarter than the average bear, obviously. "That'll have to do. Maybe we'll get lucky."

She ended the call. The sergeant turned to her. She greeted him, then filled the group in.

Haas nodded. "I want to initiate a trace on every call that comes in to you, here and at home. And I want them all recorded." He turned to Riggio. "Is the autopsy in?"

"Yes, Sarge. I picked it up last night. No new information, unfortunately. She was smothered, just like the three original SAK victims. Nails were clean. No sign of sexual assault. No defense wounds. Only the hematoma to the forehead."

"Any help there?" Sal asked.

"Pathologist believes it's a thumbprint."

White stepped in. "This guy's like a cat. Neighborhood canvas turned up zip."

Riggio took over. "Realtor promised to get back to me this morning with a list of everyone who's been through the house."

"Fingerprints?"

"ID Bureau's working on it. So far, everything's consistent with the three original killings."

"Except for the hands," Kitt said. "Big inconsistency there."

The room went silent.

Detective Riggio broke the silence first. "We have no proof this caller's not just another crank. The *Register Star* ran the story front and center this morning. This guy may have been the first to call in with a wild claim, but I hardly think he'll be the last."

"Point noted, Detective Riggio. But I'm not willing to put my money on that. Are you?"

"No, sir."

"Lundgren?"

"Chief?"

"Let us know if he contacts you again. Put in the trace orders now."

She nodded and unclipped her cell phone. "And if he does call, what do I tell him?"

"Say whatever the hell you have to to keep him on the line."

Meeting concluded, they exited the office. Out of their superior's earshot, Riggio leaned toward her. "Looks like you got what you wanted. You're in the loop."

"You have a problem with that?"

"Just don't forget who's lead on this one, Lundgren. It's my case."

"Somehow, I don't think you'd let me forget, Detective Riggio."

The woman looked as if she had more to say; Kitt didn't give her the chance. "If you'll excuse me, I have traces to order."

9

Wednesday, March 8, 2006
6:40 p.m.

M.C. dreaded Wednesday nights. Specifically, six-thirty to eight-thirty. "The Pasta Hours," she called them. That was when she—and all five of her siblings—assembled for a command performance at their mother's table. There, they would be skewered, then grilled on every aspect of their lives.

M.C. could feel the hot coals already—she was her mother's favorite entrée.

There wasn't a single thing about M.C. that her mother approved of. Nothing, nada. The big zippo. It used to bother her, but no longer. She'd realized that if she had wanted to become the woman her mother wanted her to be, she could have.

So, M.C. sucked it up week after week, only occasionally praying for a homicide that would keep her away.

She pulled up in front of her childhood home, a two-story farmhouse, minus the farm. She parked, frowning as she thought of Kitt
Lundgren and her anonymous caller.

Could the woman have fabricated the story in an attempt to ac-
tively participate in the investigation? Would she go that far?

Yes—if what she'd heard about Lundgren's obsession with the
case was true.

The suspicion left M.C. feeling uneasy and she glanced toward
the front porch. Michael and Neil stood there, deep in conversation. She smiled to herself. She'd affectionately nicknamed her five
siblings: the Overachiever, the Suck-up and the Three Ass-kissers.

Michael, the Overachiever, was the oldest. A chiropractor. In her
mother's world, the only thing better than one of her children
being called "Dr. Riggio" was their being called "Father Riggio." But
Michael—and the rest of the Riggio boy-brood—enjoyed women
and sex way too much for that particular calling, so Mama Riggio
had contented herself with "her son, the doctor."

Neil, the Suck-up, taught math at Boylan Central Catholic High
School, their alma mater, and coached the wrestling team. Very normal. He had also provided their mother with a daughter-in-law and
her first and, to date, only grandchild.

The three youngest of the boys, Tony, Max and Frank, had pooled
their resources and Mama's family recipes and opened Mama Riggio's Italian Restaurant. The trio had just opened their second location and had plans for a third, in the suburbs closer to Chicago.
The name of their restaurant had earned them the nickname the
Three Ass-kissers.

M.C. loved her brothers. Adored them, actually. Even the one
whose brainchild it had been to decorate Mama Riggio's with old
family photographs, including one of her with braces, zits and *really*
bad hair.

A photo they jumped at every opportunity to point out.

"And that's our only sister, Mary Catherine. She's unmarried, if you're interested."

Big yuk.

She climbed out of her SUV. "Hello, boys."

"Yo, M.C.," Neil called. "Looking wicked."

"Thanks," she called back, slamming the vehicle door. "Hoping to scare Mama."

And she just might. She was dressed all in black, her dark hair pulled into a severe ponytail.

"You packing heat?" Michael asked, tone teasing.

"Always. So, watch your step."

Of all her brothers, she was closest to Michael. Maybe because he had been kind to the little girl who had always been tagging after him, or because their minds worked in the same way.

She crossed to him. They hugged, then kissed each other's cheeks. She turned to Neil and did the same.

When she pulled away, he grinned at her. "I suggest you check that weapon at the door, Mama's in rare form tonight. You might be tempted to kill her."

"Justifiable homicide," she said. "There's not a judge in the city who'd convict."

Just then Benjamin, Neil's three-year-old, barreled out the door, his mother, Melody, in close pursuit. Neil's engagement to Melody—a willowy, Protestant, blue-eyed blonde—had been met with family fireworks. Marrying outside both faith and ethnicity? Mama Riggio had actually conjured chest pains over it.

The drama had taken the heat off M.C. for a good six months. Then Melody had ruined everything by becoming Catholic, then having Benjamin.

M.C. was surrounded by Suck-ups.

Benjamin caught sight of M.C. and squealed in delight. She squatted and held out her arms. He ran to her for a big hug and the treat he knew she would have in her pocket. Today it was a package of animal crackers.

"You spoil him," her sister-in-law said.

M.C. stood and smiled. "What're you going to do about it? Arrest me?"

Neil scooped up his son and helped him open the crackers. "How's the weather in there?" he asked his wife.

"Cloudy with a chance of thunderstorms. You know Mama."

They did, indeed, know Mama. They exchanged glances as if wondering whose neck would be on the chopping block tonight.

Michael looked at his watch. "The three pasta-pushers are late."

"Haven't they heard carbs are out?" M.C. said. "Again."

"Actually, I think they're back in," Neil murmured. "Again."

Just then, the three arrived, following one another in separate vehicles. M.C. saw that they were all on their cell phones. They parked and spilled out of their cars, still on their calls. Arguing. *With one another, for heaven's sake.*

They bounded up the steps, snapping their phones shut. She was immediately surrounded by the handsome, rowdy bunch. The noise level rose. Hugs, kisses and good-natured ribbing ensued.

God, she loved these oafs.

Melody broke up the reunion. "May I suggest we head inside? Before Mama—"

"Gets really ticked off," Neil offered. "Good suggestion."

They all headed in. Shouts of "Mama!" filled the house. The woman appeared in the doorway of the kitchen.

"You're late, all but Michael and Neil." She glared at M.C. "My only daughter and no help at all."

Apparently, it would be her neck. Big surprise.

"Sorry, Mama," she said, kissing her mother's nearly unlined cheeks. "I was working."

Her mother made a sound, her own unique cross between a snort and "Holy God." "Oh, yes, *that* job."

"Meaning exactly what?"

"You know how I feel about what you do. Police work? Please. That's no job for a woman."

M.C. opened her mouth to argue; Mama waved everyone to the table. As they took their seats, Melody stepped in, voice hushed. "Are you working that child murder?"

She nodded, glancing down the table at Benjamin. He seemed oblivious to everything but his animal crackers. "I'm lead detective."

"Congrats, li'l sister." That came from Michael and she smiled at him. He passed the bowl of spaghetti. She served herself, then passed it on.

"Is that madman really back?" Melody asked. "That Sleeping Angel guy?"

"It looks that way. But there were inconsistencies." Her brother handed her the platter of veal parmigiana, followed by green beans and salad.

"What kind of inconsistencies?" he asked.

She flashed him a smile. "You know I can't tell you that."

Max jumped in. "So, this could be a copycat killer?"

The table went quiet. All eyes turned to her. She thought of Kitt Lundgren's anonymous caller claiming a copycat had killed Julie Entzel. A funny sensation settled over her. "At this point in the investigation, anything's still possible."

"I'm glad I had a boy," Melody murmured. "I'd be scared to death otherwise."

"Enough!" Mama snapped. "What kind of dinner talk is this? And with the baby listening. Shame on you all."

"Sorry, Mama," they murmured in unison, just as they had been doing all their lives.

They turned their attention to their food, which was delicious. Her mother may be a supersize pain-in-her-ass, but she was a fabulous cook. If not for M.C.'s metabolism, she'd weigh four hundred pounds.

"Mary Catherine, you wouldn't believe who I ran into at the market." Mama beamed at her. "Joseph Rellini's mother."

Just call her clueless. "Who?"

"Joseph Rellini. He graduated from Boylan the year before you. Played in the band."

She vaguely remembered a dark-haired, stoop-shouldered boy. He had been pleasant enough, but she knew where this was heading and wasn't about to give her mother any encouragement. Not that she needed any.

"He's an accountant now." Mama Riggio leaned forward. "And single. I gave her your number, told her to have him call you."

"Mama, you didn't!"

"I most certainly did. *Per amor del cielo,* look at you! You could do worse."

Her brothers hooted. Melody made a sound of sympathy. M.C. glared at her mother. "I don't need a man to complete me, Mama. I'm fine on my own. Doing great."

"Every day at mass, I pray that you'll come to your senses, quit that job and bring a nice young man to dinner."

"Pardon me, Mother, but you are so full of—"

Michael cut her off. "She brought her Glock. Does that count?"

Tony jumped in. "Get used to it, Mama. She's a lesbian."

M.C. tossed her napkin at her brother. "Up yours, Tony."

"Mary Mother of God!" Mama lowered her voice. "When did this happen?"

"I'm not gay, Mama. Tony's just being a jerk."

"As usual," Max offered, refilling his wineglass. "For myself, I plan to play the field for a long time."

"You're a young man," Mama said. "But your sister's not getting any younger."

Melody, God love her, stepped in. "There's no rush. Take as long as you need to find the right guy, M.C. Life's too short to spend it in a so-so relationship."

"Speaking from experience?" Tony shot back, grinning.

Melody didn't take the bait. "Yes," she answered smoothly. "Experience married to the most wonderful man on the planet."

That brought a round of hoots and ribbing from her brothers. It also shifted Mama's focus—and gave M.C. an opportunity to escape.

She choked down enough of her meal for appearances and stood. "It's been real, gang, but I have to go."

"But we haven't had dessert yet!" Her mother exclaimed. "Cannolis. From Capelli's Market."

Capelli's cannoli was practically its own food group. It was that good.

But now that Mama had been tipped, there was no way she could stay without another round of "Roasting Mary Catherine."

She begged off, though she couldn't escape until she had made her way around the table to kiss everyone goodbye. She was nearly to her SUV when Michael called out to her.

She stopped and waited.

"Are you okay?" he asked when he reached her.

"Why wouldn't I be?"

"Like all good Riggios, you never pass on dessert."

"I guess I'd just had my fill."

He understood she wasn't talking about food. "She really does love you, you know."

"It's my life. Not hers. She needs to accept me for who I am."

"True." He nodded, his expression thoughtful. "But—"

He bit back whatever he was about to say, and she frowned. "What?"

"You won't beat me up, will you?"

"I'll shoot you if you don't speak your mind."

"Okay. It just seems to me, that door swings both ways."

"Excuse me?"

"The acceptance thing. You need to accept her the way she is."

"I do. But, she's my mother and she's supposed to be—"

"Everything you want her to be?"

"No. But she doesn't even make an effort!"

"Do you?" he countered.

Mary Catherine, like the rest of the Riggio clan, had a temper. Over the years, she had learned how to hold on to it.

This wasn't one of those times. Her temper rose; she felt herself flush. She gestured toward the house. "I'm here, aren't I? Every freaking Wednesday night."

He didn't respond and she lashed out at him. "It's easy for you. For all of you. The perfect sons. All of you have always been everything she wanted you to be. And everything Dad wanted you to be, as well. Males."

"The world's smallest violin, Mary Catherine. Just for you."

"Forget about it." She yanked open her car door. "Of all people, I would have thought you'd understand."

She slid inside the Explorer and slammed the door behind her. She started the car and drew away from the curb. She glanced in her rearview mirror and saw that he hadn't moved.

He cocked his head, grinning at her.

Muttering an oath, she slowed to a stop, lowered her window and leaned her head out. "I give up! I'll see you next week. But if you really loved me, you would have smuggled a cannoli out."

10

Buster's Bar was located in a section of town called Five Points, the spot where five major thoroughfares intersected. It was an area that seemed to fall in and out of favor, depending on what commercial endeavors—mostly bars, restaurants and clubs—happened to occupy the space at the time.

Buster's had weathered the ebb and flow of popularity. The owners served a hearty, if limited, selection of pub food and strong drinks, and offered entertainment several nights a week.

Too worked up to head straight home, M.C. had decided to stop at Buster's. The slightly seedy club wasn't an RPD favorite, but it wasn't unusual for several cops, typically detectives, to wander in on any particular evening. A drink and shop talk with a fellow detective was just what she needed to calm her down.

M.C. entered the building. It smelled of cigarettes, burgers and beer. She saw that she was in luck. Brian and his two biggest RPD buddies—Detectives Scott Snowe and Nick Sorenstein—were at the bar, talking to a third man she didn't recognize.

M.C. crossed to the bar. Snowe caught sight of her and waved her over.

"Just the man I was hoping to see," she said.

"That so?" he asked, taking a swallow of his draft.

She ordered a glass of red wine, then turned back to him. "Thought you could update me on the Entzel evidence."

"And here I thought it was my personality that interested you."

"Yeah, right."

"There's not much to update, unfortunately. The window proved a bust. Only prints on it were on the inside and belonged to the girl and her parents. Our perp no doubt wore gloves."

"Any hair? Fiber?"

"Not my area. Ask about the photos."

"Consider yourself asked."

"Dropped them on your desk on the way out tonight. Where were you? Little girls' room?"

She ignored that. "How do they look?"

"Works of art. What did you expect from a master?"

She rolled her eyes. "Nice ego."

"Yo, Riggio," Sorenstein said, interrupting the two. "I like a bar that caters to the city's underbelly."

"Bite me, bug man," she shot back.

Nick Sorenstein was ID's forensic entomologist. He was the lucky one who got to collect bugs and larvae from corpses. It was an area that had required considerable advanced training—and earned him never-ending ribbing.

Snowe took a swallow of the beer. "Riggio here was just asking about hair and fiber from the Entzel scene."

"Some interesting dark-colored fiber," Sorenstein said. "Retrieved from the bedding and the window casing. Our guy was wearing black."

"Now, that is unusual."

"A lot of cat hair," Sorenstein continued, ignoring her sarcasm. "They have a long-haired cat named Whiskers. It's all at the lab. Analysis takes time."

"Time I don't have."

Brian, yuking it up with the man she didn't recognize, saw her then and grinned. "Hey, M.C. Meet our new friend. Lance Castr'gi'vanni."

The way he mangled the name told her he had been at the bar longer than was healthy.

"Castrogiovanni," the man corrected, holding out a hand.

She took it. "Mary Catherine Riggio."

"Nice meeting you, but I've got to go. I'm on."

A moment later she understood what he meant. It was Comedy Night and Lance Castrogiovanni was the entertainment.

She hoped he was funny; she could use a good laugh.

"Bet I could bench-press that guy, he's so thin," Snowe said. "Think he'd be pissed if I tried?"

That brought a round of drunken yuks. Guy humor, she supposed. But he was probably right. Detective Scott Snowe wasn't a big man, but he was strong. She regularly saw him in the gym; a couple of times they had spotted each other at the bench press. He pressed something like two-fifty.

And the comic, now monologuing about his pathetic childhood, was tall, rail thin and redheaded.

"Actually," he was saying, "I come from a big Italian family."

That caught M.C.'s attention and she glanced toward the stage.

"I know, that's unusual for around here. Can't swing a dead cat without hitting 'family.' But really, look at me. Do I look Italian?"

He didn't. Not only did he have red hair, he had the pale, freckled skin to go along with it.

"I was adopted," he continued. "Go figure. What, did the agency lie? Yeah, he's Italian. Sure he is, that's the ticket.

"I've seen the baby pictures, folks. I was born with these freckles. And the hair? I affectionately call this shade 'flaming carrot.' I mean, instead of looking like a mob enforcer, I look like the matchstick he chews on. Do you think I can get any respect on the street?"

M.C. chuckled. He had a point.

"It just doesn't work when I say—" He motioned the way one of her brothers would, and she laughed outright. "I was always having my ass kicked.

"I tried, you know. To be Italian. One of the guys. I worked on the walk. It's a strut. Very macho. Cocky."

He demonstrated the loose-hipped swagger. Each of her brothers had it. Watching the comic, she couldn't fault his technique, but on him it looked ridiculous. M.C. laughed loudly.

He looked her way. "That's right, laugh at my pain. At my pitiful attempts to gain acceptance."

Sorenstein nudged her, dragging her attention from the comedian's schtick. "I hear Lundgren heard from someone claiming to be the Sleeping Angel."

"Yeah? Who'd you hear that from?"

"A buddy in CRU."

And she knew which one. She narrowed her eyes at Brian, who was flirting outrageously with the too-young-for-him bartender. "Passing along a crank call? Some people have way too much time on their hands."

"You so sure it was a crank?" That came from Snowe.

"Makes a hell of a lot more sense than the real killer calling and confessing. Come on."

"Strange things happen."

Suddenly irritated, she wished she had gone home. "Give me a break."

M.C. swung her stool to face the stage.

"Did we hit a nerve?" Sorenstein teased.

Snowe snickered. "What? Is Lundgren getting to you?"

"Not at all, boys, just enjoying the show."

She ignored their laughter, sipped her wine and listened to the rest of the comic's routine about growing up outside the Italian circle, looking in on them.

When he finished, she clapped loudly. He shot her a big smile, bowed and exited the stage. A moment later, he joined them at the bar. M.C. smiled at him. "Thanks. I needed that."

"Thank you. *I* need that." The bartender set a beer in front of him, obviously on the house. He took a long swallow, then glanced back at her. "Let me guess, you're family."

He was referring to her ethnicity, she knew. And with her dark hair and eyes and olive skin tone, she knew she looked the part. One hundred percent. She smiled. "You were very funny. Right on target."

"Thank you, Mary Catherine."

"Call me M.C. So tell me, how has your family reacted to your choice of comedic subject matter?"

"They hired Uncle Tony to take care of me."

"Uncle Tony?" she repeated, lips lifting. "An enforcer?"

"Much worse. An ambulance-chasing shark in a suit. He threatened me with a defamation of character lawsuit."

"You're serious?"

"Absolutely. I told him to bring it on." He took a swallow of his beer. "So what's your story?"

"I'm the youngest of six. And the only girl."

"I'm sitting next to royalty, then." He mock bowed. "Princess Mary Catherine."

"In the form of a cop."

He held up his glass in a mock toast. "To a fellow rebel and outsider."

An outsider? She had never thought of herself quite that way, but it certainly fit. She was one of them and loved, but different. And not just because she didn't fit the mold of her ancestors. Her profession made her different, as well. The way she lived. The violence and inhumanity she saw on a daily basis.

"Is this a private party, or can anybody join in?"

That came from Brian, who seemed to have given up on the bartender. Deciding she'd had enough, she stood. "It's your party now, guys. I'm beat."

As she walked away, she looked back at Lance Castrogiovanni. He caught her glance and smiled. She returned the smile, wondering if she would see him again—and hoping that she would.

11

Thursday, March 9, 2006
7:20 a.m.

Kitt stood at the grave site, shivering in the early-morning chill.
The stone read:

Our Beloved "Peanut"
Sadie Marie Lundgren
September 10, 1990—April 4, 2001

Kitt visited Sadie at least once a week. Laid fresh flowers on her
grave, removed the dead ones. Today it was daisies.

She looked up at the gray sky, longing suddenly for real spring.
Bright sun and blue sky.

"Something bad's happened, sweetheart. He's back. That man
who killed those girls. And I'm—"

She struggled to speak past the lump that formed in her throat.

Even after all the time that had passed, she still choked up at moments like this.

"I'm afraid," she went on. "For other girls. But for me, too. I can't…start drinking again. I can't let it…let him take over my life.

"Not that I have—" She shook her head and bit off the thought. She wouldn't go there. Wouldn't burden her sweet child with her problems.

"I hope you're happy. That it's good there." She paused. "I think about you every day, baby. I love you."

She bent and straightened the flowers, hating to go. Wishing with all her heart that staying would bring her daughter back. Finally she forced herself to take a step back from the grave site. To turn, walk away.

Her cell phone rang as she reached the walkway. She simultaneously answered and glanced back.

"Lundgren here."

"Hello, Kitt."

The hair at the back of her neck prickled. *The Sleeping Angel Killer. How had he gotten her cell number?*

"I'm at a disadvantage," she said. "You know my name but I don't know yours."

"You know who I am."

"I know who you say you are."

"Yes." He paused. "So, did you arrange what I asked?"

"I talked to my chief."

"And?"

"He's taking your request seriously."

"But not seriously enough to give you the case."

"PDs don't work that way."

"Another girl's going to die," he said. "You can stop it."

"How?" she asked, heart beating faster. "How can I stop it?"

"I committed perfect crimes. This one's a cheap imitator. He'll move fast. Too fast. He won't plan. The Copycat doesn't know my secrets."

"What secrets?" She gripped the phone tightly, working to keep excitement from her voice. To keep it cool, even. "Tell me, so I can help."

"I know *your* secret, Kitt."

His voice had turned sly. She frowned. "What secret would you be referring to?"

"You could have caught me. But you were drunk. That's why you fell. It was a stupid mistake on my part. But I didn't make another, did I?"

Kitt couldn't speak. The past rushed up, choking her. A call had come into the department. A mother, insisting her daughter was being targeted by the SAK. That she was being stalked.

During that time, they had gotten so many calls like that, hundreds. The department checked them all out, but they simply didn't have the manpower to watch every nine- and ten-year-old girl in Rockford.

But something about this mother's claim, about this girl...she'd had a feeling. The chief had refused to fund it, had reminded Kitt of her fragile emotional state.

They had buried Sadie the week before.

So, she had broken one of the cardinal rules of police work— she'd gone solo. Set up her own after-hours stakeout.

Night after night she had sat outside that girl's house. Just her and her little flask. The flask that chased the cold away.

At least that's what she had told herself. It had been a lie, of course. The flask had been about chasing the pain away.

A week into it, she had seen him. A man who didn't belong. She should have called for backup. Instead, she'd given chase.

Or tried. By that time, she had been stumbling drunk. She'd fallen, hit her head and been knocked unconscious. When she'd come to, he'd been long gone.

He had never given them another chance.

The chief had been furious. The SAK could have killed her. He could have taken her gun, used it on her or others.

Kitt refocused on the now, on what this meant: he was who he said. There were only two others within the department who knew the truth about that night, Sal and Brian.

Then another girl had died and the SAK had disappeared. Until now.

"Okay," she said, "you've got me. Do you know who the Copycat is?"

He laughed coyly. "I might."

"Then tell me. I'll stop him."

"What fun is there in that?"

She pictured the body of Julie Entzel. Recalled the sound of her parents' grief. The way it echoed inside her.

"I don't call any of this fun, you son of a bitch."

He chuckled, seeming pleased. "But it's my game now. And it's time to say goodbye."

"Wait! What should I call you?"

"Call me Peanut," he said softly.

In the next instant, he was gone.

12

Kitt stood frozen, cell phone held to her ear. She struggled to breathe. *Peanut.* They'd given Sadie the nickname because she'd been so small. Because of the leukemia.

How dare that monster use her precious daughter's name! It had sounded obscene on his lips. If he had been within her grasp, she would have been tempted to kill him.

Kitt reholstered the phone and walked quickly to her car. She unlocked it, slipped inside, but made no move to start the engine. He was playing with her. Somehow, he had learned her cell number. Her daughter's nickname. Which buttons to push.

What else did he know about her?

Everything. At least that was the presumption she needed to operate on. He had called this "fun." His "game." And like a masterful player, he had made it his business to educate himself on his competitor's weaknesses.

She breathed deeply, calmer now, putting the call into perspective. She unclipped her phone and punched in Sal's cell number. He answered right way.

"Sal, it's Kitt. He contacted me again. I'm on my way in."

Kitt arrived at the PSB just after Sal. She caught him waiting at the elevator. The car arrived, and they stepped inside. He punched two and turned to her.

"Well?"

"He's the real deal, Sal. He knew about that night, about my falling. Why I fell."

His mouth tightened. "Go on."

"He said another girl is going to die."

The elevator stopped on the second floor; they stepped off and headed down the hall to the Violent Crimes Bureau.

"When?"

"He was speaking metaphorically. Said the Copycat was going to move too fast. That whoever was copying his crimes was going to make mistakes."

They reached the bureau. Nan held out a stack of message slips with a cheery "Good morning."

He returned her greeting and began to thumb through the slips. "Anything urgent?" he asked the woman.

"The chief needs to push your meeting back thirty minutes. And Detective Allen's down with the flu. His wife called."

The deputy chief nodded. "I want Riggio and White. In my office, ASAP. Is Sergeant Haas in yet?"

"In his office."

"Send him in as well."

"Will do." Nan turned to her. "Detective Lundgren, you have a message as well. An old friend. Said he'd try you later."

Kitt frowned. The woman handed her the pink message slip. "Called himself 'Peanut.' Said to tell you he was looking forward to seeing you on television."

Kitt didn't comment, but by the time they had all assembled in Sal's office, she shook with anger. This brazen bastard was starting to piss her off.

Sal began. "The man claiming to be the Sleeping Angel Killer contacted Detective Lundgren again. This time on her cell phone." He turned toward her. "Detective, you want to fill everyone in?"

She took over, recounting the brief conversation, minus the incriminating comments about her fall. "He told me to call him 'Peanut.'"

Sal looked sharply at her. "Your daughter's nickname?"

She kept her voice flat. "Yes. He called the bureau this morning as well." She handed the message slip to Sal. "This was waiting for me here."

Sal swore. She shifted her gaze to the rest of the group. "Point is, he knows details of the original case and investigation that he couldn't, unless he is who he claims."

M.C. frowned. "Last time he called them his 'perfect' crimes as well. Obviously, that's important to him."

"He's arrogant," Kitt said. "He's pissed that this guy is copying his work—"

White stepped in. "And being damn sloppy about it."

"In his opinion," Riggio murmured.

"Yes." Kitt paused a moment. "I asked him if he knew who the Copycat was. He said 'maybe.'"

Sal steepled his fingers. "Do you think he really does and is being coy? Or that he suspects but isn't certain?"

"At this point, I'm not certain. If I had to wager a guess, I think he's being coy."

"Because he's playing a game with you," Riggio agreed. "His words."

"Yes. A game he called 'fun.'"

"If the Copycat makes the mistakes Peanut claims he will, we'll get him."

Kitt flinched at the other detective's use of Sadie's nickname, though she acknowledged that she had better get used to it. This wouldn't be the last time.

"But another girl will die," White offered. "Maybe more than one."

Kitt cleared her throat. "We're forgetting another thing here. If he's telling me the truth, we have two killers to catch. The SAK *and* his copycat."

The room grew silent. Sergeant Haas looked at his superior. "What's your recommendation, Sal?"

"Give him what he wants. Play along."

Riggio jumped in. "With all due respect, Chief, I disagree."

The deputy chief turned to her. "He called here, this morning. Said he was looking forward to seeing Kitt on TV."

"On television?" White asked. "What did he mean by that?"

"Press conference," Sal offered. "For whatever reason, he wants Kitt working the case and he wants proof we complied with his demand."

Riggio spoke up. "Clearly, this man's made it his business to educate himself about Detective Lundgren. He's gone to great lengths to involve her in this 'game.'" She looked at Kitt. "My question is, why?"

"I don't know."

"Seems to me, that'd be an important thing to find out."

"Agreed." Sal moved his gaze between the group. "Tom, I'm temporarily reassigning you. Riggio, it's you and Kitt on this one. Kitt's lead."

Riggio made a sound of protest. "Lead? This is my case. Let her assist, but don't—"

"My decision's final. Sorry, Riggio." He turned to Kitt. "Are you up to this? It's only round one and he's calling himself by your daughter's nickname."

"I can handle it."

He nodded. "Then, let's get busy. Call a press conference for this afternoon. Keep it simple. A straightforward FYI."

They filed out of the office. When they cleared the chief's hearing range, Kitt stopped Riggio. "This is going to get intense. It'll be important we work together, as a team."

"You don't need to lecture me, Detective. I have my priorities straight."

"I'm glad to hear that."

"With that said, do you *really* think you're ready to lead a major homicide investigation?"

"I said I'm ready, and I am."

Riggio shook her head. "Do you even know what that means anymore? The pressure of being under the departmental microscope? The press hounding you? The public demanding results? And we're not talking just any case, *the* case?"

Kitt didn't flinch, though a small seed of doubt bloomed inside her. "I'm ready," she said again.

Riggio leaned toward her. "It's my ass on the line with this one, too. I need a partner I trust watching my back."

"I'll be watching it," Kitt muttered. "Better than any partner you've ever had."

"Somehow, I have a hard time believing that."

Kitt watched Riggio walk away. She didn't blame the woman for her skepticism. Would she want her for a partner? With her history? Would she be able to trust?

Hell, no.

But none of this was her doing. A killer had singled her out for fun and games. He had demanded her participation, for what reason she didn't yet know.

She could have turned him down. Or *pretended* to play along. But she hadn't even considered either an option. From the moment another child had turned up dead, she'd wanted on the case.

Was she making a good, objective choice here? Or was she letting her own need to nail this guy rule her, thus jeopardizing the case?

Brian knew her better than anyone on the force. They had been partners for years; he had been with her as she'd slid deeper and deeper into the bottle—and into despair.

She trusted him completely. To be straight with her, no punches pulled.

She found him in his office, also located on two, just down the hall from the shift commander.

She tapped on his door. "Hey, partner. Got a minute?"

"For you? Always." He waved her in. She took a seat and he sent her one of his trademark broad smiles. "What's up?"

"Wanted to run something by you."

"Shoot." He leaned back in his chair, waiting.

"The guy called me again."

"The one claiming to be the SAK?"

"The very one. On my cell phone. Asked me to call him Peanut."

Brian was quiet a moment, as if processing all the ramifications of that. "How are you with that?"

"Royally pissed off."

He nodded. "Go on."

She filled him in on the conversation, sharing how the man had proved his identity.

"Sal put you on the case."

It wasn't a question; she answered, anyway. "Yes."

"And Riggio's not happy about it."

"An understatement." Kitt shifted her gaze, frowning. "Which brings me to you. Am I doing the right thing, going along with this? Am I ready?"

"Seems to me you don't have a choice. This guy's brought you onboard, like it or not."

"Maybe." She stood, crossed to a wall of photos. There was one of the two of them, receiving a commendation from the mayor.

That'd been more than a lifetime ago. There was one of Brian and Scott Snowe from ID at a press conference last year. She remembered it. She'd been on leave, had watched with everybody else— on the *News at Five*. They had obtained the fingerprints of a "floater" recovered from the Rock River by actually peeling the skin from the corpse's hand intact. The victim had been identified as the missing wife of a prominent city official—and her identification had quickly led to the husband's arrest for her murder.

The press had been all over it.

And Brian had gotten bumped to lieutenant.

She turned and faced him once more. "I don't trust my instincts, Brian. I'm afraid to. Last time—"

"You saved that little girl's life, Kitt."

"But I let him get away. Another girl died."

"Maybe two more would have died. You don't know."

"I screwed up."

"Yeah, you did. But what about today?"

She made a sound of frustration. "I don't know what you mean."

"Have you screwed up today?"

"Hell no."

"Then let the past go. You were a great partner, Kitt. I counted on you, and until Sadie died and your world fell apart, you never let me down."

"I'm not the cop I was back then. I don't know if I ever will be."

"So?" He leaned forward. "Has it occurred to you that you might be a better one?"

It hadn't.

"You're going to have to prove yourself, Kitt. To Riggio. To Sal and the rest of the department. But most of all, you're going to convince *you*."

"I have to do this, don't I?"

"That's the way I see it." He paused; when he spoke again, his tone was low, deep with emotion. "Go slow. Trust your instincts, but not blindly. I'll be here for you. Anything you need."

She thanked him and stood. She wasn't certain he'd given her the vote of confidence she longed for, but it would have to do.

In the end, the fact was, a killer had volunteered her for this game. She had no choice but to play.

13

Thursday, March 9, 2006
5:05 p.m.

He sat at the bar, ice-cold draft in front of him, bowl of pretzels and his pack of smokes beside that. He had arrived before the after-work crowd, to get the best seat in the house—directly in front of the TV that was mounted behind and above the bar.

He acknowledged excitement. Anxiety.

Would his Kitten come through for him this time?

He hoped so. He would be angry if she defied him again.

He lit a cigarette and sucked the smoke in. It had an instant calming effect on him. He smiled to himself, recalling watching her at her little daughter's grave. It'd been sad. And curiously sweet. He supposed he should feel bad, spying on her. Using what he learned against her.

But he didn't.

He was just that kind of guy.

Taking another drag on his cigarette, he glanced at his watch. It had been genius to ask her to call him Peanut. It had rattled her, big-time. As had calling on her cell phone. Both proved he meant business. That he knew his shit and wasn't afraid to play dirty to get what he wanted.

Genius. He liked the sound of that.

Damn but he liked being him.

The *News at Five* began in earnest. Top story of the day: "The Return of the Sleeping Angel Killer."

They showed a picture of Julie Entzel. Then of his Little Angels. Their narrative was over the top. *Typical media.*

They cut to a breaking press conference. And there she was, his Kitten. He hung on her few words. They were exploring every lead. Studying all the evidence. They had no proof they were even dealing with the same killer.

Blah...blah...blah...

The other detective was with her, Mary Catherine Riggio. Taking a back seat. Standing quietly at his Kitten's side. Expression set. Grim. Not a bit happy about this turn of events. About her sweet, career-making case being stolen out from under her nose. He almost laughed out loud.

Of course, not a word about a copycat. No mention of communication from someone claiming to be the SAK. No indeed.

She closed the brief conference by assuring the media that they would catch this monster, that he would not get away with this heinous murder.

But he already had.

He smiled to himself and stood. *Good girl, Kitten. Stay tuned, there's lots more fun to come.*

14

Thursday, March 9, 2006
7:30 p.m.

Kitt had been attending Alcoholics Anonymous for eighteen months. The department shrink, and consequently her chief, had required her to complete a twelve-step program before they would allow her back on the job.

She truly hadn't thought she needed it. That attending had been nothing more than a hoop the department wanted her to jump through. She hadn't turned to alcohol until her life fell apart. She'd thought that made her different, not really an alcoholic.

Little by little, she had seen how wrong she was.

She had realized, too, she needed the support and understanding of fellow alcoholics. They had become a kind of surrogate family. They were privy to her most secret thoughts and feelings, the demons that chased her and the longings of her heart.

She had become particularly close to three of her fellow AA members: Wally, an unemployed machine-shop supervisor who lost his job and two fingers because of drinking on the job; Sandy, a homemaker whose kids had been taken away because of her drinking; Danny, the youngest of them, who had woken up to his problem after an auto accident in which his best friend was killed. Danny had been the one behind the wheel.

They'd grown close because of the alcoholism—and because they understood loss.

"Hello, love," Danny said, taking the seat next to hers and sending her a goofy, lopsided grin.

She returned the smile. "You're chipper tonight."

"Life is good."

"Must've gotten lucky," Wally said from her other side.

"Been sober one year tonight."

Sandy squeezed his hand. "Way to go."

They chatted quietly while they waited for the meeting to begin. Sandy, it turned out, had had a positive meeting with her lawyer about establishing visitation time with her kids and Wally had gotten a job.

As the group leader opened the meeting, Danny leaned toward her. "Want to get a cup of coffee after?"

"Sure. What's up?"

"Saw you on the news. Thought we should talk about it."

From the tone of his voice, she knew he was concerned. *Stand in line, my friend.*

They didn't speak about it again until they were sitting across from each other in a booth at a local eatery called Aunt Mary's.

"I'm worried about you taking on that case, Kitt. You sure you're ready?"

"Boy, that question's getting old."

"Maybe you should consider that people have a legitimate reason for asking it." He leaned forward. "You know what your triggers are, Kitt. Don't put yourself in that position."

The pressure to perform. Being under the microscope. Stress. Despair. Hopelessness.

"The anniversary of Sadie's death is coming up," she said.

"I know, Kitt. And that's exactly my point. You're not ready for this."

She stared into her cup of coffee a moment. "I have to do this, Danny. I can't explain all the reasons—"

He reached across the table and covered her hand with his. "You don't have to. I know them."

She gazed at their joined hands, suddenly uncomfortable. Carefully, she slid her hand from under his. "It's more than my personal reasons. I can't discuss it, but it has to be me."

He was silent a moment, then nodded. "Okay. Just know I'm here for you."

He had been. They'd joined AA around the same time and had been through a lot together. She liked him. Counted on calling him friend.

He'd made it no secret that he would like to deepen their relationship. But she cherished his friendship too much to take a chance on a romance between them. Besides, at twelve years her junior, she felt like she'd be robbing the cradle.

"Joe's getting remarried."

Danny paused, a forkful of apple pie halfway to his mouth. "I'm sorry."

"It hit me hard. But I should be happy for him. He deserves happiness."

"Screw that." Danny set his fork down and leaned forward. "Wallow."

She smiled at her friend. "I tell myself life goes on. It should go on. That I need to let go."

"Let go," he said softly. "You deserve happiness, too."

"With a younger man."

Her tone was teasing. The expression in his eyes was anything but. "You know how I feel. Give us a chance." He caught her hands. "Let the past go. Allow yourself to have a future."

A lump formed in her throat. Her eyes burned. *He was right, dammit. What was stopping her? Sadie was gone, five years now; Joe was moving on.*

"I care about you, Kitt. I know who you are. I like *you*. Strong. Vulnerable. Stubborn and forgiving. We've lived through the same struggles. We understand each other. We would be good together."

"You're too young for me."

He tightened his fingers. "Biological years mean nothing. I'm an old soul."

She hesitated; he pressed his point. "If our ages were reversed, you'd think nothing of it."

That was true. An age-old double standard.

Maybe she *should* let go. Live a little.

"I don't want to lose your friendship," she said. "It's too important to me."

"You won't. I promise. Will you at least think about it?"

"Let me get this case behind me," she said, meaning it, "and I will."

Later, as she stood at the bathroom vanity in her panties and a T-shirt, she thought about that promise. Dating Danny. Dating leading to sex. Wasn't that the natural progression of things?

The thought flustered her. She'd never been with anyone but Joe. They'd been high school sweethearts. Married at twenty. Divorced at forty-five.

This was the first time since the divorce she'd even thought about it. She'd had neither the time nor the energy; hell, for the past year, she'd been in a fight to save her own life.

She had written in her journal faithfully since her therapist urged her to give it a try. It had taken a number of resentful, self-conscious attempts, but the entries had become a vehicle to pour out her anger, fear and grief. And eventually, hope.

Would a future entry read: Went to dinner with Danny. Afterward, I invited him inside to spend the night.

Good God.

She worked to shake off how the thought made her feel. No doubt Joe and his fiancée were...intimate.

Was Valerie younger than Joe? Probably. Ten years? It didn't seem Joe's style, but lots of guys did it. Why not?

Why not? A couple of the divorcées from group were always joking about getting a "boy toy." She supposed that Danny, at thirty-six, would qualify.

Kitt gazed into the mirror, imagining taking off her clothes in front of him.

The thought horrified her. She'd had a baby, for Pete's sake. Not only had she cleared her fortieth birthday—she was facing her fiftieth. She lifted her tee and stared at her aging body. She wasn't overweight, but she was out of shape. Falling in all the wrong places. Going soft where she was supposed to be firm. Dear God, what had happened to her knees? When had it happened?

Kitt dropped the tee and turned away from the mirror. When was the last time she'd worked out? She couldn't remember exactly. Before Sadie died, for sure. Ditto for going for a run.

Pitiful. She was a police officer. How would she run down a suspect? Fend off an attacker?

"Call me Peanut."

She narrowed her eyes. This son of a bitch meant business. He claimed to be a killer. And he had singled her out for fun and games, psychotic style.

She marched to her closet, dug out her running shoes, then crossed to the dresser for socks and jogging pants.

The time for being soft and vulnerable was yesterday. She meant business, too.

After dressing, Kitt clipped a can of mace to her waistband and strapped on an ankle holster. She wasn't about to take any chances, not with a maniac stalking her.

There was a lighted track at the high school, three blocks away. The route there was fairly well lit and rarely deserted. She collected her keys and headed out.

The run exhausted her. Toward the end, she felt as if her heart was going to burst from her chest. She never hit that place where the endorphins kicked in and you forgot the pain. Her legs and lower back ached, she was out of breath and sweating like a pig.

She could imagine Mary Catherine Riggio's expression if she saw her now. Or any of the guys. She'd be the watercooler joke-of-the-day.

So unbelievably uncool.

Kitt made her way home, grateful for the dark. For the opportunity to lick her wounded ego in private. Tomorrow, she would hit the gym. The shooting range wasn't a bad idea, either.

As she neared her house, she saw that something had been tacked to her front door. A note, she saw.

She climbed the stairs, crossed to the door. The note read:

Saw you on TV. Good girl. I'll be in touch.

Love, Peanut.

15

Friday, March 10, 2006
12:30 a.m.

The angel slept now. Golden hair spread across her pillow. Frilly gown carefully arranged. Just so.

She slept—but not beautifully. Not perfectly. Her blue eyes were wide with terror; her perfect bow mouth twisted into a sort of howl.

Horrible. Grotesque.

Trembling, he applied the lip gloss, smearing it. He attempted to dab up the mess, but his hands shook so badly, he made it worse. Tears stung his eyes and he fought them.

Mustn't cry. Mustn't leave any bodily fluids behind.

He backed away from the bed, to the wall. He sank to the floor and brought his knees to his chest. He clutched them, hands sweating inside the latex gloves. He felt ill. Light-headed. The angel had awakened. She had been afraid. Terrified. She had fought him. The terror and fight had ruined her. Made her ugly.

The Other One would be angry. Furious.

He was always watching. Judging him. Ready to scold. Criticize.

He was sick of it. And he was tired. So damn tired he sometimes felt he could close his eyes and sleep forever.

What if he did? Simply went to sleep, never to awaken. Like one of their sweet angels? Or if he disappeared, slipped away into the night? What would the Other One do then? How could he survive?

His mind raced; his heart beat crazily. The room spun slightly. He rested his head on his knees, struggling for control. He breathed deeply. Slowly. Remembering all the things the Other One had told him.

Stay calm. Think first, then act. Take care not to leave anything behind.

He had shown him all the tricks. Remembering them calmed him. Little by little, his heart slowed. His sweat dried.

The angel's bedside clock glowed hot pink. He watched as the minutes ticked by. He had to wait. For the hands. To pose them.

They were his. All his. Important. A surprise.

Yes, he had surprised the Other One. A difficult, near-Herculean feat. He had weathered the fury that had ensued. The punishments.

But strangely, in the end, the Other One had been pleased.

Who knew? Maybe tonight's surprise would please him as well.

Friday, March 10, 2006
7:10 a.m.

M.C. parked in front of the single-story, ranch-style home. The first officers had already cordoned off the area; one stood at the perimeter, the other was in the house with the victim.

She'd gotten the call as she stepped out of the shower; she hadn't even taken the time to dry her hair. She needed a shot of caffeine—badly—but would have to make due with the cup of instant coffee she had downed on the way across town.

She swung out of her vehicle, shivering as the cold morning air hit her wet head. She hunched into her jacket, irritated with the cold, longing for spring.

Tullocks Woods. An odd choice of neighborhood for the SAK—or his copycat—to choose, certainly different from the last. Located on the far west side, heavily wooded with large lots, the area was well removed from everything else.

A destination, M.C. thought, frowning. Neither a thoroughfare nor adjacent to one. An unfamiliar vehicle would stick out like a sore thumb.

She'd had a couple of high school friends who had lived here. They'd hosted parties down at the neighborhood clubhouse—the Powwow Club. One of them had gone on to write murder mysteries.

A murder here was hitting way too close to home.

She slammed her car door and started up the walk. Behind her, she heard the sound of others arriving. No doubt the ID guys. Lundgren. The brass.

M.C. recognized the first officer from the range. Jenkins. Real young. A great shot.

She signed the log. "What've we got?" she asked.

"Ten-year-old girl. Marianne Vest. Appears to have been suffo-cated."

"Parents?"

"Divorced. Mother found her. She's hysterical. Her pastor's on the way. A neighbor's with her now."

"Anyone else home?"

"No. Big sister spent the night at her best friend's house."

"Lucky her. Anything else I should know?"

He hesitated. "No."

She narrowed her eyes. "You're certain?"

"It's just, it's—" He shifted his gaze. "It's pretty horrible."

She nodded. "Let's keep access to the inner scene as limited as possible. Any questions about that direct them to me. Or Detec-tive Lundgren."

M.C. said the last grudgingly; she heard it in her own voice and wondered if he did, too. She stepped into the house. It smelled of burned toast. The mother sat at the kitchen table, hunched over a cup of coffee, expression blank with shock.

The neighbor stood awkwardly behind her, looking ill.

M.C. turned right, heading down a hallway. Finding the victim's bedroom wasn't difficult—an officer stood outside the door.

She reached him and nodded. "Anybody else been in?"

"No, Detective."

"Did you touch anything?"

"Took her pulse, that's it."

M.C. glanced toward the child's bed. From this position she could see the victim's hands were once again posed oddly, the right hand with the three middle fingers extended, the left in a fist.

She experienced a quiver of excitement, of expectation. They had a fresh scene. A new, best chance for catching this guy.

Maybe this time he'd slipped up.

"Morning, Detective Riggio."

She turned. Detective Scott Snowe. The first detective from ID. No doubt the chief would send the entire bureau. Snowe had his camera and video recorder. He wanted to get his initial shots before the room filled up. And before anything was disturbed.

"Detective."

Snowe motioned toward the bedroom. "This is a pretty fucked-up way to start the weekend. So much for TGIF."

"No joke. You want to get your shots?"

"If you don't mind. I'll be quick."

"Have at it."

He stopped just inside the door. "Lundgren's on her way in. She and a Channel 13 news van pulled up at the same time."

"How'd the press hear so fast?"

It was a rhetorical question and the detective didn't answer.

While he went to work, she quickly inventoried the other bedrooms. There were three in total. The teenager's looked as if a tornado had struck. The master was only slightly less chaotic, but for different reasons. Baskets of clean clothes, yet to be folded. Several stacks of paperback books on the nightstand. Romances.

Mysteries. Typical genre stuff. Two empty wineglasses beside them.

M.C. frowned. Had the woman had company last night? She bent and without touching either of the glasses, sniffed. Wine, definitely. Both white.

She shifted her gaze to the other side of the bed. Clearly, if the woman had had company, they hadn't slept on that half of the queen-size bed. It was neatly made—and covered with stacks of paperwork. She crossed to them. Mama Vest must be a Realtor. The paperwork consisted of flyers, listings, comps, things like that.

"Anything jump out as wrong?"

M.C. turned. Kitt stood in the doorway. "Not yet. You're late."

"The media's all but erecting a big top out there. Or should be."

"You wanted the job of ringmaster, you got it. Congratulations."

To her credit, Kitt let that pass. "Apparently, the local affiliates of all three networks received an anonymous call about the murder."

"Anonymous calls seem to be popular these days."

"So do murders of ten-year-old girls. Is this another SAK copycat?"

"Looks that way, though I haven't been in yet. Gave Snowe a few minutes to get his shots." She paused. "He posed her hands again. Saw that from the doorway."

Kitt nodded, and together, they headed for the victim's bedroom. M.C. noticed that the other woman was limping. "What's wrong?" she asked. "You're moving like a lame horse."

Kitt sent her an irritated glance. "I went for a run last night. Had a message waiting for me when I got home. Thumbtacked to my front door."

"Peanut?"

M.C. saw her wince at the name. "Yup. Said he saw me on TV and would be in touch. Bagged the note and brought it to ID this morning. Which, by the way, is why I'm late."

M.C. didn't comment. They reached the child's room, stepped

inside. Several more ID guys had arrived; they all stood silently by the bed.

Kitt and M.C. joined them. Snowe looked over at them, visibly shaken.

"I didn't expect this," he said.

M.C. didn't have to ask what. The Sleeping Angel they had expected to find was, instead, a work of horror. The child's once-beautiful face was screwed into a terrible scream.

Kitt took a step backward, as if propelled by strong emotion. M.C. held her ground, though not without effort. They had all worked grislier crime scenes, seen bodies mutilated beyond recognition, victims who had been subjected to vile indignities, pre- and postmortem. But this child, the terror frozen on her face, was somehow more chilling, more horrible.

"This one saw him coming," Snowe muttered.

M.C. cleared her throat. "If we're lucky, she got a good whack at him. Scratched him, pulled out some hair."

Snowe squatted, examining the oddly bent fingers. "Nothing to the naked eye. Pathologist will scrape the nails. Here he is now."

She turned, grateful when she saw it was Frances Roselli on call. She wanted all the experience she could get.

The older man reached the bed, made a sound.

"It isn't pretty, is it?"

He slipped off his glasses, cleaned them, then slipped them back on. M.C. sensed he was composing himself.

"You got your shots?" he asked Snowe.

He had, and he and the rest of the identification team moved on. He looked at M.C. and Kitt. "Detectives?"

"Anything jump out at you, other than her expression?" M.C. asked.

"Not yet," he said. "I want to get her hands bagged, then I'll give her a look-over."

They thanked him and left him to his work.

"Talked to the mother yet?" Kitt asked.

"No. Let's do it."

Mrs. Vest was still in the kitchen, only now a tall, middle-aged man was with her. The pastor, M.C. decided, judging by the cross hanging from a chain around his neck and the Bible on the table in front of him.

"Mrs. Vest?" she asked. The woman looked up, her expression naked with pain. "We need to ask you a few questions. You think you're up to that?"

She nodded, looking anything but.

"When did your daughter go to bed last night?"

"Nine. That was her...that was her regular time."

"Did you tuck her in?"

Her eyes welled with tears and her lips quivered. She shook her head. "I didn't...I was working, so I—"

She broke down sobbing. The pastor laid a comforting hand on her shoulder. M.C. noticed that Kitt looked away.

"So you what, Mrs. Vest?"

"I just...I just told her good-night."

"Where were you working?"

"In bed."

"And when did you turn out the lights?"

"Eleven." M.C. had to strain to hear her small choked reply.

"When you turned out the lights, did you peek in on her?"

M.C. knew the answer by the woman's tortured expression. Her heart went out to her. "Mrs. Vest, did you have company last night?"

"Company?" She pressed the crumpled tissue to her eyes. "I don't understand?"

"A visitor."

She shook her head. "It was just us. Janie, that's my oldest, spent the night with her best frien—" She looked up at the pastor. "How am I going to tell her about...she doesn't...dear God."

M.C. waited, letting the woman cry, the pastor comfort her. When she appeared to have regained some composure, she asked again, "Did you have a visitor last night?"

"I'm sorry, what?"

"Do you have to do this now?" the pastor asked.

"We do," Kitt replied softly. "I'm so sorry." She squatted in front of her. "Mrs. Vest, I know how hard this is. But we need your help catching the person who did this. Just a couple more questions. Please?"

The woman nodded, clinging to the pastor's hand.

M.C. continued. "There were two wineglasses on your night-stand, Mrs. Vest. You're certain you didn't have company?"

She stared blankly for a moment, as if she didn't understand, then nodded. "They're both mine. I didn't...I've been so busy, I haven't straightened up."

"Did you hear anything last night?"

She shook her head, miserable.

"Think carefully. A car passing? A dog barking?"

"No."

"Did you awaken at all in the night?"

Again, she indicated she hadn't.

Kitt stepped in. "Had your daughter expressed any concern about being followed? Or mention a feeling of being watched? Or having seen the same stranger more than once?"

That had been the case with one of the original SAK victims, as well as the almost-victim whose house she had staked out. When the mother answered "No," she tried again.

"Anything odd occur over the past weeks? Notice any strange cars in the neighborhood? An unusual number of solicitors or other calls? Sales people coming to the door? Hangups?"

Nothing. There was nothing.

Later, as they left the scene, M.C. looked at Kitt, frustration pulling at her. "Who is this guy? Houdini?"

"He's got no special powers," she replied, sounding weary. "Only the ones we give him."

M.C. stopped, faced her. "What the hell's that supposed to mean?"

"We're all so comfortable with our hectic lives, we don't notice anything. We're sleepwalking, for God's sake! He depends on that. Without it he couldn't hurt these gir—"

She sucked in a sharp breath. "Like that mother in there. Kicking herself. Wishing for a second chance. If my daughter was alive and this animal was still out there killing girls, I'd never take my eyes off her. Not tuck her in? She'd sleep with me! But it's not an issue for me, is it? Not anymore."

Kitt's voice shook. She visibly trembled. Inside the house she'd handled herself with absolute professionalism, not revealing to M.C. even a glimpse of the depth of her pain. How close to the emotional edge she was.

Now M.C. saw; she didn't know how to respond.

Kitt didn't give her the chance to come up with anything. She spun on her heel and walked away.

17

Friday, March 10, 2006
3:00 p.m.

Kitt sat at her desk. Her stomach rumbled and her head hurt. She felt as if she had been chasing ghosts all day. Ghosts, plural. Not just a killer who seemed able to manage the impossible, but her own personal ghosts, the ones that tormented her.

She hadn't had a face-to-face with Riggio since her emotional outburst. They had gone different ways—she to canvas the neighborhood, Riggio to interview the father, sister and others who'd had a relationship with the victim.

Kitt dreaded their meeting. M.C. had probably spoken with both Sal and Sergeant Haas by now; she herself had provided all the ammo needed to undermine their confidence in her.

Hell, she'd undermined her confidence in herself.

Kitt brought a hand to her head and massaged her aching temple. It was laughable, really. That first day, at the Entzel murder, she'd warned Riggio that "it wasn't about her."

But Riggio had maintained her cool objectivity; it was she who had lost it. She who had made it "about her." How had she actually believed herself strong enough for this?

Her thoughts turned to the previous evening, the note she had found tacked to her door. She had bagged both the note and the tack, careful not to destroy any prints that might have been left on them. First thing, she had taken it to ID to have it dusted. Sergeant Campo, the ID supervisor, had arranged for one of the guys to go out and dust her door for prints. She didn't think they'd find anything. "Peanut" was way too careful to make such a stupid mistake.

I'll be in touch.

She shifted her gaze to her phone. *But when would he call?*

She realized her hands were trembling and dropped them to her lap. There'd been a time that telltale tremble would have sent her scrambling for a drink. Liquid calm. She had kept a flask in her glove compartment and another tucked into a boot in her locker.

No more. That was a part of her history she would never relive.

"Hungry?"

At the sound of her partner's voice, Kitt looked up. M.C. stood in the doorway holding a brown paper sack. From the grease spots on it, she guessed the contents were from the deli across the street.

"Starving," she said cautiously, half expecting M.C. to say "Good" and pull out a big sandwich to eat in front of her.

Instead, Riggio crossed to her desk, pulled up a chair and sat. "Figured you hadn't stopped to eat, either." She reached into the sack and pulled out two sandwiches. "Reuben or pastrami and swiss on rye?"

Kitt frowned slightly, feeling off balance by the younger woman's thoughtfulness. "You choose," she said.

Riggio passed her the pastrami and cheese. "I got chips, too. Mrs. Fisher's, of course."

Mrs. Fisher's was a Rockford brand; their hearty, kettle-style chips a local favorite. When Kitt was growing up, her mom bought them from the factory in three-gallon tins.

They unwrapped the sandwiches—both topped with a big dill pickle spear—and began to eat.

"Canvas turn up anything?" M.C. asked around a bite of the greasy Reuben.

"Nada. Not even a dog barking." Kitt washed the sandwich down with a sip of water. "This guy chooses a residential, out-of-the-way neighborhood. He leaves his car for *hours* on this quiet cul-de-sac, but nobody notices. Nobody hears a thing. Nobody needs to take a midnight leak, passes a window and sees the car. Who is this guy?"

She thumbed through her notes, looking for something she might have overlooked. She shook her head. *There was nothing.* "Poor little thing turned ten just a month ago."

M.C. opened her bottle of water and took a drink. "Maybe he lives in the neighborhood."

"Makes sense. He didn't drive in, he walked." She ripped open the chips. "Thanks, by the way. What do I owe you?"

"Nothing. You buy next time."

Mary Catherine Riggio was full of surprises.

"Why are you being so nice?" she asked around a bite of sandwich.

"I'm no Mother Teresa, Lundgren. Fact is, you're no good to me if you're not thinking clearly. You need to take care of yourself."

Or maybe not so full of surprises.

"Let's run a background check on every Tullocks Woods resident sixteen and up."

"Already begun." Kitt popped a chip into her mouth and leaned back in her chair. "He doesn't know all my secrets," she murmured after a moment. "He'll make mistakes. Move too fast. Screw up."

M.C. took another swallow of water. "What are you talking about?"

"What the SAK said to me." She met her partner's eyes. "Both times he called, he described his crimes as 'perfect.'"

M.C. wiped her mouth with a paper napkin. "Right. That's why he's pissed. Somebody's ripped him off. And he doesn't think this somebody is doing it right."

"So, what makes the perfect crime?"

"Easy. Getting away with it."

"And who gets away with it?"

"The smart ones. The ones who are careful. The ones who plan."

"Exactly." Kitt sat forward, feeling a stirring of excitement. "He told me, 'This one will move fast, he won't plan.'"

Kitt saw that M.C. was getting excited, too. "When you move fast, you're sloppy. You miss things. You're seen. You leave things behind at the scene."

"The lack of evidence was one of the most frustrating things about the original SAK murders. He left us nothing to work with."

"He knew what he was doing. He was highly organized."

They fell silent. M.C. reached across and helped herself to one of Kitt's chips. "So far, this one's no different," she said. "He's left us nothing."

"That we've uncovered yet," Kitt corrected. "And he certainly has moved fast. Two girls in three days."

M.C. munched on the chip, expression thoughtful. "What else made the original SAK murders unsolvable?"

"The randomness of the choice of original victims was a huge roadblock. We never found a link between them. Yeah, they were all blond, blue-eyed ten-year-olds, but all from different sides of town, backgrounds, schools, you name it."

Usually a serial chose victims from a specific area, one he knew well and traveled often; or he chose them from a walk of life, such as prostitutes.

It was unusual for them to operate outside their comfort zone.

"So, how did he choose them?"

"Exactly." Kitt held out the bag of chips for her partner. "And don't forget, he stopped at three. With each victim, the odds of capture are raised. Hell, Bundy admitted to twenty-eight murders and may have actually committed more. The SAK didn't give us that."

"Why did he stop?" M.C. wondered aloud. "That's another anomaly. Usually, they don't."

"He was busted," Kitt offered. "Ended up doing time on an unrelated crime. Took him out of circulation."

M.C. nodded. "It happens."

"Presuming my caller is telling the truth about a copycat, maybe these two met in prison?"

M.C. agreed again. "That killing duo, Lawrence Bittaker and Roy Norris, met in prison. Went on to jointly kill five teenage girls. Your caller is pretty proud of himself. I don't see him hiding his 'work.' Probably bragged about how he pulled it off."

"But not to just anybody. It had to be somebody he trusted. Child killers are not beloved, even in the joint."

"And even if we assume these girls are his and not a copycat's, prison still makes sense. It's been five years since the last Sleeping Angel murder. We need the names of anyone recently released from the state pens."

Kitt sat back, mulling over the pieces, thinking aloud. "The original SAK committed three murders. He executed each crime exactly six weeks apart. Then he stopped."

She shifted her thoughts to his calls, the things he said. "He believes his crimes were perfect. That's important to him, maybe even more important than getting away with the crime. What does that say about him? Who is this guy?"

M.C. narrowed her eyes. "He's arrogant. Cocky. Out to prove he's the best."

"He thinks he has proved it," Kitt offers. "Then along comes this 'copycat.' Our SAK is pissed. He doesn't think this guy has the ability to pull 'perfect' off. He'll make him look bad."

"He won't be as careful," M.C. says. "He'll leave evidence behind.

Or his victims won't be random. Or he won't have the self-control to stop. He's already blown it by killing two girls in three days."

He'd seen this coming. Absolutely.

He knew who the killer was.

Kitt opened her mouth to say just that, then swallowed the thought as another jumped into her head.

Self-control. Dear God.

"What are you thinking?" M.C. asked.

"If the SAK wasn't in prison, if he was able to consciously stop in order to lessen the chances of being caught, he's a whole different breed of serial. One with uncommon control over his urges."

"Which would make him that much more dangerous."

"Exactly."

M.C. stood. "Evidence is what it is."

"We have no way of knowing if and when he'll stop."

"So we focus on finding a commonality between the victims."

"Bingo." Kitt followed her to her feet, grabbing her jacket from the back of her chair. "Let's fill Sal and Sergeant Haas in. Then talk to the girls' parents."

18

Friday, March 10, 2006
4:20 p.m.

Julie Entzel's mother was still in her bathrobe and bed slippers when she answered the door. When she saw them, a look of fear came into her eyes, followed by one of hope.

"Have you found out something?" she asked.

"Nothing definite yet," M.C. said gently. "We wanted to ask you a few more questions."

Margie Entzel looked crushed. She nodded and wordlessly opened the door wider. She shuffled deeper into the house, to a small family room. The television was on. The Weather Channel.

She picked up the remote, hit Mute, then looked at them. "I like watchin' it 'cause I don't have to think."

Kitt murmured her understanding and leaned forward. "Mrs. Entzel, I'm Detective Lundgren. I'm so sorry for your loss."

The woman's throat worked; she struggled to speak. "I seen you on TV the other night. Today, I seen where another girl got killed."

"Yes." Kitt glanced at her partner, then back at Margie Entzel. "We are going to catch him. Soon. You can help us."

The mother clasped her hands on her lap, expression growing determined. "How?"

"We're trying to find a link between your daughter and the other girl who was killed. Did you know her or the family?"

She shook her head that she didn't. They ran through the list of possible places their paths intersected: school, church, pediatrician, the places they shopped, restaurants they frequented. M.C. took notes while Kitt listened and prodded the mother's memory.

"Any out-of-the-ordinary stops or events in the past few months?"

Margie Entzel thought, expression tight with effort. "Girls' softball tryouts. My uncle Edward's seventieth birthday...Julie's birthday party."

"When was that?"

"Her birthday was January 21. It was a Saturday. She was so...excited to be having her party *on* her birthday. That doesn't happen that...often."

Marianne Vest's tenth birthday had been in February.

Kitt glanced at M.C. She hadn't made the connection yet.

"You had a party for her? Where?"

She plucked a tissue from the box and dabbed her eyes. "The Fun Zone. She loved it there."

This time M.C. looked at Kitt. Kitt sent her the slightest nod, which she returned. M.C. closed her notebook and stood. "We'll talk to the other girl's family, cross-reference this list. Hopefully, something will intersect."

Kitt stood and held out her hand. "Thank you, Mrs. Entzel. We'll be in touch."

Margie Entzel took her hand. Hers was damp. "I wish I could have helped more," she said.

"You helped more than you know. If you think of anything else, don't hesitate to call."

They waited until they were in the car to speak. Kitt started the car, then looked at M.C. "Julie Entzel's birthday was in January, Marianne Vest's in February. Coincidence?"

"I bet not. Or maybe I should say, I hope not."

Within the hour, their hunch proved correct. Marianne Vest had also had her tenth birthday party at the Fun Zone.

Friday, March 10, 2006
5:40 p.m.

The Fun Zone was an indoor play place that catered to children from ages two to fourteen. For the little ones there were rides, a ball pit and maze; for the older ones, laser tag, a rock-climbing wall and a game arcade the size of a small university. As an added incentive, the Fun Zone mascots, Sammy and Suzi Squirrel, roamed the place, handing out hugs and signing autographs.

They showed their badges to the teenager manning the front door and asked for the manager. She pointed toward the ticket counter, located just inside. A Mr. Zuba.

M.C. cocked an eyebrow at the name. "What?" Kitt asked.

"My brother Max went to school with a Zuba. Zed."

Kitt shook her head. "What kind of a sick puppy names their kid Zed Zuba?"

The other woman shrugged. "Called himself ZZ, for obvious reasons and because he was crazy about the rocker ZZ Top. It's probably not the same guy, ZZ was a hell-raiser. Gave his parents never-ending shit."

"No doubt getting back at them for the name."

They waited in line behind a family with four kids under the age of six, all four of them talking at once. Since the noise and activity level inside was mind-boggling, the four youngsters fit in just fine.

They reached the front of the line and asked the bored-looking teenager behind the counter for Mr. Zuba. The kid nodded and called over his shoulder, "ZZ, you got visitors!"

A man standing at the other end of the booth turned. His gaze landed on them and recognition lit his features.

"Oh, my gosh! Mary Catherine Riggio?"

"ZZ." She smiled. "I haven't seen you since Max called and begged me to come pick you guys up in Beloit." Beloit, Wisconsin, a quick, thirty-minute trip across the state line from Rockford, was a college town and favorite of Rockford teens. "You were drunk off your ass."

"And you were a saint for picking us up. An angel of mercy." He shook his head. "Those were some crazy days. I'm settled down now. Got two kids. Boy and a girl." He looked past her. "You here with your family?"

"No." She showed him her badge. "This is my partner, Detective Kitt Lundgren. Can we speak to you in private?"

He paled slightly. "Sure. Hold on."

He gave strict orders to the teen, exited the booth and motioned for them to follow him.

"Is it always like this?" M.C. asked, nearly shouting to be heard.

"Friday nights are big. Second only to Saturdays between ten in the morning and two in the afternoon."

He unlocked a door that led into the stockrooms, which were considerably quieter. M.C. said a silent thank-you. When they reached his office, he invited them to have a seat.

She saw a photo of his wife and kids on the desk. Pretty lady. Cute kids. She told him so and he beamed.

"Judy and I met at Rock Valley. Isn't she great? And that's Zoe." He pointed to the picture of a pretty, dark-haired toddler. "She's two now. And the baby. Zachary."

Zoe and Zach Zuba. She ran the nickname possibilities through her head: ZZII, Zgirl, ZZ-redux, Zuper-kid.

She wanted to shake him and demand, "What were you thinking?"

Instead, she asked, "The noise level doesn't drive you nuts?"

"Nah. I love kids. Besides, they're just having fun."

ZZ. Who would have thought?

"What's up, M.C.?"

"We're investigating the recent Sleeping Angel murders. Apparently, both victims had their birthday parties here. The Entzel girl in January. The Vest girl in February."

He moved his gaze between them, looking uneasy. "When I saw them on TV, I thought they looked familiar, but I see so many kids. Now that I know they… Oh, man, this is really horrible. How can I help?"

"What kind of screening do you put prospective employees through?"

"Criminal-background check with the state police and a drug test. We ask for references, which we check."

"You get many adults in here without children?"

"We're real careful about that. The Fun Zone prides itself on being a safe place for kids. We advertise it."

He opened the top drawer of his desk and took out a package of wristbands. "They're numbered—a family or group all have the same number on their bands. We check wristbands as people exit. A child is never allowed to leave without the adult they registered with.

"In addition, an adult walks in solo, without a kid, my door employee is instructed to ask what party or group they're meeting. If they're not, they call me or one of my assistants and we suggest they've come to the wrong place. I mean, what kind of adult would come *here* for fun? Get real."

"What about video surveillance?" Kitt asked.

"At the front entrance and in both restrooms. Also at the registers."

"Do you save the tapes?"

He shook his head. "They turn over every seventy-two hours. They're mainly for insurance liability."

M.C. leaned forward. "We'll need any tapes you have. Plus, from this minute on, no rolling over."

"But—"

She didn't give him a chance to argue. "In addition, I'm going to need to get a list of your employees. Current and terminated in the past year."

For the first time, he looked uncomfortable. He shifted in his chair. "Like I said, M.C., the Fun Zone prides itself on being a safe environment for kids. If—"

"If what, ZZ? If Julie Entzel and Marianne Vest's killer found them here, you wouldn't want the press to find out? Afraid it might hurt business?"

He flushed. "Of course not. But our employees are clean. Hell, most of 'em are teenagers."

"Then you have nothing to worry about. Right?"

He reached for the phone. "Let me get Mr. Dale. He's the owner, so it's his call."

M.C. ended up speaking with the man herself. She convinced him that actually, in the end, it was *their* call. He instructed his manager to give them whatever they needed; M.C. promised she would do her best to keep the Fun Zone out of the news.

They left with a list of the Fun Zone's employees, both part- and full-time; the records from the day of both girls' parties and forty-eight hours of the play place's video surveillance.

As they belted into M.C.'s Ford, Kitt looked at her. "Angel of mercy? No offense, but I can't see it."

"He's forgotten I refused to do it unless they each gave me fifteen bucks."

"There's the Mary Catherine Riggio I've come to know."

"Hey, it beat the hell out of Mom and Dad finding out. Max would have been grounded for the rest of his life." She eased away from the curb. "By the way, remind me never to have kids."

Kitt turned to her. "Why's that?"

"One visit to that place is enough for a lifetime."

"It's not quite as bad when you're there with your own kid. They love it so much, it sort of eases the pain."

M.C. grimaced. "Like I said, remind me never to have kids."

"Do you really mean that?"

M.C. thought of Benjamin, how much she loved him. "Sure," she said. "Who needs 'em. You've got to admit, they're nothing but troub—"

As soon as the words passed her lips, she realized her mistake. "I'm sorry, Kitt. I wasn't thinking, I—"

"Don't worry about it," she said, looking away.

M.C. noticed Kitt's hands clenched in her lap. She wanted to kick herself. Of all the stupid, graceless and insensitive things she could have said. "I'm such a jerk. Really, I'm sorry."

Kitt shook her head. "Forget about it. Let's talk about the case."

M.C. jumped at the familiar—and comfortable—territory. "It's going on seven. Your choice. Keep going or call it a night?"

"I vote we run these names through the computer. See how far we get."

"You got it," M.C. replied, heading for the Whitman Street Bridge. "To hell with Friday night."

20

Friday, March 10, 2006
10:35 p.m.

They made it three-quarters of the way through the list before
M.C. suggested they call it quits. She was tired and hungry, and the
most exciting thing they had turned up was a DWI, Driving While
Intoxicated. Kitt had agreed and they'd planned to resume the next
morning—there was no such thing as a weekend off when neck-
deep in a high-profile homicide investigation.

M.C. was beginning to think they'd gotten their hopes up for
nothing. Truth was, the Fun Zone could still be the link, but their
UNSUB could be some freak with kids of his own. He brings his
own kid in, looks like Dad of the Year; whole time he's scouting his
next pretty little victim.

That scenario would make him much more difficult to nail.

M.C. eased into her driveway, shifted into Park, but made no move to kill the engine or get out of the car. She'd left Kitt at the computer only because she had assured M.C. she would be on the road five minutes behind her.

M.C. let out a long breath, thinking of the day. Of Kitt. The pain in her eyes and voice as she had spoken of her daughter—and of her regrets.

And of her parting words tonight, as M.C. had headed home.

"Hey, Riggio." She had stopped, looked back at her. *"For the record, being a mom was the best thing I ever did."*

A lump formed in M.C.'s throat. The image of Marianne Vest filled her head, followed in quick succession by one of Julie Entzel's mother in her robe and slippers at four in the afternoon.

They made all her little dramas seem pretty insignificant.

M.C. swallowed hard, gazing at her dark house. She hadn't left a porch light on. She didn't own a dog, cat or any other creature.

Growing up in a house with five boisterous brothers and a constant menagerie of pets, friends and relatives underfoot, she had looked forward to someday living alone. To having her personal space, to using the bathroom whenever she needed to, no waiting. To spending as long as she wanted in the shower, without fear of running out of hot water.

Quiet. Calm. Just the way she liked it.

So why didn't she want to go inside?

Because she couldn't face the quiet tonight. Not yet, anyway. She needed people. A few laughs. A drink or two. Or four.

But where to go? Buster's Bar, she decided, and acted on the impulse. She checked her rearview mirror, shifted her SUV into Reverse and backed down the drive.

She made it across town to Five Points in fifteen minutes. Unlike the other night, the place was packed. And instead of funny man Lance Castrogiovanni on the stage, a country-western singer was attempting a version of Shania Twain's "Any Man of Mine."

M.C. wound her way through the crowd to the bar. There she saw Brian Spillare and several of his RPD buddies. Judging by the decibel of their laughter, they had been there a while.

Brian caught sight of her and waved her over. The group made room, and Brian ordered her a glass of wine. "I was just thinking about you," he said.

She let that pass, though it set her teeth on edge. "Really, Lieutenant?"

"So formal?" He swayed slightly on his feet. "It's Friday night, loosen up."

"Looks to me like you're loose enough for both of us." The bartender set her wineglass in front of her. After paying for it, she turned back to him. "Is your wife with you? I'd love to tell her hello."

"Nope. She's having a girls' night out. I'm a free man."

Oh, brother. She couldn't believe she had fallen for his lines, naive rookie or not. "Lucky her. Excuse me, Lieutenant, I have—"

He caught her arm. "I need to talk to you, M.C. Privately."

"Can't it wait? I'm beat. And as you said, it's Friday night."

"It's about the SAK case."

She frowned. "What about it?"

"Not here." He motioned toward the back of the bar, the hall that led to the restrooms.

Although she didn't like it, she nodded and followed him.

He stopped at the end of the corridor and faced her. "You still totally do it for me. I wanted you to know that."

She stared at him, not quite believing what she knew she had heard. "Are you hitting on me?"

"I'm just being honest." He caught her hand. "Putting myself out there. For you."

She made a sound of disgust. Apparently, they had very different definitions of *honest*. Her definition didn't include tricks or infidelity.

She jerked her hand away. "This is sexual harassment, Lieutenant. I don't think you want to go there."

"Whatever happened to us?" he asked, leaning toward her, forcing her backward. "We were good together, weren't we?"

She realized then just how inebriated he was. Too inebriated to listen to reason. "You were married. You still are."

"But it was good, wasn't it?"

"Back off, Brian. You're drunk."

"Not that drunk." His voice took on a whiny tone. "Come on, it could be good again."

"There you are, M.C.," Lance Castrogiovanni said, coming up behind Brian. "Sorry I'm late."

She gratefully grabbed the out. "My date," she said, ducking past the startled lieutenant. "Brian, you know Lance. Excuse us."

The comedian put his arm around her and steered her out of the hallway. She leaned toward him. "Thanks, that was getting uncomfortable."

"Thought you looked like you could use saving." He pointed toward a table in the corner. "For a moment, I thought he was going to pulverize me."

"Brian's big but harmless."

"Didn't look so harmless to me." They reached the table. He held out a chair and she sat. "Aren't you two colleagues?"

"We are. He's also a superior officer—and a mistake from my days as a rookie."

"Ouch."

"No joke. Of course, he wasn't a lieutenant back then. But I wasn't a detective, either."

"Young people make mistakes. I made my share, that's for sure."

She held her glass up. "To mistakes and lucky breaks."

"Lucky breaks?" he asked.

"That you were here. Because of my past relationship with Brian and his position on the force, I have to be very careful."

"So kneeing him in the balls would have been a bad thing?"

She laughed. "A very bad thing, yes."

He leaned toward her, expression amused. "You really weren't that lucky, Detective Riggio."

"No?"

He shook his head. "Typically, when I'm not working, I avoid these places like the plague. Too much smoke and desperation."

"Which would make me unusually lucky to find you here."

"Except...I was here looking for you."

"Funny."

He met her gaze, his serious now. "That's not part of my act. It's true. In fact, this is my third time in. If you were a no-show tonight, I was moving on to plan B."

"Which was?"

"Call you at work. I wasn't thrilled by plan B."

"You have something to hide, Lance Castrogiovanni? A skeleton or two in your closet?"

"Don't we all?" He laughed. "Actually, as long as it's confession time, cops give me the willies. Except for you, of course."

"I'm honored, I guess."

"I know an open-all-night diner that serves the best homemade cream pies in the world."

"That is so *not* Italian," she teased.

"Exactly." He held out a hand. "My treat."

"In that case, you've got a deal."

They agreed to each take their own car. The diner, appropriately named the Main Street Diner, was located at the corner of North Main and Auburn Streets, an area that had fallen on lean times.

As they entered the brightly lit establishment, the woman behind the counter—middle-aged with a net over her gray bob—greeted Lance by name. When she did, a man peered out from the kitchen.

"Lance, buddy, where've you been?"

"Working. A good thing, by the way. Keeps me in pie."

"Who's that with you?"

"A friend. Mary Catherine Riggio, Bob Meuller. His wife Betty. Mary Catherine's a cop, so be nice."

"I'm always nice," he said.

Betty snorted. "More like, always crusty. That's why I keep him in back."

Just then a group of rowdy young people stumbled into the restaurant. M.C. could tell they were all about three sheets to the wind—except for the designated driver, who looked irritated. She kept jiggling her car keys and rolling her eyes.

Lance waited until the kids had picked a table, then chose the one farthest from them.

"You must live near here," M.C. said.

"I do. Just up the block. Eat here at least once a day. Sometimes more."

"Those the owners?"

"Yup. Couldn't find reliable night help, so they pull the shift themselves. Nice people. Down to earth."

"They seem that way."

He handed her a menu. "Everything's good, by the way."

"I don't even have to look. If I don't try this famous cream pie, I'll be thinking about it for the next month. Which one do you suggest?"

He couldn't recommend only one, he said, so he ordered one of each: coconut, chocolate, strawberry and lemon, along with two cups of coffee. When Betty brought them out, M.C. made a sound of surprise: they were huge, at least six inches high.

"You looked hungry," he said.

They spent the next couple of minutes passing the slices. Lance gave her the first taste of each. The rowdy teens, obviously influenced by their cream pie extravaganza, ordered four slices of pie as well.

"Okay, I've got to admit, this is the best pie I've ever had."

"Favorite?"

"Coconut. Followed closely by chocolate."

He smiled. "Me, too. But followed by lemon."

She took another bite of the coconut, then set aside her fork, vowing to breathe a while before taking another bite.

"How's work?" she asked.

"It's a joke."

"Professional humor?"

"I can't help myself." He took another forkful of the dessert. "It's good. I've been busy. How about you?"

"It's murder."

She said it deadpan, and he hooted. "Professional humor?"

"Absolutely."

"What's it like being a cop?"

"What's it like being a comic?"

He didn't seem to mind her turning the question back to him. "Rewarding, painful, exhilarating, frustrating. When the audience is with you, it's the highest high ever. When they're not, nothing is more horrible. And it's everything in between, including trying to earn enough money to keep on doing it—and eating."

"Why do you? Keep doing it?"

"Because I have to," he said simply. "It keeps me sane."

She liked his honesty, she decided. She liked that he didn't pretend to be something he wasn't, didn't self-aggrandize.

Her cell phone rang, and she held up a finger as she answered. "Riggio here."

"It's Kitt. We've got him."

M.C. straightened, instantly focused on the case. "Who is he?"

"Derrick Todd, a registered sex offender."

"Working at the Fun Zone? I'll be right there."

She ended the call and reclipped her phone. He made a sound of regret. "You've got to go," he said.

"I'm sorry." She took a swallow of her coffee and stood. "I enjoyed this. Thanks for the pie."

He followed her to her feet. "Can I see you again?"

She didn't hesitate. "Absolutely. I'll look forward to it."

It wasn't until she was halfway to the PSB that she realized she hadn't given him her phone number—if he wanted to see her again, he'd have to resort to plan B.

Saturday, March 11, 2006
12:05 a.m.

M.C. found Kitt at her desk, reading a printout. "You said you were right behind me," M.C. said, acknowledging her irritation. But at what? Having been outworked by the other woman? Or having been pulled away from an enjoyable evening?

Kitt looked up. M.C. saw her excitement. "I meant to be. Just kept punching in 'one more name.' Our man Derrick popped up at the bottom of the list. Last man, in fact."

Kitt handed her the printout. "Twenty-four years old. A maintenance engineer at the Fun Zone. Skills he probably acquired in the pen. Did two years at Big Muddy River for indecent liberties with a child."

Big Muddy River was a correctional facility with a treatment program for sex offenders. "When did he get out?"

"Less than a year ago. Which works with our theory that the SAK and his copycat met in the joint."

M.C. flipped through the pages, frowning. It was all petty stuff. Shoplifting. Truancy. DUI. Possession. Then the sex offense.

But it painted a picture of a kid sliding downhill.

"He would have had to register. Probably quarterly." Working at a place like the Fun Zone was a violation, just like living within five hundred feet of a school or volunteering as a Little League coach would be.

Mr. Todd was going back to prison, ASAP.

"How in the hell did this guy slip through the Fun Zone's screening process?" M.C. asked.

"Good question. One I suggest we get an answer to. Think ZZ's up?"

"I'd bet not. But I'd be happy to get him up. Besides, I'm an old friend, how annoyed could he get?"

Pretty damn annoyed, it turned out. His wife answered the door; she nearly fainted when she learned they were cops. She called ZZ, who stumbled out of the bedroom, looking dazed and confused. The commotion awakened the baby, who began to wail. Which in turn woke the toddler, who appeared at the top of the stairs, crying.

"Mary Catherine?" he said, blinking at her, then Kitt. "Detective?"

Kitt grabbed the lead. "I apologize for the hour, Mr. Zuba, but we have a few questions that couldn't wait until morning."

ZZ's wife stopped halfway up the stairs, expression frozen with fear. "Zed?"

"It's okay, Judy. Take care of the kids."

She hesitated a moment, then hurried up the last few stairs and scooped the toddler up. When she had disappeared from sight, ZZ turned back to them. "Kitchen," he said, pointing.

They followed him and all sat at the round oak table, which still bore the evidence of an evening meal with very young children.

The bleary-eyed manager looked at them. "You scared the crap out of my wife. This had better be good."

"Again, Mr. Zuba," Kitt said, "I apologize for the hour. It was necessary, however. In an investigation like this, every minute—"

"Counts," M.C. said, jumping in. "What if it were one of your kids? Would you want the police to wait until everybody had their full eight hours?"

The man looked less disgruntled. "No, of course not. You want coffee or anything?"

They both refused; M.C. began. "What can you tell us about Derrick Todd?" she asked.

"Derrick?" he repeated, appearing genuinely surprised. "He's all right. A quiet guy. Keeps to himself."

"You hire him?"

"No. Our owner did. He came highly recommended."

"By whom?"

"I don't know."

M.C. cocked an eyebrow. "But you were the Fun Zone's manager at the time?"

He nodded and yawned. "I was pretty new, though. Just on board, I don't know, a matter of months."

"He go through the usual employment screenings?"

ZZ straightened slightly, as if he was finally awake enough to realize what was going on. "Can't say for certain. I was new and Derrick was the owner's hire."

"As maintenance engineer, how much interaction does Derrick Todd have with Fun Zone patrons?"

ZZ shifted uncomfortably. "He's on the floor a lot. Maintenance engineer covers a lot of territory for us. Janitorial. Game repair. Sound system, coin and drink machines. Not heavy-duty repair, you understand, but tinkering. He's good at that."

"What would you say if I told you Derrick Todd is a registered sex offender?"

The manager's expression would have been comical in a different situation. "That's impossible. Derrick can be surly sometimes, but...he's good with the kids, just has a way with..."

His words trailed off. Maybe he heard how they sounded. Or maybe he had heard the stats about pedophiles: that they "loved" kids, that they chose jobs or professions that put them in contact with children, that they could not be rehabilitated.

"Zed? Is everything all right?"

They looked toward the doorway. Judy stood there, expression concerned. It was no wonder; ZZ looked like he was going to throw up.

"Everything's fine, Mrs. Zuba," Kitt responded, standing. "We apologize for disturbing your family."

"Is this about those girls who were killed?"

"They say Derrick's a registered sex offender."

She brought a hand to her mouth. "My God. He's been over to the house."

M.C. followed her partner to her feet. She passed behind her old friend's chair and patted his shoulder. "You should call Max. I know he'd love to hear from you."

He nodded but didn't rise. M.C. suspected he was busy dealing with the ramifications of this information getting out. And even worse, what would happen if Derrick turned out to have killed Julie Entzel and Marianne Vest?

When M.C. reached the kitchen doorway, she glanced back at ZZ. "The Fun Zone's owner, Mr. Dale, does he live around here?"

His wife answered. "He lives on the east side. In that swanky neighborhood, Brandywine Estates."

Moments later, they were outside, heading toward the car. "Interesting," M.C. said. "Hired by the boss, coming 'highly recommended.' We'll definitely need to talk to Mr. Dale in the morning."

"Why do tomorrow what we could tonight? If he's not awake already, he will be in a matter of minutes."

When ZZ called. M.C. suspected her old friend wouldn't waste a minute notifying his employer of the turn of events. She just prayed ZZ's story was true and that he hadn't been lying to save his ass.

They reached the Explorer, unlocked it and climbed inside. "I suggest we let Mr. Dale stew a bit. Besides, a rich guy like him has an army of lawyers to call when he gets pissed off." M.C. started the car. "Let's pay the kid a visit instead."

Derrick Todd rented in a neighborhood that aspired to "crummy." To get to it, they passed Lance's diner. As they did, M.C. smiled to herself.

"What?" Kitt asked.

"Nothing."

She cocked an eyebrow, clearly suspicious. "When I called, what were you doing? Not home sleeping."

"Eating. Cream pie. Four different kinds."

"Sounds like somebody has an issue with sweets. Have you tried to find help?"

"What makes you think it's *my* issue with sweets?"

"Want to tell me about him?" Kitt asked.

"Hardly."

"Not even a name?"

"Nope."

"That's what I love about this partnership," Kitt said, tone dry, "the sharing and camaraderie." She pointed to the intersection up ahead. "Right turn there."

They came upon the building in a matter of minutes. Ramshackle. Overgrown. Just the kind of place one would expect a twenty-four-year-old ex-con to live.

M.C. cruised to a stop in front of the apartment building. Light showed from several windows. "Should we go in?"

"I'm thinking yes." Kitt checked her weapon. "You?"

"Absolutely."

"Flashlight?"

"Yup." She opened the glove box. "Got it."

They exited the vehicle and made their way up the walk to the building's front doors. The structure itself was a big rectangle-shaped box. Brick. Built in the forties, M.C. guessed. Probably a pretty nice place in those days. Never the Ritz, but certainly not the dump it was now.

The interior hallway was dimly illuminated by the one bulb that wasn't burned out. It smelled musty, as if it needed a good airing out, and of someone's dinner.

Cabbage, M.C. guessed. Nasty stuff. Luckily, Italians didn't eat a lot of cooked cabbage.

"Third floor," Kitt murmured. "Unit D."

They climbed the stairs and made their way down the corridor to D. Music spilled from the apartment across the hall. Kitt rapped on Todd's door. It creaked, then swung open.

Kitt glanced at M.C., who nodded. Kitt drew her weapon, then rapped on the door again, pushing it wider with her foot. "Derrick Todd?" she called. "Police."

Nothing. M.C. snapped on the pencil light and directed it into the interior. A crappy dump. Kid was no housekeeper, either.

Kitt looked at her again, for confirmation. M.C. nodded. "Door was open. Justifiable entry. We were concerned about the man's health."

Kitt turned back to the apartment. "We're coming in, Mr. Todd. Just to make sure you're okay."

Yeah, right. M.C. drew her weapon. They made their way into the apartment.

There was little to it other than the front room. Kid slept on a dirty-looking futon. The small bathroom didn't even have a tub, just a stand-up shower. The place was a mess, but not the kind that indicated foul play.

M.C. itched to take advantage of the situation and initiate a real search. But anything they found would then be inadmissible—and their asses would be in a major, big-time sling.

If Todd proved to be a good suspect—which she believed he would—securing a search warrant would be a piece of cake.

Back in the hallway, Kitt belted the flashlight. She repositioned the door as they had found it. Music still blasted from the neighbor's apartment. Other than that the floor was quiet.

They made their way downstairs and outside. After they had climbed into the SUV, Kitt turned to her. "Want to hang around? See if Todd shows up?"

"I'm game."

"You got anything to eat in this vehicle?"

"Bag of nuts and some soy chips."

"Soy chips?" Kitt repeated. "Very uncoplike. Now, if you'd said pork rinds or pretzels, I might have bought it."

M.C. opened the console compartment, pulled out two snack bags. "Something's got to balance all my mother's pasta. They're actually not bad."

"I'll take the nuts. Thanks."

M.C. watched the woman rip open the bag and begin to eat. She most probably hadn't had a thing since the sandwich and chips late that afternoon.

She was an interesting woman, M.C. decided. Certainly not the "head case" she had labeled her. She was extremely focused. Smart. Ambitious. She could see how those traits could, under the right circumstances, mushroom into obsession.

The right circumstances. The death of your own child, the murder of several others, an elusive killer and a pressure-cooker investigation.

Kitt shook out some nuts, popped them into her mouth. "Cashews. My favorite."

"Mine, too. A guilty pleasure."

Kitt nodded as she munched on the nuts. "Weight's never been one of my issues. Don't know why. I enjoy eating."

"It's my heritage," M.C. said. "Italian women get to a certain age and unless they're careful, they get round. Very round."

"Your Mom?"

"Round. Very."

"My Mom was svelte until the day she died."

"When was that?"

"A couple years ago."

Her daughter. Her marriage. Her mother. She had lost them all in a matter of a few years. M.C. couldn't imagine. "I'm sorry."

She said the words, though they felt lame to her own ears. Inadequate.

Kitt didn't reply. They fell silent.

After several moments, Kitt asked, "How do you want to do this? Shifts?"

"Okay by me." M.C. glanced at her watch. "One hour or two?"

"Let's shoot for two. You sleep first. I'm wide-awake."

M.C. agreed, though she wasn't sleepy, either. Mind racing, she leaned her head back and closed her eyes. Beside her Kitt hummed very softly under her breath. A lullaby, M.C. realized.

As she listened, she wondered what made Kitt Lundgren tick.

Saturday, March 11, 2006
8:30 a.m.

Derrick Todd never showed. Kitt could offer a number of different scenarios for why, but she feared any minute she would get a call informing her that another girl was dead.

After all, the Copycat didn't just kill his victims, he spent the night with them.

She and M.C. had decided that their best course of action would be to station a uniform at Todd's apartment, freeing them to move on. They needed to fill in the chief, acquire both a search and arrest warrant for Todd, and interview the Fun Zone's owner. Food, a shower and change of clothes were high on Kitt's list of priorities as well. They arranged to rendezvous back at the PSB.

Kitt beat the younger woman there and used the time to retrieve Mr. Dale's address from the computer.

"I'm starting to get a complex."

Kitt looked over her shoulder at M.C. "About what?"

"You outwork me last night, this morning you manage to eat, shower and change clothes at the speed of light. How'd you do it?"

Smiling, Kitt stood. "I keep a change of clothes in my locker here. I showered in the ladies' dressing room, ate peanut-butter crackers from the vending machine and fortified myself with a cup of been-sitting-in-the-pot-all-night coffee."

"Has anyone ever told you you're an overachiever?"

"Once or twice." Clearly, M.C. had a competitive streak. Amused, Kitt crossed to her. She held out the address. "Brandywine Estates, just like ZZ's wife said. You want to drive or should I?"

"I will." M.C. snatched the paper from her. "And snack crackers for breakfast is not a healthy start. You'll be hungry in an hour."

Roy Lynde, the detective at the desk across the aisle from Kitt's, chuckled and M.C. sent him an annoyed glance. "What's so funny?"

"Nothing." He held up his hands as if warding off an attack. "Just hanging out, watching the show."

That brought guffaws from a couple of other guys. One of them said, "Looks like somebody's met her match."

Roy piped up again. "Don't take it personal, Riggio. Even Wonder Woman comes up short sometimes."

Kitt saw her partner's jaw tighten but didn't comment until they were headed down the corridor for the elevator. "Want some advice?" she asked.

"Not particularly."

"You know I'm going to offer it, anyway."

"I'd prefer if you didn't."

"Don't take it all so seriously. Lighten up, sometimes."

M.C. stopped, looked at her, expression incredulous. "*You're* telling *me* to lighten up?"

"Yeah. You got a problem with that?"

"For obvious reasons, yes."

"Obvious reasons?" Kitt said, keeping her voice low. "You mean ones like outworking and out-investigating you? Or being able to take a joke?"

M.C. flushed. "Let's see, Detective Intensity, you basically 'go postal' over the SAK case, blow it and several others, climb into a bottle and end up suspended. By the grace of God—or some mighty powerful strings—you're back at work and I'm stuck with you. Yeah, I have a problem with you telling me to lighten up."

They glared at each other. Kitt acknowledged being angry—as much at herself as Riggio. For letting the woman engage her and for stepping into the "wise mentor" role in the first place. If Mary Catherine Riggio wanted to be humorless and unlikable, it was her life.

"You know what, Riggio? We have to work together, so get over it."

Kitt didn't give her a chance to respond; she turned and started for the elevator. M.C. fell into step beside her. They reached the elevator and simultaneously moved to punch the call button. Same for the floor number.

They didn't speak again until they were halfway across town. Kitt broke the silence first. "My daughter died. My marriage fell apart. I didn't handle it well. You called it 'going postal.' Whatever. It's in the past. Or at least, I'm working hard to put it there."

For a long moment, Riggio didn't respond. When she did, her voice was tight. "I overreacted," she said finally. "Being taken seriously is a big deal for me. I had to fight for it all my life." She paused. "I shouldn't have said those things to you."

"Fact of the matter is, neither one of us was lying," Kitt answered.

M.C. smiled suddenly. "If we ever need to speak in code, you're 'Going postal.'"

"And you're 'Taking a joke.'"

"But I still don't trust you to watch my back."

"Ditto."

The remainder of the drive passed in silence. But a less prickly one this time, one Kitt used to assemble her questions for Sydney Dale.

Mr. Dale, they discovered, lived in a large, contemporary home. The house sat on a beautifully landscaped lot—two acres or more, Kitt guessed, with pool, cabana and natural pond with rock waterfall.

They parked in the circular drive, behind a white BMW convertible. They crossed to the door, but before they could ring the bell, it swung open. An attractive teenage girl ducked past them, blond ponytail swinging. She trotted to the BMW, slid inside and started it up.

As the engine roared to life, a man thundered out the door, nearly knocking Kitt down. "Sam!" he shouted. "I did not give you permission to—"

"Gotta go, Dad. I'm late!" The teen stepped on the gas and sped down the drive.

Kitt watched, part amused, part disgusted. *Classic case of teen ruling the roost. When she was growing up, either of her parents would have chased her down, then soundly kicked her butt.*

"Mr. Sydney Dale?" M.C. asked.

He looked at them then, as if just realizing they were there. "Yes?"

He was a big man, though not particularly attractive. His nose occupied too much of his face, and his pitted skin spoke of teenage years besieged by acne.

A problem his daughter did not have. Of course, these days well-heeled parents spared no expense on their spoiled children: facials, professional manicures and pedicures, salon styling Kitt couldn't even afford. She had even heard about breast augmentation as high school graduation gifts.

Geez. Her Mom had given her a ten-karat-gold cross necklace.

Kitt showed him her shield. "Detective Lundgren, Rockford Police Department. My partner, Detective Riggio."

M.C. flashed her badge; the man didn't even glance at it. "I was wondering when you'd get here. And just to let you know up-front, I've already spoken to my lawyer about this matter."

Typical rich asshole. "What matter is that?" Kitt asked.

"My employment of Derrick Todd, of course. Isn't that why you're here?"

"It is. I guess my confusion stems from why you'd think you'd need to consult a lawyer over a few questions about one of your employees."

He frowned. "Don't play games with me, Detective. We both know why a man like me would consult with his lawyer over this. I have a lot to lose from liars, scam artists or bad press."

That was true, and she appreciated his candor. "And what did your lawyer advise you to do, Mr. Dale?"

"Answer your questions honestly and help you in any way I could, then send you on your way."

"That sounds fine to us, Mr. Dale."

He closed the door behind him. "My wife's still sleeping."

Lucky her. Kitt took out her spiral-bound notepad. "I understand you own the Fun Zone."

"Yes. It's one of my investments. I leave the running of it, including the hiring and firing, to my manager."

"Mr. Zuba."

"Yes."

"You say you leave the 'hiring and firing' to your manager, but that's not always true. Is that right?"

He hesitated, just slightly. "Once in a while I offer suggestions."

"As you did with Derrick Todd?"

Again, he hesitated. "Yes."

"Mr. Zuba told us you 'highly recommended' Mr. Todd."

"I did. He was our yard and pool boy for several years. He did a good job, seemed like a nice kid. He quit when he went back to school."

"Where'd he go?"

"RVC."

Rock Valley College was a local junior college. Many a high school senior from the area attended "The Rock," as they called it, before moving on to a four-year university. The school also drew older students, looking to better their chances in the work force.

"When was this?"

He thought a minute. "Four, four-and-a-half years ago."

Kitt glanced at M.C. She was watching the man carefully, gauging his truthfulness by his body language and eye movement.

"Then what happened?"

"He approached me about a job. I promised I'd see if there was anything available at one of my business endeavors. The Fun Zone had an opening. I recommended Mr. Zuba consider him for it."

"And that's it?"

"Yes."

"You didn't tell your manager to hire Mr. Todd on your recommendation alone?"

"Without a background or criminal check? That would be very stupid, don't you think?"

"I do, Mr. Dale. But somehow that's what happened."

"I certainly don't know how." He glanced away, then back at her. "Some sort of communication foul-up, I suppose."

Kitt's hackles rose. He sounded almost bored. "That *communication foul-up* may have cost two young girls their lives."

He blinked quickly, three times. She had hit a button with that one. Why? Guilt? Or fear?

"So, you had no idea that Derrick Todd had run afoul of the law after leaving your original employ?"

"Would I have recommended him if I had?"

He all but bristled with indignation. Kitt cocked an eyebrow. "I don't know, Mr. Dale. Would you have?"

"I have nothing more to tell you, Detectives. If I could help you more, I would."

Yeah, right. And pigs fly.

They thanked the man and headed for M.C.'s car. When they were buckled in and on their way, Kitt looked at M.C. "Did you notice he never commented on the reason we were investigating Todd? Never expressed regret, concern or denial?"

"Yeah, I noticed. He was too busy covering his own ass. Prick."

Kitt nodded as they turned onto Riverside Drive. "If it turns out Todd is guilty of the Copycat murders, Dale's making certain your friend ZZ takes the fall."

"He had his story down pat, no doubt about it. What a sweetheart."

"Let's run Mr. Dale through the computer, see if he's as fine and upstanding as he'd like us to believe."

M.C. nodded. "But first, let's swing by the Fun Zone and have another chat with ZZ. Give him a little heads-up. See if his story changes."

They arrived at the Fun Zone before the doors officially opened for the day. ZZ and his employees were busy readying themselves for the Saturday onslaught of screaming kids.

He looked anything but happy to see them.

"Could we have a word in private?"

He nodded. "Come on back."

When they reached his office, M.C. didn't mince words. "ZZ, we have a problem. Your boss insists he only recommended you look at Todd. Not that you hire him. And certainly not that you skip any of the screening process."

ZZ blanched. "That's not true. He told me quite clearly that he was 'hired.' That he could personally vouch for him."

"That's not his story. I'm sorry."

Visibly upset, he ran a hand through his hair. "I don't know why he would say that."

M.C. held his gaze. "ZZ, you gotta be straight with me here. 'Cause if Derrick Todd turns out to be a killer, it's going to get ugly. Real ugly. If you've twisted the story to save your own ass, you'd better tell me now."

"I didn't. I swear."

Kitt studied the man. Why *would* he lie? Besides, they had questioned him cold; Dale had been primed by ZZ. That had given him plenty of time to prepare his story.

"Thank you, ZZ. We'll be in touch."

"Wait!" The manager looked confused. "Why do you think Mr. Dale said that?"

"Maybe you should take that up with him?"

His expression changed, realization coming over him. He knew. His boss was setting him up, just in case.

Hang the little guy out to dry. No big mystery there.

Kitt felt bad for the man. Reality checks sucked, big-time.

Her cell phone rang. She unclipped the device, brought it to her ear. "Lundgren here."

"Kitt, it's Sal. Derrick Todd made an appearance. Officer Petersen picked him up."

"Good. Stick him in an interrogation room. We're on our way."

Saturday, March 11, 2006
Noon

Derrick Todd was an angry young man. Big on bad attitude. Small on smarts. Not to say he wasn't intelligent. M.C. had no idea if he was or not—he had enough brainpower for her not to have ruled it out yet.

He seemed like one of those kids who consistently made the wrong choice, then blamed somebody else for it.

This cycle always ended badly, in squandered opportunities, jail-time—or worse.

Kitt wandered in, carrying a coffee mug, a newspaper and a box of doughnuts. The doughnuts were a cliché, but that was the point. They figured Mr. Not-So-Bright probably had a chip on his shoulder about cops and would buy right into it.

As they had rehearsed, she dropped the latest edition of the *Register Star* on the table, well within Todd's line of vision. The headline screamed Copycat Or Not—Will He Strike Again? There was a picture of both little Julie Entzel and Marianne Vest. There were also smaller photos of the original SAK victims.

Most serials loved the limelight. They loved to read about themselves in the news. Loved reliving the act. Got off on it. And on the fact they had people in a panic and the cops on the run.

If he was the killer, once he saw the headline, he wouldn't be able to take his eyes off it. It was a psychological trick that had been developed by the Behavioral Science Unit of the FBI. The trick also worked with items from the crime scene, photos of the victim, murder weapons.

The first time M.C. had tried it, the suspect had actually moved his chair to get a better view of the item, a lavender knit cap the victim had been wearing at the time of her murder.

They would start out easy, they had decided. Lull him into a false sense of security. M.C. would play the "bad cop," Kitt the "good one."

Kitt set the box of pastries smack on top of the paper. "Sorry I'm late," she said. "I was taking a coffee break."

"Cops," the kid muttered.

"Excuse me?"

He rocked back in his chair, expression cocky. "You never disappoint, that's all."

"Doughnut?" She motioned to the box. "Help yourself."

"No thanks."

"M.C.?"

"Sure." She made a great show of choosing one, then taking a bite.

"Why am I here?"

"I think you know, Mr. Todd."

"So I got a job at the Fun Zone. Big fuckin' deal."

"Where were you last night, Mr. Todd?"

"Out."

"Out where?"

"At a friend's."

"Name?"

"Don't have one. Met her in a bar."

No accounting for taste. "Which bar?"

He hesitated. "Google Me."

"You don't seem so sure about that."

"I'm sure. Just don't want you pigs to know where I hang out."

Another indication of low IQ: insulting people who carry guns *and* hold your fate in their hands.

Duh.

M.C. glanced at Kitt. She was watching Todd intently, the expression in her eyes fierce. She could guess her thoughts: *Look at the paper, damn you.*

But he didn't. Almost pointedly. Could he be on to them? She didn't think this one had the native intelligence to know what they were up to, but she needed to put it to the test.

"Kitt, can I have a word with you outside?"

The other woman met her eyes, immediately understanding what she was up to. They exited the interrogation room, locking the door behind them. They went around the corner to the surveillance room. There an assistant D.A., a thirtyish young man sporting Harry Potter spectacles and prematurely thinning hair, Sal and Sergeant Haas were watching the video monitor.

All homicide interrogations were videotaped, a relatively recent addition to the RPD's investigative arsenal. The videotape provided a permanent account of the interrogation to study at length later, and a means for the department to cover its ass against rights violations and brutality charges.

Other than a quick glance in their direction, the trio never took their eyes from the monitor. M.C. pulled up a chair; Kitt stood. Todd thrummed his fingers on the table. He stood and paced. He sat again, looked at the camera and flipped them the bird.

But he didn't give the paper more than a cursory glance.

"Maybe he can't read," M.C. muttered.

"He's not the one," Kitt said. "He's not going for it."

"You don't know that for certain," M.C. shot back.

"Yeah, I do. Dammit!"

"Hold on," the assistant D.A. said, "he's taking the bait."

M.C. swung back to the monitor. Sure enough, Todd was inching his chair closer to the paper. As they watched, he leaned forward, as if craning to read the headline around the box of doughnuts.

She held her breath. *Move the box. Get yourself a real good look at that paper. Read all about it, you bastard.*

Instead, he spat into the box of pastries, then settled back into his seat, smiling.

"That little son of a bitch," Sal muttered. "I was going to have one of those."

M.C. looked at Kitt. "Let's take the gloves off."

Kitt frowned slightly. "That's not the way we rehearsed it."

"So?"

"So, we go the way we rehearsed it."

M.C. made a sound of frustration. "He needs more heat."

Kitt pulled rank. "We give it another minute or two. Then up our ante."

M.C. wanted to argue, but saw Sal frown. He would not have his detectives arguing over methods, and certainly not at this important juncture. "Okay, let's go."

They returned to the interview room. Todd grinned at them. "Doughnut, detectives?"

"You're a nasty little prick, aren't you?"

He shrugged. "Whatever."

"Whatever," she repeated, pulling a chair out, angling it to face him. "Funny you would patronize a place called Google Me. After all, you wouldn't want to be Googled, would you, Mr. Todd?"

"Fuck you."

"Do you think that woman you spent the night with would have let you near her if she had known you're a registered sex offender? Or maybe she wasn't a woman at all. How old was this "friend" last night?"

Kitt stepped in before he could respond. She kept her tone low, without the edginess of her partner's. "Who at the Fun Zone hired you?"

"The owner. Sydney Dale." He said the man's name on a sneer.

"No love lost there?" she asked. "Even though he gave an ex-con a job?"

"No love. You could say that. The guy's a dick."

"When he hired you, did he know your history?"

He shrugged. "Don't know, don't care."

M.C. took over. "Really? A children's play center seems a strange place for a child molester to work. Or maybe not so strange…at least from the pervert's point of view?"

His face turned red. "I'm not a child molester!"

"A jury disagreed, didn't they?"

She grabbed the newspaper and tossed the front page on the table in front of him. She tapped Julie and Marianne's photos. "Ever see either of these girls before?"

"No."

"You sure about that?"

He stared at the paper. The headline. He put it all together. And looked ready to puke.

"Care now?"

"I never saw those girls."

"Did you work Saturday, January 21?"

"I don't remember."

"I can help with that," Kitt said. "I had Mr. Zuba check your time card. You did."

"How about Saturday, February 11?"

"I don't remember. Probably."

"You did," Kitt offered, cheerfully.

"So?"

He tried for his earlier confident attitude, but came off scared and queasy instead.

"Both those girls had birthday parties at the Fun Zone. Julie Entzel in January. Marianne Vest in February. That's a pretty big coincidence, don't you think? A convicted sex offender working at the place two murdered girls had their birthday parties?"

He went white. Sweat beaded his upper lips. "I want a lawyer."

"I'll just bet you do, Mr. Todd." M.C. straightened. "Come on, Kitt, let's get Mr. Innocence here an attorney. Obviously, he needs one."

"I didn't do anything!"

Kitt took the motherly role. "Derrick, this looks bad. You know that. I want to help you. I want to catch whoever is hurting these girls. If you didn't do this—"

"I didn't, I swear! I never even saw those girls at the Fun Zone. There are birthdays there all the time!"

"So, why are you working at the Fun Zone? What are we supposed to think?"

"I needed a job!" he cried. "Dale owed me. That's all!"

"Dale owed you? What's that supposed to mean?"

"I know my rights! I'm not saying another fucking word until—"

"You get your lawyer," M.C. finished for him, and stood.

24

Sunday, March 12, 2006
9:20 a.m.

Out of breath and sweating, Kitt slowed her pace. She had kept the promise she'd made to herself to get back in shape. On the couple of days she had wanted to sleep in, she pictured the much younger Mary Catherine Riggio and suddenly found the energy to get her forty-eight-year-old butt up and moving.

She knew it was ridiculous to try to compete with the other woman, but she couldn't help herself. She looked at Riggio and saw the detective she had been twenty years ago. Confident. Her entire career ahead of her. Her entire *life* ahead of her.

Kitt had been acutely aware of the differences between them during their interrogation of Todd. M.C. had insisted on charging forward. Taking control. Kitt had wanted to go slower, not push too hard.

Was that because it would have been the better approach? Or because she had been afraid of making a mistake?

Would she ever not feel as if she was groping around in the dark?

After their interrogation of Todd, the investigation had ground to a halt. He had been booked for violating the state's sex offender registration law. The search of his apartment and vehicle had turned up nothing to connect him to the Entzel and Vest murders.

She hadn't been totally surprised by that. On paper the kid looked like a good suspect, but her instincts, such as they were, told her he wasn't their guy.

For one, he hadn't gone for the bait. And two, if he had been guilty, he would have been on better behavior from the get-go.

Besides, the kid had been convicted of exposing himself to a minor. Fondling himself while he did. A logical next step might be sexually assaulting a child. But the SAK and Copycat victims hadn't been molested.

Her bungalow came into view. Someone sat on the front porch, waiting. As she drew closer, she saw it was Danny. Reading the paper and sipping from a Starbucks Venti-size cup.

"Hey you," she said when she reached him.

He looked up and smiled. "I was just about to give up. Thirty minutes was my limit."

She sat next to him. "I'm glad you didn't. Is that for me?" She indicated a second Starbucks cup.

"It is. Vanilla latte." He handed it to her. "I guess I should have made it a sugar-free skinny?"

"I would have been pissed if you had. I'm exercising to keep up with the competition, not to lose weight."

She sipped, making a sound of pleasure as the sweet, barely warm beverage flowed over her tongue.

"Your partner?"

"Mmm. Mary Catherine Riggio."

"You say the name like she's a snake you're afraid is going to bite you."

Kitt leaned back on her elbows. "I think she already has."

He pursed his lips. "Want to talk about it?"

"Maybe. That for me, too?"

He handed her the pastry bag. "What's left of it. I got hungry waiting."

She peered into the bag at the half-eaten muffin. "Not that I don't appreciate the thought, Danny, but I think I'll pass."

"No problemo." He grinned and helped himself to the last of the muffin.

"So, what's up?" she asked, eyeing him.

"Wanted to check on you. See how you're doing."

"I haven't melted down, if that's what you're asking." She winced at the defensive edge that had crept into her voice.

"I'm not waiting for you to fail, Kitt. I'm not expecting you to."

"Just want to be here when I do, right?"

"No," he chided gently at her sarcasm, "just want to be here if you need me. You know me better than that."

She did. Damn. "Sorry. So I guess the stress *is* getting to me."

"Or the partner."

The partner. Right. Kitt took a swallow of the coffee. "She's young. And smart."

"Attractive?"

"Yeah, that, too."

"And this bothers you why?"

"I would think the reasons are quite obvious."

"Not to me."

"Be serious."

"You're smart, Kitt. And, if I may say so, damn attractive."

"You're my friend, you have to say that. And——" She held up a hand, stopping him. "I'm not young."

"But you are wise."

He delivered that with a grin. She groaned. *Great. The wise, grandmotherly one.* "I'm a screwup."

"Now you're just feeling sorry for yourself."

Kitt was quiet a moment, acknowledging that he was right. "I suppose the thing is, she makes it look effortless."

"The work?"

"No. Believing in herself."

He didn't comment, simply gave her a quick hug. "I need to go."

She followed him to his feet. "So soon?"

"I promised a friend I'd help him move."

She watched him walk away, then turned and crossed to her door. And found it unlocked.

She frowned. Surely she hadn't left it that way.

Had she?

She searched her memory, retracing her steps. She couldn't clearly remember locking it—but it was one of those things she did automatically. She was a cop, after all.

She examined the door and casing. There weren't any signs of the lock being jimmied or forced. Could she have been so distracted she'd forgotten?

She could have, Kitt realized, dismayed. She had better pull herself together.

She let herself in, pointedly locking the door behind her. A shower, then a good breakfast, she decided. The latte would hold her until then.

She peeled off her damp T-shirt as she entered the bedroom. She tossed it at the hamper, then froze, the hair at the back of her neck standing on end.

Her nightstand drawer stood partly open. The drawer she kept her gun in.

The blood began to pound in her head. An officer always carried a weapon. When she ran, she wore a fanny pack or an ankle holster. Today it was a fanny pack.

Still, she knew she had not left that drawer open.

Kitt crossed to the nightstand and slid the drawer the rest of the way open. Her journal. A pen. Several favorite photos of Sadie. The empty space where her Glock usually rested.

Someone had been in her house. Who? She pictured Danny, waiting on the front porch. Surely, not—

Peanut.

He knew where she lived. He was, obviously, adept at breaking and entering. He had decided to take his toying with her to a new level.

He could still be there.

She unzipped the fanny pack, removed the Glock and began a systematic search. In the end, she found nothing out of place save for the original drawer and her unlocked front door.

Was she imagining things? Had she left both the door unlocked and the nightstand drawer open?

Was she losing it? Again?

The hell of it was, she couldn't be certain. She didn't trust herself, her instincts. Which left her more uneasy than *knowing* a dozen monsters like the SAK had been in her home.

Monday, March 13, 2006
8:00 a.m.

Kitt sipped the just-brewed coffee. The rest of the day before had slipped by without incident. She had spent a good part of it wrangling with herself over whether the SAK had been in her house or not and whether she should share her suspicions with M.C. or Sal.

She had decided against sharing. The last thing she needed was anything that made her look overwrought or would shake their confidence in her state of mind.

She was shaken enough, thank you very much.

M.C. arrived then, looking slightly bleary-eyed.

"How was your day off?" Kitt asked.

"Frankly, it sucked. I spent it doing laundry, cleaning and paying bills."

"The fun never stops for us cops. The kid's lawyer left a message."

"Yeah? What'd he have to say?"

"That Todd's innocent, of course."

"I like the kid for this. He's the best we've got."

"Actually, I think the Fun Zone's the best *lead* we've got. It links the victims, something we were never able to do with the original SAK murders. By the way, Sal authorized an undercover officer working the place. He thought you'd be the perfect choice."

That brought M.C. fully awake. "The perfect choice? I scare the crap out of most kids. Plus, if I have to spend another ten minutes in that place, I won't be responsible for my actions."

"That's what I told him. Reminded him, too, that both of us have been on TV in regards to the case."

"And?"

"He's putting Schmidt on it."

"Lucky Schmidt. So he gets the previous security tapes, too?" When Kitt nodded, she added, "I suppose I owe you for that one."

"What're partners for?"

Before M.C. could comment, Kitt's desk phone rang. "Detective Lundgren."

"Are you running in circles, dear one?"

Him. Kitt signaled M.C. The other woman was immediately on the phone to CRU, initiating the trace.

"Who is this?"

"You know who this is. Your beloved Peanut."

Kitt gritted her teeth at his sly tone. "I wondered when you'd call. Thought maybe you were welching on our deal."

"I don't welch on my deals."

"Good. We gave you what you wanted, now it's your turn. Give us the Copycat."

M.C., still on with CRU, bent and jotted *cell phone* on the folder on the desk in front of her.

Dammit. She had to keep him on five minutes to get the trace.

"How does it feel having another girl's death on your hands?" she asked.

"Not on mine. Yours, Kitten." He laughed. "Besides, I don't care if my hands have blood on them. A child's blood. But you care."

"My conscience is clear."

"Is it? What of your daughter? Is her blood on your hands?"

It took everything she had to stay focused. He wanted her to lose it. He got off on being in control. She wouldn't give him what he wanted.

"This isn't about me," she said. "You promised information, I expect you to keep that promise."

He laughed again, the sound somehow reptilian. "How's the investigation going?"

"We're following some very strong leads."

"Who? That kid from the Fun Zone?"

That blindsided her. She fought to keep from revealing it. "How do you know about Todd?"

"I know everything. I'm omnipotent."

"I'm sorry, did you say you're impotent?"

She darted a glance at M.C. who put a hand over her mouth to keep from laughing out loud.

Kitt supposed it wasn't a very good idea to piss him off, but she wanted to test his limits. Locate his buttons, see how he responded to her challenging his authority.

In the process, she learned what made him tick.

"Don't do that again," he told her, voice shaking slightly.

He was angry.

He took himself very seriously.

She glanced at M.C. and pointed at her watch. The other woman held up three fingers.

Two more to go.

Piece of cake, she told herself, though the truth was, two minutes seemed an eternity right now.

"Sorry. My sense of humor gets away from me sometimes."

"Just see that it doesn't again."

Word had spread through the bureau and a group of her colleagues gathered around. Kitt gave them little more than a glance. "We could meet, you and I. Get to know each other better."

"I don't think that'd be a good idea, Kitten."

"I'd come alone. We could have a drink or two. Talk."

"I'm worried about *your* health, Kitten. Not mine. I know you're trying to trace this, so don't play games. Loves Park Self-Storage. Unit seven."

He ended the call. Kitt jumped to her feet. "Did we get it?"

M.C. held up a hand, then swore. "No. You were just shy of five."

"Dammit!" Kitt grabbed her jacket. "I want a search warrant for that self-storage unit."

"Under way."

"Get me two cruisers, minimum. Call ID. Have them meet us there."

26

Monday, March 13, 2006
9:40 a.m.

Loves Park was a small community that sat adjacent to Rockford, on the north side. The running joke held that women from Loves Park all had big hair, and the men, big pickup trucks.

Kitt wasn't certain how the gag had gotten started, the trip from one community into the other was seamless save for a small sign announcing the change. Simply, Rockford held itself in higher esteem than its neighbor; it had been that way as long as she could remember.

Loves Park Self-Storage, it turned out, was located between a Chinese restaurant and a burger joint. As Kitt climbed out of her vehicle, the smell of grease hit her hard. Not even ten in the morning and somebody was frying something. She had no doubt that a number of the guys they'd brought with them—three patrol units and most of the ID Bureau—were already wondering about lunch: Chinese or burgers?

If they were still here at noon. Who knew? The locker could be empty. The tip could be a ruse. Obviously "Peanut" got his jollies from making her jump through hoops.

But the storage unit could contain anything. The key to the investigation. A direct lead to the Copycat. Or one back to the SAK.

"Hoping Santa brings you everything you're wishing for?" M.C. said from the other side of the car.

"You know it's true. Shall we?"

They made their way around the vehicles and fell into step together. Behind them, she heard the rest of the team arriving.

Delivering a search warrant was a mixed bag. It could be an exhilarating moment. Triumphant. Because, as a cop, you knew *this was it.* That this scumbag, who had done whatever, was about to get nailed. You just *knew* it. A cop's instincts.

Other times, it made you feel lousy to be the law. Because of the innocent bystanders. Family members or loved ones who either had no clue what kind of creep they had been living with or were too young to have a clue.

She had experienced everything in between as well. Suspects who pulled weapons or tried to run, ambivalence, lawsuits.

They stepped into the leasing office. It wasn't much more than a desk, file cabinet and sitting area. Very small. Barely serviceable.

"Good morning," Kitt said to the woman behind the desk, who not only did not have big hair, but sported a sleek little bob.

So much for stereotypes.

"Can I help you?" she asked, smiling.

"Afraid so." She crossed to her and handed her the warrant. "I'm Detective Lundgren from the Rockford Police Department. This is Detective Riggio. I have a warrant to search unit seven."

The young woman looked confused, then flustered. "I'm sorry. I don't understand."

"A search warrant. For the contents of unit seven and that unit's renter information. It's all there on the warrant."

"I'll have to call my boss and get his okay."

She reached for the phone; Kitt noticed her hand was shaking. "Call him if you like," Kitt said, "but a judge already gave me permission. By the way, the law requires you or the owner be present during the search. If you think that's going to present a problem, you might want to call someone else in."

"Wait! I don't have a key to that padlock. How are you going to get in?"

Kitt stopped in the doorway and turned back. "Don't worry, we've got it covered."

By the time she made it to number seven, one of her colleagues had already cut the lock and rolled back the metal door. The interior was dim, even with sunlight pouring through the open door. The three uniforms snapped on their flashlights.

"We're going to need scene lights," Kitt said.

M.C. nodded. "I'll call."

The unit, Kitt discovered, was very full. She shone her flashlight beam over the interior. The contents ran the gamut from furniture to bikes, boxes to books, even a dressmaker's mannequin.

For the next two hours, Kitt and the rest of the team carefully picked through the items, opening boxes, leafing through folded garments, books. Looking for the obvious. Photos. A family Bible or other inscribed items. Weapons. Body parts. A recognizable trophy.

There was something here. She felt it.

Or were those her shot instincts talking to her?

She crossed to Snowe. "What do you think?" she asked.

Snowe turned his ball cap backward on his head. "It's going to take days, even weeks, to get through everything in here."

She had thought the same thing but had hoped for better.

"I don't have that kind of time."

"We can't give you a miracle. Wish we could."

"What about an inventory?"

"No analysis? Less time. A few days."

Civilians watched television shows like *CSI* and figured every case got that kind of attention. If only it were so.

At any given time, an urban PD had hundreds of ongoing investigations, new crimes being committed continually and limited manpower and budget. Even cases as high profile as the SAK and Copycat killings faced time-and-money constraints.

"Do your thing," she said. "I'm going to follow up on the renter." Kitt motioned one of the uniforms over. "Get the renter's information and run it through the databases. I want to know who this guy is, where he lives and if he has any priors."

Each patrol unit traveled with an MDT, or Mobile Data Terminal. It allowed them to access pretty much everything about a suspect but the size of his morning dump.

The man nodded. "You got it, Detective."

M.C. sidled up to her. "We need to talk."

Kitt felt herself stiffen. "That so?"

"I'm thinking this is a setup. Another hoop for you to jump through."

Kitt fought the defensiveness that rose up in her. "Why?"

"It has the feel of a stage set to me. It's too perfect."

Kitt moved her gaze over the contents, the picture they made. The dressmaker's mannequin, the two old Schwinn bikes, propped up against the far wall. The steamer trunk and cracked mirror.

Like a movie set.

One working hard to be part of a story.

"He's dicking with you, Kitt."

"But there's something here. I feel it. He's planted it."

"If he did, he buried it. To tie you up. Keep you chasing shadows."

Chasing shadows. Sadie. Joe. The Sleeping Angels.

"You gotta ask yourself, why?" M.C. said.

Kitt resisted the idea. "Are you suggesting, Detective, that I not pursue this?"

"No. Just—" M.C. looked away, then back. Kitt had the sense that she struggled with something. Or that she was stepping into an arena not only foreign to her, but uncomfortable as well.

"Just be careful," she finished.

The other woman had surprised her. Concern was the last thing Kitt had expected her to want to communicate. "Thanks for caring," she said gruffly, "but I don't think I have anything to worry about from either the SAK or his copycat. I'm not ten years old anymore. And these days I'm only blond because my hairdresser's a genius."

M.C. didn't smile. "You can lose a lot more than your life, Kitt."

They both knew many things could be taken from a victim besides her life.

What M.C. didn't realize was, Kitt had already lost most of them.

"Detective Lundgren? I've got him."

The two women hurried out to the patrol car. "Andrew Stevens. Twenty-eight. Engineer with Sundstrand. Lives on Boulder Ridge Drive. Record's clean. Not even a traffic violation."

"Great." Kitt looked at M.C. "You in the mood to ride shotgun?"

"Absolutely."

As they hoped they would, they caught Stevens at work. He possessed one of those broad, honest-looking faces that didn't mean squat.

"Is this about my wallet?" he asked, after they had introduced themselves.

"Your wallet?" Kitt asked.

He looked frustrated. "Was stolen. The day after Christmas. I reported it. Never heard a thing back."

"I'm sorry, Mr. Stevens. We're here about your storage locker."

"What storage locker?"

"Loves Park Self-Storage. Unit seven. You rented it on January 3."

He stared at them a moment, frowning. "I didn't rent a storage facility, my wallet was stolen. Can't you guys get anything right?"

Nice. "I'm sorry you feel that way, sir." Kitt handed him a copy of the rental agreement. "But according to this, you did."

He scanned the document, frowning, then handed it back. "This isn't me. It can't be."

"And why's that?" M.C. asked.

"I was in San Francisco on January 3. On my honeymoon."

Monday, March 13, 2006
3:00 p.m.

By three that afternoon, Kitt was mighty pissed off. M.C. watched the woman as she paced. "At this rate, you're going to wear a hole in the floor. Or your shoes."

"Screw 'em both. Another dead end. Dammit!"

"Apple?" M.C. asked.

Kitt stopped pacing. "I'd rather have snack crackers."

"No junk food." M.C. tossed her the apple. "You're already on edge."

Kitt caught it. "He's screwing with me. And it's starting to piss me off."

"I told you so."

"Don't you start with me now. One is most definitely enough."

"You've got things backward," M.C. said. "I'm the young, brash hothead.You're the mature, seasoned veteran who's counseling me. Remember? Lighten up? Go with the flow?"

Kitt took a bite of the apple. It was crunchy and tart, just the way she liked them. "I never said go with the flow."

"Let's pretend, then. Now, take your own advice."

"Excuse me?"

M.C. stood. "Yeah, he's screwing with you. And doing a damn fine job of it, don't you think? Stop letting him get to you. Stop running in circles and being pissed off about it."

"You irritate the hell out of me."

M.C. smiled, perversely pleased. "Better me than him."

Kitt took another bite of her apple, never taking her gaze from M.C. "I still think there's something there."

"But what? It's not Stevens. His story checked out. He reported his wallet stolen. He canceled all his credit cards and changed the locks on his doors. The airline confirmed Mr. and Mrs. Andrew Stevens traveled with them, the hotel confirmed the couple stayed at their San Francisco property for six nights, beginning January 2 and checking out January 8."

"So our guy steals a wallet. Uses the ID to rent a storage locker. Pays a year in advance."

"But which guy? The Copycat? Or Peanut?"

M.C. saw Kitt's involuntary cringe at the nickname. This guy knew how to get to Kitt, no doubt about it. She made a mental note not to refer to him by the name again.

"I don't know." Kitt drew her eyebrows together in thought. "He didn't tell me whose storage locker it was, so I assumed—"

"It was the Copycat's. As he knew you would."

"But instead, it's part of his game."

"It looked like a stage set, because it was one. He's sent you on a kind of scavenger hunt."

Kitt perched on the edge of the desk. M.C. could see that she had forgotten she was pissed off. "So, it's up to me to find the clue hidden there."

"Buried, you mean. Like a needle in a haystack. If there's anything at all."

"There is, I'm certain." She tossed the apple core into the trash can under her desk. "Because if there wasn't a clue, he'd be cheating. What fun is that?"

M.C. arched her eyebrows, unconvinced.

"Think about it. He's playing with me. He's enjoying the game. He's called it 'fun.' Cheating isn't fun, there's no satisfaction in winning an unfair game."

"To *you*. You're talking about a killer." She took a bite of her own apple, chewed a moment before speaking again. "That's a stretch, Lundgren. Sorry."

"I know it is. But I have a feeling about this."

"Do you really think you're in a place to trust your gut right now?"

Kitt looked momentarily stricken. The moment offered M.C. a glimpse of how vulnerable her partner really was. How hesitant.

A very bad place for a cop to be.

M.C. let out a long breath, working to help herself make sense of all the pieces. "You have to question everything he says. Because it's a game, you have to look at each statement through that filter. Ask yourself why. First question, why you, Kitt?"

"Because I was lead on the original SAK case," she said quickly. "He thinks I'm a worthy opponent, a pushover or whatever. I don't think that's important."

M.C. didn't buy Kitt's glib reasoning and she disagreed that targeting Kitt was insignificant. The reason the SAK was calling Kitt was of paramount importance.

"There's a specific reason he's involved you," she insisted. "Think about it, he could have called me or anyone else on the force. But he chose you."

Kitt made a sound of frustration. "What difference does it make why he chose me? I'm more interested in how he and the Copycat know each other."

"Maybe they don't. Or maybe they're one and the same person. Or in cahoots with each other. Maybe this is a game they're playing with each other?"

"And I'm simply a pawn?" Kitt brought the heels of her hands to her eyes. "Which brings us back to square one. Seven days and another girl dead, and we're no closer to an answer than before."

They both fell silent, M.C. lost in her own thoughts. After a moment, Kitt looked at her. "How do you think he knew about Derrick Todd?"

A good question. And one they hadn't spent much time considering. Yet.

"He could be following us," M.C. offered. "He could be involved with the case."

"A cop?"

"Unlikely. But we can't rule anything out." M.C. pursed her lips in thought. "Who knew about Todd?"

"For certain? You and me. The chief. ZZ. His wife. And Sydney Dale."

M.C. nodded. "We both felt Dale was being evasive. The man recommended Todd, hired him without instituting the normal safeguards. Todd said Dale 'owed' him. Why?"

"I suggest we put the answer to that at the top of our list."

"Speaking of lists," Kitt murmured, motioning behind M.C. "Could we be so lucky?"

M.C. looked over her shoulder. Detective Snowe was striding toward them, a shit-eating grin spread across his face.

"Got your inventory," he said when he reached them. He laid it carefully on the desk. "Sorenstein and I worked most of the night. We were as detailed as we could be, considering."

M.C. thumbed through the list. Fifteen single-spaced, typed pages. "We owe you."

"You sure as hell do. Buy me a drink some night."

"You've got it."

He started off, then stopped and glanced back at her. "Remember that comic from Buster's?"

"Lance Castrogiovanni. What about him?"

"I saw him downstairs a few minutes ago. He was asking for you at the information desk. I'm thinking you have an admirer."

Detective Allen peeked around his cubicle at them. "A boyfriend, Riggio? And here I thought you and Lundgren were an item."

M.C. made a sound of disgust. "Grow up, boys."

She exited the VCB and, five minutes later, crossed the lobby to where Lance sat, looking every bit the fish out of water.

"Are you lost?" she asked when she reached him.

He stood and smiled. "I was. Not anymore."

Something in his tone left her feeling as if she had done something wonderful. "What brings you into the belly of the beast?" she asked.

"I was in the neighborhood…well, the general vicinity, and decided to look you up. Figured it'd be harder to turn me down in person."

"Turn you down for what?" she asked, though she had a pretty good idea.

"A date."

"What did you have in mind?"

"You and me, food and drink. A few laughs. Hopefully more than a few, considering."

She laughed at that. "When?"

"I've got a gig every night this week but Wednesday."

She would have to miss the family dinner. Her mother's interrogation. Lance Castrogiovanni had an excellent sense of timing.

M.C. smiled. "Unless I get hung up here, you're on."

28

Tuesday, March 14, 2006
7:30 a.m.

The sounds of the busy coffeehouse swirled around him. He liked being out among people. Blending in, interacting.

No one had a clue. Who he was. What he was capable of.

No one suspected his secrets.

Even his Kitten. Or maybe, especially her.

He leaned back in his chair and sipped his espresso, smiling at a woman who glanced his way.

He often played this game: studying people—like that woman— and then imagining what she would do if he revealed himself to her. Imagined the fear creeping into her eyes, the noise she might make—a small squeak, like a terrified mouse.

He almost got hard just thinking about it.

The word Lundgren had called him—*impotent*—flew into his head, sucking the pleasure from the moment.

She had made him very angry.

But worse, she had known it. Until he had regained control, she'd had all the power.

He had been powerless.

It'd been a smart move on her part. She had surprised him and earned his admiration. But also his ire.

He couldn't let her get away with it. She would have to pay. A small price this time, as it was her first offense. But not so small she didn't feel its sting. A warning, of sorts, he decided, pleased with himself.

But what?

The woman at the next table caught his eyes and smiled again. Maybe he should ask her? *"I need to scare the shit out of someone. A woman. As a warning. A punishment for bad behavior. What do you suggest?"*

No, he didn't suppose that would do at all, but it was fun to imagine. Taking his espresso with him, he crossed to the woman and introduced himself.

Tuesday, March 14, 2006
4:30 p.m.

Every spring, the local chapter of the Leukemia Society of America held a fair to benefit children stricken with the disease. Held at Rockford's Discovery Center Museum, the fair included food and games, performances and a silent auction. Though it hurt, Kitt always attended. If she could help someone else's child beat this disease, it was worth any amount of distress she might experience.

This year, for the first time, she was attending alone. The past two, although they had been divorced, she and Joe had gone together. They had clung to each other despite their personal differences.

This year, she supposed, he would be clinging to his fiancée.

She wondered if she would see him there. And if Valerie would be with him.

If he bothered to come. Maybe this was another piece of his past he'd chosen to let go.

Kitt strolled through the fair. She bought tickets for games she had no intention of playing, bid on several items she didn't want and ate a piece of pizza she wasn't hungry for.

Lastly, she purchased a luminaria for Sadie. Every year, the fair created a memorial garden to honor those who had been stricken by the disease. The luminarias consisted of a plain white paper bag—on which you wrote your loved one's name, then decorated with markers—and a tea light to be placed inside.

Kitt scrawled *Sadie Marie Lundgren* in purple, Sadie's favorite color, across the bag. She couldn't bring herself to do more, it hurt too much.

The memorial garden was located at the very center of the main hall, cordoned off by a white picket fence. She found the location appropriate—for weren't the victims of the disease at the heart of the drive to find a cure?

Kitt handed the attendant Sadie's bag and watched as the woman placed it, then lit the candle.

She wasn't the first to place a light for Sadie.

Joe was there.

A lump in her throat, Kitt stared at a second luminaria with her daughter's name on it.

Our Peanut. Sadie Marie.

The lump became tears. They burned her eyes. God, she missed Sadie. And Joe. Being a mom.

She missed her family.

"Kitt?"

Joe. She didn't want him to catch her crying. Especially if he wasn't alone. Blinking to clear her eyes, she turned.

"Joe," she said stiffly. "Hello."

She shifted her gaze to the woman with him. She looked to be a good ten years younger than he was, with soft brown hair and eyes.

Joe's fiancée looked nothing like her. Even their builds were different—Kitt was tall and angular, Valerie petite and curvy. She wasn't sure why that was such a surprise—or why it upset her so much. Perhaps she had imagined he'd picked a clone of her. A sort of stand-in because he still pined for her.

"I'm Kitt," she managed to say, and held out her hand.

"Valerie." The woman smiled and took it. "I've heard so much about you."

She sounded nice. She looked sincere. Kitt wished she could hate her, but that only made her feel worse.

A pretty, fair-haired girl rushed up to Valerie, face aglow with excitement. She held up a plastic zipper bag, half-filled with water. A pitiful-looking goldfish swam inside.

Kitt stared at the child, guessing her age to be nine or ten. Her fingers went numb. A rushing sound filled her head.

Valerie had a child.

Joe was going to be a father again.

"This is my daughter, Tami. Tami, this is Detective Lundgren."

The child peeked at her, then turned her face into her mother's side.

"I'm sorry," Valerie said. "She's extremely shy. It's partly because of her—"

Kitt didn't let the woman finish. Blinded by tears, she turned on her heel and hurried toward the exit.

Valerie had a child. A daughter.

Joe was replacing Sadie.

"Kitt, wait!"

She began to run, wanting nothing more than to be away from him. And the girl with the soft brown eyes and shy smile.

He caught up with her just outside the main doors. He captured her elbow and turned her to face him.

"Let me go, Joe!"

"Not until we talk."

"About what? You trying to replace our daughter?"

"It's not that way."

"How old is she?"

His expression said it all, and her breath caught on a sob. "How could you do this?"

"I need to live again, Kitt. I need to move on."

"Start a new life," she said bitterly. "A new family."

He caught her other arm. "Wanting a life doesn't dishonor our daughter's memory. Wanting what I had and lost doesn't dishonor her memory. It celebrates it."

"Let me go," she said. "I don't want to hear your self-serving justifications."

"Sadie would hate what we've become. She would hate what you've become. Think about that."

She jerked her hands free, shaking with the force of her anger and betrayal. "I'm never going to forgive you for this, Joe. Never!"

For long moments, they stood that way, gazes locked. Kitt couldn't bring herself to walk away. She longed to throw herself into his arms and weep for all they had lost—and beg him not to marry Valerie.

Finally, he took a step back from her. "I'm really sorry, Kitt. But I can't...I can't do this anymore."

He turned and walked away. She watched him go, crushed. Her marriage was over. Soon Joe would belong to another woman. Be part of another family.

A sound of pain caught in her throat. Until now, this very minute, she had still thought of him as hers.

"For you, pretty lady."

She shifted her gaze to the clown who had come up to her. His painted face serious, he held out one of the balloons he was selling. A pink one.

Her vision blurred, she shook her head, unable to speak.

Stubbornly, he held the balloon out. "To make you smile again."

The clown had seen the exchange between her and Joe. Perhaps he had heard it as well. He felt sorry for her.

But not as sorry as she felt for herself.

Helplessly, she took the balloon. He bowed, his orange wig bobbing with the movement, then shuffled off.

Clutching the pink balloon, Kitt headed for her empty home.

Tuesday, March 14, 2006
11:00 p.m.

The shrill scream of the phone awakened her. Kitt cracked open her eyes, head and vision swimming. She moved her gaze over the dark room, disoriented.

The phone screamed again. She reached for it, sending something on the nightstand tumbling. A glass, she realized.

An empty glass.

One that had been filled with vodka.

She brought the device to her ear. "H'lo. Lun'ren here."

"Kitt? Is that you? It's Danny."

"Danny?" she repeated, struggling to shake the cobwebs from her head. Shake off the effects of the alcohol.

She had fallen off the wagon. Given in to her feeling of betrayal and her despair. How could she have been so stupid and weak?

"Are you okay?" he asked.

"Fine. I was sleeping." She cleared her throat and dragged herself up to see the clock. "What time is it? It feels like the middle of the night."

"About eleven."

She heard the disappointment in his voice. The suspicion. A drunk recognized another drunk's bender.

"What's up?" she asked, trying to sound normal. Sober.

He was silent a moment. "Nothing. I was thinking about you. We haven't spoken since last week and...I just wanted to make certain you're doing okay."

"I'm doing great." She cringed as the chirpy-sounding lie sprang from her lips. "I mean, as great as can be expected. Considering."

"Considering that your ex-husband is engaged and you're embroiled in a carbon copy of the case that sent you over the edge?"

"Exactly." She closed her eyes and prayed he didn't ask her if she had been drinking. She didn't know if she could bring herself to tell him the truth.

"You could have called me, Kitt. Or another member of the group."

"I don't know what you're talking about."

"Right." He paused, as if collecting his thoughts or giving her a chance to change her answer. "I thought we were closer than this. Call me when you're ready to be real."

"Danny, wai—"

But he had hung up. For long moments she sat, dial tone buzzing in her ear. She felt like crap—physically and emotionally. A year of sobriety, down the toilet. With one binge, she had slipped right back into behavior she found personally abhorrent—not just the drinking, but the evasions and lies.

Kitt dropped her head to her hands. They shook. She felt ill. She needed Danny to help her through this. She needed her group, her support system.

She jumped as the phone jangled again. Danny, she thought. He hadn't been able to leave it this way between them.

She snatched up the receiver. "Danny, you were right. I'm so sor—"

"Danny? Should I be jealous, dear one?"

Not her friend.

Him.

"What do you want?" she snapped.

"That's not very nice, Kitten."

"I'm not in a nice mood."

"And after all I've done for you."

"And what would that be? The wild-goose chase you sent me on? Thanks."

He chuckled. "It may have seemed that way to you. You have to have faith."

"I have faith, all right. That I'll find you and your copycat, and you'll both rot in prison."

"You don't sound yourself tonight. Didn't you like the balloon? Didn't it lift your spirits?"

For one dizzying moment, she thought she had misheard him. But she hadn't. *He had been there.*

Had he been lying in wait for her? Did he know her routine so well?

A clown. Dear God, was that how he scouted victims?

"Cat got your tongue, Kitten?"

Gooseflesh crawled up her arms at his self-satisfied tone. "Go to hell," she said, and hung up.

Almost immediately, the phone rang again. As she'd expected, it was him.

"Don't ever do that to me again," he said, voice vibrating with the force of his fury. "Do you understand? You won't like what happens."

She smiled, experiencing a tingle of victory. For him, the thrill was in terrorizing and manipulating her. Anticipating her emotions. He hadn't anticipated her hanging up that way. She had momentarily wrenched the upper hand away from him.

If she could manage to do it again, could she force him to make a mistake? Maybe reveal something he hadn't intended to?

"And what'll that be?"

"Don't push me." She heard the strike of a lighter, the hiss of a cigarette being lit. "I know where you live, Kitt Lundgren. And I know what hurts you."

Her hands were shaking. She simultaneously cursed the vodka of earlier and longed for more. "You don't know me as well as you think you do. I promise you that."

"Tell yourself that, dear one. If it reassures you."

"I'm done being controlled and intimidated by you. You know what, I think you're full of shit. You want to be this big badass, but you're just a coward."

For a moment she wondered if he had hung up on her, then she heard the sound of his breathing. He was angry again. "There were others, you know. Others who died. Other perfect crimes. Mine."

Her breath caught. "Other children?"

"You never connected them to me. No one did."

"Were these others children?" she asked again. "Tell me!"

"Did you like the balloon?" he asked. "Did it remind you of Sadie? Or of the other girls who died? It was thoughtful of me to give it to you, don't you think?"

"What others?" she asked again. "Tell me, damn you!"

"Sleep well, Kitten."

He hung up. She swore, certain they didn't get the tap. A moment later the officer monitoring her phone confirmed it.

She tossed the phone onto the bed.

Bloody hell.

Climbing out of bed, she strode to the bathroom. Her legs felt rubbery, her hands shook. After splashing cold water on her face, she headed to the kitchen. There, the half-empty bottle of vodka mocked her. She stared at it, furious. At herself for succumbing. At Joe. At this child-killing monster.

Fueled by her fury, she crossed to the sink and dumped the remainder of the alcohol, then rinsed the sink to remove its smell. They would not beat her. None of them.

While a pot of coffee brewed, Kitt paced. He'd claimed he'd killed others. Plural. Children? she wondered, then discarded the thought. No way could the murders of children have slipped past the RPD radar.

But if not children, who?

The coffee burbled. She crossed to the pot, needing the caffeine. She needed to chase away the last of the alcohol fog. Mug poured, sugar and milk added, she made herself a peanut-butter sandwich.

While she consumed both, she turned her thoughts to the other things he had said to her. He had been at the charity event. He claimed to be the clown who had given her the balloon. She worked to recall details of his appearance.

Tall, maybe six feet. Medium build. Caucasian. His features had been concealed by the clown getup: white face, big red nose, eyes made up to look wide and surprised. Blue, she thought. His eyes had definitely been blue. Hair color had been obscured by the neon-orange wig.

What to do? She glanced at the wall clock. Still well before midnight. If M.C. wasn't still up, she should be.

This couldn't wait until morning.

She returned to the bedroom and snatched up the portable phone. She dialed her partner's cell number. She answered after the second ring, tone wary.

"You awake, partner?"

"Kitt?" The word came out half growl. "This better be good."

"You decide. He contacted me again. Claimed other victims, ones we never linked to him."

She heard the woman's sharply indrawn breath, then what sounded like her climbing out of the bed. "You think he was telling the truth?"

"Don't know. I'm going to headquarters now. Figured I'd get on the computer, see if I can find anything."

"They're not going anywhere, you know. It'll wait till morning."

"I know. But I won't be able to sleep, anyway." She cleared her throat. "There's more. Apparently, he and I were face-to-face tonight."

"You've got me now," M.C. said. "I go right past your place on my way to the PSB. I'll pick you up."

31

Wednesday, March 15, 2006
12:05 a.m.

As the crow flew, Kitt didn't live that far from her. M.C. parked in the driveway of Kitt's cottage-style home, climbed out of her Explorer, crossed to the door and rang the bell.

It took several minutes for Kitt to come to the door. Her hair was wet, her face flushed.

"That was fast," she said. "I didn't expect you for at least fifteen minutes."

"I should have warned you, I was still up and dressed."

"No problem. I took a quick shower. Mind if I take a minute to dry my hair?"

"Go ahead. Is that coffee I smell?"

"A nearly full pot, help yourself. Kitchen's dead ahead."

M.C. found the kitchen, then the cabinet that held the mugs. A box of sweetener sat open on the counter. Obviously, Kitt had already had a cup. And, judging by the empty plate by the sink, something to eat.

Before she called? M.C. wondered. Or after?

M.C. filled a mug, sweetened it and sipped. From the other part of the house she heard the hum of a hair dryer.

She crossed to the refrigerator. A half-dozen photos, held in place by magnets, graced its front.

Sadie, she realized. And Joe.

She studied the images, one by one. Sadie had been a beautiful little girl. Blond and blue-eyed, with an endearing smile that included dimples. Joe, also fair-haired, was a handsome man. Strongly built, like someone whose job kept him active. She saw where Sadie had gotten her dimples.

M.C. sipped the coffee. But it was the pictures of Kitt that surprised her most. She almost didn't recognize her, she looked so young in the photographs. So lighthearted.

What must it feel like to lose your family?

She had lost her father, and it had been awful. But losing your child? Then your marriage? She couldn't imagine the pain.

"I see you found the coffee."

M.C. whirled around. Some of her coffee sloshed over the rim of her cup, onto her hand and the floor.

Kitt crossed the kitchen, ripped off a paper towel and handed it to her. "Sorry I startled you."

M.C. mopped up the mess, then turned back to Kitt. The other woman's gaze was on the photographs, the yearning in her expression painful to see.

"She was a beautiful little girl."

A smile touched Kitt's mouth. "Inside and out."

"I'm really sorry. It's got to be...horrible."

Kitt didn't respond, but crossed to the sink and rinsed her plate and cup, then stuck them in the dishwasher. "You said you weren't asleep. Out with the guy?"

"Working. Going over the storage-unit inventory list."

"Anything jump out?"

"No. It's a major mishmash of crap. Clothing, books, old calendars, the dressmaker's dummy, an aluminum Christmas tree, old record albums. And that's just the beginning. It reads like the contents of someone's attic."

"But whose?"

"My fear is, it's no one's. That your anonymous friend went to Goodwill or a few garage sales and assembled a bunch of junk to throw you off." M.C. crossed to the sink, dumped the remainder of her coffee and rinsed her cup. "Garbage in here?" she asked, opening the cabinet located under the sink.

"No! I'll do—"

M.C. saw what Kitt was trying to hide. An empty vodka bottle. A bottom-of-the-barrel brand.

The kind a drunk would buy.

M.C. stared at the bottle, realizing what it meant. This was what she had feared when they'd been assigned to work together. Kitt had sworn she was rehabilitated. She had been fool enough to believe her.

Was this a first offense? Or had it been happening all along?

Did that even matter?

M.C. tossed the soiled paper towel into the trash, then retrieved the bottle. She turned to Kitt and held it up, furious. "What is this?"

Kitt stared at the bottle, expression devastated.

"Dammit, Kitt! You've been drinking."

"I can explain."

"No, you can't. You're an alcoholic. You can't drink. Not ever."

"I know." She took a step toward her, hand out. "Just listen. Please."

"I've got to go to Sal with this."

"It won't happen again. I promise."

"You can't promise that. And I can't allow you to jeopardize this investigation."

"He'll suspend me. And I don't have…being a cop is all I have left."

"You should have thought of that before you knocked back a fifth."

"It wasn't like that… It—"

"This partnership is over, Kitt."

"Joe's remarrying!" she cried. "The woman has a daughter. Sadie's age. He…I found out tonight. They're going to be a family. They're going to have—"

She bit the words back, but M.C. imagined they went something like *They're going to have everything I lost.*

A lump formed in M.C.'s throat as she struggled with the pity she felt for the other woman. It was okay to feel bad for her, but she couldn't allow Kitt to put the investigation at risk. Her responsibility was to the force, to the trust the public—and her superior officers—had in her.

As she watched, Kitt crossed to the table and chairs. She sank onto one of the chairs and dropped her head into her hands.

"It broke my heart," she whispered. "The thought that he could do this. Just replace Sadie that way. Replace…me."

M.C. wavered in the doorway a moment more, then crossed to Kitt. She squatted down in front of her. "Tell me what happened," she said softly. "I'm listening."

"It's a fund-raiser for pediatric leukemia. We go every year. I ran into Joe there, with his fiancée. Valerie. That's when I learned—" She sucked in a deep breath. "When I learned about her daughter. Tami.

"We had words. I was so angry. Felt so…betrayed. I stopped at a store on the way home, bought the vodka and…proceeded to drink most of it."

She swallowed hard, then looked up at M.C. "That's what I did when Sadie died. I drank to fill up the empty place inside. To dull the pain. Dull the ache of missing her.

"Before that, I didn't drink. Occasionally, socially. Drinking wasn't a part of my life growing up. My paternal grandfather was an alcoholic and because of that my dad never drank."

She squeezed her hands into fists; M.C. saw that her knuckles were white.

"Then *he* called. Tonight. So proud of himself. Smirking and so arrogant. He was there, at the leukemia event."

"He told you?"

"Yes."

"He gave me a pink balloon." Kitt went on to explain about how, after her confrontation with Joe, a clown had approached her with a balloon. "On the phone, he asked if I liked the balloon he had given me."

A clown. Is that how he chose his victims?

M.C. stood. "What else did he say?"

"He said there were other victims, ones the police never connected to him."

"But nothing else about tonight?"

"No." Kitt laced her fingers. "I was sober for a year, M.C. I screwed up tonight. I hate myself for it. But it won't happen again."

M.C. didn't know a lot about alcoholism. Thankfully, no one in her family had succumbed to it. She knew it was a disease. That some people were "genetically" susceptible. That the alcoholic couldn't be cured through willpower alone.

Should she give her another chance? Could she afford to?

Dammit, she hated being in this position!

"This once," she found herself saying, "I'll give you the benefit of the doubt. But just this once. If you screw up again, I'm going to the chief."

Even as the words passed her lips, M.C. wondered if she was making a big mistake. A mistake that would cost her dearly —more than a few rungs up the ladder.

Maybe even her life.

Wednesday, March 15, 2006
3:30 a.m.

The Other One had not been pleased. He had been very angry. Punishing and cruel.

He stared into the small mirror above his bathroom sink, steamy from his shower. Using his hand, he wiped the moisture away. Before he could get a clear look at himself, it clouded again. How could the Other One treat him so? They were a part of each other. Not two, but one. It had been so for as long as he could remember.

Not two, but one.

He covered his face with his shaking hands. Hadn't he suffered enough? He couldn't rest. Couldn't close his eyes without seeing that last angel. The image tormented him. Day and night.

Horrible, horrible.

He had been responsible for transforming her into a beast.

Beast. What he had secretly begun calling the Other One, when certain he wouldn't hear.

For that's what he was. A beast. And a bully.

Anger surged through him, with it defiance. How dare he scold! Had he asked permission to play games with that detective? To call her, doling out information as he pleased?

No. Absolutely not.

Who had decided the Other One controlled their fates? Not him, certainly.

Beast! Bastard!

He dropped his hands. A darting image in the cloudy mirror caught his eye, and he whirled around.

He was alone in the bathroom. The door was shut but not locked. His imagination was running away with him. Or was it? It wouldn't be the first time the Other One had come to spy on him.

And what of the angels? Perhaps one—the horrible one—had come to seek revenge for what he had done to her.

He sank to the floor, the ceramic tile cold against his naked backside. He scooted toward the wall, until he was pressed into the corner facing the door.

The minutes passed as he waited, his pounding heart marking off the seconds. Finally, eyes burning, he blinked. And she filled his head, her terrible, ugly countenance. He whimpered and cringed, bile rising in his throat.

He had to be rid of her. But how? How?

Another one. Another angel to take her place.

Perfect and beautiful.

The Other One be damned. He had no one's permission to ask but his own.

33

M.C. wouldn't admit it to anyone but herself, but she was nothing but a big chicken. At least when it came to her mother. If she'd had her "big-girl pants" on, she would be able to call her mother and tell her she wouldn't be at dinner. That she had a date.

She would also be able to handle the grilling that followed her announcement with ease and aplomb.

Instead, she was going to take the coward's way out and get her big brother to do it for her.

Michael took his last appointment at 5:00 p.m. and was home by 5:45, like clockwork. She always joked that he had trained his patients well.

He lived in a beautiful, old residential neighborhood called

Churchill Grove. He'd bought a house built in the twenties and had been renovating it little by little over the years.

She climbed the colonial's front steps, crossed to the door and rang the bell. He came to the door carrying a pint of ice cream and a spoon.

"That stuff'll make you fat," she said.

He swung open the door. "Want a bite? It's Chunky Monkey."

"Appropriate, Michael." She stood on tiptoes and kissed his cheek. "Work through lunch again?"

"Mmm." He closed the door behind her, then gestured for her to follow him to the kitchen.

The house smelled of lemon cleaner. "Service come today?"

"Yes, thank God." They reached the updated but still charming kitchen. She especially liked the retro black-and-white tile counters and floor.

He returned the ice cream to the freezer, then faced her. "A visit from my favorite sister, what a treat."

Code for: I know you want something, spill it.

"I'm your only sister, Michael."

"But you're still my favorite. You want a beer?"

"Thanks."

She watched as he moved around his small kitchen, totally comfortable. He took a bottle of Corona from the fridge, uncapped it and handed it to her. Then he got one for himself.

"Beer on the heels of Chunky Monkey? Michael, please."

"Don't knock it until you try it. How's the investigation going?"

"We're working our butts off."

"I saw you had a new partner. That woman."

"Kitt Lundgren. She's heading up the case now."

"I'm sorry."

M.C. shrugged and took a swallow of the beer. "She was put on the case for reasons that had nothing to do with my abilities or hers. I'm living with it."

They stood in silence for several moments, her brother waiting, obviously, for her to share the reason for her visit. She knew that after she told him, he was going to ask a lot of questions.

Talent for interrogation ran in the Riggio family.

"I'm not going to be at dinner tonight. I was hoping you'd pass along the message to Mama."

His eyebrows shot up. "No good, Mary Catherine. Wednesday nights are not an option."

"Tell her I have a date."

"Is that the truth? You know I won't lie for you."

He never would, even when they were kids. The rat. "Yes."

"With a guy?"

He smirked at her and she slugged him. "Yes, with a guy."

"Bring him along. I'm sure Mama and the rest of the family would love to meet him."

"I'm sure they would. But I actually may want to see him again."

"You want to tell me about him?"

"Not yet."

"How about a name?"

"Not yet." She smiled. "Sorry."

"Just tell me, is it an Italian name? So I can pass something along to Mama."

M.C. laughed and took another sip of the beer. "Yes, for heaven's sake. The name's about as Italian as they come."

The rest of the date wasn't. But that was another story.

He rolled the bottle between his palms, expression in his dark eyes thoughtful. "You like this guy?"

"I don't know. Maybe."

He pursed his lips. "You don't date much, Mary Catherine. Just be careful."

She pictured Lance and laughed. "I'm a cop, Michael. I'm trained in self-defense, am a second-degree black belt and carry a loaded Glock. You don't need to worry about me out on a date."

COPYCAT

He didn't smile. "You and I both know, there are ways of being hurt that all the bullets and self-defense classes in the world can't protect you from."

Tears pricked at her eyes. "That's so sweet, Michael." She hugged him. "I love you, too."

Michael had been right—she didn't date much. Never had. She supposed she had been so busy rebelling against her gender that she hadn't allowed herself much interest in the opposite sex. Certainly not the overwhelming interest many women had.

Or maybe she had rebelled so much that the opposite sex hadn't been interested in her.

Whichever, her experience in that arena was relatively limited. "Relatively," because she wasn't totally inexperienced. She had dated, had a few steady boyfriends and sex.

Even so, as she crossed the bookstore parking lot, she wondered what the hell she had been thinking, agreeing to go out with Lance. She should be at the PSB with Kitt, buried in the case. Not traipsing off to a date with a guy who she knew almost nothing about except the fact that he could make her laugh.

They had arranged to meet in the bookstore's café. It'd been a good, neutral choice and he had earned points for making it. The last thing she was interested in was a bum rush. She entered the bookstore, which seemed busy for a Wednesday night, and headed for the café.

He had already arrived, she saw. He sat at a table with a clear view of the entrance.

He stood when he saw her. She smiled, waved and crossed to him.

"Hi. Sorry I'm late."

"No problem."

He pulled a chair out for her, a gentlemanly gesture that surprised her. "I had to stop at my brother's to get him to pass along my regrets to Mama."

"Mama?"

"Wednesday nights are pasta night at my mother's house."

"You gave up dinner with your family? I'm sorry, you should have told me you had plans."

She shook her head. "Believe me, it wasn't a hardship. Let's just say, Wednesday nights can be a...trial."

"I wouldn't know anything about that."

He delivered the line deadpan, but she laughed. Because, of course, she had heard his act and knew he understood *exactly* what she was talking about.

"Michael, my brother, suggested I bring you."

"We could still go."

"You don't know what you're saying. I wouldn't wish *that* on my worst enemy."

"We're talking enough material for a new act, aren't we?"

"Enough for two new acts. Plus, chances are, I'd never see you again. I've never had a boyfriend who survived a meal with my family."

He fell into his comedy schtick, pretending to pick up a mike, face an audience. "I met my girlfriend's family for the first time last night. My God, this family puts the 'fun' in dysfunctional. Mama's an Italian tank with breasts. And one eyebrow. She doesn't use tweezers to pluck that monster, she pulls out hedge trimmers. No, wait. That's for her mustache."

M.C. laughed. "You *have* met my mother."

He grinned. "I want to hear more, but *after* I get us some coffee."

For the next hour, their conversation volleyed between her telling him about her family and him keeping her in stitches with a running commentary on everyone and everything, sometimes dry and caustic, others screwball.

It wasn't until they announced the store was closing that M.C. realized how much time had passed.

They stood, tossed their cups in the trash and started for the entrance.

Outside, the night was mild, the sky starless. He walked her to her vehicle. There, she faced him.

"This was a lot of fun. I don't know when I've laughed so much."

"I don't know when I've made anyone laugh so much." He lowered his voice. "I wish it didn't have to end," he said.

"Me, too."

"If I kissed you, would you pull a gun on me?"

"I'll pull the gun if you don't kiss me."

So he did, softly, slowly. When he drew away, her knees were weak.

"Are you hungry?" he asked.

God yes. "Starving."

"We could go to my favorite diner? Or…I have most of a Mama Riggio's supreme pizza left in my fridge."

"My brothers' restaurant."

"Best pizza outside the Chicago Loop."

She hesitated. She knew what she *should* do. But God help her, that's not what she wanted to do.

"I'm a sucker for pizza," she said. "Especially when it's the family recipe."

34

Wednesday, March 15, 2006
9:30 p.m.

Kitt sat alone at the computer terminal. M.C. had left several hours ago for a date. With "the funny guy," as she had called him. The detective shift had ended at 6:30 p.m. and the Violent Crimes Bureau had emptied almost on the hour. Slow crime day, apparently.

She and M.C. had spent a good part of the day searching the cold-case files. They had started with 2001, the year of the original SAK murders, and searched through to present day.

Nothing had jumped out at them. Gang killings. Prostitutes found dead. The occasional Jane or John Doe. Nothing that appeared serial in nature. Nothing that seemed to fit the SAK's profile.

So, Kitt had decided to search backward in time, thinking the "others" the SAK spoke of had been pre-Sleeping Angels.

Kitt glanced at the clock. Her head, neck and shoulders ached. Her eyes burned.

She longed to pack up and go home.

But to what? Her empty house? The television? She couldn't even head out to one of the bars frequented by other cops. She didn't trust herself around alcohol. Not now. Not after the night before.

Kitt refocused on the terminal. Another thirty minutes and she'd call it a night. By the time she got home, she would be exhausted. She could make herself a peanut-butter sandwich and a cup of chamomile tea, then go to bed.

And sleep. If she was lucky. If not, she could turn to the sleeping pills her doctor had prescribed—or stare at the ceiling for hours.

April 3, 1999. Marguerite Lindz. Eighty-two. Bludgeoned to death.

Kitt stared at the entry, frowning. There had been another elderly woman beaten to death. She had read the entry just minutes ago.

She surfed back until she found it. *February 6, 1999. Rose McGuire. Seventy-nine. Bludgeoned to death.*

Kitt took a deep breath, working to control her rush of excitement. Old women beaten to death couldn't be more different from the Sleeping Angel murders; the crimes being related was improbable at best.

She scrolled back in time. And found another, Janet Olsen. Exact same MO.

That was three. There could be more, though her instincts told her there wouldn't be. She initiated a global search, then while the computer chomped on that, she went for the official case records.

Kitt collected the files, then swung past the vending machines on the way back to her desk. She got herself a pack of snack crackers and a Diet Coke. Files tucked under her arm, she ripped open the package and stuck one of the cracker sandwiches into her mouth.

As she munched on it, she read the package label. Partially hy-drogenated oil. High-fructose corn syrup. Yellow dye #6. M.C. was right. She had to stop eating this garbage. It was loaded with trans fat and sugar, no protein, all bad carbs.

Tomorrow. She'd start eating well then.

By the time she returned to the terminal, the search was com-plete, and no other similar killings had been found.

That meant there had been three. Same as the original Sleeping Angel killings.

Kitt settled into her desk chair and opened the first woman's file. *Janet Olsen. Seventy-five. Beaten to death in her home. No sign of sexual assault. Robbery had not been a motive.*

The same held true for the other two victims. Killer had duct-taped their mouths.

Kitt took a swallow of her cola, washing down the last cracker. The investigating detectives had identified the cases as being serial in nature but had never discovered a link between them. The killer left the scenes strangely clean. The lack of physical evidence had hindered the investigations and the cases had gone cold.

Kitt drew out the crime-scene photos. The scenes were grisly. Bloody. The killer had beaten the women to the point of being un-recognizable, the shiny silver duct tape grotesque on their pulver-ized faces.

He had applied the tape postmortem.

Kitt straightened. She set her Diet Coke can down with a thud. So, he hadn't applied the tape to silence them.

They had already been silenced. Permanently.

Kitt stood. She began to pace. Mentally comparing the crimes. The SAK applied lip gloss postmortem. This killer applied tape.

To the mouth. *The mouth.* What did it mean?

She could see why no one had considered these cases related to the Sleeping Angel deaths. They couldn't be more different—the crimes or the choice of victims.

In their differences was a pattern: old versus young; violent versus serene; ugly versus beautiful.

There were similarities as well: three victims; the postmortem attention to the victim; the lack of evidence.

Acting on a hunch, she crossed to her desk, jotted down the dates of the three murders, then pulled out a calendar.

The "Granny" murders had each been eight weeks apart. Exactly.

The SAK murders had been six.

This guy was one highly organized asshole.

The son of a bitch. The chicken-shit. He built himself up by preying on the weak.

The images from the photos filled her head. The old ladies first, then the little girls.

Fury took her breath.

Shaking with it, she grabbed her cell phone, then the Copycat case files. She opened it, found what she was looking for—a list of every cell number "Peanut" had called her from.

She stared at the numbers, heart racing. Every call had been made from a different number; no doubt he had disposed of each device after use. Why would he keep them?

But hanging on to them didn't expose him in any way.

Acting on emotion, not giving a damn that she was breaking protocol, Kitt punched in the last number he had called from. She banked on the fact that if he still had the device and it was on, that he would recognize her number and pick up.

The call went through. She waited, trembling with rage, while it rang. She hoped he hadn't destroyed this phone and acquired another. She wanted the son of a bitch to answer. To hear his voice. So she could tell him exactly what she thought of him.

A moment later, she got her wish. "Calling me now? Kitten, I'm honored."

"I was sitting here, looking at pictures of your handiwork.

Thought I'd give you a call. Tell you how sickened I am by you. How disgusted."

"That hurts. It really does."

"Old ladies and little girls? And you're proud of that?"

"So, you found them."

They were his. "It wasn't that difficult. Just look for victims who are too helpless to fight back."

"Careful, Detective."

"Is that what it's all about? You find victims who can't defend themselves and then you get to call your crimes 'perfect'?"

"They are perfect. Picking out the right victim is the first step—"

She cut him off, voice vibrating with anger. Even as she warned herself to regain control of her emotions, she lashed out at him. "You're pathetic. You actually believe your own schtick, don't you."

"I've had you and your entire department chasing your tails for years. I beat all of you! Police investigators? Detectives?" He all but spat the words at her. "Imbeciles! Idiots!"

"You're a coward. You pick victims who can't challenge you. Sleeping children and the geriatric? Why stop there? What about the handicapped?"

"Shut up."

"Killing a paraplegic sounds like fun. They can't fight or run away. Or how about sneaking up on a blind person? What a challenge!"

"You want me to level the playing field, Kitten?" His voice quaked with rage. "Pick someone healthier?"

"Yeah, I do. How about me, you bastard? Up the ante. Bring it on."

"Maybe I will. Maybe I'll—" He bit the words back. "You'd like that, wouldn't you? Because you don't care about yourself. If you're dead or alive. Isn't that right?"

He hit a nerve; she fought from letting it show. "Obviously, yellow's your favorite color. I have less than zero respect for you."

"Good try. You almost had me." She heard amusement come into his voice. "I actually do think you'd rather be dead. No child. No marriage. Nothing to live for."

"I have something to live for, all right. Nailing sick pricks like you. I live to see you behind bars."

"No, Kitten, it's the children you care about. The little girls."

He was right. Dammit. He had turned the tables on her.

"You like the idea of prison?" she pressed. "You have any idea what the rest of the prison population thinks of child killers? You like the idea of a boyfriend named Big Bubba?"

He went on as if she hadn't spoken. "Maybe I *should* up the ante? Isn't there a little girl in your life right now? In the periphery of your life? Are you strong enough to protect her? Smart enough? How fast and how hard would you run to save another little girl? Another Sadie?"

Kitt lost it. She felt something snap inside. A bitter-tasting fury spewed out. "You bastard! You know who this killer is. Tell me! Give me his fucking name, or I'll tear you apart!"

He laughed, the sound high-pitched, gleeful. "Thanks for calling, I enjoyed our talk so much. Keep your eyes on the little girls and whatever you do…don't blink."

"You son of a bitch! When I get my hands on—"

"Call anytime, Kitten. Bye-bye."

Thursday, March 16, 2006
9:00 a.m.

M.C. sat at her desk, staring into space, thinking of the previous evening and her date with Lance. She had slept with him, for God's sake. On their first date. What had she been thinking?

She hadn't been. Not rationally, anyway. He had swept her off her feet. With laughter, of all things.

She crossed her legs under her desk, remembering. Who would have thought she could laugh and orgasm at the same time?

And that the combination would be so incredible? Her abdominal muscles, already contracting with laughter, had spasmed with orgasm. It'd been like an orgastic explosion; she had thought she was going to die. She had actually fallen on top of him, momentarily paralyzed.

Afterward, he had teased her about it. But in a sweet way, one that made her feel sexy and beautiful.

Big mistake, though. And one, God help her, she wouldn't be making again.

"I found them."

M.C. blinked, focused. Kitt had arrived and stood before her, clutching several file folders to her chest.

M.C. frowned. "What happened to you? You look like hell."

"I didn't sleep."

"At all?"

"That doesn't matter." She shook her head. "I found them. The others."

M.C. straightened, fully engaged now. She shifted her gaze to the file folders. "Are you certain?"

"Yes. Absolutely."

"Children?"

"No. Look for yourself." Kitt dropped the file folders on the desk in front of her.

M.C opened the first file and began to read. As she did, Kitt paced.

When she closed the third file, she returned her gaze to Kitt's. "The MO's totally different."

"I thought the same thing at first. But their very differences link them."

"You should have gotten more sleep."

"Just listen. Three crimes, obviously the work of the same person. The crimes a study in extremes. Same with the Sleeping Angel killings."

M.C. nodded, reluctantly intrigued. "Go on."

"Think about it. Violent versus serene. Old versus young. Bloody versus clean. These murders were committed exactly eight weeks apart, the SAK's, six. Then there's the tape. Like the lip gloss, applied postmortem."

"Postmortem?" M.C. repeated. "It's interesting. Worth exploring."

Kitt rested her palms on the desk and leaned toward the other woman. She lowered her voice. "They're his. He admitted it."

"He called you?"

"I knew before he admitted it," Kitt said. "Outwardly, they couldn't be more different. But they had the bastard's signature all over them."

M.C. narrowed her eyes. "What aren't you telling me?"

"I've been thinking about Sydney Dale," she said. "I want to have another talk with him. Thought I'd pay him a visit. See if we could get those questions of ours answered."

M.C. sat back in her chair. Clearly, Kitt wanted out of the bureau before she said any more about her call last night. Why?

Whatever the reason, she decided to play along. "I ran Dale through the computer. He's clean. Squeaky clean."

"Guy doesn't get to be that rich without dirtying his hands a little bit."

"True, but that kind of stuff doesn't end up in our data banks."

"I don't trust him. Fact is, he hired Todd. Told his manager the kid was 'hired.' Why?"

"Like he said, he knew the kid before he'd gotten himself in trouble. Figured ZZ would do the appropriate background checks and drug screenings."

"Do you believe that?"

"Hell no. The guy was lying, at least about what he told ZZ."

Kitt perched on the edge of the desk. "What if he did know Todd was an ex-con and a registered sex offender? Why would he hire him?"

M.C. had an idea where Kitt was heading and held her hands up. "Stop there. Are you thinking Dale might have deliberately put Todd there as a way to deflect suspicion? In case we found the connection between the girls and the Fun Zone?"

"A fall guy. What's wrong with it?"

"Dale's a solid citizen. A businessman of standing. Probably a deacon at his church."

"So was Ted Bundy. And Dennis Rader, the BTK serial killer." Kitt leaned toward her once more. "He's smart. And he's slick. And he was lying. Another chat would be a good thing."

"Has Schmidt gotten anything from the tapes or surveillance of the Fun Zone?"

"Nada."

M.C. gazed at the other detective. She may not trust her—but there was a kind of fire that burned in her eyes, one she responded to.

The woman she had labeled a burned-out has-been, had more intensity than any cop she had ever worked with. "You've had entirely too much coffee this morning. And way too little sleep."

"You have a point?"

"Yeah, I might try it myself." She pushed away from the desk. "Let's go."

M.C. offered to drive. Kitt took the offer with what M.C. thought was relief. They made their way to the parking garage and her SUV. Once they were belted in and on their way, she glanced at Kitt.

"We're alone now. What didn't you tell me in there, about last night's conversation with the SAK?"

"He didn't call me. I called him. From my cell phone."

She paused a moment, as if knowing M.C. needed a moment to digest what she'd said.

She was right.

Kitt went on. "I knew if he still had the phone and saw it was me, he'd answer."

"And you did this how?"

"I just tried the last number he called us from."

For a full ten seconds M.C. said nothing. It had been an outrageously ballsy move. And one that could earn Kitt a severe reprimand.

"Did you involve the CRU?"

"No."

"Another officer present?"

"No."

"So, obviously, not recorded." The light ahead changed; she slowed to a stop. "Dammit, Kitt! Do you have a clue how out of line that was? Do you realize we only have your word of what transpired?"

"Yes. To all of it."

"What the hell were you thinking?"

"I wasn't. I knew he'd done that, to those old ladies. I saw red. I took a chance. It paid off."

"Dammit!" she said again. "What else did you get?"

"I know him better. What drives him."

"In other words, nothing."

"Not nothing. I kept him on the line. I can do it again."

"You guess. You hope." M.C. gripped the steering wheel tightly. "Were you drinking?"

"No. Absolutely no. I made a promise about that, I mean to keep it."

For what it was worth, M.C. believed she meant it. But the behavior was off. Impulsive. Risky.

"He's obsessed with his crimes being perfect," Kitt went on. "Unbelievably arrogant about it."

Obsession. That was it, M.C. realized. It explained Kitt's behavior. The light in her eyes. The long hours, the chances she was taking.

Is that what had happened to her before she tumbled over the edge and into a bottle?

M.C. stopped at another red. She turned to the other woman. "You're getting too close to this case, Kitt."

"I have it in perspective."

"Do you?"

The other woman's cheeks reddened. "I challenged him about his choice of victims. Accused him of being a chicken-shit for picking children and geriatrics. I challenged him to pick on someone stronger. More capable."

Behind them a horn blared. The light, M.C. saw, had changed. She eased forward. "Someone like you?"

"Yes."

"Did he take the bait?"

She hesitated a moment, then shook her head. "No. He became angry. And defensive. Insisted part of committing the perfect crime was choosing the perfect victim."

"So his victims aren't an emotional choice. They're an intellectual one."

"Exactly." Kitt angled toward her. "No serial kills simply for intellectual satisfaction. That means the emotional drive lies in another direction."

M.C. turned onto Riverside Drive, which led to the entrance to Brandywine Estates. "You cornered him. You pissed him off. And he struck back. How?"

"How do you know he struck back?"

"A cornered animal defends itself," she replied simply.

Kitt fell silent. M.C. wound her way through the hilly neighborhood, letting the other woman compose her answer.

When she spoke, her tone was steely with resolve. "He threatened the little girls, ones I might care about. But...there are none."

He had gotten the best of Kitt. Because, unlike her, Kitt's caller was not emotionally involved.

They reached Sydney Dale's drive and M.C. pulled in. She brought the car to a stop and faced Kitt. "You say you're learning what makes this guy tick. That may be, but he's learning the same about you, Kitt. And it seems to me, that's a dangerous place to be."

36

Thursday, March 16, 2006
10:10 a.m.

Sydney Dale wasn't home. But his young, blond-haired trophy wife was. She came to the door in a pretty silk pantsuit. She directed them to his office, located in the Strathmore Professional Complex off Mulford Road.

As they turned to go, Kitt stopped and looked back at her. "What can you tell me about Derrick Todd?"

Her expression subtly altered. "Who?"

"He worked for you and your husband about four years ago. He was the yard and pool—"

"I'm the new Mrs. Dale," she told them, yawning. "I wasn't around then."

"Would you know where we could find the 'old' Mrs. Dale?"

"Ask Sydney. I don't keep track of her."

As they climbed back into the SUV, Kitt looked at M.C. "The new Mrs. Dale is so young she was probably a teenager when Todd worked here."

M.C. arched her eyebrows. "I wonder how many Mrs. Dales there have been?"

"And if each one was younger than the last?"

They passed the rest of the ten-minute drive in silence. When they reached the office, they parked near the appropriate suite number and climbed out.

"You mind if I do this?" Kitt asked as they crossed the parking lot.

M.C. hesitated, then nodded. "You seem to have the eye-of-the-tiger thing going—have a ball."

The receptionist was as young, attractive and blond as the "new" Mrs. Dale, and Kitt wondered if he used the office as a screening ground for prospective wives.

As she had suspected would be the case, Dale was not happy to see them. "Detectives," he said with barely veiled annoyance, "this is a surprise."

"We have a few more questions about Derrick Todd."

"I can't imagine. We've fired him. Naturally. I don't know what more you could want from me."

"An explanation of why you hired a registered sex offender to work around children."

"I gave you that explanation."

"But it didn't quite make sense to us."

"Do I need to contact my lawyer?"

"If you feel it's necessary, go ahead." Kitt paused, allowing him a moment to think it over. When he didn't make a move, she continued. "Perhaps you could tell us again *why* you asked your manager to forgo background checks and hire Mr. Todd?"

"I never told Mr. Zuba not to do the customary background checks." He spread his hands. "A classic case of miscommunication."

"Problem is, he tells a more convincing story than you do."

"That's your problem, Detectives. Not mine."

"Actually," M.C. said, stepping in, "it is your problem. Because when we're not convinced, we keep digging. We're like a dog with a bone, Mr. Dale. And it's not pretty."

"Are you threatening to harass me?"

"Absolutely not. Just giving you a glimpse into the investigative process."

"We need to speak to your ex-wife as well," Kitt said. "We need her name and address."

"Is this really necessary?"

"Afraid so." Kitt waited, pen poised above her tablet.

He glanced at his receptionist, then pointed to his office. "We can talk in here."

They followed him into the office; he shut the door behind them. "I gave Todd a job because she lied."

"Who lied, Mr. Dale?"

"My daughter. She's the one he was convicted of exposing himself to."

She pictured the pretty blonde roaring off in the BMW. "Sam?"

"No. Jennifer. She lives with her mother now."

Kitt glanced at M.C. The other woman raised her eyebrows.

"How do you know she lied?"

"I found her diary." He looked genuinely sickened and for the first time M.C. thought of him as human. "Her mother and I were going through a messy divorce. Our lives were in chaos. The girls were traumatized. Jen made up the whole thing in an attempt to keep us together. And to keep her and Sam together."

"It didn't work. Obviously."

"No. My ex-wife would have no part of staying together."

"Your ex-wife?"

"Yes." He looked away, then back. "I know what you're thinking. I see it on your faces. I loved my wife, not that it's any of your business. She left me for another man, not the other way around."

Kitt didn't respond in any way, though she experienced a prickle of guilt at having jumped to exactly that conclusion.

M.C. jumped in once more. "We're not here to judge your personal life, Mr. Dale. Just to get the truth about Derrick Todd and his job at the Fun Zone."

"Exactly," Kitt confirmed. "Once you learned the truth, did you go to the D.A.? Try to secure an early release for him?"

He shook his head. "I was afraid of the...ramifications. From Todd. And the state."

Afraid that he'd be sued.

The "human" label once again became suspect.

"So, Mr. Todd doesn't know that you believe him innocent?"

"No. I told him I suspected it didn't go down the way Jen said. And I offered him a job. He was grateful."

She would bet he was. That kind of label wasn't easy to live with. And it made finding a job damn difficult.

Kitt thought of Derrick Todd, his surliness, his anger at the police. The blatant disrespect.

No wonder. He had been convicted of a crime he hadn't committed. No doubt he had proclaimed his innocence to the heavens. Yet, he'd gone to prison. Suffered God only knew what while in the pen and would have to carry the stigma of sex offender with him for the next ten years.

Now he had no job and was being questioned about another crime he hadn't committed.

No wonder he was bitter. She'd probably dish some serious antisocial attitude, too.

In one fell swoop, she had gone from longing to smack the cocky smirk off the kid's face to pitying him.

"Do you have the diary?" M.C. asked.

He hesitated, then nodded. "In my safety deposit box. I kept it just in case I needed it someday."

"'Someday' has come, Mr. Dale. I'll need you to retrieve that journal today and bring it to us. Understand, I'm not going to keep this information a secret. Not from Todd, his attorney or the state."

He nodded, looking ill.

As they left his office, Kitt stopped and turned back to him. "By the way, Mr. Dale, where were you the nights of the sixth and the ninth of this month."

He frowned. "I don't know for certain. Nancy keeps my calendar. Let's go see."

He led them back out to the waiting area. The receptionist produced his day planner. On the sixth he had been out of town on business. An overnight stay. On the ninth he and his wife had attended a Burpee Museum fund-raiser, then had gone home to bed.

"I suppose you can produce documentation and witnesses to confirm both?"

For the first time, he looked shaken. "Of course."

"Thank you, Mr. Dale. Bring that item in before day's end."

Kitt and M.C. walked to the car in silence. When they'd reached the Explorer, climbed in and buckled up, Kitt turned to the other woman. "Do you believe Dale's story?"

"Unfortunately, yes."

"Puts Todd in a whole new light, doesn't it?"

"And puts us back to square one."

"Thanks for mentioning that," Kitt muttered, then shook her head. "No, not square one. The Fun Zone's still a connection."

M.C. started the car. "Could be a coincidence."

"Could be. But I'm not buying that. Not yet, anyway."

They drove in silence for several blocks. As they slid through the light at Riverside and Mulford, Kitt murmured, "Your date last night, how was it?"

"That's sort of personal."

"It must have been very good, then."

M.C. shot her an irritated glance. "Whatever."

"Who was he? That Lance guy who came to the PSB to see you?"

"Yes. Satisfied?"

Clearly, she didn't want to talk about it. Which, perversely, made Kitt want her to. "You went to bed with him, didn't you?"

"Excuse me?"

Kitt smiled. "I'm multitalented. Both nosy and psychic."

"More like multi-pain-in-the-ass."

"Whatever," she said, tossing M.C.'s indifferent word back at her.

They drove for several minutes in silence. Then, as they neared the PSB, M.C. made a sound of exasperation. "Okay, how did you know I slept with him?"

"Simple. When I walked into the squad room this morning, you were staring dreamily into space and smiling to yourself."

"I was not!"

"It was one of those satisfied little grins that speaks volumes."

M.C. opened her mouth as if to argue, then shut it.

Kitt laughed. "I think it's sweet."

"I've never aspired to sweet."

"You like this guy."

It wasn't a question; M.C. answered her, anyway. "Yeah, I like this guy. But I'm only admitting it in the hopes you'll shut up." She glanced out the window, then back at Kitt. "Where do we go from here?"

"Personally, I think you should back off on the sex and get to know him better. But maybe that's my age talking."

"Thanks, Mom, but I was talking about where you and I should go. With this investigation."

"Let's talk to the chief. Fill him in on the latest."

"Then what?"

"Hell, if I know."

"Now, there's a definitive answer."

"You asked. Besides, I suspect the chief is going to have a strong opinion on what comes next. He always does."

"He's going to have your ass for what you did."

Trying to turn the tables on "Peanut." Calling without clearing it first.

Stepping outside the chain of command—again.

"He doesn't have to know," Kitt said.

"And how are you going to explain being certain Lindz, McGuire and Olsen were victims of the SAK?"

"I just will be."

It took a second or two, Kitt saw, for her words to register. "You're out of your mind if you think I'll lie for you."

"I won't ask you to."

"You screwed up, Kitt. Face the music and move on."

"I don't see it that way. A good cop follows her gut. Sometimes that means making a move that's left of protocol."

"Left of protocol? I don't think so. I want my career to move forward, not the other way around. If I take part in that meeting and don't reveal all I know—"

"Then don't take part in the meeting."

"That's bullshit." She cruised into the PSB garage, parked and shut off the engine. She turned to her. Kitt saw that she was angry. "You're losing it, Detective. I suggest you take a big step back, before it's too late."

M.C. opened the car door. Kitt caught her arm, stopping her. "You think sleeping with that guy was smart?"

"That doesn't have anything to do with this."

"You followed your gut. Whether you regret it now or not, that's what you did."

"That was personal. This is work. There's a difference."

"No, there's not. We go through our lives acting on our instincts, our gut feelings. About people. Choices that range from which job to accept to whom to trust. The good cop tunes into those instincts, follows them."

"You are so full of shit, Kitt." She shook off her hand. "For a while I wondered how such a good cop could have ended up the way you have. Now I know."

37

Thursday, March 16, 2006
3:40 p.m.

He watched the girl play. She was perfect. A perfect angel. Care-free. Lovely. More perfect than any of the others had been.

Why? He cocked his head. She was blonde and blue-eyed and pretty. But the others had been also.

No, this one was special because of Kitt. He had made a threat. And a promise. A threat to the little girls around his Kitten.

And a promise to himself. To win. At all costs.

She cared about the girls. Hurt them and he hurt her. And this one she would blame herself for.

Funny, now that he had determined her punishment, and real-ized how utterly effective it would be—he wasn't angry with her.

Yes, she had defied him again. Challenged him again. But he saw it as fighting spirit. And truly appropriate.

He leaned against the park bench and let the sweet breeze flow over him. What a devastating blow it would be to her when this girl died. Poor Kitten. Would she be able to overcome it? Would it send her back to the bottle? Or maybe, this time, for her service weapon.

One shot to the head and all the pain would go away.

A part of him hoped she took that path. She had endured so much already. But another part was rooting for her to fight on.

Interesting how attached he had become. How connected to her struggles.

It was too bad this scenario could only have one outcome—Kitt Lundgren's death.

38

Thursday, March 16, 2006
6:20 p.m.

M.C. stood at her kitchen window, leftovers Melody had dropped off earlier heating in the microwave. She and Benjamin had stayed for animal crackers and a chat. Ben, of course, had been more interested in the crackers than the talking. M.C. had learned that in her absence at the previous evening's dinner she had been her mother's main course.

The microwave chimed and she retrieved the cannelloni. She carried the plate to the table, sat but didn't eat. Truth was, she wasn't all that hungry. M.C. hated the position Kitt had put her in. She had overlooked Kitt's lapse into the bottle. Now she expected her to overlook this. What next?

She had done as she'd threatened and boycotted Kitt's meeting with the chief. A small thing, but one Sal would make note of. Even so, she wasn't at all certain that move had been the right one.

Yes, Kitt had acted outside protocol. But it had been a ballsy move. The "no guts, no glory" kind that sometimes paid off big-time.

M.C. wasn't a gambler. She couldn't afford to be associated with risky behavior. Brash, ballsy cops weren't the ones who became chief of detectives, let alone the chief of police. Because those big risks backfired as often as they paid off.

No, the cops who climbed the ladder were steady. They followed protocol, were brilliant strategists and excellent politicians. Admittedly, she had a ways to go in those areas, but she had time. If she kept her eyes on her goals, she would achieve them.

The doorbell rang and for a second she thought it was the microwave again. She made her way to the door, peeked out the sidelight. Brian Spillare stood on her porch, hands jammed into the pockets of his faded blue jeans.

She opened the door. "Brian? What are you doing here?"

"Can I come in?"

She hesitated, then opened the door wider. He stepped through and she closed the door behind him. "What's up?"

"I needed someone to talk to. Someone I could trust."

An epidemic, apparently. At this moment no one would be better to discuss Kitt with than Brian. After all, he had been her partner.

She smiled. "Coincidentally, so do I. How about a cup of coffee?"

"You have anything stronger?"

Typical Brian. "Beer?"

"Perfect."

He followed her into the kitchen. His standing in the doorway that way brought back memories. Ones that weren't unpleasant, but had no place in their present relationship.

"Something smells awfully good."

"Leftovers of Mama's cannelloni."

She thought about offering him some but didn't want him to get the wrong idea. Sharing a meal in her small kitchen was just a little too intimate for comfort.

She handed him the longneck bottle, eschewing a glass. He had always preferred drinking out of a bottle. She was pretty certain in his case it was somehow a phallic thing—the man really was all about his ding-dong.

"Thanks." He took the beer. Their fingers brushed and she drew her hand away.

"You're not drinking?" he asked.

"No. Not tonight."

He rolled the bottle between his palms. "Ivy kicked me out."

"When?"

"Two days ago."

"I'm sorry," she said. And she was. Not that she blamed the woman. She had certainly put up with a lot in her years married to the hard-partying cop. "Maybe she'll take you back? She has before."

"I might not want her back." He took another swallow of the brew. "Other fish and all that."

They had been married twenty-some years and had three children together and "other fish" was what he had to say? No wonder she kicked him out. *You go, girl.*

"You wanted to talk to me about something?" she asked.

"Us."

"Oh, please." She pushed away from the counter, irritated. "I don't have time for this."

He caught her arm. "Can you just listen?"

"Brian—"

"I've never gotten over you."

She stood stiffly, working to control her annoyance. "This is so interesting, Brian. Your wife kicks you out and suddenly you've never gotten over me."

"It's true."

She shook her head, disgusted. With him, his adolescent behavior. With herself for ever getting involved with him. And for allowing him into her home tonight.

"We shared nothing but a few weeks of sex."

"But it was great sex."

She shook off his hand. "Grow up, Brian."

He took a step forward, weaving slightly. "That'd hurt if I believed you really felt that way."

He'd been drinking. Dammit, why hadn't she noticed that before she let him in?

"I think you should go."

"Don't be that way, baby."

He made a move to grab her; she sidestepped him. This situation presented a big problem. The man was a superior officer. Well liked and well connected within the force. He could make trouble for her. The kind of trouble that could affect her climb up the ladder.

She eased toward the front door. "I'm seeing someone. Regularly."

"It doesn't have to be love. It can just be fun."

"Not interested, Lieutenant. Please go."

M.C. reached the front door. She grabbed the knob; he laid his hand over hers. "Who're you seeing? Not that scrawny comic from the bar?"

"Yes, if you must know."

He snorted. "What do you see in him?"

"He makes me laugh. Let go of my hand, Brian."

"Bet he's not as good as I was."

"You're a legend in your own mind. But nobody else's."

His mouth thinned. He made a grab for her; she swung sideways, grasped his upper arms and kneed him square in the nuts.

He doubled over, moaning and muttering a string of curses, all directed at her and her gender.

"Sorry, Brian. I didn't want to do that, but you left me no choice." As he started to straighten, she opened the door and pushed him through it. "I'm willing to pretend this never happened. But if you *ever* try this crap again, it'll cost you more than sore balls."

39

Thursday, March 16, 2006
11:00 p.m.

As she'd threatened Kitt that she would, M.C. had taken a stand. Kitt had faced the chief alone, her partner's absence pointedly noted. Sal was sharp. He suspected something was up but had supervised detectives long enough to understand the wisdom of giving them space. Most issues eventually resolved themselves, one way or another. And if they hadn't, he'd stepped in with appropriate action.

What the chief didn't know wouldn't hurt him. At least at this juncture.

Or so Kitt told herself.

She didn't blame M.C. her decision. If this blew up in Kitt's face, her partner didn't want to be taken down with her. As M.C. had said, she had ambitions.

But if they cracked this case, nailed the SAK and the Copycat, M.C. would take part of the credit. Even if it was directly a result of the "left of protocol" move M.C. so strongly protested, she would move up her rung.

Kitt would be happy for her; everybody would win—but especially the children.

Kitt sat at her kitchen table, files spread around her. Her mind raced. The chief had agreed—study the Olsen, Lindz and McGuire case files, look for a commonality between them and the SAK killings, something the original investigating officers missed. Brian and Sergeant Haas had worked it. That'd been just before she and Brian had been partnered up; Sal had been sergeant then.

Kitt frowned. She was starting to understand this bastard. This time, she was going to nail him. If it was the last thing she did in this lifetime, his ass was going down.

She pushed away from the table, stood and stretched. Her body ached, and the muscles in her neck and back were knotted. She rolled her shoulders in an effort to loosen them, then tipped her head from side to side.

It momentarily relieved the tension, and she began to pace.

Three old ladies, beaten to death. Vicious murders. Gruesome. Scenes surprisingly clean, considering. One had lived in an assisted-living community, one in an apartment, another a home. All had lived alone. None had been sexually assaulted. Robbery had not been a motive. No witnesses. No hair, fingerprints or bodily fluids.

Frustrated, she turned and strode back to the table. Her doorbell sounded and she glanced at the clock. It was after eleven, late for a visitor.

Danny, she saw when she went to the door. He stood in the circle of light, looking tired and tense.

"Danny?" she said as she opened the door. "What are you doing here?"

"Can I come in?"

"Sure." She stepped aside and he entered her small foyer. After she closed the door behind him, she nodded toward the kitchen. "I have a pot of coffee brewed."

He followed her, though he refused the drink. "I'm coffeed-out."

She poured herself a cup, aware of him watching her, then turning his gaze to the case files.

"Your hands are shaking," he said.

She smiled. "I'm probably coffeed-out, too."

"Then maybe you should cut yourself off?"

"I've got a lot to do. I need the caffeine if I'm going to make it."

"I'm worried about you, Kitt."

"Me? Why?"

"What day is this?"

She stared at him, realizing she didn't know. Or rather, she couldn't access the information.

"It's Thursday, Kitt."

AA. She had missed group.

"I'm so sorry. I was working…it totally slipped my mind."

He took her cup and set it on the counter, then caught both her hands with his, holding them tightly. "The other night, when I called. You'd been drinking."

She wanted to deny it, but to deny it would be as bad as the drinking itself. "Yes."

"And tonight you skipped group."

"Forgot, didn't skip. There's a difference."

He said nothing. He didn't need to speak, his expression said it all.

She hurried to reassure him. "It was just that once, I swear. It's not going to happen again."

"Before you fell off the wagon, wouldn't you have sworn it couldn't happen at all? That you had a handle on it?"

"That was before…something happened. Joe…his fiancée has a daughter. A ten-year-old."

Her friend's expression softened with understanding. And regret. For her. "Kitt, damn...I'm so sorry."

Danny, like her other AA friends, knew her heart. They knew all her hurts and fears, all the things that had sent her into the bottle in the first place.

He brought his arms around her. She rested her head on his chest, suddenly overwhelmed with emotion.

And tired. So very tired.

"It hurt so bad," she said, voice small. "I felt...feel so betrayed."

He gently rubbed her back, rhythmically smoothing his fingers over her knotted muscles.

"He's replacing Sadie," she murmured, tipping her face up toward his. "And I can't bear the thought...I can't bear the thought of them all living together, being a family."

"But drinking isn't going to make it better. It only masks the pain. And when you come off the binge, you feel worse."

"I know, Danny, and I promise you, I'm not falling back into the trap."

He searched her expression. "You're particularly vulnerable right now. You need us, more than ever."

"I'm fine. I—"

"Fine? You're not! Jesus, Kitt, you're an alcoholic. You can't just turn it on and off. It'll grab a hold of you again and—"

"It won't. I have it under control." She saw that he meant to argue with her and went on. "I can't think about anything but the case right now. It consumes my every waking thought. I have to catch him, Danny."

He took a step back from her. "Listen to yourself. Don't you see what you're doing? Don't you recognize what's happening to you?"

"Yeah, I recognize it. I'm alive again. I have purpose. Resolve. And you know what? I like it."

"That's addictive behavior. You're substituting one compulsion for another."

"You don't understand the nature of police work."

"That may be, but I understand the nature of addiction." She tried to turn away; he stopped her. "Are you sleeping? Taking time to eat? Real food, not crap? And what about downtime? Catching a movie or calling a friend?"

"I'm in the middle of a *murder* investigation. I don't have time for things like movies or girlfriends."

He closed the distance between them. "Dammit, Kitt, you're driving me frigging nu—"

He kissed her. For a split second she was too shocked to respond, then she pushed him away, furious. "What the hell was that?"

His face flooded with color. He looked angry. "Nothing. It was nothi—"

He bit the last back, turned and strode toward the door.

"Danny, wait! Let's talk about this."

He didn't stop and a moment later the door slammed shut. She ran after him, through the door and onto the porch. "Danny! Come on, it's—"

Too late, she saw as he started his car and roared away from the curb. She watched until his taillights disappeared from sight, then turned and went back inside.

She locked the door behind her, then rubbed her arms, chilled from the night air. She would call him tomorrow, after he'd had a chance to cool down. Get over what was undoubtedly anger and embarrassment caused by her rejection.

Dammit. She didn't want to lose his friendship. She valued it. But she wasn't attracted to him. That wasn't going to change.

She felt suddenly drained. Why'd he have to pull this now? She didn't have the time or energy to deal with this. She had a killer to catch. Make that two killers—one of whom had made her mission personal.

"No, Kitten, it's the children you care about. The little girls."

He had turned the tables on her. He knew her, her deepest fears. How had he managed it?

She began to pace, her fatigue falling away. Replaced by a kind of nervous energy. She went over what he'd said.

"How fast and how hard would you run to save another little girl? Another Sadie?" And then, *"Aren't there some little girls in your life right now? Are you strong enough to protect them? Smart enough?"*

She stopped pacing. She realized her heart was pounding. Her hands shaking.

Little girls. In her life.

Are you strong enough to save them? Smart enough?

It hit her all at once then. Joe. His fiancée's ten-year-old daughter, Tami. The Leukemia Society fair. The clown and his balloon.

Dear God. The SAK knew about Tami.

Tami was the little girl at the periphery of her life.

Fear grabbed her in a stranglehold. She pictured Tami, her shy smile and pretty brown eyes. She had to warn Joe. She had to warn his fiancée.

Kitt found her shoes, slipped into them. Her sweatshirt jacket was next, followed by a search for her car keys. She located them, grabbed her purse and headed out into the cold night.

The drive to the Highcrest Road home she and Joe had shared took less time than normal because of the hour. The house was dark; his pickup truck sat in the driveway. She wheeled into the drive, stopped behind the truck, slammed out of her car and ran to his front door.

She rang the bell, then pounded on the door. "Joe!" she called. "It's me, Kitt! Open up!"

She pounded again, calling out, growing desperate.

Finally, she heard the dead bolt slide back; a moment later the door opened.

He'd thrown a robe on over his boxers. "Kitt?" he said. "What—"

"Tami's in danger," she said. "We have to warn Valerie."

He blinked and she had a sense that he was only waking up now. "Tami," he repeated. "In danger?"

"Yes. From the SAK. Because of me."

He gazed at her a moment, then opened the door wider. "It's cold. Come in."

She stepped into the foyer; he closed the door behind them. It smelled like *him* she realized. Not like them, their family, anymore.

She faced him. "You have to call Valerie. Now. Tonight. It's that important."

"Slow down, Kitt. You're talking crazy. How would this madman even know Tami?"

"The Leukemia Society fund-raiser. He was there. Dressed as a clown, selling balloons."

Joe's eyebrows shot up. "A clown? Selling balloons?"

"Yes, dammit! He saw our exchange and gave me a pink balloon. He called me later, asked me if I liked it."

"This is madness."

"True. But that doesn't mean I'm crazy. He threatened me."

"He threatened you?"

"By threatening the little girls. The ones I care about, the ones in my life."

"Kitt—"

Her hackles rose at the way he said her name. Patiently. As if talking to a headstrong child. Or a nutcase.

"He said 'little girls at the periphery of my life.' I just realized tonight that he was talking about Tami. Don't you get it? Tami's at the periphery of my life. She's the only one."

"Goddammit, Kitt, just stop!"

The words exploded from him and she took a step back, shocked. Joe rarely swore, and certainly not *that* epithet. She could count on one hand the number of times he had lost his temper and yelled.

"It's happening again, isn't it? The same thing that happened to you last time. You're losing it, falling apart."

"It's not like that! Just listen."

"No. Look at you. You're not sleeping, are you? Not eating right. You can't think about anything but the case."

"No...no...listen. I think he's been in my house. He's stalking me. He knows—"

"Are you drinking again? Because if you're not now, it's next."

"I'm different now. That's not going to happen." She grabbed his hands. "I know Tami's in trouble. Because of me, she's caught the attention of a killer. I couldn't bear it if— If she was hurt because of me. If something happened to her."

He curled his fingers around hers. "It's not your fault that Sadie died. You couldn't have saved her. Or the girls that monster murdered. None of their deaths are your fault."

"You don't understand, Joe." She shook her head. "You don't see."

"You've got to let it go."

"I can't," she whispered. "The girls need me."

"What if I needed you, Kitt? What would you do?"

"This isn't about you, Joe, it's about Tami. Her safety."

He tightened his fingers. "I'd hoped...I'd thought maybe, just maybe, you'd pulled it together. I see now that you haven't."

Everyone in her life was telling her the same thing—that she had lost perspective, had become obsessed.

She hadn't. Why couldn't they see it? This was real.

She told him so. Begged him to call Valerie.

He said he would, though she didn't believe him. Maybe it was the pity she saw in his eyes. Or the way he had snapped the door shut behind her. With a kind of finality.

Her car sat in the driveway, just beyond a streetlight. She started around to the driver's side, then stopped as marks on the passenger-side panel caught her eyes.

Someone had keyed her.

No, she realized. Not just keyed her. They had left her a message. *He* had left her a message. Scratched into the paint, across the car's door and front panel.

Don't blink.

Friday, March 17, 2006
1:45 a.m.

M.C. called herself fourteen kinds of fool. It was nearly 2:00 a.m.and here she was, at Lance's door. She had been unable to sleep. Unable to quiet her mind. Her conflict with Kitt, Brian's sleazy come-on, the investigation, life in general.

The only thoughts that brought her pleasure were ones of Lance. Is this how an addiction started? she wondered. This thought-stealing need to experience pleasure again? To acquire the potion that would calm the nerves, bring sleep, peace or whatever the psyche—or soul—needed?

She knew he was home. She had seen his car parked on the street out front. If she knocked, two things could happen. He could invite her in. Or rebuff her.

The way her day was going, she should walk away now.

She tapped on the door instead. The first time tentatively. Then more forcefully.

He opened it. From inside came strains of classical music. Something soothing.

He frowned. "M.C.? What are you—"

"Doing here? Your guess is as good as mine."

He didn't move to open the door more and it suddenly occurred to her that he might have a guest. He looked as if he had been in bed—hair mussed, shirt open, trousers half buckled. The thought made her feel ill.

"I should have called." She took a step back. "So sorry. I don't know what I was—"

"Silly." He caught her hands and drew her inside, against his chest. He buried his face in her hair. "You smell so good."

He didn't have someone there. She brought her arms around him. He felt too thin, his skin cool. As she held him, he warmed.

"Are you all right?" she asked him.

"I am now."

She smiled. "Me, too."

He locked the door and led her into his small living room. Pin neat with homey touches that surprised her. Most bachelors' places were anything but "homey."

"Bad day?" she asked.

"Bad night."

"They didn't laugh?"

He looked as if she had slapped him. She brought a hand to his cheek. "What?"

"No. No laughing tonight."

"I'm sorry. I—"

He brought a hand to her mouth.

Wordlessly, he led her to his bedroom. There, they made love. But this time, without laughter.

Without any sound at all.

He muffled them, with his mouth, hands. Drinking them in, absorbing them. She allowed him to lead, her pleasure feeding on the silence. The need to cry out grew inside her, strangely erotic. Like a separate, building orgasm, straining for release.

And when the release came, it reverberated inside her with the power of a nuclear explosion.

It was the most incredibly erotic experience she'd ever had.

He broke the silence first. "Wow."

She smiled and rubbed her face against his damp shoulder. "My sentiments exactly."

"Hungry?"

She shook her head slightly. "Sleepy. Happy."

"You weren't earlier. Earlier, you were Grumpy. Next thing I know, you'll be Sneezy or Doc."

She smiled at his reference to the dwarfs in Snow White. "Are you suggesting I have a multiple-personality disorder?"

"Don't all women?"

She pinched him, and he yelped. "I'm also a cop and carry a gun. I'd remember that, if I were you."

He mock shuddered. She yawned and nestled closer to his side. "I had a particularly trying day and night."

"Want to talk about it?"

She thought a moment, then shook her head again. "Absolutely not."

"So, what do you want to do?"

She tipped her face up to his. "I'm open to ideas."

Turned out he had plenty of them. Ones that proved both innovative and exhilarating.

M.C. came instantly awake. She knew immediately what had awakened her.

Lance had left the bed.

She lay stone still, listening. He hadn't gone to the bathroom. Nor to the kitchen for a snack. Though this wasn't her home, she knew this to be true by the sound of his footfalls, their number.

It was a cop thing. A heightened awareness of surroundings brought on by a job that demanded it to stay alive.

M.C. couldn't locate him. She may have slept with him—twice now—but she didn't know him well enough to be comfortable with that. She slid quietly out of bed, bringing her Glock—which she had tucked just under the mattress near her head—with her. She snatched her shirt and panties from the floor and slipped them on.

M.C. made her way silently from the bedroom to the hall. She found Lance standing at the front window, naked, gazing out at the street. When he turned to look at her, his expression was heartbreakingly sad.

"What's wrong?" she asked.

"I couldn't sleep." He looked pointedly at the gun, the ghost of a smile touching his mouth. "That seems a bit reactionary."

"Just being cautious." She laid it on the back of the couch. "You want to talk about why you couldn't sleep?"

"The truth?"

"Truth's always best."

He took a quick breath and she prepared herself for the worst. Was he wondering what he had gotten himself into? Did he want out?

It wouldn't be the first time she'd had a guy tell her their relationship had been a mistake. A big one.

"I think I like you too much."

She couldn't have predicted that one in a million years. She stared at him, nonplussed. "Give me a break, funny man."

"I'm not joking. For once."

She crossed to him, tipped her face up to meet his. She studied his expression, searched his gaze. He wasn't joking, she realized.

Which in a strange way, was more frightening than if he had been giving her the brush-off. Where did they go from here? Where did she want them to go? Did she want to open herself up to the possibility of a relationship?

Yes, she supposed she did.

She smiled at him. "I think I like you too much, too."

"Really?" He searched her gaze, as if for proof that *she* wasn't joking. Convinced, he smiled. "This not-sleeping thing works for me."

She laughed and rested her head against his shoulder. "Me, too."

From the bedroom, she heard the shrill scream of her cell phone. A call this time of night only meant one thing—somebody was dead.

Because she was being called, she feared the worst. The Copycat had struck again.

She prayed she was wrong.

Lance tightened his arms. "Ignore it?"

"I can't." She stepped out of his arms. The phone screamed again.

She hurried to the other room, grabbing her gun on the way. When she snatched up the phone, she saw from the display that it was, indeed, headquarters.

She answered. "Riggio."

"We've got another girl, Detective."

She hated it when she was right.

While the dispatcher filled her in, she turned to the doorway. Lance had followed her. He stood there watching, expression concerned.

"I'm on my way," she finished, then ended the call.

"You have to go."

"Yes. I wish I didn't but—"

"I understand. Go."

She collected the remainder of her clothing, started toward the bathroom, then stopped and looked back at him. "Another girl is dead."

He spread his hands, expression helpless. "I'm sorry. What can I do?"

"Think of me while I'm gone?"

"Nothing but you."

She crossed to him, pressed a kiss to his mouth, then went to dress.

41

Friday, March 17, 2006
5:20 a.m.

When M.C. arrived at the scene, she saw that Kitt was already there. She parked beside the Taurus and got out. She gazed at the vehicle, at the words scraped into its dark gray paint and frowned. *Don't blink?* What was that all about?

She found Kitt sitting on the home's front step. "What the hell happened to your car?"

"Peanut. He left me a message."

The other woman's voice was curiously devoid of emotion. "When?"

"Last night, I guess. I noticed it around midnight."

M.C. wanted to ask what occasion led her to her car at 12:00 a.m. but let the question pass in favor of another. "What does it mean?"

"It's a warning about the little girls. To stay on my guard. To watch them carefully. If I don't, one will—"

She bit back the word. M.C. knew what it was—die. "This isn't your fault, Kitt."

She lifted her face. Her eyes were red. "This is number three."

M.C. nodded. "You've been inside?"

"Briefly."

"Detective Riggio?" That came from the officer standing at the edge of the sidewalk.

She turned. "Yes?"

He held out a clipboard. "Could you sign in, please?"

She'd walked right past him, she realized. "Of course. Sorry."

She signed in, scanning the log as she did. ID. Sal. The Sarge. Looked like everybody but the chief of police himself. She wouldn't be surprised if he made an appearance, too. "Anything I should know?" she asked.

"I've filled Detective Lundgren in."

"Good. Thanks."

M.C. turned back to her partner. "Kitt? Are you all right?"

"Puked in the bushes."

"Excuse me?"

"I threw up." She dragged a hand through her hair. M.C. saw that it shook badly. "You going to go to the chief with that? Have me pulled from the investigation?"

"Do I need to?"

"Fuck you."

M.C. didn't know what to say. The silence stretched between them until Kitt cleared her throat. "Victim doesn't fit the profile. She's a brunette. Very brunette. Brown eyes."

"A brunette," M.C. repeated, processing what this meant. "His ritual is changing."

"Or maybe he's just giving up the pretense of being the SAK. He knows we're onto him."

"We *suspect* he's not," she corrected. "Is everything else the same?"

Kitt stood. With the light directly on her face, M.C. saw how tired she was. "From what I could tell, yes. The nightgown, the lip gloss, the posed hands. She was smothered. It looks as if he came in the window."

"The scene?"

"Looks clean." Kitt took a deep breath. "Mother thought she heard something and came to check on her daughter."

"When was that?"

"Fourish. Found her this way. Called 911."

"Father?"

"MIA. Six years now."

"Any reason to suspect him?"

"From what I've heard so far, no. He took off and the mother said 'good riddance.' She never even tried to tap him for child support."

"Name?"

"Webber. Catherine. Mother's Marge. A friend's with her." Kitt stuffed her hands into her windbreaker's pockets. "I don't think he's going to stop with three."

"We don't know that, Kitt." M.C. said it as firmly as she could, but Kitt didn't respond. M.C. sensed she was mired in her own dark thoughts.

They headed into the home. Modest. Neat. Tiny foyer. Equally tiny dining room to the right, family room to the left.

Two women sat on the couch. M.C. had no trouble picking out the victim's mother. She caught M.C.'s eyes before she could look away.

Their gazes held. Something in the mother's affected her like a slap. Before she realized what was happening, Marge Webber was on her feet and across the room. She grabbed M.C.'s right arm. "You let this happen!" she cried. "How could you do that?"

M.C. stared at her, shocked.

"She's not blond!" The woman tightened her fingers; they dug into M.C.'s arm. "Her eyes are brown! Not blue!"

Mary Catherine couldn't find her voice. Even if she could have, she didn't know what she would say.

"Marge, honey," the friend cooed, crossing to them, "come on, sweetheart."

"No! No!" Her voice rose, taking on a hysterical edge. "My baby!" she wailed. "He's taken my baby!"

After prying the woman's fingers from M.C.'s arm, she drew her away. As M.C. watched, Marge Webber crumbled, sobbing in her friend's arms.

M.C. realized she was shaking. That her chest was tight. She struggled to breathe evenly. Past the guilt that had her in a choke hold.

Now she understood Kitt, her obsession, her actions. Marge Webber had made her understand.

"Any means necessary," she muttered.

"What?"

She looked at Kitt. "I don't care what we have to do to get this son of a bitch, how many rules we need to break. I want him."

Kitt held her gaze for a long moment, then nodded. "Yes," she said. "Any means necessary."

42

Friday, March 17, 2006
11:20 a.m.

Kitt sat at her desk, staring at the notes spread out before her. She liked to make notes on Post-its. They were like puzzle pieces. She could move them around, shuffle them, tack them up, create a time line.

M.C. sat slumped in a chair across from her, lost in her own thoughts. They had just endured a lengthy meeting with not just the Sarge and Sal—but *their* boss as well. They had been grilled for forty minutes over the case, their progress—or lack of—and the latest murder.

The chief didn't want to accept the fact that Derrick Todd wasn't their man. He was too perfect. A convicted sex offender working at a kid's party place. He insisted they take another look at the ex-con. An arrest would go a long way to reassuring the public.

Never mind that the poor bastard didn't do it.

She picked up the Post-it that read *Derrick Todd* and crumpled it. He was out of it. He couldn't have committed this last murder— his ass had been sitting squarely in jail for violating the state's sex-offender-registration law.

Of course, she doubted he would be in there much longer. Dale had delivered the diary to her. She, in turn, had handed it over to Todd's lawyer.

Her phone rang and she reached for it. "Detective Lundgren."

"Sorry about the angel," he said.

Kitt snapped her fingers to get M.C.'s attention, then pointed to the Post-it with "Peanut phones" written on it. She nodded and dialed CRU, initiating the trace. That done, M.C. wrote *Cell/11:41* on a card and set it on the desk in front of Kitt.

"Was she yours?" Kitt asked.

"Did I kill her? No, Kitten, I didn't."

"And you expect me to believe you? Just like that? After the little warning you left me?"

"I hope it doesn't devalue your ride too much. I wanted to be creative."

"I suppose you consider picking a brunette this time your idea of 'creative'?"

"I told you, I didn't have anything to do with this girl." He lowered his voice to a husky drawl. "I would choose someone closer to you, Kitten. Someone you have a connection with."

Tami. "Give me a name, asshole!"

"You don't play well with others, do you?"

"Fuck you. I'm tired of your games."

He laughed, clearly pleased. "I hate it when we fight. Can't we make up?"

"Tell me what I want to know and you're my best friend again. We're both on the same side. We both want to stop the Copycat."

"We are indeed two of a kind," he said, sounding pleased. "Hurt by people who were supposed to love us. Betrayed by them. Cheated out of the life we deserved."

She took a stab. "And we're fighters. Both of us."

He was quiet a moment. When he replied, his voice sounded deeper. "Yes. Fighters."

"Then help me. Please."

He ignored that. "What's it like to bury your child?" he asked.

"I don't want to talk about my daughter. I want to talk about the Copycat."

"But it's my show, Kitten. Give me what I want and maybe...maybe I'll give you what you want."

Kitt experienced a tickle of excitement. She glanced at the clock. "You're a professional at delivering death, maybe you *should* know how it feels for those left behind. Sadie's death left a hole inside me, a yawning chasm that nothing could fill. I wanted to die myself. Wished I was dead. Considered doing it. Killing myself."

"Why didn't you?" he asked, tone rapt.

"I don't know," she answered simply, honestly. "Or perhaps I did try, one drink at a time."

"What brought you back?"

"AA, the people I met there." She paused, thinking of Danny, the night before, how she had hurt his feelings. "They reminded me that I'm not the only one in the world who hurts. That we're all inter-connected."

"And that Sadie wouldn't want you to give up."

She paused, caught off balance. How did he know that? "Yes," she said.

M.C. set another card on the desk. 11:43.

Three *minutes* to go.

A group had gathered. Sergeant Haas, several of the other de-tectives, Sal. They were all watching the clock, praying, she knew from experience, that this time they'd nail him.

"You think you know me so well?" she asked.

"Yes."

"How?"

"Now, Kitten," he chided her, "you don't really expect me to tell you all my secrets?"

"Why not? I tell you mine, you tell me yours. A partnership."

"A partnership," he repeated. "I like that. In fact, I like you, Kitt. I respect you, despite your screwups."

"That's good to know. But will you still like me when I bust you?"

He laughed. "Maybe more. Of course, that's not going to happen."

"You're so certain?"

"Yes."

She glanced at her partner, who held up two fingers. "How?"

"Because I'm better than you," he said simply. "I'm sorry if that hurts, but it's true. I'm better than you all."

"I'll take that challenge, Peanut." The ease with which the nickname slipped off her lips surprised her. "Let's make it official."

"Competitive, even when you feel so hopeless. When you're so lost. See why I admire you?"

"But I feel neither hopeless nor lost."

"I feel so hopeless," he said, tone mocking. *"As if nothing will ever be good, or right, again. I wonder sometimes, should I just end it? But thoughts of Sadie stop me—I fear taking my own life would keep me from being with her in the afterlife."*

Kitt felt ill. She recognized her own words, her thoughts and feelings, being spit mockingly back at her

An entry from her journal.

He had been in her house that day. Maybe more than once.

Kitt fought to keep how exposed that made her feel from showing. "So, you *were* in my house. You read my journal. Make you feel like a big man?"

He ignored that. She heard the flick of a lighter, the hiss of a cigarette catching, coming to life. "Did you warn the little girls? The ones in the periphery of your life?"

"There are no little girls in my life."

He clucked his tongue. "Now who's playing games, Kitten?"

"I don't play games."

"We all do. In fact, life's one big game. We're all vying to come out the big winner. Top dog. King of the hill."

"Queen of the hill, thank you. Besides, playing at life and really living it are very different things."

"I would love to continue this discussion but our time's up."

"No, wait! You promised—"

"I said maybe, no promises."

"That's not fair! I gave you what you wanted, I—"

"Life's not fair, dear one. Bye-bye."

He hung up; she swung toward M.C., already on the line with CRU. She met Kitt's eyes, expression jubilant. "Got him!"

"Six cruisers," Sal ordered. "No chances. Everybody wears Kevlar. No mistakes." He turned toward White and Allen. "Backup Lundgren and Riggio."

Everybody scrambled. Before they even reached the address, they had learned it was a twelve-unit apartment building. As Kitt pulled up in front of the building, HQ was in the process of running the building's individual addresses through the computer.

Definitely not the most desirable real estate in the metro area.

The cruisers were already there, officers at the ready, weapons drawn.

Kitt climbed out of the car. "Nobody leaves," she ordered. "ID everybody."

White and Allen joined them, and they made their way into the building. The hallway was dim and smelled of urine. The trace had pinpointed the address, but not the unit number.

"Super's usually on the first floor," Kitt said. "If the building's got one." The detectives split into pairs, each taking one side of the hallway.

Kitt and M.C. struck pay dirt right off.

The super was a sixtyish man with an impressive beer belly and a face lined from years spent in the sun. She noted his hands—big, callused and fish-belly white. From inside the apartment came the sound of the TV. *All My Children,* she recognized. While on leave she had become addicted to it.

"Detective Lundgren." She held up her shield. "Detective Riggio. We need to ask you a few questions."

M.C. stepped in. "Are all these units occupied?"

"All but two. Those folks vacated a couple weeks ago. Skipped on their rent." He narrowed his eyes. "I bet you're lookin' for that freak in 310."

"Why's that?"

"Caught him lookin' at pictures of kids."

"Pictures of kids?"

"You know, that kiddie porn. Wanted to puke. Thankful my kids are grown. Warned everyone in the building with kids."

Ex-con. Sex offender. Promising.

"His name?"

"Brown. Buddy."

"Know if he's home right now?"

"No clue. Haven't seen him in a week or so. But he slips in and out, all hours. Like the freak he is."

M.C.'s cell rang. She separated herself from the group. "Riggio. Thanks. Got it."

Kitt excused herself, crossed to her partner. "HQ?"

She nodded. "They discovered Brown, too."

"Sex offender?"

"No. Burglary and assault. They're still working on the other tenants. So far nothing's jumped out."

"Brown's our man. I feel it." She crossed back to the super and thanked him for his help. "For your own safety, I suggest you return to your apartment. Remain there until I give you the go-ahead to leave."

He looked almost gleeful. Kitt suspected this was the most excitement he'd encountered in some time. *All My Children* just couldn't compete. "The freak's behind on his rent," he called after them. "You need me to let you in, just give a shout."

Kitt, M.C. and the two other detectives converged on 310.

Kitt rapped on the door. "Mr. Brown, open up! Police!"

From inside came a sound, like a glass shattering.

"Let's go!" White reared back and kicked the door in. The four burst through, guns drawn. A cat darted past their feet and into the hall. Otherwise, the unit seemed devoid of life.

"Mr. Brown!" Kitt called again. "Police!"

She didn't need to search the apartment to know it was empty. Brown had already flown the coop.

They fanned out, anyway, searching the one-bedroom unit. It smelled of cat excrement and spoiled food. Kitt found what she was looking for on a soiled futon near the front window. A cell phone. He'd left it when he ran.

She crossed to it, snapped on a latex glove, squatted down and retrieved the last number called.

The department's main number.

She scrolled back. A virtual plethora of numbers. Any one of which may lead them to the Copycat.

M.C. joined her. "Sent White and Allen to question the other tenants."

Kitt nodded. "He figured we got the trace, took off. Called me from this phone."

"I'll report it. Get the units downstairs to start canvassing the area. He could be close."

"He have a car?"

"A Ford Escort. It's out front."

"Let's get it impounded."

M.C. nodded, then frowned. "You notice there's no cat box in here."

She looked at her partner, surprised. She hadn't noticed.

"No food or water bowl, either."

"No wonder the creature took off the minute the door opened. Poor thing."

"It's weird."

"What?"

"An outdoor cat in an apartment? No pet door? Why didn't the cat bolt when Brown exited earlier?"

"That's a good question, isn't it? Clearly the cat belonged to Brown and had been here a while."

"Judging by the amount of cat doo."

Kitt arched an eyebrow at the expression. "Doo?"

"You know, as in doo-doo. Aka shit."

"New usage for me. I associate 'do' with prom hair."

M.C. wrinkled her nose. "Nice image, Lundgren. Let's get ID in here for a complete search."

"Done."

While M.C. made the call, Kitt poked around. In the bottom of the bedroom closet she found a shoe box. She flipped the lid back.

Yellowed newspaper clippings. All concerning the same events— the original Sleeping Angel murders.

A lump in her throat, she carefully leafed through them. She recalled each as if burned in her memory. In a number of them, she was named as lead detective on the case.

In every news story, he had highlighted her name with a fluorescent yellow marker.

"M.C., come take a look at this."

Her partner joined her and thumbed through the clippings. "Looks like somebody has a crush on you," she said dryly.

"Lucky m—" She bit the word off. At the bottom of the box was a tube of lip gloss. Maybelline. The kind that could be purchased at every drug store in America.

The color—*Pretty in Pink*.

Friday, March 17, 2006
3:50 p.m.

Buddy Brown's parole officer was not happy to see Kitt and M.C., a fact that had nothing to do with them. Another con breaking his parole agreement meant more paperwork, more irritation and more discussions with officials.

Wes Williams motioned toward the chairs in front of his desk. "I wouldn't have figured Brown as one of those who'd end up back in the pen right away. Some of these guys, yes. Brown *really* didn't like prison."

Some did? Kitt glanced at her notes. "He always make his weekly meeting?"

"Like clockwork. Until a week ago."

"He didn't show?"

"Yup."

"What did you do?"

"Reported him."

"That he was in violation of his parole didn't come up on our computer."

He spread his hands. "What can I say? The wheels of bureaucracy move slowly."

M.C. jumped in. "What else can you tell us about the man?"

"One of those who always got caught. Started as a wild teenager and became a bad adult." He flipped through the pages. "Robbery. Arson. Drugs."

"He seem like the type who could kill someone? A child?"

His gaze sharpened. "A child killer? Brown?"

"Yes."

"I've been around long enough not to be surprised by anything, but my gut impression? No."

"The building super claimed he caught him with child pornography. Brown into that?"

The man looked surprised. "Not that I know of. Nothing in his file about it."

"What about smarts?" Kitt asked.

"Not the brightest bulb. The smart ones don't get caught."

"How'd he get out early?" M.C. asked.

"Same way they all do, Detective. By convincing the review board he no longer posed a threat to society. The fact prisons are filled to bursting doesn't hurt. Out with the old to make room for the new."

Clearly, this guy had been around a long time. Long enough to acquire a very hefty cynicism.

"How many times has he been sent away?"

"This last time was two. He seemed to understand that getting convicted a third time would be very bad, but like I said—"

"Not the brightest bulb."

"Exactly." He glanced at his watch. "I have an appointment in a few minutes. Is there anything else I can help you with?"

Kitt stood and M.C. followed her to her feet. "Thank you, Mr. Williams. If he contacts you or if you think of anything else, please call us."

"He won't contact me, I can assure you. But if he does, I will."

They stopped at the door. Kitt glanced back. "Do you know if he had a cat?"

"A cat?" the man repeated, clearly caught off guard by the question. "Not that I know of."

They started through the door, but he called them back. "Wait, I did forget one thing. His employer called. Said he'd fired the man for not showing up."

"Before or after Brown was a no-show for his weekly?"

"Just before."

Interesting. "Who was his employer?"

"Hold on." He shuffled through his papers, then looked up, expression odd. "Lundgren Homes."

44

Friday, March 17, 2006
4:20 p.m.

M.C. waited until they were in the car to comment. "Lundgren Homes. Any relation?"

"My ex-husband's company."

"Thoughts on that?"

She shook her head, brow furrowed with thought. "I'm still processing."

M.C. started the engine, then eased away from the curb. She had thoughts on what they had just learned, ones she would keep to herself until Kitt was ready.

"We need to interview him."

Kitt nodded. "Let's check back in at the PSB first. See what ID collected. White and Allen should have finished their canvas of Brown's building and neighborhood. Maybe something turned up."

M.C. agreed and merged into downtown traffic. "Brown being the SAK doesn't add up for me."

"It wouldn't have anything to do with his being dumb as a stump, would it?"

M.C. ignored the sarcasm. "Partly, yes. We've already ascertained the SAK is damn clever. That he has uncommon self-control over his urges. That he's arrogant. That doesn't sound like Buddy Brown."

From the corner of her eyes, she saw Kitt massage her temple.

"Nor is Brown a killer."

"But we found the phone that was used to call me. My number was the last one dialed, that's concrete, not speculation."

"True."

"We also found newspaper clippings about the original SAK murders and a tube of lip gloss we're assuming was used on the Sleeping Angels."

"Facts aren't always what they seem."

Kitt turned to fully face her. "Say what you're thinking, dammit!"

"Where does your ex fit into this?"

"He was Brown's employer."

"Don't you think this is all too coincidental?"

"Meaning what? That maybe *Joe* is the SAK?"

M.C. held her tongue a moment, then murmured, "I'm not discounting anything, Kitt. Are you?"

The other woman bristled. "I can tell you that Joe Lundgren is one of the most decent, caring men I've ever met. He was a wonderful husband and father and would never hurt a child. Never, M.C."

"Okay, so what else could this mean? Put the pieces together. What do we know?"

"That three girls are dead, killed in the same way as the Sleeping Angel murders. Someone has been calling me, claiming to be the SAK and claiming his crimes are being ripped off. And today we know that someone called me on a cell from an apartment rented to an ex-con named Buddy Brown."

Kitt fell silent then. M.C. sensed she was mulling over the pieces, reshuffling the deck, as it were. "Brown's stint in prison works, in terms of his being the SAK," she said finally, slowly. "Timewise."

M.C. nodded, navigating around a bus. "The Angel killings stopped because he ended up in the slammer."

"There he met another inmate whom he confided in. One he told all his secrets to."

"He's arrogant. Proud of his accomplishments. Brags, big-time."

"They're both released. The confidant begins reenacting these 'perfect' crimes. Brown's pissed. Wants him stopped."

"But why not stop him himself?" M.C. asked. "One phone call is all it would take. Why involve you?"

Kitt frowned. "It doesn't add up."

"What if it's all about you?"

"Excuse me?"

M.C. pulled into the PSB parking area reserved for police vehicles. She parked. They climbed out, slamming their doors in unison. "What if there is no copycat?" she said. "The new murders are also the SAK's? What if Brown's just a pawn?"

M.C. saw Kitt's frustration. That she wanted to completely discount the theory, but couldn't.

"Okay, I'll bite. Why's it all about me?"

"That, partner, seems to be the question of the hour."

"You think Joe's involved?"

"He's a link between you and the caller, we know that for a fact. What it means is still speculative."

They made their way into the building and up to the second floor. As they stepped off the elevator, Kitt stopped dead, causing the officer exiting behind her to spill his coffee.

"Son of a bitch!" he exclaimed.

Kitt apologized even as she drew M.C. to the side. "Tami," she said. "That's how 'Peanut' knew about her. Because of Joe."

"Who?"

"Joe's fiancée's daughter. Remember, he threatened the little girls in my life. She's the only one."

She started for the bureau office, expression determined. "It's either Brown or someone working with him. They know about Tami because Brown worked for Joe. They got my cell phone number the same way. My God, it would have been so easy! Most of the time Joe's not in the office. His office manager, Flo, comes and goes. Joe's so trusting. He wouldn't think twice about letting one of his crew go into the office to use the phone, bathroom or whatever."

She stopped again and swung to face M.C. "That's how this bastard knows so much about me! A lot of those guys have worked for Joe forever. They knew Sadie. Her nickname. How her death devastated us. My drinking. Everything!"

She swung on her heel and started back toward the elevator.

"Where're you going?" M.C. called, starting after her.

"To see Joe." She looked back at M.C. "Brown's free. He threatened Tami. And if he's the man I've been communicating with, he's going to see my tracing his call as a betrayal. I don't want him to take that betrayal out on her."

Friday, March 17, 2006
5:35 p.m.

They found Joe in his office, preparing to leave for the day. As he shuffled papers, he looked tired. Kitt would swear his hair had gone grayer, just since she had seen him last.

"Hello, Joe," she said.

He paused midshuffle. "Kitt?" he said, obviously surprised to see her. His gaze moved from her to M.C. "What's up?"

"This is my partner, Detective Riggio. We need to ask you a few questions about one of your employees."

"My employees?" he repeated. "Who?"

"Former employee," M.C. corrected. "Buddy Brown."

His expression tightened. He waved them into the office. "What do you want to know?"

"How long did he work for you?"

"Three weeks."

"You knew he was an ex-con?" M.C. asked.

"Yes. He had construction experience. He seemed pretty desperate for a fresh start."

"Why'd you fire him?" M.C. asked.

"Didn't show up for work two days in a row. I'm very clear with these guys, you're here every day, ready to work. Or you're gone. I need people I can count on."

"You said 'these guys.' You hire ex-cons before?"

"I believe in giving people another chance." He shifted his gaze back to Kitt. "What's going on? What'd he do?"

"We have reason to believe he's the man who's been calling me, claiming to be the Sleeping Angel Killer."

His expression went from blank to thunderstruck. "The Sleeping Angel Killer? Do you really think Buddy Brown's...that he could be the one?"

"We're fairly certain he's the one who's been calling me," Kitt said. "Whether he's the SAK or not, we don't have enough proof, one way or the other."

M.C. stepped in. "We believe your fiancée's daughter may be in danger."

"Tami...my God—" Joe looked at Kitt, his expression stricken. "I never called Valerie. I didn't believe you. I thought you were losing it, like before. I never thought—"

He reached for the phone. She saw that his hand shook. "I'll call her now."

Kitt stopped him. "We'd like to speak with her first. It's important we do it this way."

He hesitated. She saw his conflict. "Trust me," she said.

He nodded and jotted her phone number and address on a message, then handed it to her. "She's a nurse. She should be off her shift now."

"Thanks, Joe." Kitt took the address. "If you hear anything from Brown, contact us immediately."

"I will." He looked slightly dazed. "Tell Valerie to call me, so I'll know she's okay. Tell her I..."

He didn't finish the last, just let the words trail helplessly off. Kitt wondered what he had been about to ask. For her to pass along that he loved her?

She didn't know for certain, but was honest enough to admit the thought bothered the hell out of her.

46

Friday, March 17, 2006
6:10 p.m.

Valerie Martin opened the door to her cottage-style home. It was located off Springbrook, near the junior college. Though still a well-respected area, it no longer had the cachet it once had. She wore her uniform, though she had changed into slippers. By her expression, M.C. suspected she recognized Kitt.

No doubt Kitt realized that as well, but she introduced herself, anyway. "Valerie, Kitt Lundgren. Joe's ex-wife."

"I remember. We met at the leukemia event." She glanced at M.C., then returned her gaze to Kitt's. "How can I help you?"

"This is my partner, Detective Riggio. We're here in an official capacity. May we come in?"

"Official capacity?" she repeated, eyes widening. "Is Joe…has something happened to—"

"Joe's fine," Kitt said quickly. "May we come inside?"

"Of course." Valerie stepped away from the door.

Kitt entered first; M.C. followed. The interior was homey and comfortable, with pretty feminine touches. Tami sat cross-legged on the floor, a box of markers and drawing pad on the coffee table in front of her. She didn't look up at them.

"Do you mind?" She looked toward the kitchen, which they could see from where they stood. "I was getting dinner together."

They said they didn't and followed her to the other room. She had, indeed, been preparing dinner. Looked like leftover spaghetti and a salad. She crossed to her chopping board, picked up the knife and went back to work.

"You work at Hillcrest Hospital?" M.C. asked, though it wasn't a question. She still wore her hospital name tag.

"Yes. The pediatric ward."

"Been there long?"

"My whole career."

Kitt cleared her throat. "You're aware of the recent murders of three ten-year-old girls?"

The woman's movements stopped. She looked up, fear creeping into her eyes. "Yes."

"We have reason to believe Tami may be in danger."

The knife slipped from her fingers and clattered against the board. Without a word, she crossed to the kitchen door and opened it. She peered out, as if to reassure herself her daughter was fine, then turned back to them.

"What makes you… Why do you think this?"

M.C. sidestepped the question with one of her own. "Have you noticed anyone out of the ordinary lately? Someone hanging around, a stranger, or strange vehicle, in the neighborhood?"

"No."

"Think carefully, Valerie. A face you registered seeing before, even a sense of being watched or followed."

"I need to sit down." Valerie crossed to one of the stools at the breakfast counter and sank onto it.

"I don't think... No," she said again. "Nothing comes to mind."

"Did a clown approach you at the leukemia event?"

She stared blankly at them. M.C. sensed she was working to process what they were telling her—and all the ramifications of it.

"He was selling balloons," Kitt added.

"Tami had a balloon," she said. "A pink one. Joe bought it for her, I think."

M.C. glanced at her partner. To her credit, Kitt's expression registered nothing of the turmoil she must have been experiencing.

"Please," Valerie said, "tell me why you suspect Tami's in danger."

"We have no concrete proof that she is," Kitt said gently. "I received a threat that spoke of little girls at the periphery of my life. Tami fits that description."

Valerie pressed her lips together, though she looked slightly relieved.

"We aren't about to take any chances, Ms. Martin. With that in mind, I suggest you're extra-careful right now. Don't leave Tami alone, particularly at night. I suggest that until we catch this killer, you allow your daughter to sleep in your bedroom."

She nodded, blinking rapidly, as if fighting tears. "I will. Thank you. If anything happened to Tami, I don't know what I'd..." Her voice trailed off and she glanced at Kitt, cheeks pink. "I'm sorry."

"No need to apologize," Kitt said stiffly. "If you think of anything or notice anything out of the ordinary, don't hesitate to call us."

The woman walked them to the door. This time, as they neared the girl, she peeked up at them and shyly smiled. M.C. smiled back. Most kids, including her nephew, would have had the TV blaring. She found it refreshing to see a child entertaining herself another way.

It had grown dark and Valerie flipped on the porch light for them. As they started across, M.C stopped and turned back. "Ms. Martin? How did you meet your fiancé?"

From the corners of her eyes, she saw Kitt look at her in surprise.

"At the hospital."

"Surely not in the pediatric ward?"

"Actually, it was." She smiled. "Joe came in to entertain the kids with magic tricks."

"Magic tricks? Is he good?"

"Quite good. For an amateur."

M.C. glanced at Kitt. She was frowning. "That was nice of him," she said.

"That's what I thought. The kids love him. It takes their minds off being in the hospital."

"He still do that?"

"He comes in every couple of weeks. Once a month at the outside."

M.C. thanked her again, and she and Kitt walked to the car. Once inside, she turned to Kitt. "Your ex is a magician?"

"Calling him a magician makes him sound professional. He does magic tricks, pretty basic sleight-of-hand stuff. It was a hobby."

"He visit hospital children's wards before Sadie died?"

"When Sadie was in the hospital, he used to cheer her up with his tricks. Sometimes other kids came in to watch."

M.C. didn't comment. She started the car and turned on the lights. As she pulled away from the curb, she noticed another vehicle half a block behind her do the same.

M.C. moved her gaze from the rearview mirror to the road. "That must have been difficult for you," she said, changing the subject. "Her being engaged to your ex and all."

"I'm fine." The edge in Kitt's voice suggested otherwise. "Can we focus on the case?"

"Sure. Martin seemed on the up-and-up. Like a real nice lady who loves her kid a lot."

M.C. navigated traffic, grateful the rush hour was over. "Did Joe hire ex-cons while you were married?"

"Not that I know of." Kitt frowned. "First the magic tricks, now the ex-cons. What are you getting at?"

"Something's not right here."

"Why? Because he does philanthropic work?"

M.C. backed off, not quite ready to confront Kitt. "You want to get some dinner?"

"Thanks, but I'll pass. I'm beat."

"That's cool. Tomorrow, same time same station?"

Kitt agreed, and after dropping her at the PSB, M.C. stopped at Mama Riggio's for takeout, but ended up eating in and catching up with her brothers' antics. In true Tony, Max and Frank fashion, when a couple of their single friends came in they introduced her, then wasted no time pointing out her fourth grade "geek squad" photo.

Why she still loved them, she had no clue.

She left the restaurant, climbed into her Explorer and headed for home. As she exited the parking lot, she noticed the lights of another car in the lot come on. A moment later, the other vehicle eased into traffic behind her.

M.C. frowned. Was someone following her?

As she drove, she kept watch on her "friend." He stayed with her at a discreet three-car distance. She slowed, giving the driver a chance to pass. He didn't, instead falling back himself to maintain his distance.

The stoplight up ahead was about to change from yellow to red; instead of slowing to a stop, she hit the gas and sped through. She saw in the rearview that her shadow, if he or she had even been one, had been forced to stop at the light. She made a turn, then several more. Certain she was no longer being tailed, she headed home.

Hours later, unable to sleep, she stood at her front window. She couldn't stop thinking about the events of the day, couldn't shake the question of whether Joe Lundgren's involvement with Buddy Brown was more than that of employer and employee.

As she gazed at the street, a car cruised slowly past her house. A Ford. Like the one that had pulled out after her earlier tonight, when she'd left the restaurant. And before, at Valerie Martin's.

An unmarked police car.

Someone was keeping tabs on her.

Who?

Without turning on the porch light, she slipped out of the house and crossed to the far end of the porch. From that vantage point, she'd be able to answer that question when the driver passed under the streetlight.

She didn't have to wait long. As if the driver had simply made a loop of her block, he rolled by again. And as she had predicted, she got a clear look at the man behind the wheel.

It was Lieutenant Brian Spillare.

Saturday, March 18, 2006
8:10 a.m.

When M.C. called, Kitt was on her third cup of coffee and still trying to shake the cobwebs out. She had stayed up most of the night, reviewing Brown's file. Picking it apart. Nothing in it suggested great skill or intelligence. A two-time loser, he seemed to have been picked up for everything he'd ever done. He more than likely would have spent most of his life behind bars if not for lawyers and legal loopholes.

"Yo," Kitt answered.

Her partner didn't mince words. "They found Brown. But before you get too excited, he's dead."

It took Kitt a moment to process that. When she had, she hurried to the bathroom. "How?"

"Only know where. Paige Park."

"Son of a bitch!" She pulled down her pajama bottoms and sat on the toilet. "You on your way out there?"

"Pulling myself together. Are you peeing? That's so gross."

"It was an emergency." She stood, flushed and crossed to the sink. "So sue me."

"I'll think about it. See you out there."

Twenty minutes later Kitt pulled up next to M.C.'s Explorer. Anna Paige Park was located on the far north side of town. If a body was going to surface in a park in Rockford, Paige Park would head the list.

Kitt climbed out of her battered Taurus, clutching a travel mug of coffee. Her partner stood beside her vehicle, hands stuffed into the pockets of her down vest.

"You look like hell," M.C. said.

"Here's a clue, so do you."

She smiled grimly. "I blame the job. It sucks."

"How's a girl going to get her beauty sleep?"

M.C.'s smile was sudden and took Kitt by surprise. "Exactly."

They crossed to the first officer and signed the log. Outdoor sites posed specific investigative problems. Rain and wind destroyed evidence. Wild animals had been known to decimate crime scenes, including the body. Weather conditions altered the decomposition process.

When it came to crime-scene investigation, nothing beat the two C's—control and containment.

"What've we got?" she asked.

"Body in a gully, just beyond that ridge of trees. Jogger and his golden retriever found him. One Buddy Brown. Wallet was on him. Cash in the wallet."

"How much?"

"Enough to buy a fifth of something cheap or dinner at McDonald's."

Robbery hadn't been a motive.

"Anything else?"

"Looks like he was killed at another location and dumped here."

"Great."

"All the appropriate parties are on their way. My partner's with the body."

They nodded and started for the ridge, consisting of thick pines and spindly hardwood trees. Pine straw, leaves and other natural debris crackled under their feet—the same debris with which the killer had attempted to conceal the body.

Kitt and M.C. started down the hill. The uniform lifted a hand in greeting and they crossed to him, introducing themselves.

"You two are the first."

"Lucky us." Kitt crossed to the body, squatted down beside it. He lay faceup on a black tarp. The killer hadn't bothered digging a hole, had simply covered him with the leaves.

He hadn't been too worried about the body being uncovered.

She recognized Brown from the pictures in his file. Medium-size man—midtwenties. Medium complexion. Brown eyes and hair.

She gazed at him, working to picture him as the one who had taunted her, calling himself Peanut. The man who had arrogantly described his crimes as "perfect."

He looked like every other, quite ordinary, penny-ante criminal.

"He's been dead a while," M.C. said, squatting beside her.

"Mmm." The decomposition process was, indeed, well under way.

"Got a guess?"

"Too many variables, I know I'll be off. But it wasn't yesterday, that's for certain."

Which meant Buddy Brown had not been the one on the phone with her.

Which changed things dramatically once again.

Exactly when he had died would be established by the pathologist. Kitt moved her gaze over the victim. "No gunshot wound, no blood."

From behind them came the sound of ID arriving. Kitt glanced over her shoulder. Sorenstein and Snowe. The pathologist, Frances Roselli.

She stood, M.C. with her. "Day late and a dollar short," she called. "Couldn't drag yourselves out of the sack?"

"Bite me," Sorenstein answered. "It's Saturday."

As they neared, Kitt saw that with the exception of the pathologist, the men looked a bit green. The smell of the victim was not helping their condition.

"Overdo it last night?" she teased. "No one to blame but yourself."

"Kiss mine," Snowe grumbled.

"This your suspect?" Sorenstein asked. "The ex-con?"

She cocked an eyebrow. "Bad news travels fast."

"Neck was broken," pathologist said. He squatted and pointed. "See the angle of the head?"

"Think that's what killed him?"

"Doesn't make much sense to break somebody's neck after they're already dead, but you never know."

"How long you think he's been this way?"

For a long moment, the pathologist was quiet. "It's been dry. Cool. That'd slow the process. I'm thinking two to three weeks, depending. Autopsy will give us a more specific time." He glanced at Sorenstein. "And whatever's feasting on this sorry shit."

Snowe laughed. "Ready to go buggy, buddy?"

Sorenstein hunched deeper into his jacket. "Damn, I hate this job."

Kitt and M.C. backed off to let the others do their thing.

Two to three weeks? Three weeks ago Julie Entzel had been alive.

M.C. turned to her. "What now?"

"Figure out the connection between the SAK, Copycat and Buddy Brown."

"And you," M.C. added.

And me, Kitt silently agreed.

48

Monday, March 20, 2006
8:40 a.m.

Kitt entered the PSB. She crossed the lobby, heading straight for the elevators and caught one that took her to the second floor. It'd been a busy weekend. Roselli had performed the autopsy and determined that Brown had, indeed, been dead two weeks, give or take a few days. That excluded him from the Copycat killings and the calls to her.

The man's neck had been broken. It had taken both strength and skill on the part of the killer. Since the autopsy hadn't turned up any defensive wounds, he had taken Brown by surprise.

Which suggested Brown had known his murderer.

Kitt felt strongly that the two men had met in prison, that Buddy Brown had been killed by her caller, who was, indeed, the Sleeping Angel Killer.

The SAK had taken up residence with Buddy Brown, either before or after he had killed him. ID had sent the lip gloss to the lab
for comparison to the samples taken from the SAK and Copycat victims, and ID was dusting the clippings for prints.

Kitt yawned widely as she exited the elevator. They had done a
search for inmates who had served time with Brown and were now
free. She and M.C. had spent much of Sunday tracking the men
down.

She reached the bureau, greeted Nan and headed for the coffeepot.

Nan returned the greeting. "Detective Riggio's in Interrogation
Number One. They've just begun."

Kitt looked over her shoulder at the woman. "Who's just begun
what?"

"Questioning the suspect. Sergeant Haas and Detective Riggio."

"The suspect? In what case?"

The secretary looked at her as if she had lost her mind. "The
Copycat killings."

The case they were working nearly round the clock.

Who the hell had Riggio brought in?

Kitt finished doctoring her coffee and started that way.
"Thanks, Nan."

"Oh, Detective?"

She glanced back. The receptionist held up several message slips.
"Shall I hold on to these?"

"No, I'll take them. Thanks." She crossed back, took the messages
and stuffed them into her jacket pocket. "I'll be in Interrogation. If
anyone needs me, I've got my cell."

All five of the Violent Crimes interrogation rooms were located
on the same hallway. In addition to a table and chairs, a door with a
window, room one was fitted with a ceiling-mounted video recorder.

Kitt reached room one and peered through the window. M.C.
was standing, blocking her view of the suspect. The sarge was sitting, expression impassive.

She lifted her hand to tap on the glass; M.C. moved. Kitt's breath caught.

Joe. They were questioning Joe.

Disoriented, she stared through the window at her ex-husband. It couldn't be Joe sitting in that chair. Not steady, even-tempered, kind Joe. Not *her* Joe.

Kitt shifted her gaze to the other woman. When had M.C. decided to do this? And did she really think she was going to let her get away with going behind her back this way?

She tapped on the window, struggling to stem her sudden rush of anger. The three looked her way. So angry she shook, Kitt kept her gaze trained on her partner. She didn't think she could meet Joe's eyes without losing it.

She motioned for M.C. to come outside. As soon as the door closed behind her, Kitt drew her away from it.

"You made it," M.C. said. "I had Sergeant Haas sit in until you got here."

"Cut the bullshit. What the hell's going on?"

"I brought Joe in for questioning."

"Without consulting me. We're partners. I'm lead on this. That's unacceptable."

"I felt the element of surprise would work best."

She felt herself flush. "My surprise? Or Joe's?"

"Frankly? Both." She lowered her voice. "When it comes to your ex, you have blinders on. You've made that pretty clear."

"How do you figure?"

"Look at the facts, Kitt. Your ex-husband was Buddy Brown's employer."

"So that makes him a killer?"

M.C. ignored that. "While you two were married, your husband did not hire ex-cons. Your words."

"I said I didn't *think* so. He may have."

"While you were married, magic tricks were simply a hobby. Now he entertains sick children with them."

"Please! It was a logical next step. He saw how his magic helped kids while Sadie was in the hospital."

"Highcrest Hospital rang a bell. So I spent some time digging through the case files. Three months ago, Julie Entzel's cousin Sarah was a patient there. She spent a full week in the pediatric ward."

"You think Joe's the Copycat?" The utter disbelief in her voice would have been comical in another situation.

"And your caller. Yes."

"But I know this man," Kitt argued. "I grew up with him, was married to him for nearly twenty-five years. What you're suggesting is simply not possible."

M.C. leaned toward her. "Why, Kitt? That's what I've wondered all along. Why involve you? This makes sense."

"Not to me." Kitt grabbed at straws, thoughts whirling. "What about the clown at the leukemia event? He gave me the balloon, called me later. But Joe was there. He couldn't—"

"He saw the clown give you the balloon." She held up a hand, stopping the denial. "And don't ask about not recognizing his voice, we both know that anyone who can access a computer can buy a voice altering device online. And some of them are damn good.

"He's punishing you," she went on. "For leaving him. For focusing on the case instead of him. For caring about the little girls more than him or your marriage. Choose any one to fill in the blanks; they all work."

Kitt spun away from the other woman. Joe knew everything about her. Her hopes and fears. He knew about her falling and hitting her head; that she had been drinking.

He knew everything about her.

No. This wasn't possible.

"I called Julie Entzel's mother."

Kitt looked over her shoulder at M.C.

"They saw Joe's magic show. Little Julie was quite taken with it."

My God.

It couldn't be how it looked.

"Can you do this?" M.C. asked. "Or shall I keep the sarge in?"

"I can do this, dammit. Give me a minute."

M.C. didn't comment. Kitt heard the interrogation room door click shut. She closed her eyes. How did she get her arms around this? How did she even muster enough objectivity to go in there and ask the important questions?

How the hell did she look Joe in the eyes?

She flexed her fingers. Everything M.C. said was true. If the man sitting in that room was anyone else, she would have been in his face.

Kitt sorted through the points M.C. had presented to her. He was a physical link to Buddy Brown. And between her and Brown. Now there was a connection between him and one of the victims. M.C. had provided a plausible motivation for the calls to her.

He could have seen the clown as an opportunity to throw suspicion away from him.

When she'd warned him that Tami might be in danger, she'd told him about the clown. The balloon. The clown's call.

He hadn't said a word about having bought the child a balloon.

The truth of that rushed over her in a chilling wave. No, none of it made sense to her. None of it jibed with the man she knew—and loved.

But how often did family of the accused express shock, astonishment and disbelief over their loved ones' actions?

More often than not.

Kitt drew in a deep, fortifying breath. It didn't change her feelings about the way M.C. had gone behind her back. But she had a job to do, and she meant to do it. Although, if this went any further she would be out of it. With personal connections to a prime suspect, she would be pulled from the case. At this stage, however, she could be a big asset in the interrogation process.

She crossed to the door, pulled it open. "Taking over, Sarge," she said.

He nodded and stood. On his way out, he squeezed her arm reassuringly. She wondered if he had been a party to M.C.'s decep-
tion and hoped he hadn't been.

"Hello, Joe," she said, taking a seat across from him at the table.

"Kitt?" She cringed at the relief in his voice. "What's going on here?"

"Just some questions. That's all."

"You already asked me questions. Why here? I would have answered anything you asked at the office."

"Riggio here likes things official."

The bad cop, obviously.

She smiled reassuringly, feeling like a fraud. "Everything's going
to be fine."

"Okay." He nodded. "So let's get this going, I've got a crew waiting for me."

Riggio began. "Your fiancée told us you met at the hospital where
she works."

"That's right."

"What were you doing in the pediatric ward, Mr. Lundgren?"

He frowned. "Valerie didn't tell you? I perform magic tricks for
the kids. I was there doing one of my shows."

Kitt stepped in. "When did you start doing that, Joe?"

"A year or so ago. I was lonely...missed Sadie and—" He cleared
his throat. "I had a lot of free time. To fill it, I worked on my magic.
I remembered how the kids at the hospital had enjoyed it and approached the hospital about performing for the kids every couple
of weeks."

"Is Highcrest the only hospital you visit?"

"No. I go to The Ronald McDonald House. Children's Hospital.
I even performed at a couple of nursing homes."

Kitt saw M.C. make a note. She would check those places and
see if any of the other victims had a connection to them.

"Seems like all this philanthropy would take a lot of time away
from work," M.C. said.

"Work isn't everything, Detective. Life is about giving back."

"How would you respond if we said you had met one of the Copycat's victims?"

He looked from Kitt to M.C. "I'd say you're mistaken."

"Julie Entzel. She saw one of your magic shows."

"At Highcrest Hospital."

The color drained from his face. "I didn't know. I saw the picture in the paper...but I didn't recognize her as one of the kids who..."

His voice trailed off. Kitt recalled how he had said the Entzel girl "meant nothing to him." That he didn't even "know her."

He looked ill. M.C. changed direction. "Let's talk about Buddy Brown."

He didn't comment, just nodded. "How did he come to be working for you?" she asked.

"He contacted me. And he had some experience. So, I hired him."

"He was up-front with you about his past?"

"Yes."

"That didn't worry you?"

"Look, somebody's got to hire these guys. How can they go straight if they can't support themselves?"

"So you consider it your civic duty?"

He frowned. "Not really. I still expect a full day's work for a full day's pay. I'm not a charity."

"Where were you the nights of March 6, 9 and 16?"

"May I consult my planner?"

She said he could, and he pulled out his PalmPilot. After navigating through the menu, he said, "The night of the ninth I was with Valerie."

"All night?"

Kitt didn't look away, though she wanted to. He shifted in his seat, clearly uncomfortable. "I don't normally. But Tami spent the night at her grandmother's."

"What about the other two nights?"

"Nothing. Valerie, Tami and I went to dinner on the sixth. I had a homeowner's association meeting on the sixteenth."

"You were home by what time?"

He thought a moment. "Both nights, 10:00 p.m. No later." Joe looked at her. "Do I need to get a lawyer, Kitt?"

Riggio answered for her, quickly. A fact that once again proved the other woman didn't trust her. "A lawyer is your right, of course. Only you know if you need one."

A trick used to make a suspect feel as if he was incriminating himself if he lawyered-up. She had certainly used it enough.

So why did it feel so wrong now?

M.C. stood. "I'm sorry, but could you give us a few minutes?"

He looked at his watch, obviously frustrated. "How much longer do you think—"

"Not much."

He looked at Kitt as if for reassurance. She longed to give it to him but couldn't.

"Could I have a word with you?" he asked her. "Alone?"

"I'm sorry, Joe. That's not possible. Not right now."

Something passed across his features. An understanding. Realization.

Hurt.

"I think I would like to call a lawyer," he said stiffly. "As you said, it's my right."

M.C. looked sharply at Kitt. "Of course. I'll make a phone available to you right away."

"I'd also like to call my crew foreman, so he can get started."

"That shouldn't be a problem." She motioned toward the door. "The hallway, Kitt. Now."

They exited the room and stepped away from the door. M.C. whirled to face her. "What the hell was that all about?"

"Excuse me?"

"Did you signal him or something?"

Now M.C. had pissed her off. "That's insulting. I'm not even going to dignify that with an answer."

"One look at you, and he lawyered right up. What would you think?"

"I'd think he was a bright guy. For God's sake, M.C., he lived with a detective for twenty-five years. Do you think I never talked about interrogating suspects? That he doesn't know the techniques we use?"

M.C. opened her mouth as if to argue, but Kitt didn't give her a chance. "If we're going to partner, even if only for this one case, we have to trust each other. Can you do it?" she asked, throwing the other woman's earlier question back at her.

For a long moment, M.C. was silent. But instead of answering in the affirmative, as Kitt had, she murmured, "I'll try. Right now, that's the best I can do."

Monday, March 20, 2006
10:10 a.m.

M.C. had decided to get someone out to question Valerie, ASAP. She hadn't needed to tell Kitt she wanted to make certain Joe didn't have the opportunity to give his fiancée a heads-up-and a chance to lie for him. Nor had she needed to tell Kitt that if Valerie Martin didn't corroborate, she would recommend an arrest.

In the end, M.C. had decided to call on Valerie herself. She had taken Detective White with her, leaving Kitt to oversee Joe's meeting with his lawyer. Kitt supposed that displayed trust. Or not, thanks to the trusty video camera.

Kitt was acutely aware of how Joe's being a suspect had reversed their positions on the case. M.C. was calling the shots now. Though it was as it should be, Kitt couldn't quite quell her feeling of resentment toward the other woman. M.C. would be *certain* the shadow of impropriety didn't fall over her.

Kitt glanced at her watch, wondering what was happening. If Valerie didn't confirm Joe's story about their spending the night of the ninth together, Joe was going to be in some very deep shit. Either way, M.C. would go for a search warrant. And Kitt didn't see a problem with a judge granting it—even with the alibi, they had probable cause.

Joe's lawyer hadn't arrived yet. While she waited, she'd decided to review the transcripts of her calls from "Peanut." She scanned the first of the recorded calls, noting the way he put words together, his choice of words.

Joe didn't talk like this. Yes, a voice changer could alter a person's voice. But not the way they spoke.

She narrowed her eyes, considering the content next. He had known about Derrick Todd. How? He had claimed omnipotence. Had opened their conversation with a comment about her chasing her tail.

Could "Peanut" be a cop?

It would make sense. Her history wasn't a secret around the force. Someone nosing around asking the right questions would learn some damn personal stuff about her.

And, clearly, the SAK had understood crime-scene investigation. He had left the scenes nearly pristine; it had always seemed as if he knew what their next step would be.

Of course, it wasn't unusual for a serial killer to be a crime- or law-enforcement buff. Some had even been known to listen to police scanners.

She switched to the second transcript. More generic. He had taunted her about the balloon. And about her mood.

"After all I've done for you," he'd said.

"And what would that be? The wild-goose chase you sent me on? Thanks."

"It may have seemed that way to you. You have to have faith."

Have faith. In him? In the clue he had given her? Or both?

"Kitt?" She turned. Sal stood in the doorway, expression grim. "My office."

She stood and followed him. "Close the door, please," he said when they were inside. "Update me."

"As I'm sure you're aware, M.C. brought Joe in for questioning. He's requested a lawyer. He claims an alibi for the night of the ninth. M.C.'s checking that out now."

"I want you out of this. Immediately."

"Yes, sir. And if the lawyer arrives before M.C. returns—"

"Sergeant Haas or I will sit in." His expression softened. "I'm sorry, Kitt."

"For taking me off the case?" The bitter edge in her voice didn't surprise her. The sudden lump in her throat did.

"No, for the reason I'm taking you off the case."

"He's not involved, Sal."

"You're certain?"

"Absolutely. And not just because of my personal relationship with him."

For a long moment, he held her gaze. Then he nodded slightly, as if in acknowledgment of her feelings. "If Joe's cleared, you're back in charge. I have zero choice in this."

"Understood." She turned and walked to the door. There, she stopped and looked back. "Request permission to follow up on evidence unrelated to Joe. Specifically to go through the contents of the storage locker."

"Seems like a good use of your time. And, Kitt, for what it's worth, I hope you're right about Joe."

She thanked him and returned to her desk. She gazed at the transcript, feeling suddenly lost. In need of a friend.

Brian, she thought. If anyone would understand, it'd be him.

Kitt headed for his office. When she reached it, she found the door closed. She lifted her hand to knock on his door, then froze as she heard M.C.'s voice. "Enough! Stop following me."

"I don't know what you're talking about."

"Bullshit. I saw you roll by my house the other night. You were tailing me earlier that same night. I don't want to have to go to the chief with this."

"I bet you don't." Brian snickered. "Don't want anyone to know you slept your way into the VCB."

Kitt heard M.C.'s sharply drawn breath. "That's a lie, you prick."

"You know how fast news travels in the RPD. Speed of light, babe."

Clearly the two had had a sexual relationship. When? Had Brian used his influence to get M.C. assigned to the Violent Crimes Bureau?

"Try it," M.C. said, "and you'll regret it, I promise you that."

"Are you threatening me, Detective?"

"Whatever you want to call it. Back off."

The last was delivered in a voice akin to a growl. Kitt dropped her hand and took a step backward. She had heard enough. Her respect for both colleagues had plummeted.

She took another step; Brian's door flew open. M.C. stormed out, stopping short when she saw her.

"Kitt!" she exclaimed, face red. "What a coincidence, I was just coming to find you." She glanced toward Brian's door, then back at Kitt. "Joe's alibi checked out."

"I thought it would."

"Doesn't mean he's not guilty."

"You're getting a search warrant."

It wasn't a question; she answered, anyway. "Yes. Should have it within the hour."

"Sal took me off the case. Temporarily."

M.C. nodded. Obviously, if she hadn't already known, she had expected it. "I'll keep you posted on our progress."

"I'd appreciate that."

Kitt watched her go, then tapped on Brian's door casing. He was on the phone; he waved her in.

"So call me," he said. "I miss you. Okay?"

He hung up, the picture of misery.

"What's up, Brian? You look like you lost your best friend."

"Ivy and I have split up. Her idea."

Brian was a good cop and had been a wonderful partner and friend. But no way would she want to be married to the man. He had a serious case of Peter Pan syndrome.

"Sorry to hear that. Anything I can do?"

He dragged his hands through his hair. Kitt saw that they shook. She noticed how much of his red mane had been replaced by gray. When the heck had that happened?

"I wish. This time I...I think she means it."

Because of an affair with the much younger M.C.? Or something—someone—else?

He jumped to his feet, visibly shaking off his mood. "That partner of yours was just in here."

Kitt cocked an eyebrow at his choice of words. "I saw that."

"She told me about Joe."

Did she? Odd. "What did she say, exactly?"

"That he was a suspect. A good suspect. And that you're off the case."

"Temporarily," she corrected. "Until Joe's cleared."

"I'm sorry, Kitt. It really sucks."

"He's not a part of this. I know he's not."

He began to pace, as if agitated. "She was almost gloating about it. I found that curious. I thought you two were getting along?"

Kitt frowned. The part of the conversation she'd overheard had nothing to do with Joe, but why would Brian lie to her?

"We're tolerating each other pretty well."

Or at least, she had thought so until this morning.

He stopped, turned and faced her. "Can I give you some advice?"

"Always, Brian."

"With that one, watch your back. She's ambitious...and she'll do anything, to anyone, to get what she wants."

With that off his chest, he seemed to relax. He settled onto the corner of his desk and folded his arms across his chest. "Did you come down here just to shoot the shit, or was there something specific you needed?"

"Wanted to pass something by you."

"Go for it."

"I was reviewing the transcripts of my calls with Peanut. Could the SAK be a cop?"

"A cop?" he repeated. "Geez, Kitt, how could you even think that?"

"The way he talks. That he knew about Derrick Todd. Think about it." She leaned forward. "He knows the process. That's how he's gotten away with it."

"Yeah, sure. But why?"

"Could it be someone who feels slighted? Someone passed over for promotion? Fired or dressed down in some way?" This time it was she who stood, who started pacing. As she did, she fitted the pieces together, thinking aloud. "He's arrogant. Proud of his 'perfect' crimes. He's made a big deal about how we've all been chasing our tails."

He nodded slowly. "Theoretically, it makes some sense. But a cop? Cops might take a couple dollars under the table here or there, accept a favor or a free cup of coffee, but serial murder?"

She refused to back off. "A cop with an ax to grind."

"Why involve you?"

"He wanted to boast. This Copycat came along, it pissed him off. Or maybe I'm a symbol of the fallen cop. The total screwup."

"Maybe." He rubbed his jaw. Kitt noticed that he hadn't shaved. At the same moment, she noticed he looked as if he'd slept in his clothes.

"Any names come to mind?" she asked.

He thought a moment, then shook his head. "Have you mentioned this to Sal?"

"Not yet. I wanted to run it by somebody first." She smiled. "I picked my old friend."

"I appreciate that vote of confidence." He smiled and stood. "I tell you what, before you say anything to Sal, let me put my thinking cap on. Look through some records, see if I can come up with a name or two."

She thanked him and headed for the door. There, she remembered the three women the SAK claimed were his. "I've been meaning to ask you about three cases you and Sergeant Haas worked on, back in '98 and '99."

"Ask away."

"Three elderly women, all beaten to death. Duct tape applied to their mouths postmortem. You remember them?"

He made a face. "How could I forget? What do you need to know?"

"Ever find a link between the three women?"

"Never. We knew the same UNSUB killed all three, but that's as far as we got."

"The SAK claims they're his."

Now she had him. "MO's completely different."

"True. But that's the point." Kitt explained how she had found the three cases and her "ying and yang" theory. "I confronted him, he said they were his."

Brian nodded. "Plus, there were three. And the scenes were strangely evidence-free."

"Exactly."

"During the SAK investigation, I never even considered them related. Boy, do I feel like an idiot."

"Who would have? If he hadn't teased me with his claim of having 'done' others, I never would have gone looking."

"How can I help?"

"Can you recall anything that stuck out as particularly odd about any of the witnesses? Any suspicions that you followed up on but led to nothing? Do you remember anyone you questioned being vague or uncommunicative?"

He was quiet, as if running through the case, refamiliarizing himself with it. He shook his head. "It was a horrendous case to work. Everyone was stunned by the brutality. Jonathan and I spent the most time trying to find the link between the women, thinking it might lead us to the killer."

He spread his hands. "We came up empty."

"Thanks, Brian. I'm going to be reviewing the case files, if I have any questions—"

"I'll be here." He smiled, but as Kitt exited his office, it occurred to her that something about the curving of his mouth seemed false.

50

Monday, March 20, 2006
3:30 p.m.

As M.C. had predicted, a judge granted the search warrant for Joe Lundgren's home, vehicles and business. The language of a warrant had to be specific; law enforcement could not simply go on a fishing expedition. Each address and vehicle had to be specifically named in the warrant or it was off-limits. Likewise, a warrant that was too specific could hamstring investigators.

They had begun with the business office, for no other reason than his connection to Brown was through Lundgren Homes. There, they had pulled employment records; communication with the Illinois Parole Board, cell phone bills, bank statements, his computer.

M.C. hoped to find a payoff to Brown, receipts for the cell

phones used to call Kitt, or something that would tie him to Kitt's caller or Brown's murder—or any of the others, for that matter.

From the business office, they moved to the man's Highcrest Road residence. M.C. wondered if this was the house he and Kitt had shared when they were married. Something about the lived-in feeling of the California cottage-style home suggested that it was.

She stood in the living room, surveying the row of family photos on the fireplace mantel. They were all from the time before Sadie's death, when they had been a family. Many of the photos included Kitt. A smiling, carefree-looking Kitt.

A wife and mother. Happy. Loved.

A visual record of Kitt's loss.

M.C. shifted her thoughts away from her partner. How did Valerie feel about the photos? M.C. had seen ones similar to these in every room of the house. Did they make her feel threatened? Jealous?

"Detective?"

She turned. One of the officers assigned to search Lundgren's truck stood in the doorway. "Find anything?" she asked.

"It was clean. You want me to have it impounded?"

"Do it." Although they weren't looking for biological evidence from the Copycat murders, Buddy Brown had been killed then transported to Anna Paige Park. "Detective White's with Lundgren's lawyer?"

"Yes. In the basement."

The lawyer had followed them around while another uniform had kept a confused yet indignant Lundgren company just outside.

She turned back to the photos, frowning. Something about this didn't feel right. Was Joe Lundgren as good a suspect as she'd originally thought? It had made sense to her, the idea that Joe was punishing Kitt. She had painted him as angry and jealous.

Would a man with so much anger toward his ex-wife keep photographs of her displayed this way?

If he was smart, yes. If he was a cool customer, acting with his intellect instead of his emotion.

Which brought her right back to her problem. She didn't see him as that man. And it certainly didn't fit her theory.

Nor had they found the proverbial "smoking gun."

Her thoughts turned to her argument with Brian. Had Kitt overheard it? M.C. hoped not. Depending on what or how much she had heard, she could have a big-time wrong idea.

Now, unless she brought it up, she would never know. And Kitt could continue to have the wrong idea.

Should that bother her? Yes, she decided. For despite not fully trusting the woman or her methods, she had grown to admire her. And in a strange way, they didn't make too bad a team.

It was almost five-thirty by the time M.C. made it back to the bureau. Sal looked up from the report on his desk. "How'd it go?"

"It'll take a while to sift through the minutiae, but not great."

"What now?"

"Put Kitt back on."

He cocked an eyebrow. "You're certain that's wise?"

"Lundgren's not our man."

"That's a big reversal from earlier today, Detective."

"Yes, it is. But I'm standing by it."

He sat quietly a moment, then nodded. "Limited role until all the 'minutiae' is studied. I can't allow even a hint of impropriety here."

"You've got it. I'm going to break for dinner, then begin picking through it."

What M.C. hadn't told Sal was that she didn't plan on eating alone. Lance had been in her thoughts all day; she had decided seeing him was just what she needed.

She didn't call, simply stopped at Wok to Go, then headed to his place. "Hey," she said when he opened the door. She held up the take-out bag. "I brought Chinese."

"My angel of mercy."

She entered his apartment. The normally pin-neat living area looked as if a tornado had struck. She moved her gaze over the disaster. Books. Photos. Notebooks. Papers that had been crumpled and tossed. Empty coffee cups, soda cans, an extra-large pizza box and an overflowing ashtray.

She frowned. "You smoke?"

He grimaced. "A friend stopped by. He chain smokes." He crossed to the couch and cleared a space for her, then collected the pizza box and a half-dozen cans and cups.

"Sorry about the mess. I'm working on some new material. It's a painful process."

"Apparently. Looks like you hosted a World Wrestling Federation event in here."

"An apt analogy. Creation. Birth. Demon wrestling."

"You want to pass anything by—"

"No. Thanks."

Stung by his gruff reply, she didn't comment.

Moments later, they were eating in silence. After a while, he set down his chopsticks. "I'm sorry," he said.

"For what?"

"What I said…about my stuff. The process is so raw…I'm just not ready. Thanks, though, for offering to listen."

She smiled, touched by the apology. "It's okay."

"I don't think it is."

Something in his eyes and voice told her he was no longer talking about his apology. "What is it, Lance?"

"I'm falling in love with you."

Just like that, she thought. He laid the words between them. Gave form to whatever was growing between them.

What did she say to that? How did she feel? Elated. Terrified. Hopeful. Confident. Vulnerable.

"What are you thinking?"

"That you must be crazy."

"To be falling in love with you? Or just in general?"

She smiled. "To be falling in love with me."

"That makes *you* crazy."

Was she? She thought yes. Definitely.

She laughed. "I might be falling in love with you, too."

A smile pulled at his mouth. He stood, held out his hand. She took it and they went to the bedroom. And there they made love.

Afterward, they lay quietly, holding each other. M.C.'s thoughts whirled with the events of the day—Kitt's response to her bringing Joe in for questioning and her temporary removal from the case. The evidence awaiting her at the bureau. Her argument with Brian, his threat.

Remembering it, a knot formed in her stomach. He would do it, too. She didn't know why, after so long, he was behaving this way. It was as if Brian had become another person.

"What's wrong?" Lance rubbed her back. "You're tense."

"Remember that guy from the bar? The one you saved me from?"

"The pushy creep?"

"Yeah, that one. He's been following me."

Lance propped himself up on an elbow, expression concerned. "When did this start?"

"A couple days ago. Last week he showed up at my house, drunk. He came on to me again. When I turned him down, he started following me."

"What's this asshole's problem?"

"I don't know, it's weird. I cornered him today. Told him to back off."

"Or else?"

"Pretty much."

He searched her gaze. "And he didn't take that well?"

"No." She rolled onto her back and stared at the ceiling. "He threatened to start a rumor that I slept my way into the VCB."

"With him."

"Yes."

"So he can smear you and boast at the same time. What a jerk."

"He's a superior officer. Decorated. Well-thought-of. People will be more likely to believe him than me."

"Maybe I should have a man-to-man with him?"

She had a big picture of that. Lance would end up in jail—with an emergency room stop on the way. "Thanks, hero. But I think I've got it covered."

"I want to be your hero, Mary Catherine Riggio. Just say the word."

M.C. liked the sound of that and leaned across and kissed him, then drew regretfully away. "I can't stay," she murmured. "I wish I could."

"Duty calls?"

"Unfortunately."

"So, that's the way it is—eat and run."

He was teasing; she teased back. "More than just eating, or have you already forgotten?"

"Never. Just an insatiable appetite, that's all."

She smiled and kissed him again. "I've got to go."

As she climbed out of the bed, he caught her hand. "When will I see you again? Tonight?"

"I don't know how late I'll be. Call me?"

"You call me. I'll be here."

M.C. agreed she would try, then she hurried to dress.

51

Monday, March 20, 2006
6:30 p.m.

The RPD evidence room was located in the building's basement. Kitt had spent the day there, sifting through the items collected from the storage unit Peanut had directed them to.

His comment, "You have to have faith," suggested she had given up on it too quickly. Of course, it could be his way of sending her on another wild-goose chase.

She sat back, frowning. She had hardly made a dent in the locker's contents, yet a theme had already begun to emerge. The items were decidedly feminine in character—they had either belonged to a woman or a woman had selected them to create this tableau.

Interesting. All along, they had assumed the SAK to be a man.

Most serial killers were men, true. But women who killed typically chose "softer" means of death, like poison or suffocation. They eschewed guns, knives, clubs and anything else that caused a mess.

The Sleeping Angel deaths were nothing if not "clean." In fact, the SAK took great pains to "prettify" his victims.

Or was that *her* victims?

Kitt rubbed her forehead. Big problem: The three bludgeoning deaths Peanut had claimed responsibility for.

The SAK wasn't a woman.

The Copycat was.

The truth hit her like a ton of bricks. She stood up quickly. Was this the clue? What Peanut had meant for her to find? He expected good detective work out of her. He refused to make it easy.

This made sense. Didn't it?

She retrieved her bottle of water and sat on a carton filled with books. She took a swallow of the water, mind racing.

A man had rented the storage locker. An assumed man, she corrected. With a stolen ID. A man they didn't have a photo of; just the vague recollection of the storage-facility salesperson.

Could she be right? Was the Copycat a woman?

"I heard you were down here, Lundgren. Working hard, I see."

She turned and smiled at Scott Snowe, choosing to ignore his sarcasm. "Detective Snowe? What brings you out of the ID cave?"

He sauntered in, grinning. "I have a present for you. Analysis of fibers retrieved from the Entzel and Vest scenes."

He held out the report, looking very pleased with himself. She took it.

"Tyvek," he said. "Consistent with a Hazmat suit."

Kitt scanned the analysis. Crime-scene techs wore "clean" suits mostly for protection. The Tyvek was disposable, durable and fluid repellant. Some techs and law-enforcement professionals wore them to protect the scene from contamination, as well. Most were coverall style, some with booties and hood. In addition to the hood, a mask with a breathing apparatus was also worn anytime the threat of airborne contaminants existed.

"Gray," Kitt said. "Not as common as the white. Which will help to narrow down the source."

The RPD used white, the standard. She had seen the gray, however. One of the city's emergency management teams used them.

"True, though I've seen white with gray booties."

She nodded, then murmured, "It makes sense. He wears the clean suit. It reduces the possibility of his leaving trace behind."

"Exactly. Thought you'd want to know, ASAP."

"Thanks." She looked back up at him. "Has M.C. seen this?"

"Not yet. You want to do the honors?"

"Maybe not." She held the report out. "I'm off the case."

"I heard. And in my not-so-humble opinion, it's all bullshit." He slid his hands into his pockets. "You do it."

She hesitated, then nodded. "You done for the day?"

"Oh, yeah. It's Miller time."

As he turned to leave, she called after him. "Thanks, Scott. I appreciate this."

He waved off her thanks and disappeared through the evidence room door. For long moments she gazed at the now-empty doorway, thoughts on the evidence report. Tyvek. An unexpected turn. And one that certainly lent credence to her "SAK as cop" theory.

This was one smart SOB.

She let out a weary breath, the elation she had felt before Snowe's visit gone. She was tired, hungry and intellectually spent. She flat didn't have the energy for the puzzle right now.

She thought of Snowe, leaving for the night. Meeting his buddies for a drink. Didn't a beer sound like heaven about now? Along with a big, greasy burger. Or even a couple of slices of an artery-clogging, all-meat pizza.

The closest she was going to get was a bag of snack crackers and a Diet Coke.

Kitt unclipped her cell phone from her belt. She saw she had a message waiting and frowned. She hadn't heard it ring. She flipped the device open and saw why—no signal.

She stood and exited the evidence room. Once again she had a signal and she dialed M.C.'s cell, making a mental note to check her messages later. The other woman picked up almost immediately.

Kitt hadn't spoken to M.C. since that morning, and at the sound of her voice, she recalled the things Brian had said.

"She told me about Joe. She was almost gloating."

"She's ambitious…and she'll do anything, to anyone, to get what she wants."

Like go behind a partner's back. Get them removed from a case. "M.C.," she said stiffly. "It's Kitt. How's it going?"

"As well as can be expected," M.C. responded, tone guarded. "Sifting through some pretty boring stuff."

Joe's stuff. "White abandoned you?"

"Sent him home. His wife called, he heard the baby crying and the other two kids fighting in the background. She sounded three-quarters of the way toward a breakdown."

Kitt couldn't help wondering if she had sent him home because she was all heart, or because she wanted all the glory?

She hated thinking that way. She wanted to trust M.C. Until this morning, she had begun to—and begun to think that growing trust had been a two-way street.

"You in the building?" she asked.

"On two. You?"

"I'm in the basement. I'm coming up. I've got some interesting information to share."

When she made the VCB, she discovered that M.C. had ordered a pizza. Extra-large. Extra-cheese. Extra-everything. Seeing it was after hours, she had also scored a six-pack of beer.

"That's a mighty big pizza, Detective. PMS week?"

A smile touched her mouth. "My brothers' idea of a joke. I order a small, they deliver this. Join me?"

"And here I was prepared to beg."

Kitt dragged a chair to the other woman's desk. "You've been here all evening?"

"Almost. Had an errand to run earlier."

Kitt simultaneously handed the fiber analysis report to M.C. and reached for a slice of the pie. "I must be psychic, I was just thinking about pizza."

"Great minds and all that. What is this?"

"Fiber analysis from the Entzel and Vest scenes." She popped the tab on the Diet Coke she had brought up with her. "Take a look."

She did and a moment later, straightened. "Tyvek? Holy crap."

Kitt cocked an eyebrow at the saying. "Not quite my sentiment, but close."

After a moment, M.C. laid the report aside. "Interesting. Do you think he wears the coverall to the scene or puts it on there? Let's say, outside the girl's bedroom window?"

"My guess, wears it there. Puts the hood up outside her window."

"Then, afterward, he destroys the garment. And any evidence on it that might link him to the crime."

"Him," Kitt agreed. "Or her."

M.C. straightened. "Excuse me?"

"I believe there's a strong chance the Copycat is female." Kitt shared her theory with the other woman, starting with her observations of the locker's contents and finishing by recalling the traditional profile of a female serial killer.

M.C. sat back in her chair, bringing her beer with her. She took a long swallow, then rolled the can between her palms. "The Copycat a woman? Interesting."

Kitt leaned forward. "I want to run one additional thought by you. Could the original SAK have been a cop?"

"You're joking, right?"

"I wish I was. I reviewed the transcript of my recorded conversations with Peanut. He knew about Todd. How? Who else knew he was a suspect?"

"Outside the department, damn few. ZZ. Sydney Dale. ZZ's wife."

"Exactly. Of course, since I'm not officially on the case, take it for what you think it's worth."

"You're back on."

"First I've heard of it."

"Limited involvement until I've finished going through all this." She motioned with her hand to her desktop and computer. "I'm doing my best to plow through it tonight."

Kitt cocked an eyebrow. "That come from Sal?"

"My recommendation to Sal was for full reinstatement. He added the caveat."

"You want me to thank you?"

The edgy question landed between them. M.C. leaned forward, expression earnest. "I screwed up, Kitt. I'm sorry."

"Because the search of Joe's turned up nothing?"

"No, because we're partners. It wouldn't matter if we had found a journal detailing the crimes, I would still be apologizing. This isn't about Joe. Or the case. It's about how you deserved to be treated."

"And the search?"

"Let's just say, I don't believe Joe's as strong a suspect as I did."

Kitt nodded, slightly mollified but unconvinced. She couldn't dismiss the things Brian had said about M.C. They had been friends a long time; he had earned her trust. Why would he lie to her?

"So, what do you think, Kitt? Can you work with me?"

She avoided the question with one of her own. "A better question might be, can you trust me?"

"I'll do my damnedest. How's that for honesty?"

"Not bad. Now it's my turn. I overheard your argument with Brian."

M.C. stiffened. "I was afraid of that."

Which would explain the sudden magnanimity.

Kitt recalled the last thing Brian had said, *"Are you threatening me, Detective?"*

Her expression must have given her away because M.C. swore and stood. "I was afraid because I knew you'd get the wrong idea."

"From what I heard, I'm not certain there could be a 'right' idea. You had an affair with Brian?"

"Yes. Had. Years ago. I was a rookie and he was a detective in the VCB. He was separated from his wife.

"It was stupid," M.C. continued. "I was young. Naive. I looked up to him…he was like a god. The hotshot, macho detective. He knew everything, had seen everything."

Kitt remembered the younger Brian. Big and good-looking with the kind of swagger that screamed "I'm all that." Female catnip.

"So, what happened?"

"I realized sleeping with a colleague was a mistake. He went back to his wife. No harm, no foul."

"Until now?"

M.C. frowned. "Yeah. And I don't get it. Years go by, we have a fine working relationship. Suddenly, he's all over me. Hitting on me. Following me. It's weird."

It *was* weird, Kitt thought. That behavior certainly wasn't typical of the Brian she had known for years. He had always been a womanizer. A love 'em and leave 'em kind of Romeo. More faithful to his wife at some times than others.

But none of his affairs, that she knew of, had ever been serious. Certainly none had ever crossed this kind of line.

What was going on with Brian? Middle age and a crumbling marriage? Something more?

Or was M.C. lying?

"A word of advice, Kitt. Watch your back with that one."

"What are you thinking?" M.C. asked.

"That it's time to go." Kitt finished her slice of pizza and wiped her mouth with a napkin. "My tail's dragging."

"That's it? You're not going to say anything else?"

Kitt met her gaze evenly. "I'm not certain what to say. Brian's my friend. My good friend."

"Well," she said, tone bitter, "you said you'd be honest."

"I'm trying to be fair, too. I'm sorry."

"Don't be." M.C. crossed to the pizza box and closed the lid. "That's life."

"M.C.? I—" Kitt bit back the conciliatory words she had been about to say. "I'll see you in the morning."

"Sure. See you then."

Kitt exited the bureau, feeling as if she should say something more, but not knowing what. She knew M.C. felt she was taking Brian's side, but that wasn't the case. She simply wasn't siding with M.C., either. Weirdly, she didn't fully trust either of them right now.

She made her way to the elevator, which took her to the parking garage. As she crossed to her vehicle, she remembered her waiting message. She checked it. It was from Brian.

"Kitt. It's me. I did a little nosing around. You're not going to believe what I found. Call me on my cell."

52

Excited, Kitt jumped into her vehicle. The message could mean only one thing—Brian had found something that might implicate a cop in the SAK and Copycat cases. After buckling up and starting the engine, she dialed him back. The device went automatically to his voice mail.

"Dammit, Brian, don't leave me that kind of voice mail, then go into hiding. Call me back."

Thirty minutes later, home and changed into her comfortable jeans, he still hadn't called. She tried his cell again with the same results. Frustrated, she decided to try Ivy. Maybe he was with his kids. Or reconciling with his wife.

If she struck out there, she would begin trying his hangouts. No doubt he was at one of them.

She dialed the man's home number. His wife answered. "Hi, Ivy. It's Kitt Lundgren."

"Hello, Kitt. Brian's not here."

"He told me you guys were separated. How're you doing?"

"Great." A bitter note crept into her tone. "For a fortysomething, soon-to-be-divorced woman."

"I'm really sorry."

"Me, too. I just wish I'd divorced him years ago."

"Maybe he'll change? Once he realizes you mean it."

"He won't change, Kitt. Old dog. Hound dog."

For a moment, Kitt was silent. It was true. She wished she could console the woman, but Brian had been a womanizer as long as she had known him. "He does love you, Ivy."

"He has a unique way of showing it, doesn't he?"

Kitt felt bad for the other woman. She wanted to remind her that at least she had her children, but knew the comment wouldn't be appreciated. "Do you know how I can reach him?"

"He's got his cell phone."

"He didn't answer. Any idea where he's staying?"

"Same crappy dump where he used to rendezvous with his girl-friends, the jerk. The Starlight, on Sixth Street."

She knew the place. It *was* a crappy dump. The kind of place that could be rented out by the hour.

"Thanks, Ivy. If you hear from him, let him know I called."

The woman didn't respond, just hung up.

Things were bad between them.

Kitt called the Starlight's front desk. She learned Brian was, in-deed, registered there. She asked the man to ring his room.

He did. And after fifteen rings without an answer, she hung up and called the deskman back. "He didn't answer. Have you seen him this evening?"

"I haven't looked, lady."

"Is his car in the lot?"

For a long moment, the man said nothing. Then he let out a patient-sounding sigh. "I don't spy on the guests. If you've got worries about your old man, get your sagging ass down here yourself." With that, he hung up.

What, did her voice sound like it was attached to a sagging derriere?

She redialed. He answered on the second ring, voice wary.

"This is Detective Kitt Lundgren with the Rockford Police Department," she said. "I'm trying to reach one of your guests. *Lieutenant* Brian Spillare. Since he's not answering his phone, I need you to check the parking lot for his vehicle. This is not a negotiable request. Is that clear?"

The man's voice took on a whiny edge. "How would I know which car is his? We got lots of—"

"It's a blue Pontiac Grand Am. You took his plate number when he checked in. Look for it. Now."

For a moment, she thought he was going to argue. He didn't. "Hang on," he said, then put her on hold.

A couple of minutes later, he returned. "It's here. You need anything else before I go back to my job?"

She ignored the sarcasm, already on her way to her vehicle. "What room's the lieutenant in?"

"Two-ten."

She ended the call and slid into her Taurus, thoughts racing.

Brian's car in the lot. No answer on his cell or the room phone.

"I did a little nosing around. We need to talk."

She didn't like the feeling that settled in the pit of her gut. A vague uneasiness. A feeling that something wasn't right.

As she sped toward Sixth Street, Kitt tried to reason it away. He could be currently involved in one of those "rendezvous" Ivy had mentioned. Or out with one of his RPD drinking buddies, who had driven.

But a detective answered his cell, radio or beeper. Always, no matter what he was in the middle of. It was a cardinal rule of police work. She'd been called out of church, movies, dinners out. While making love with her husband.

Brian was in trouble.

She made it to the Starlight in good time. She leaped out of her car and ran up the stairwell to the second floor. She reached 210 and tapped on the door. From inside came the sound of the TV. "Brian! It's Kitt."

He didn't answer and she knocked again, harder. When he still didn't reply, she tried the knob. And found the door unlocked.

Her unease growing, taking on a horrible form, Kitt drew her weapon. With her free hand, she eased the door open.

A cry slipped past her lips. Brian lay on his back in the doorway, eyes open, vacant. He was shirtless; he'd been shot twice in the chest. A pool of blood ringed his body.

She crossed to him. With shaking hands, she checked his pulse. She found none and stepped away, a hand to her mouth.

Her mind raced. A knot of tears choked her. Kitt turned her back toward her friend, unclipped her cell phone and dialed the CRU. It took three tries before she could say the words clearly enough for the woman to understand.

"Officer fatality. Starlight Motel, Sixth Street and Eighteenth Avenue."

53

Monday, March 20, 2006
10:20 p.m.

M.C. roared into the motel parking lot. She was not the first to arrive; parking spots were scarce already. Patrol cars. The coroner's Suburban. Vehicles she recognized as unmarked police cars. News of a fatality involving a police officer spread fast. No doubt Sal and Sergeant Haas were on the scene already; the chief of police himself would make an appearance.

An officer was down. A lieutenant.

M.C. simply stopped her SUV and climbed out. Heart thundering, she slammed the door and hurried toward the stairs, pausing only long enough to sign in.

Kitt had called her, told her what happened. Bluntly, without emotion.

M.C. hadn't been fooled. Kitt and Brian had been partners. Good friends. She was taking this hard.

M.C. reached the second floor. A number of officers milled about on the covered walkway, anxious, awaiting word—of what had happened, how they could help. Nobody spoke. The silence was grim.

M.C. crossed to the officer manning the door. She showed him her ID and he waved her in. Her first look at Brian knocked the wind out of her. She stopped cold, fighting to regain her equilibrium.

She had seen him just that morning. Very much alive. Bigger than life.

She had been angry. Furious.

"Try it and you'll regret it, I promise you that."

"Are you threatening me, Detective?"

"Whatever you want to call it."

Mouth dry at the memory, she lifted her gaze. Kitt stood to the right of Brian, silently watching as the forensic pathologist examined him. She looked up. M.C. lifted a hand in greeting and made her way toward her.

"How are you?" she asked when she reached her.

"Not great."

"I'm sorry."

She nodded, glanced away, then back. "This afternoon I asked Brian to look into any police officer who might have had a grudge against the department. This evening, he left me a message saying he'd found something. That's how I ended up here."

"My God—" M.C. lowered her voice "—you believe this somehow relates to the SAK or Copycat?"

"Yes. I'm thinking Brian might've questioned the wrong person about it."

M.C. digested that. "His death coming on the heels of your conversation and his message could be a co..."

She let the word—*coincidence*—trail off. It was almost too preposterous to utter.

They fell silent. M.C. moved her gaze over the room. The TV was on. ESPN, she saw. His shoulder holster, with holstered weapon, hung on the back of the desk chair. The shooter had caught him mid–Big Mac. The bag and food sat on the bed by the remote. Two Miller longnecks, one empty, the other half-drunk, sat on the nightstand by the bed.

His cell phone was attached to his hip.

The sound of the teams climbing the stairs filled the quiet. ID, M.C. thought. Sure enough, a moment later, ID Detective Sorenstein and Sergeant Campo entered the room.

Kitt glanced from them, to her. "Anybody besides me overhear your argument with Brian?" she asked quietly.

The elephant in the middle of the room. M.C. appreciated her bringing it up. "Not that I know of. But that doesn't mean no one did."

"May I make a suggestion?"

"You've never hesitated before."

"This could cause you problems. Head it off. Go to Sal. Tell him everything before he asks."

The thought of revealing her affair to the chief made M.C. squirm. It would go on her permanent record; a mistake that would shadow her for the rest of her career. "There's nothing to tell. I had nothing to do with this."

It was their last opportunity to speak privately. Sal and Sergeant Haas arrived. They caught sight of her and Kitt and started toward them. M.C. noticed how the chief kept his gaze fixed on them, never lighting on Brian's body.

"Detectives," he said by way of greeting, then turned fully to Kitt. "Brief me."

"Brian left me a message. I couldn't get him on his cell, so I tracked him down here."

"Here?"

"He and Ivy were separated. I called her, she told me where he was staying. I found him this way, checked his pulse and called in."

Sal nodded and turned to the pathologist. "Anything you can tell us, Frances?"

"Judging by the gunpowder tattooing around the bullet wound, the shooter was standing no more than eighteen inches away." He indicated the gunpowder particles imbedded in a circular pattern in the skin around the bullet hole. "I haven't a doubt that's what killed him. First bullet entered in the lung area, the second his heart. I'm guessing the order by the tattooing. First bullet hit and Lieutenant Spillare took a step backward. Changing the shot's distance changed the gunpowder pattern."

"How long ago?" Sal asked.

"Not long. A few hours. Temperature and stomach contents will help us pinpoint the time." Roselli stood and removed his gloves. "He gets priority, of course."

"He knew his killer," Sergeant Haas said.

"I agree." Sal turned to Kitt. "The scenario seems pretty clear. He opened the door and was shot."

Considering the scenario and the fact she was the one who had found Brian, she came under suspicion. Kitt unsheathed her weapon and held it, grip out, for the superior officers. "My weapon," she said.

Every time a gun was discharged, particles of primer and burned gunpowder deposited on the hands of the shooter, as well as the barrel of the gun. Sergeant Haas took the gun, examined it for such residue, then handed it back. "Keep it for now."

"Thank you, Sarge," she said, and reholstered it. "There's something else about tonight." Kitt glanced her way and for one horrifying moment M.C. thought she was going to tell them about her affair with Brian. "About the message he left me. Could we step outside?"

They agreed and headed out onto the walkway. As it was far from private, they took the stairs to the first floor, then crossed to stand beside Kitt's Taurus.

"This afternoon I approached Lieutenant Spillare with a theory. That the SAK was a cop."

Sal narrowed his eyes and Sergeant Haas drew a sharp breath. "And what led you to this theory?"

She repeated what she had told M.C. earlier that evening. "I reviewed the tapes of my calls from Peanut. He knew about Derrick Todd, that we were 'chasing our tails.' He understands the process. That's how he got away with his crimes. He takes great pride in that. As if he has something to prove to us. A chip on his shoulder."

"He could be a crime or police buff. Or have family in law enforcement."

"All true. But he could also be a cop, or former cop, with an ax to grind with the department, some sort of grudge."

She paused, as if to give them a moment to comment. When they didn't, she went on. "Brian offered to check employment records, see if any names popped up."

She drew a breath, moved her gaze between the two men. "In his message, Brian said he had 'nosed' around. That he needed to talk to me."

Her two superiors were silent a moment, as if digesting what she'd said. "You saved the message?"

"Absolutely."

Sal swore suddenly. "Trace Lieutenant Spillare's steps. I want to know who he talked to, every file he opened, every piece of paper he touched. If a cop's responsible for this, I'll tear him apart myself."

54

Monday, March 20, 2006
11:57 p.m.

It was nearly midnight when Kitt arrived home. She pulled into her driveway, shut off the engine and sat. The sky rumbled ominously. The weather forecast had called for thunderstorms tonight; they had been threatening for hours.

Brian was dead. Her friend and confidant. Her champion.

And she had gotten him killed.

Tears burned her eyes and she didn't fight them. They rolled down her cheeks. Slowly at first, building until the force of her sobs shook her.

He had made her laugh. Had reminded her daily of the good things about being a cop. He'd been like family.

Family. Three daughters, now fatherless.

Kitt pressed her lips together, thinking of Ivy. Sal had decided he should be the one to tell her. Sergeant Haas had offered to accompany him. More than likely, they were doing it now.

She brought the heels of her hands to her eyes. Why had she approached him with her "cop with a grudge" theory? Why hadn't she investigated it herself?

Maybe it would be her in the morgue now, two bullet holes in her chest.

Better her than Brian. She wouldn't have left anyone behind.

The minutes ticked past. As they did, her tears abated, her grief twisting into a kind of exhausted anger. The kind that brought thoughts of revenge, of finding the son of a bitch who pulled the trigger and making him pay.

She had used grief to fuel her anger many a time before. As a way to keep going, do her job, face a new day.

She climbed out of the car, made her way up the walk. A package waited for her on the front steps. A brown-paper grocery sack. As if some kindhearted neighbor had brought her a meal, and finding her not home, had left it for her. The way they had when Sadie died.

Kitt stared at the bag, anger building, tightening in her chest. A neighbor hadn't left this. Peanut had. She knew without looking.

The bastard wanted to gloat.

She turned and strode back to her car for her investigation kit. It contained latex gloves and evidence bags, among other things. She unlocked the car, retrieved a pair of gloves and a couple of bags from the kit, then the flashlight from her glove box. She stuffed the bags into her jacket pocket, then tucked the Maglite under her arm. As she walked back to the porch stairs, she fitted the gloves on.

"Okay, you bastard," she muttered. "Let's go."

She carefully opened the bag, then aimed the flashlight's beam inside. A cell phone, she saw. She also saw by its blinking green light that it was on. And she had a message waiting.

She drew the device out of the bag. Her fingers brushed against something attached to its back.

She turned it over. A lock of blond hair, she saw. Tied with a slim pink ribbon.

A little girl's pretty blond hair. The hair of an angel.

Her heartbeat quickened. Her breath with it. She worked to control both. What was she looking at? A lock of hair from one of the Sleeping Angel victims? Or from a future victim?

Or was this simply another of Peanut's head games?

Kitt carefully loosened the tape, then removed the hair. After sealing it in an evidence bag, she flipped open the phone. It was a Verizon phone, same service she used. She accessed the message service, and a prerecorded voice asked for a password. Possibilities ran through her head: Peanut, Kitten, Sadie. He wanted her to be able to retrieve the message, so it would be something easy.

Angels.

Of course.

She punched in the password, exchanging letters for numbers— 2-6-4-3-5-7.

The password accepted, the message began to play.

"You were wrong," he said. "I did take trophies. I'm sharing one with you."

Kitt began to shake. Revulsion rose up in her. As she held the phone to her ear, it rang.

"Hello, you son of a bitch," she said.

"Kitten," he admonished, "name calling? I thought we were friends."

"Yeah," she said, scanning the street, the dark cars and windows, the pools of shadows. *He was here, somewhere. Watching her. Amused.* "We are friends. Come on out and play."

He laughed. "I've been waiting for you. Where've you been all night?"

"Cut the crap. Did you call to gloat about Brian? About killing him?"

"I don't know what or who you're talking about."

"Lieutenant Brian Spillare." To her horror, her throat closed over his name. "My friend. My former partner."

For long moments he said nothing. "I'm sorry for your loss."

"I should believe you, right? A liar and a murderer? Are you a cop, too? Are you, Peanut?"

He sucked in a sharp breath. She pressed on. "Did he get too close? Ask the wrong question? So you killed him."

"Not mine, Kitten. You'll have to look elsewhere this time."

He attempted to be flip, but Kitt detected the slightest tremor in his voice. She had shaken him. Why? If he was being honest and hadn't killed Brian, why care?

Because she'd asked if he was a cop?

"A child killer and a cop killer." She paused. "But I forgot the little old ladies. We could rename you the Granny Basher."

"The cop's not mine," he said again. His voice rose. "That's not why I called."

"Why did you call, *Peanut?* Not to gloat? Then why? Why bother me?"

"To talk." His voice shook. "To make you understand. Without others listening."

She laughed at him, at the tremor and the notion that she should listen to him. "Understand what? That you're a yellow son of a bitch. A chicken-shit who murders children and grandmothers?"

"Careful—"

"Why should I be? No one's listening, remember?" She spun around, facing the dark street. She held out her free arm. "Come get me, asshole! Here I am!"

"You're hysterical. Calm down."

"And you're a monster. Go to hell."

"I'm not a monster!" He fell silent; she heard the crackle and hiss of flame touching tobacco. His deep inhalation. "I'm not one of those animals who kills for pleasure. I get no thrill from taking a life."

"Then why?" she asked.

"It's an intellectual pursuit. Like chess. Crime and investigation. Criminal and cop. Don't you see?"

"Nobody dies in chess."

"Higher stakes, that's all."

Kitt thought of the dead children, their families. She thought of the three old ladies he claimed were his victims, that they'd been someone's mother, sister, grandmother. She made a sound of disgust. "Those girls were playing a game with you? Give me a break."

"No, Kitten." She heard the admonishment in his voice, the disappointment. "You and I are playing. Now. And five years ago."

"I'm not playing with you now. I wasn't then."

"You are. You were. Five years ago, I won."

"Winning is getting away with the crime?"

"Yes. Outsmarting and outmaneuvering you. The police."

"And if I win, I catch you."

"Yes," he agreed. "We both want to win. I have the edge, of course."

"Why's that?"

"I'm not emotionally involved. You are."

He wasn't, she realized. Which made him a true psychopath. No remorse. No empathy. No moral sense of right and wrong.

It also made him that much more difficult to catch.

"Taking a life is not a game move."

"To you," he said softly. "Exactly why I have the advantage."

"Are you the Copycat?"

He paused. "No. I'm not."

No innuendo this time, no infuriating maybe. She sat down hard on the front steps as the realization hit her: Two killers. Six dead children. A span of five years. And she was no closer to an answer.

She couldn't do this.

She didn't have a choice.

"Giving up, Kitten?"

He knew her so well. Did he read her mind? Or the tone of her voice? Or was he a distorted version of herself, a cop obsessed with committing crime instead of stopping it.

"Never. I'll never give up or stop searching for you."

"I'm sorry." The regret in his voice sounded genuine. "It's hard for you to lose, isn't it?"

"I've already lost everything. This is nothing."

"Not your life. Surely, you fear death?"

She pictured Sadie and smiled. "No. Death isn't an ending, but a beginning."

"Then why fight so hard to hold on to life?" His voice deepened, took on the quality of a caress. "Why the outrage when it's taken?"

"Because life has value. It's a gift, a blessing from God. And it's not yours, or anyone else's, to take."

"My Kitten has a spiritual side."

"Whose hair is this?"

"That's what DNA testing is for."

"Is it one of the original Angels'?"

"Yes."

"Do you know who the Copycat killer is?"

"Yes."

In the past he had been coy with her. Tonight he seemed bent on taking their "game" to a new level. Or was it their relationship he wanted to take to the next level? she wondered. A step past teasing, toward the intimacy of real sharing.

He thought of this as a relationship, she realized.

She worked to keep her excitement at bay. "Give me a name. I'll get him—or her—out of the picture. Then it'll be just you and me."

"Her?" He sounded pleased.

"Is that what you planted for me to find in the storage locker?"

"No. But you've surprised me. Until now I've been…less than impressed with your deductive skills."

There was something else there.

She tucked that away for later. "A name. Then it'll be just you and me. I'd like that. Wouldn't you?"

"Things like that aren't free."

"What do you want in return?"

"You, Kitt." She could almost hear his smile. "I want to know you better."

"I invited you to come out of the shadows. There's no one here but me."

"We do not have to see each other for me to know you. I want inside your head. I want to know how you think, what you feel. Your dreams. And your fears."

"But you already know," she said softly. "Don't you?"

"Not enough," he said simply. "I want more. Tell me about your marriage."

"My marriage?" she repeated, off balance.

"About Joe. Your love affair."

She hadn't expect this. He seemed determined to peel back her self-protective layers and peer beneath. What did he intend to do with her once he had examined each and exposed her soft, inner core?

He meant to kill her.

No, he meant to destroy her.

As if once again reading her thoughts, he laughed. "A name, Kitt. Do it for the children."

The children. The angels. That he used them as a bargaining chip infuriated her. "Bastard. Ask me a question."

"How did you meet?"

"We were high school sweethearts," she said grudgingly. "We met when I was a freshman and he was a sophomore."

"How?"

His questions, coming so close on the heels of Joe being interrogated, were weird.

"It's a cliché. He bumped into me, I dropped my books. He

helped me pick them up." She drew a deep breath, realizing that she was trembling. "He had the bluest eyes I'd ever seen."

"And you fell in love with him, just like that?"

"Yes. Just like that."

"Love at first sight, how sweet."

She could tell he was laughing at her. That *sweet* was synonymous with *naive* and *ridiculous*. "I didn't know that's what it was. Only now, in retrospect."

"Why him? The blue eyes?"

"Joe's kind. The kindest, most gentle man I've ever known." She smiled to herself, recalling. "Not just to me. He loves others. Appreciates people. Their differences. Even their flaws."

"He's a fucking saint, isn't he? Saint Joe."

"We had the same dreams," she went on, his ugliness rolling off her. This wasn't about him, she realized. The SAK or Copycat; it wasn't about the investigation.

It was about her.

And it was healing.

"We had the same beliefs. About life, its beauty and sanctity, about the afterlife. About the things that truly mattered. Love. Family. Faith."

As she spoke, memories came flooding back. Good ones. Of times she hadn't thought about in years.

Of laughter. Making love. Sharing their successes. And fears. Celebrating the birth of their daughter. Of Joe's hand curled around hers as the doctor informed them Sadie had leukemia.

Memories she had locked away, in a strongbox deep inside her. Why was that? How had she allowed the pain to swallow the joy? Bad memories to overshadow good?

Thunder rumbled again, sounding closer this time. The leaves began to rustle. She shivered.

"So what happened?" he asked. "When did your dreams change?"

"What?" she asked, surprised.

"You had the same dreams and beliefs. And you loved him. Why did it all change?"

She'd changed, she realized. Her dreams, her beliefs.

"Because Sadie died," she said softly. "I lost faith. The ability to dream. To love."

"Yes," he said. "Life is cruel. It preys on the weak. The idealistic. Those who love deeply. Better to crush than be crushed."

"No," she said, "you're wrong."

"Am I, Kitten?"

"And I was wrong. To give up. To turn away from love."

"I think I'm going to puke."

Tears filled her eyes. Ones of joy. She had loved Joe from the first. *She loved him still.*

She told him so.

He laughed. "You're a fool. He's engaged to another woman. He doesn't love you."

"Only a fool doesn't love." The rain started then, a drop, then sprinkle. *The heavens preparing to open up.*

"The name," she said. "I gave you what you wanted. It's your turn. Who's the Copycat?"

"Look at the victims again. The victims are talking to you."

"No! That's not—"

He hung up. A crack of thunder shook her. She jumped to her feet, grabbed the bag and darted onto her porch just as the sky unleashed a flood.

Shivering, she watched the rain. He'd played her for a fool again. Tricked her into doing what he wanted, giving her what he wanted.

Kitt unlocked her door, stepped into the dark house. She still had the latex gloves on, she realized. She set the paper bag containing the bagged lock of hair and the phone on the top of her console, then removed the gloves.

She curled her fingers around the empty gloves, a laugh bubbling to her lips. He had tricked her, but she had won.

He'd given her something she had been unable to give herself. Forgiveness. Healing.

Love.

Her thoughts filled with Joe. Her heart filled. She looked at the phone, started toward it. No. She had to apologize. For today. Yesterday. Everything.

She had to beg his forgiveness.

Snatching up her keys, she ran out into the storm.

Tuesday, March 21, 2006
1:30 a.m.

The rain came down in blinding sheets. Kitt pulled into Joe's driveway, threw open the car door and darted for the house. Already wet, she was drenched by the time she reached his door.

With the storm, the temperature had dropped. Her teeth chattered. Her hands and feet were numb.

She didn't care about the rain. Or the cold. Only Joe. Sharing what she had learned tonight. Begging his forgiveness. Even if it was too late for them to make another start, he deserved her apology.

She had been so wrong. About everything.

She rang the bell, then pounded on his door. "Joe!" she shouted. "It's me! Kitt!"

The house remained dark. She rang the bell again. And again. "Joe! Open up!"

A light snapped on inside. Then above her head. He peered out the sidelight. She nearly cried out in relief when she saw his face.

"Let me in! I have to talk to you!"

He opened the door and she stumbled inside. "I had to tell you," she cried. "Now. Tonight."

He recoiled slightly. She supposed she would, too, if a crazy person was pounding on her door in the middle of the night, soaking wet and wild-eyed.

"About the case?" he asked.

The case? She blinked, confused, then realized that of course he thought that. He had spent most of his day either being interrogated or watching his home and business be searched.

"No." She shook her head. "This is about me. And you." She clasped her hands together. "I'm sorry. For pushing you away. For shutting down after Sadie died. You needed me and instead I—"

She broke down and sobbed. In the way she hadn't allowed herself to before now. After several moments, he drew her stiffly into his arms.

She clung to him until her tears stopped. "I'm sorry," she said, taking a step back.

"Don't worry about it."

She swiped at tears with the back of her hands. "I didn't cry after Sadie. Instead I drowned myself in the Sleeping Angel investigation. When I didn't have that anymore, I turned to the bottle."

She drew a tear-choked breath. "If I didn't grieve, I didn't have to let go."

"Why are you telling me this?"

"I could have turned to you. I should have. I see that now."

"Water under the bridge."

"No, Joe, it's not. I still love you. I'm still *in* love with you."

For long moments, he simply gazed at her. What was he feeling? she wondered, unable to read his expression. Was he angry? Happy? Relieved? Annoyed?

Or after all this time, did he feel nothing at all?

Tears welled in her eyes and trickled down her cheeks. He caught one with his index finger. "It's going to be okay, Kitt. I love you, too."

It took a full ten seconds for his words to sink in. When they did, a cry rushed to her throat. She threw herself into his arms, cheek pressed to his chest.

His arms went around her. "You're trembling. And so cold." He rubbed her back, then eased her out of his arms.

She saw that his T-shirt was wet and made a sound of distress. "I'm sorry, I—"

"Come." He led her into the house, to the master bathroom. He gave her a fluffy bath towel and his white terry-cloth robe. "Take a shower, if you like. I'll be in the other room."

She couldn't find her voice and nodded. The intimate surroundings felt both odd and invigorating. When he had exited the bathroom, she started the shower. She removed her clothes, laid them over the side of the tub, then stepped into the shower.

Within moments under the hot spray, she was warm. She quickly washed; the shower filled with the scent of Joe's shampoo and soap. After drying and slipping into the big, soft robe, she padded out to the bedroom.

And found Joe sitting on the edge of the bed, head in his hands.

A lump in her throat, she crossed to him. Kneeling in front of him, she gathered his hands in hers. He met her eyes.

He had been crying.

She wanted to ask him whether they were tears of joy or despair, ones for the past or the future.

Instead, she cupped his face in her palms and kissed him. Softly at first, then deeply, with growing passion. That passion drove them to want more, to take more.

To make love.

Afterward, they lay in each other's arms. Kitt felt at peace for the first time since Sadie died. She pressed her face to Joe's chest, breathed in his familiar spicy scent.

He stroked her hair. "Not that I care, but what brought all this on?"

Brian. Her psychotic caller. The investigation. "I don't think I should tell you. Not now, anyway."

He tipped his face down to hers and frowned. "Why?"

"Because it'll ruin this." Her throat closed and she cleared it. "And I want to hang on to now, this moment, as long as I can."

Even as she said the words, the ugliness seeped in, licking at the edges of her happiness.

She wondered if she would ever get it back again.

56

The next morning, Kitt awakened to the smell of bacon. Eyes closed, she breathed deeply. Joe's famous bacon-and-egg breakfasts. Another thing she had missed about the man.

She cracked open her eyes. Sun trickled in around the blinds. To stay in bed, she thought. The way they used to when they were first married. Be lazy, make love—sometimes they hadn't gotten out of bed until one or two in the afternoon.

She smiled at the memory, sat up and stretched, then climbed out of bed. She snatched up her panties, stepped into them and crossed to the bureau. Joe had always stored his T-shirts in the second drawer down.

He still did, she saw when she opened the drawer. She drew one out and brought it to her face. It smelled liked him and was soft from wear and washings.

Kitt slipped it on, then padded out to the kitchen.

Joe stood with his back to her as he scrambled the eggs. The kitchen looked as if a small hurricane had hit: he had always been a horrendously messy cook.

"Good morning," she said.

He looked over his shoulder at her and smiled. "You're up."

"I should have been up a while ago." She dragged a hand through her hair. "I'm going to be really late."

He poured her a mug of coffee and held it out. "You were so soundly asleep. I couldn't bring myself to wake you."

A deep, dreamless sleep, she thought. Real rest. For body and soul.

She crossed to him and took the coffee. "Still buying into the 'breakfast is the most important meal of the day' theory, I see."

"Absolutely."

She sipped her coffee and watched as he took two plates from a cabinet, utensils from a drawer, and plucked napkins out of the holder near the stove.

It felt odd to be doing nothing. Joe had always been the breakfast chef, but in the old days she and Sadie would have been setting the table. Cleaning up after him as he went.

It was a strange sensation, being in the home that had been hers but wasn't anymore. Seeing that he had left some things organized the same way she had, but that others had been moved.

She wondered if her lame hovering felt odd to him, as well?

Kitt shifted her gaze. It landed on the plates. She and Sadie had picked out the stoneware pattern. White with a sunny-yellow-and-black geometric pattern on the edge.

Like bumble bees! Sadie had exclaimed.

When they divorced, Kitt had given him everything. She hadn't wanted the reminders of their life. Their family.

A lump in her throat, she ran her fingers along the plate's patterned edge. Now she found herself hungry for those reminders. For the memories.

She found Joe watching her. "Sadie picked these."

"Yes."

"These, too." She picked up the Mickey Mouse and Pluto salt-and-pepper shakers. "From our trip to Disney World. Remember?"

"I remember everything, Kitt."

Something in his tone took her breath.

She couldn't bring herself to meet his eyes. She scolded herself for being a coward, a ninny. What was she afraid of?

The moment passed and he spooned scrambled eggs—he'd made them with mushrooms, onions and cheese—onto her plate. "Bacon?"

"Silly man. Of course, bacon."

He laid two strips on her plate and pointed her toward the already toasted and buttered English muffins.

While they ate, they talked about nothing of consequence. The weather. Food. News of mutual acquaintances and family members. When they'd finished, Joe said her name softly. She lifted her gaze to his.

"Are you ready to talk about what brought you here?"

It all came crashing back. *Brian. The call from Peanut. His questions.* She felt the euphoria of the last hours slipping away.

She fought to hold on to it, at least for a few more moments. "Besides the promise of great sex and a real breakfast?"

"Don't do that. Don't make it all a joke and shut me out. That's what you—"

He bit the words back and pushed away from the table. He carried his plate and utensils to the sink, then turned back to her. She saw that he shook. "You broke my heart, Kitt. We lost Sadie. Then I...lost you."

"I know. I'm sor—"

"No," he cut her off, "you don't. You can't imagine what it was like for me to watch helplessly as you self-destructed. You can't imagine how it hurt to have you close enough to touch, but a million miles away. I needed you so...much."

His words hurt. She pressed her lips together, wishing she could deny them. Defend herself.

But how did one defend herself against the truth?

"I grieved for a long time," he continued. "Then I became angry. So angry, I...I thought it would consume me."

He'd never revealed that anger to her. Not through words or actions. Or maybe she had been too absorbed in her own feelings to notice his.

Last night's pretty dream of a happily-ever-after with Joe seemed ridiculous now.

In the heat of self-realization—then passion—it had been easy. Simple. She loved him. He loved her. This morning, in the harsh light, she saw how difficult—and how complicated—that dream really was.

"You must hate me."

"I discovered," he said, "that the line between love and hate is thin, indeed."

Kitt held his gaze, though it hurt to look at him. She felt she owed him that. "I don't know what to say besides I'm sorry."

"I'm sorry, too."

Tears choked her. She fought her way past them. Even without a happy ending for them, she was so much better off than she had been twenty-four hours ago.

Now, at least, she recognized her feelings. Had the ability to love again.

"Brian's dead," she said quietly. "He was murdered last night."

"Brian? My God."

"I can't go into the reasons why, but I believe his murder is related to the Copycat killings."

Joe crossed back to the table and sat heavily. He looked dazed. She went on. "The one claiming to be the Sleeping Angel Killer called again last night. He asked me to tell him about you. About us. Our courtship and marriage.

"In return, he promised to give me the name of the Copycat killer."

"Did he?"

"No. He gave me another clue instead."

"And you ended up here?"

"In the process of telling him about us, I opened a door. And everything I'd locked away came spilling out."

This time it was she who needed to stand, to walk away. When she had organized her thoughts, she turned back to him. "I always knew I still loved you. But I didn't think I could let go of the pain enough to really love you. The way you deserve to be loved."

"And now?"

"Remember at the leukemia event, how you told me you wanted to live again. I want to live again. To let go of the pain and stop hurting."

He caught her hand, curled his fingers around hers. It reminded her of that day, so long ago, as they had faced Sadie's doctor. Bracing themselves for whatever came next.

Together. Always. Irrefutably.

"Things are more complicated than you and me," he said. "You know that, right?"

She knew that. *Valerie. Her child.*

Too much time had passed to catch their happily-ever-after.

She held his hand tightly. "Just tell me, can you forgive me, Joe?"

"I already have."

57

Tuesday, March 21, 2006
9:20 a.m.

*W*here was Kitt? M.C. checked her watch for what seemed like the dozenth time since she had considered Kitt undeniably late. She had expected her in first thing, considering the events of the night before.

A pall hung over the department. One of their own had been cut down.

M.C. hadn't slept much, for a complicated set of reasons. Every time she'd closed her eyes, she'd relived the murder scene. She recalled Brian in life, that he had a family. She worried about her argument with him and what she should do. Go to her superiors, come clean about her and Brian's history together and their argument, or hope they never became wise to it.

Brian's murder had her spooked. If he had been killed because he'd asked a fellow officer the wrong question, that left both her and Kitt vulnerable. Particularly Kitt.

She had called her home and cell phone. The woman had answered neither. Again, weird.

M.C. drummed her fingers on her desktop, considering other scenarios. She could have fallen off the wagon and be home, sleeping it off.

After all, just a week ago Kitt had lapsed, blaming the emotional trauma of discovering Joe was going to be a stepfather. Last night Kitt's good friend and former partner had been murdered. Kitt felt partly responsible. Enough emotional trauma to send even a teetotaler running for the bottle.

It beat the hell out of the first scenario—Kitt lying just inside her own doorway, shot twice in the chest.

Screw it, she decided, standing. She'd just take a little road trip over to Kitt's to check on her.

She got no further than the decision when her cell phone buzzed. She answered without looking at the display, certain Kitt was calling.

"Riggio here."

She learned immediately she was wrong. "I missed you last night," Lance said.

She smiled. "I missed you, too."

"I hoped you'd call. Waited until the wee hours."

"Things took a turn for the worse here. I couldn't get away."

"What about today?"

"I don't know, but it doesn't look good." Sergeant Haas appeared in the doorway. "I've got to go. I'll call you."

She hung up, then turned her attention to her superior. "What's up, Sarge?"

"Sal wants to see you in his office. Now."

M.C. didn't like his tone. Too official. "Kitt's not in yet."

"We don't need Kitt for this one."

When they reached the deputy chief's office, she saw why not. Sal wasn't alone. A detective she recognized from Internal Affairs was with him.

The question about whether she should come clean about her argument with Brian had become moot. They already knew.

Another realization followed on the heels of that one:

Kitt had told them about it.

That's why she was late this morning. Why she hadn't answered her cell phone. She hadn't wanted to face M.C. until after IA finished with her.

Bitterness mixed with betrayal. She supposed she deserved it, after the way she had gone behind Kitt's back about Joe. She had been naive to believe they had worked through that.

"Come in, Detective Riggio. This is Detective Peters, from Internal Affairs."

She nodded in greeting. "I recognize Detective Peters. We spoke during the Caldwell investigation."

"That's right," the man agreed, the barest smile shaping his mouth. "Have a seat."

She sat and folded her hands in her lap.

"Do you have any idea what this meeting might be about, Detective?"

Tell the truth and look paranoid or guilty? Or play it dumb and cool? Both came with advantages and risks.

She took the middle road. "One of the investigations I'm working on would be my best guess."

"And they are?"

"The Copycat killings and Lieutenant Spillare's murder."

"A rather small caseload."

"But intense."

"Indeed." The man steepled his fingers. "How would you categorize your relationship with Lieutenant Spillare?"

"Good. Until recently."

"Until recently," he repeated. "Could you tell us what happened to change your relationship?"

"The lieutenant began hitting on me. When I refused his advances, he began following me."

"That would be sexual harassment."

"I suppose it would."

"Why didn't you approach one of your superiors. Or us?"

"I thought I could handle it myself."

His gaze sharpened. "And did you?"

"If you're asking did I kill him, the answer is 'hell no.' We argued. Yesterday, in fact."

Sal spoke up. "Why didn't you come to me with this last night? You had to know how your argument would be overheard. And how it would look. It's just plain stupid, Riggio!"

No joke.

As had been trusting Kitt.

Peters stood and crossed to stand directly before her. "I think Detective Riggio had her reasons. Isn't that right, Detective?"

Rather than cock her head back to meet his eyes, she stood. They were nearly nose-to-nose. "That is right, Detective Peters. You're very astute."

If he noticed the edge in her voice, he didn't comment. She turned toward her superiors. "Brian and I had an affair, years ago. I was a rookie, he was a detective. It was a mistake and didn't last long. I really didn't want to share that. I'm not proud of it. That's why I didn't come forward."

For a moment the men were silent. Then Sal spoke. "You weren't the first rookie to fall under Brian's spell, nor were you the last."

She nodded. "With all due respect, knowing others were as stupid as me doesn't make me feel any better."

Peters cleared his throat and redirected them. "Is it true that you threatened Lieutenant Spillare?"

"Actually, he threatened me. When I told him if he didn't back off, I intended to report him, he said he would spread that I slept my way into the VCB."

"And how did you respond?"

"I told him he had better not."

"And that's it?"

"Yes."

"You didn't threaten to shoot him?"

"Absolutely not."

"We'll need your weapon for ballistics testing."

She slipped the Glock .45 from the holster and handed it over. She knew the drill. Upon firing, every gun created a sort of "fingerprinted" bullet, marks on the metal caused by tiny imperfections in the gun's barrel. And like human fingerprints, no two weapons left identical impressions on their bullets. Likewise, with cartridge casings.

To obtain the comparison casing or bullet, they would fire it into a box of thick gel, retrieve the bullet or casing, then compare it to any that had been recovered from the scene of Brian's murder.

Sal accepted her weapon. "You'll have it back this morning."

"Thank you." She moved her gaze between them. "Was there anything else?"

They said there wasn't and she exited the office. Word of her being questioned by IA—and no doubt why—had traveled fast. A number of other officers milled around Sal's office, hoping for some dish. A few of them had the decency to avert their gazes, but others openly stared at her.

This was just the kind of attention she had worked hard to avoid.

Recalling Kitt's advice about going with the flow, she shook off her irritation and passed by them with her head high.

She found that Kitt had made it in and was at her desk. "Returning to the scene of the crime?" she asked from the doorway.

Kitt looked up. "Excuse me?"

"You made it in. Finally."

"I heard about Internal Affairs. How was it?"

M.C. ignored her question and crossed to Kitt's desk. "Where were you this morning?"

Kitt shifted her gaze slightly and M.C. frowned. "That's what I thought. Thanks a lot."

"I'm totally lost now. You want to clue me in?"

"You wanted to get back at me for Joe, didn't you? I hope we're square now, because I don't think I'm up for another sneak attack."

Kitt stood, placed her palms on the desk and leaned toward her. When she spoke, her voice was low and vibrated with anger. "You think I went to the sarge and Sal about your argument with Brian?"

"Didn't you?"

"It wasn't me, M.C. I don't go for that behind-the-back crap. I said what I needed to last night. If another issue comes up, you'll be the first to know."

The other woman gazed at her a moment. "Then who?"

"Someone overheard you. Or Brian told someone about it, which I find pretty unlikely." She lowered her voice. "How deep in shit are you?"

"Slap on the wrist for not stepping forward. They're going to run ballistics on my weapon. Most of all, I just look bad."

"We all make mistakes. I certainly have."

"That's reassuring."

She said it deadpan and Kitt laughed. "I suppose it's not, is it?"

"No."

"Look, Peanut called me last night. He—"

"Detective Riggio?"

They looked up. Sal stood in the doorway. He held out her Glock. "Your weapon."

"That was fast."

"Got the preliminaries back on the type of gun used to kill Lieutenant Spillare. The bullet was fired from a standard-issue, .45 caliber Smith & Wesson revolver."

Most urban forces had begun switching from revolvers to the semi-automatic pistols in the 1970s. RPD officers had the choice between two, both .40 caliber—the Glock or the Smith & Wesson 4046.

She took her weapon and holstered it. "The old policeman's favorite," M.C. said, referring to the revolver. "An interesting choice."

Sal nodded. "No self-respecting gangbanger or street thug's going to choose the revolver."

"Can we have a minute?" Kitt asked.

The deputy chief checked his watch. "Can it wait until after—"

"I heard from Peanut last night. He left a trophy from one of the original killings. A lock of blond hair, tied with a pink ribbon."

Kitt had his full attention. He nodded tersely. "My office. Now would be good."

58

Tuesday, March 21, 2006
10:40 a.m.

Once they had all assembled in Sal's office, Kitt described the events of the evening before, starting with finding the package on the doorstep and finishing with Peanut ending their call.

"He claimed the hair was from one of the original Sleeping Angels. He wouldn't tell me which one. Told me 'DNA' would tell the tale. ID has it and the phone already. They were going to photograph and catalog them, then send the hair to the crime lab.

"I asked him several questions point-blank," she continued. "If he was the Copycat. If he knew who the Copycat was. He answered that he was not, but that he did know who he was. In addition, he claimed no knowledge of Brian's murder."

"What do you think?" Sal asked. "Was he being honest?"

"I think so. Let's face it, he hasn't had a problem claiming responsibility for other crimes."

"But Brian was a cop," Sal pointed out.

"And the Angels were children," Kitt countered. "I accused him of being a cop himself. It unnerved him."

That brought silence. After a moment, Sergeant Haas cleared his throat. "But if he didn't kill Brian—"

"Maybe the Copycat did. Maybe the Copycat's a cop. Maybe they both are."

It was the first time she had considered it aloud. She suddenly realized that she had also speculated that the Copycat was a woman.

Considering both she and M.C. fit that relatively rarified category, she didn't particularly like the option.

Sal frowned, obviously unimpressed with her suggestions. "Maybe neither of them are. Maybe Brian's murder had nothing to do with your investigation."

He turned his gaze to her. "Kitt, I want you to retrace Brian's steps yesterday, from the time you spoke with him until you found him dead. Get into his computer, see what files he accessed. I want a log from his cell and desk phones. Get Allen to assist you."

"You want me on it as well, Sal?" M.C. asked.

"No. You stay on the Copycat. When we're finished, call down to ID. They should have a bead on the cell phone number already."

As if on cue, Kitt's phone buzzed. It was Sorenstein in ID. She listened, thanked him, then turned back to the group when she had ended the call. "The phone belonged to a dead guy. He was killed in a car wreck over the weekend. With everything going on, the family hadn't realized it was missing."

"Our UNSUB seems to have a pretty good grasp on acquiring untraceable numbers," M.C. said. "Nobody can call this one dumb."

Sal sent M.C. an irritated glance. "But how did he get the device?"

"Could be someone at the scene, like an EMT. Or someone at

the hospital. Could be our UNSUB lifted it before the wreck even happen—"

"I don't give a damn about all the ways he could have gotten it. I want to know definitively how he got it!"

He all but roared the last at them and they both jumped to their feet. Sal rarely raised his voice, but when he did, it was advantageous to take note and respond.

They exited the deputy chief's office. "Why share a trophy with you now?" M.C. asked. "It's like he wanted to prove something to you."

"I think he did. He was all about our being in a competition. That's what the perfect crime is to him. Not just getting away with it, but outmaneuvering us. Outthinking us. Winning."

"And is he?"

"Hell, yes!" She felt her frustration rise, her anger with it. As she did, she recalled something else he'd said. About her being emotionally involved. That he had the advantage because of it.

She told M.C., who nodded. "That's it, then. He gave you the trophy as a way to stir your emotions. He's counting on you not thinking as clearly because of it."

"He's a smart SOB." She narrowed her eyes. "But not smart enough."

They reached Kitt's desk. M.C. perched on a corner while Kitt paced. "So, what do we have?" M.C. asked. "All the pieces?"

"Two killers. Nine murders, six of them children, three of them grandmothers. A span of eight years."

"Thanks for narrowing it down, partner. It's all so much clearer to me now."

"Sarcasm suits you."

"Thanks." M.C. rolled her eyes. "Can we break it down a little more?"

"Demanding, aren't we?"

"An Italian princess. Just ask my mother."

Kitt relaxed slightly, pulled out her chair and sat.

M.C. grabbed a legal tablet. "What do we know about the SAK and his crimes?" she asked.

"He killed three ten-year-old girls. He has claimed responsibility for the murders of three elderly women. The means of death between the girls and the grandmothers was completely different."

"Ying and yang."

"He claims his victims are not emotional choices. That they are intellectual ones."

"He's proud of his crimes. Calls them perfect."

"We're painting a portrait of a guy who's out to prove himself. To the world."

"Or to someone in particular."

"Mother? Father? Someone who criticized and belittled him."

Kitt felt the stirrings of excitement. This was him. The one she had come to know through their phone calls. "The duct tape to the mouth. Symbolic for shutting this person up. With the Angels, adding the lip gloss—also bringing attention to the mouth.

"It's why control is so important to him," Kitt said. "There was a time in his life he was powerless. That's why he became so angry every time I challenged him."

"And yet he preys on the powerless."

"Classic self-loathing."

"Along comes this Copycat."

"He knows who the Copycat is. From the joint, maybe."

"He calls *you,* Kitt. Wants you to catch him. Says he will help you."

"But the offer comes with strings," Kitt continues. "He wants to toy with me. Watch me jump through hoops."

"He's in control. Proving his superiority."

"And doing a damn good job of it, I might add."

"Why'd he choose you?" M.C. asked.

"Because he saw me as vulnerable," she said, though she hated the characterization. "He picks on the powerless."

"Yes." M.C. got to her feet. "Winning's so important to him, he stacks the deck. He calls it being 'smart.'"

"And the Copycat—"

"There isn't a Copycat, Kitt." M.C. swung to face her. "He's SAK and Copycat. It's not about killing the girls. It's about engaging *you*."

Kitt didn't want to believe it, but it made sense. All the pieces fit together to create this scenario. "The hands—"

"Mean nothing. They were a way to pull you in. Get you involved, assigned to the case."

It could be. A way to pull her in *and* keep them chasing their tails. "And the clean suit—"

"Proves he's smart. That he knows about evidence and investigation. How to get in and get out, what we'll be looking for. The minutiae we can nail him with."

"He's kept us running. He understands trace technology, what we can and cannot do."

"He used Buddy Brown. Led us to him, knew we would run with the lead. He may, or may not, have counted on us finding his body as quickly as we did."

They fell silent a moment. M.C. broke the silence first. "And Brian? How does he fit in?"

"After I talk to Allen, I'll head down to ID, see how the ballistics search is coming along, then start retracing Brian's steps." Kitt glanced at her watch. "I think we should take one last crack at the contents of the storage unit."

"Agreed. I'll do it." M.C. glanced at her legal pad, then back up at Kitt. "We've pretty much exhausted our options with the Angels, past and present. But what about the grandmothers?"

"I reviewed the case files. Brian and Sarge were the original detectives assigned to the case. I spoke with Brian about it yesterday."

"What about questioning family and friends of the victims?"

"It was on my short list."

"Since we've linked them to the SAK murders, there might be something there that makes sense now, that didn't then."

"From my short list to yours?"

"Bingo. Files?"

Kitt retrieved them from her desk. "Call me crazy, M.C., but I feel we're close to nailing him."

"Woman's intuition?"

"Damn right." She handed her partner the files. "You want to argue about it?"

"No way. God gave women 'intuition' to make up for childbirth."

"Spoken like a woman who's never given birth. Intuition *so* doesn't cover it."

59

Tuesday, March 21, 2006
11:55 a.m.

Traditionally, comparing firearms evidence from one crime to another had been damn near impossible. An investigator had to actually suspect the same weapon had been used in the commission of different crimes, then compare the evidence. Difficult enough within a single jurisdiction, but outside it? To compare to regional, even national, crimes?

The National Integrated Ballistic Information Network, or NIBIN, had changed all that. NIBIN was a national, networked database of fired cartridge casing and bullet images. By way of a microscope attached to the system, images were scanned and stored within the system. An investigator could compare fired bullets and casings from a regional or national area.

Even so, without a suspect weapon, bullet or casing, the comparisons could take weeks—and unlimited manpower. Because, no matter how quickly the system could bring up the comparison images, the firearms examiner still had to visually study them and determine if there was a hit.

Sorenstein sat at the NIBIN terminal. Kitt crossed to stand behind him. Narrowing the type of gun the bullet had come from had been relatively easy. Now the tedious work began.

"How's it going?" she asked.

"As well as can be expected. This one felt like a regional search. Figured I'd widen the net if I needed to."

She nodded. "Let me know if you get a hit."

"Goes without saying."

"Sal wants me to trace Brian's steps. Do you know if you have a call log yet?"

"Cell and landline. On Snowe's desk."

"Thanks." Kitt crossed to the other detective's desk and retrieved the logs. "Catch you later."

Sorenstein didn't reply and Kitt exited the Identification Bureau and headed back upstairs. On the way, she got a call from CRU. She had a visitor—Valerie Martin.

Joe's fiancée.

Guilt rushed over her. She had slept with another woman's man. Never mind that she felt as if Joe still belonged to her, a ring said he didn't.

Had she found out about her and Joe? How could she have? Maybe Joe had told her. Broken their engagement. He hadn't said that was what he was going to do, and they certainly hadn't parted with any promises. He had forgiven her—but made it clear that it was more complicated than the two of them.

Maybe he had come clean and begged Valerie's forgiveness for the lapse.

And Valerie had come to the PSB to kick her ass. Figuratively, of course.

Kitt's knees went weak. She could face a killer across a table, but the thought of facing Joe's fiancée made her want to run fast and hide well.

She told the desk officer to send her up. She would meet her at the elevators on two.

Kitt was waiting when the elevator doors slid open and Valerie stepped off. She wore her nurse's uniform. She looked shaken.

"Hello, Valerie. How can I help you?"

"I need to talk to you," she said. "It's really important. But...I'm on my lunch break. I don't have a lot of time."

Kitt nodded. "Follow me."

She led her to an empty interrogation room. Neither her desk nor the break room would give them the kind of privacy this conversation required.

They sat. Kitt thought about simply telling her everything—her love for Joe, how she had realized it. Then beg her forgiveness.

Shame kept her from speaking.

"I don't know how to say this," Valerie began, clasping her hands in her lap.

Kitt saw that she still wore Joe's ring. "Just say it, then."

She nodded, took a deep breath and began. "I lied to your partner. When she asked me about Joe. About our being together the night that little girl died."

Kitt struggled to shift gears. To place what she was saying. "What do you mean, you lied?"

"Joe and I weren't together all that night."

Joe's alibi for the night of Julie Entzel's murder. He didn't have one, after all.

How did she know Valerie was being truthful now?

Kitt struggled to keep her thoughts from showing and to pull herself together. Fact was, ethically, she should turn this over to another detective right now.

She should. But she couldn't. Not yet.

That didn't mean she was so stupid as not to cover herself—or protect the investigation.

"Valerie, because of the nature of this conversation, I need to both record it and take notes. Is that all right?"

The younger woman hesitated a moment, then nodded. "As long as it doesn't take much time."

"It won't, I promise."

Within moments, Kitt had set up the video recorder and was sitting across from Valerie, a tablet on the table in front of her. "Could you repeat what you told me earlier?"

She did, repeating it almost verbatim, adding, "I couldn't stop thinking about what you said, about Tami being in danger. And I couldn't stop thinking about the girls who had died."

"Let's start at the beginning, Valerie. Detective Riggio visited you while you were working at the hospital."

"That's right. Highland Park Hospital. She asked me some questions about Joe. Whether we were together all night on March 6. I said we had been."

Kitt leaned forward slightly. "Now you're saying that's not true?"

"Yes." Valerie looked down at her hands, then back up at Kitt. Tears sparkled in her eyes. "I shouldn't have lied. I just…all I could think about was protecting Joe."

"What made you think Joe needed protection?"

M.C. had attempted to avoid this very thing by questioning Valerie before Joe had the opportunity to call her.

"Joe had told me about that ex-con who was working for him. That you'd been asking questions. He'd said it was making him uncomfortable."

Valerie let out a shaky breath. "I knew there was no way Joe could have anything to do with…that. So I lied."

"And now? What caused your change of heart?"

"I keep thinking about what you said, about Tami being in danger. And about...all those other girls. And I can't live with myself."

She wrung her hands. As she did, her diamond solitaire caught the light. It was a pretty ring, Kitt thought. Certainly bigger than the one she'd gotten. She and Joe had been kids when they'd gotten engaged; they'd had little but the roof over their heads.

Valerie glanced at her watch. "I'm still certain he couldn't have had anything to do with hurting a child. But I couldn't be party to the lie anymore."

For long minutes after Valerie had left, Kitt sat in the interrogation room, staring at the empty doorway, trying to objectively evaluate Valerie's story. Something about it didn't ring true.

But was that because it wasn't—or because she didn't want it to be?

Kitt glanced down at the log of Brian's calls. A number leaped out at her. One she knew by heart.

She knew it by heart because, once upon a time, it had been hers as well.

60

Tuesday, March 21, 2006
12:30 p.m.

M.C. started with Rose McGuire, the second victim, simply because she had lived in an assisted-living community rather than a private residence. Even though seven years had passed, M.C. hoped there might still be someone on staff from the time of the murder. If so, they would remember. An incident like that was not easily forgotten. In addition, it had no doubt resulted in sweeping changes in the center's security.

The Walton B. Johnson Assisted Living Center had been named after the Rockford millionaire philanthropist whose brainchild the center had been. Or so the center's director informed M.C. as they walked to her office. It had been the first of its kind in the city, providing a much-needed living alternative for the elderly. His foundation continued to underwrite needy residents, up to ten percent of occupancy. Their newest, a man named Billy Hatfield, had moved in just that day.

They passed a line of wheelchairs filled with ladies—their gray hair ranging in shades of silver to lavender. Some napped, others waved at her and called greetings, others seemed to be grousing about something.

"What are they waiting for?" M.C. asked.

The director smiled. "Mr. Kenneth comes in to do hair on Mondays. Every Tuesday after lunch we put up the sign-up sheet. As you can see, Mr. Kenneth is very popular with the female residents."

They reached the woman's office. A plaque on the door read Patsy Anderson, Director.

She unlocked the door and led M.C. inside. After they had both taken a seat, she asked, "What can I do for you, Detective?"

"I was hoping you could tell me something about Rose McGuire."

Her smile slipped. "Surely you don't mean—"

"I do, indeed, Ms. Anderson. We're looking into reopening the investigation."

She didn't look pleased at the news. M.C. didn't blame her. If the case was reopened, it would attract media attention—which would be bad publicity for them.

Worse than she knew.

"That was so long ago."

"Seven years."

"I wasn't even on staff here. I was hired in 2002."

"Is there anyone on staff who was?"

She frowned. "Offhand, I don't recall. I'd have to go into the personnel records."

"Would you, please?"

"It'll take a bit of time."

"When do you think you could have the information to me?"

She glanced at her desk clock. "End of the day, latest."

"I'd appreciate that."

"You know," she went on, "the previous director retired, but she lives here in town. I bet she'd be happy to talk to you. She took the murder really hard. In fact, it's why she retired when she did. Why don't I call her, see if she's home and tell her you're coming over?"

Twenty minutes later, M.C. greeted Wanda Watkins, a small, energetic woman with a lovely silver bob and eyes so big they took up an inordinate amount of her face.

"Thank you for seeing me, Mrs. Watkins."

"Call me Wanda. Come in."

She led M.C. into her small living room. A big calico cat perched on the back of the floral sofa, another sprawled across the cushions.

Unfortunately, M.C. was allergic. She felt her nose twitch.

"My babies," the woman said. She scooped up the one and shooed the other. "Please, sit."

M.C. did. She took out her notebook and pen. "As Patsy told you over the phone, we're looking into reopening the investigation into Rose McGuire's murder. We have a possible new lead."

"Thank God." She stroked the cat. "It's been difficult, knowing her killer was never caught. Not just because he was still free, but because Miss Rose was such a sweet woman. Always a smile, never a complaint."

Wanda leaned forward. "They're not all like that, you know. Some are cantankerous. Some bitter. They miss the independent lives they used to have, they don't feel well or they're just grieving having gotten old." She smiled. "I loved them all, even the crabby ones."

"You really liked your job."

"I did. Very much."

"Why'd you retire?"

"After Rose...I felt I should step down. Let someone younger take over." Her eyes grew bright. "I felt, perhaps, if I had been more observant or more forward-thinking about security, it wouldn't have happened."

Another of violent crime's victims—those left behind who blamed themselves.

"It wasn't your fault," she said softly. "There was nothing you could have done."

"I tell myself that but... You know how it goes."

She did, indeed. "How did the murderer get into the building? I noticed you had a keypad and call-box system. The main doors are kept locked twenty-four hours a day. Was anything different at the time of the murder?"

"We've added video surveillance, but that's it." She shook her head. "We believe a resident let him in. They would do that, see some 'nice person' at the door and buzz them in. We warned them not to...but they're so trusting."

"And now?" M.C. sneezed.

"Bless you. Can't say. After Rose...died, we cracked down. Things may have become more lax. Time dims the memory."

But not hers, obviously. Not about this.

M.C. thanked her and sneezed again. "Sorry," she said. "I'm allergic to cats."

Wanda handed her a box of tissues. "What a shame. You're a dog person, then?"

She had never thought about it. "I guess I am."

"Without my four-footed friends, I don't know what I'd do."

M.C. redirected her. "Who found Miss Rose?"

"I did, Detective." She buried her fingers in the cat's long fur. "We hadn't heard from her that morning, so we called her apartment. When we didn't get an answer, I offered to go check on her. That was, and still is, I believe, standard procedure. Her door was unlocked and..."

Her mouth trembled. "I'm sorry, Detective, must I go on?"

M.C. didn't need her to paint a picture—she had seen the photos. "Can you tell me anything about the days leading up to Rose McGuire's death? Was there anything special that you remember? Anything different?"

She thought a moment. "We'd had the birthday party for the center just a few days before. I remember so clearly because Miss Rose was dancing. Believe me, some of those oldsters, as I called them, could really cut a rug."

A birthday party? The back of M.C.'s neck prickled. *Julie Entzel and Marianne Vest had also attended birthday parties before they were killed.*

"Not like people from your generation," Wanda Watkins continued, "just standing there and swaying. No offense, of course."

"No offense taken." M.C. sneezed twice, then grabbed a tissue. "The party was held at the center?"

"That's right. Other than Christmas, it was our biggest event of the year."

"Tell me about it."

"It was different every year, of course. But there was always some sort of show. Music and dancing. A special meal. Even a champagne fountain. Sparkling grape juice." She leaned toward M.C. "Even though it was nonalcoholic, some of the residents still got tipsy."

"That year, what was the entertainment? Do you remember?"

She screwed her face up in thought. "A clown. He was quite good."

A clown.

Holy shit. Kitt had been right.

M.C. straightened. "Did you share this with the officers investigating at the time?"

"I'm sure I didn't. It never came up."

"What was the clown's name?"

"I don't recall. It's been years."

"Did you use a service?"

She shook her head. "We got a recommendation from someone." She frowned in thought. "Who was that? The relative of one of the residents. But...I can't remember who."

"Has the center used him since?"

"We tried the next year, but the number was no longer in service and we couldn't find a listing."

"Could the name still be on file at the center? Or can you think of anyone who might recall his name? It could be important."

Wanda would have had to be deaf to miss the urgency in M.C.'s voice. She looked stricken. "You don't think...surely that nice clown—"

M.C. cut her off. "Is there a chance the man's name is still on file at the center?"

"Probably not. When we couldn't reach him the next year, I'm sure we took his name out of the Rolodex. Keeping up-to-date records was an obsession of mine."

"What about a record of payment?" M.C. asked, knowing that most businesses kept their financial records a minimum of seven years, if not indefinitely

She nodded. "I bet there would be. We weren't allowed to pay anyone cash."

M.C. stood, excited. This could very well be nothing. But it didn't feel that way. It felt like a big something.

She thanked Mrs. Watkins and handed her one of her cards. "If you even get a glimmer of a recollection as to this clown's name, call. No matter the time. On my cell."

The woman said she would and trailed her to the door. M.C. could tell she had questions, ones she knew better than to ask.

M.C. wouldn't answer, of course.

She hurried out into the bright day. She had to call Kitt. They had checked the Fun Zone's employees, but they hadn't asked the victims' parents if their children had been entertained by a performer from *outside* the Fun Zone. They also had to check with the Olsen and Lindz families to find out if they had also been entertained by a clown.

She dialed Kitt; got her message service. "Kitt, it's M.C. I think we've got him. A clown performed at a party at Rose McGuire's assisted-living community. I'm going to contact the other families, see if they remember a clown. I'll keep in touch."

Tuesday, March 21, 2006
1:00 p.m.

Kitt stared at the phone log, at the damning number. *Brian had called Joe last night.* Kitt checked the time. *At 5:20. Just before he had called her.*

Her vision blurred. Why? What possible reason could he have had?

He'd been looking for her. It made sense. He'd left her a message, had obviously needed to speak with her so—

She and Joe had been divorced for three years, why would Brian call there, looking for her?

What had Joe said this morning? *That he'd discovered that the line between love and hate was thin, indeed.*

Dear God, how thin?

She felt ill. All along, M.C. had thought Joe was a good suspect.

She hadn't believed it. She still didn't. Not Joe. Not the man she had loved almost her whole life.

But if he had lied about the alibi…

What else had he lied about?

She reached her desk. On it sat two calendars. One from 1989, the other from 1990. Both were promotional, from the Society for the Deaf.

There was a note on top from M.C. *From the storage facility. Could be something. Call me.*

"Hey, Lundgren? You okay?"

She looked up. Detective Allen stood beside her desk, staring quizzically at her.

She worked to regain normalcy, her sense of balance. "Fine. What's up?"

"Been looking at Brian's computer. He spent a good bit of time yesterday searching old cases."

He handed her a printout. "Some of them are cold cases, others were solved."

Kitt quickly scanned the page. He had pulled up the files of Marguerite Lindz, Rose McGuire and Janet Olsen. In all of those, she knew, he had been one of the investigating officers. The other cases she didn't recognize.

She handed the list back. "With the exception of these three, could you look up who the investigating officers were on the cases? I'm going to question some of the folks Brian called yesterday. I'll have my cell phone if you need anything."

A partial truth, she thought as she exited the VCB. She intended to speak with Joe—and see where that led her.

Her cell phone buzzed and from the display she saw it was M.C. She started to pick up, then hesitated. She couldn't tell her about Valerie recanting Joe's alibi. Not just yet.

She needed to speak with Joe first.

She reholstered the device and hurried down the elevator to the parking garage.

As she exited the elevator, the phone rang again. This time it was Danny.

She hadn't spoken to her friend since the night she rebuffed his advances.

"Hi, Danny," she said.

"I was hoping we could talk about the other night."

"This isn't a good time."

He was quiet a moment. "When would be a good time?"

She frowned. "Truthfully, I don't know. This investigation is really heating up."

"How about after group?"

"I don't know if I'll be there, it depends on the—"

"Investigation."

The word dripped sarcasm and irritation rippled over her. "It's my job. And sometimes, me staying on the job is the difference between life and death."

"Right, how could I have forgotten?"

"Look, I'm sorry about the other night. We're friends and I value that too much to get romantically involved with you."

She expected him to apologize. For getting pushy. For putting her in a position that jeopardized their friendship. Instead, when he spoke, he sounded angry. "I know you, Kitt. I know what drives you—and what drives you to drink. You need us. You need *me*."

Something about the way he said it raised her hackles. "I've got to go. I'll be back to group as soon as I can."

She hung up and went in search of Joe.

Kitt tracked him down with Flo's help, at one of his building sites.

"Hi," he said, breaking into a smile. He moved to kiss her and she backed away.

His smile slipped. "What's wrong?"

"We have to talk."

"Okay. Sure."

He glanced around. The house was in the process of being framed in. Joe's crew was everywhere.

"How about my truck?"

Kitt nodded and followed him to his pickup. They climbed in the cab and she turned to face him.

"Valerie was in this morning," she said, not mincing words. "She told me she lied about the night of March 6, said the two of you did not spend the night together."

He frowned. "I don't understand."

"She recanted, Joe. You don't have an alibi now. For any of the Copycat murders. You want to change your story?"

"No! We were together. All night."

"She says not."

"And you believe her?"

"I don't want to. But—"

"I thought you knew who I was, Kitt."

"I do. But I have a job to do." She heard the quiver in her voice and acknowledged that she was out of her depth here. That M.C. had been right to take this out of her hands.

Cool-eyed objectivity. She had it.

Yeah, right. What a joke.

"Did it occur to you that maybe she changed her story out of anger? Because I met her this morning and broke our engagement?"

"She was still wearing your ring. I figured you would—"

"Stay engaged to her? After last night? What kind of man would I be if I did that?" He caught her hands. "I love you, Kitt. I never stopped."

"Then why—"

"Because I wanted a life. A family. I thought Valerie and I would be good together. And she needed me, because of Tami, her handicap."

He gazed into her eyes. "I'd given up hoping you'd ever need me again."

"I always needed you," she said. "I was just in too much pain to—What handicap?"

She saw by his expression that he was confused. "Tami," she repeated. "What handicap?"

"Tami's deaf," he said. "I thought you knew."

Tuesday, March 21, 2006
1:40 p.m.

As M.C. was leaving the Walton B. Johnson Center for the second time that day, her cell phone rang. The foundation's headquarters in Chicago housed all records over a year old; they had been contacted and would begin a search. It would take longer than M.C. would have liked, because they didn't know exactly who they were looking for or the date the check had been written.

"Riggio here," she answered, certain it would be Kitt on the other end.

Not Kitt. Lance. "I need to talk to you," he said, tone urgent. "It's important."

She frowned. "Is everything all right?"

"Yes…no. I haven't been able to stop thinking about you. About how much you mean to me."

"From where I'm standing, that sounds like a good thing." She darted across the parking lot to her SUV.

"There are things you need to know about me. My past. They may affect the way you feel about me."

He had her full attention now. "What kind of things?"

"About my family. How I grew up."

"I doubt your family could change the way I feel about you."

"That's because you never met them."

The way he said it made her laugh. "Well, you haven't met mine yet, either." She unlocked her vehicle and slipped inside. "This is a really bad time, Lance. The investigation—"

"Ten minutes," he said. "Fifteen, tops."

She glanced at her watch. She hadn't eaten yet and was getting a headache. "I have to grab a bite, maybe we could—"

"Come here," he said. "I'll have a sandwich ready for you. And I make a pretty mean ham and cheese."

"Mayo and lettuce?" she teased.

"Absolutely. Although, I'm warning you up-front that my story might ruin your appetite. My family's pretty weird."

"Weird families are right up my alley. I'll be there in ten minutes."

63

It took a moment for Kitt to process what Joe was saying. *Tami was deaf?*

How could she not have known? Kitt replayed the times she had been in the girl's company. At the leukemia fair, Kitt had been reeling over discovering the girl's existence. She had been in her presence only moments before hurrying off. At Valerie's home, Kitt had been taken with how quietly Tami played, been impressed by the absence of TV. She hadn't commented as theirs hadn't been a social call.

It made sense. It—

The calendars, she realized. The ones that M.C. had left on her desk that morning, from the Society for the Deaf. Peanut hadn't been lying—there had been a clue for them in the storage unit. They just hadn't dug deep enough until now.

"Kitt?" Joe was looking at her strangely. "What's wrong?"

"I have to bring you in. I believe you. But if it looks like I covered this up or behaved inappropriately it'll be worse—for both of us. You have to trust me."

He didn't hesitate. "I do. Let me give my lead guy some direction."

They both climbed out of the truck. Kitt watched as he jogged across the site to one of his workmen, then turned and jogged back.

"Shall I follow you?" he asked.

"Leave your truck. I'll drive."

He nodded, expression tight. "Don't want me to try to make a run for it, right?"

She caught his hand, laced her fingers through his. "I know that's not going to happen. I'm acting with an abundance of caution."

They crossed to her Taurus and climbed in. Kitt started it up, thoughts racing. She had heard some of the divorcées in the RPD discussing how hard it was to find a guy when you had kids. She imagined it would be doubly hard if you were the mother of a handicapped child.

Could Valerie have created this elaborate scheme to get away with murdering her own child?

The idea was sickening. Repugnant. As it would be to any sane person. But, as her years on the force had proved, human behavior often proved anything but "sane."

Valerie had a connection to both Buddy Brown and the pediatric ward where Julie Entzel had visited her cousin. Kitt had thought from the beginning that the contents of the storage unit had either belonged to a woman or been assembled by one.

And now, Valerie had a motive—freedom.

"Tell me more about Tami," Kitt said as she headed toward the PSB.

"What's this all about, Kitt?"

"I can't say." She glanced at him, then back at the road. "Just trust me, okay?"

He nodded tersely and began. "She's been deaf since birth, though they didn't realize it until she was about two. She goes to a school for the deaf and reads lips and signs. She's very well adjusted and an all-around good kid."

"What about Valerie? What's her story in all this?"

"It's been really hard on her. Her husband left her when they learned Tami was deaf. He 'just couldn't handle having a handicapped kid.' His words."

"Before you, did she date much?"

"She tried. But when men found out she had a handicapped child, they never called again."

"Except for you."

"Yeah. Except for me."

Kind Joe. Patient and loving. In a way, Sadie's disease had been a handicap. She certainly hadn't had what the world would call a "normal" first ten years.

Kitt tightened her fingers on the steering wheel. The clown who'd given her the balloon was her caller, the original SAK. And Valerie was the Copycat.

How the hell did they meet? And were they in cahoots? Or adversaries?

Perhaps they were lovers?

She stopped on that.

Lovers. In cahoots.

She glanced at Joe, an uncomfortable sensation creeping over her. From living with her, Joe knew police procedure. He knew everything about her—her fears and dreams. Her nightmares. He knew about her letting the SAK escape because she'd been drunk.

Peanut's knowledge of that incident had been the cornerstone of her belief in his being the SAK.

Brian had called Joe, just hours before he died. Joe had hired Buddy Brown.

But the clown had given her the balloon. He'd called and—

M.C. had pointed out the faulty thinking in that already. Joe had seen the clown hand her the balloon and used it as a way of proving himself innocent.

She struggled to think clearly, to separate fact from fear. What she was considering was insane. Impossible. She had known this man most of his life. Even with a voice-altering device, she would recognize his voice patterns and—

That was bullshit. A sophisticated voice-changer could make an old voice young, a male voice female—or vice versa—and all manner of adjustments in between.

But if her caller was the original SAK...

Maybe the original SAK had never been involved. They wouldn't even have needed him. It could be wholly their plot.

The three old ladies, she realized. If the SAK hadn't been the one calling her, how had he known about them?

He couldn't have.

What if that were a lie, too?

Kitt's head whirled with questions and answers to them—ones she both feared were true and prayed weren't.

She was aware of Joe looking at her. The hair at the back of her neck prickled. She hadn't cuffed him. Hadn't searched him for a weapon.

Of course she hadn't.

This was Joe.

She glanced at him, forcing a smile. As long as he believed nothing had changed, he would go along with her. "Almost there."

"Are you thinking Valerie's in some sort of trouble?"

"What makes you say that?"

"Ever since I mentioned that Tami was deaf, you've been acting a little strange."

She couldn't bring herself to lie to him. So she told him the truth. Her by-the-book truth. "I can't discuss what I'm thinking with you. I'm going to need to talk to Sal and he'll want to talk to you."

Kitt reached the PSB and pulled into the underground parking area. She parked and turned to him. "Ready?"

He grabbed her arm as she reached for the door handle. "What's going on here, Kitt?"

"A murder investigation. I thought you knew that."

He tightened his grip on her arm. "Do you love me?"

She held his gaze. A lump formed in her throat. Would she, if it was proved he was a child killer? Or an accomplice to one? How could she? But for now, this moment, even with her suspicions, she did.

"Yes," she answered softly. "I do."

He released her and they climbed out of the car. On their way in, they were joined by Sorenstein and Snowe, obviously just returning from lunch. The smell of fried chicken still hung on them, and she realized it'd been hours since she'd eaten.

"Yo, Lundgren," Snowe greeted her, then looked at Joe. "Scott Snowe. I think we met before."

"We probably did. I'm Joe Lundgren, Kitt's ex-husband."

They shook hands. Sorenstein introduced himself as well. If the detectives thought it was strange she was with her ex, they didn't mention it.

"By the way, nothing yet," Sorenstein said, anticipating her asking how the ballistics search was going. "I'm taking another crack at it this afternoon."

"Let me know if—"

"You'll be the first, I swear."

The elevator arrived and she and Joe stepped on. "What now?" he asked.

"I'll put you in one of the interrogation rooms, then go talk to Sal."

"When he questions me, will you be with him?"

She shook her head. "I've already been too involved."

"I'm on my own?"

"Afraid so." They reached the second floor and exited the elevator. She led Joe to the hall where the six interrogation rooms were located. Number One was empty, she opened it and flipped on the light. "I'll be as fast as I can be."

He nodded; she crossed to the door, stopped and looked back at him. "By the way, Joe, did Brian call you last night?"

"Brian Spillare?"

She nodded.

"No. Why?"

For the space of a heartbeat, she wanted to scream "Liar!" Instead, she forced a reassuring smile. "He was looking for me, that's all. Let's get this show on the road."

64

Tuesday, March 21, 2006
3:00 p.m.

Kitt shut the interrogation room door, heart in her throat. Joe had lied. Brian had called him, it was in the log. What could Brian have found that implicated Joe?

Kitt went in search of Sal. She learned from Nan that he and Sergeant Haas were in his office. Taking a deep breath, she tapped on Sal's partially closed door.

He called out for her to come in. "Kitt," he said, sounding annoyed, "what can I do for you?"

"I need to bounce something off you. It's important."

He waved her in. "Bounce away."

She crossed to the chair in front of his desk and stood behind it, gripping the back for support. "I may have had a breakthrough in the Copycat case." His expression altered subtly, and she went on. "I'm still wrestling with this, but it's a scenario. I have to lay it out for you."

Both men's gazes were riveted on her. "Valerie Martin was in this morning. She claimed she lied about being with Joe the night of Julie Entzel's murder. She was his only alibi."

Sal frowned. "M.C. was with you?"

"No. She was tracking down possible links between the three grandmother murders and the SAK."

An angry flush climbed his cheeks, but he held his tongue. She knew what would come when she'd finished and he'd assessed what he considered "the damage."

"I videotaped her statement."

"Glad to hear you used *some* sense."

No doubt he would retract that comment with her next. "From there, I called on Joe."

He looked alarmingly like he might pop. "Alone?"

"Yes."

Sergeant Haas stepped in. "You want to explain how you went from tracking Lieutenant Spillare's movements yesterday to——"

"Brian called Joe last night. Shortly before he called me. Joe's number was on the call log."

That brought silence. Kitt went on. "I questioned him, brought him in, though he came of his own volition. He's in Interrogation One. Here's where it gets weird."

She began by explaining about the Society for the Deaf calendars M.C. had found, then learning from Joe that Valerie's daughter was deaf.

"A lightbulb went off. Valerie works in the hospital pediatric ward Julie Entzel visited. She would have known of Buddy Brown, through Joe. Had access to personal information about me, including my cell phone number. And I had strongly considered during the course of the investigation that the Copycat was a woman."

She paused. "The Copycat killings were nothing but a smoke screen to cover up the murder of her own daughter."

"Why?"

"Freedom. She was tired of being tied down to a handicapped child."

"The child's father?"

"He left her when they learned Tami was deaf."

"Okay, I'll bite. Valerie Martin's the Copycat. How did she and the SAK meet?"

"Exactly what I asked myself. Where did they meet and what was the nature of their relationship? Were they adversaries, as Peanut claimed? Or were they partners? Or even lovers? And I took the logical next step."

Sal nodded. "Which led you to—"

"Joe." Her voice trembled slightly. "Joe knows everything about me. He knew about that night I let the SAK slip away. Which was the basis of my belief that Peanut was the SAK."

Sal and Sergeant Haas exchanged glances. "So you're saying the original SAK was never involved in this? That the plot was hatched wholly by the two of them?"

"Yes."

"What about the lock of hair Peanut left for you? Or the box of clippings and lip gloss found at Buddy Brown's apartment?"

"Until DNA comes back we don't know if they're for real, do we?"

"But why, Kitt?" Sal asked. "Why would he do this?"

She cleared her throat. "I don't know. To punish me."

"I can't believe what you're suggesting," Sal said. "You're talking about Joe here."

"I know. A part of me, a big part can't... But it's a scenario. I had to present it."

"If Joe and Valerie were partners in this scheme, why did she recant the alibi?"

Kitt tightened her grip on the chair back. "She found out Joe and

I slept together. Joe claims she's recanting because he ended their engagement."

"Which may be true."

"Yes. It's all speculation and circumstantial evidence."

"You're out of it."

"I wish I was never 'in it,' Sal."

"Dammit, Kitt!" He leaned forward. "By the books, you promised me. I should suspend you."

"Yes, sir."

Obviously, he wasn't ready to let her off the hook. "What the hell were you doing talking to Valerie Martin, anyway? Didn't you learn anything from screwing up the SAK investigation? The minute she walked through that door, you should have turned it over to M.C. or somebody else."

"Yes, sir."

"Then you run straight to the suspect, tipping him off. Who do you owe alleg—"

Nan buzzed in and he snatched up the phone. "What!" he barked into the receiver. "Say again?"

Scowling, he laid a hand over the mouthpiece and looked at her. "Did you authorize someone named Danny coming up?"

"Danny?" she repeated, confused. "Coming up where?"

"Here, the bureau. He appeared in the office, looking for you."

A confrontation with her friend was the last thing she needed right now. "I did not," she said, standing. "I'll get rid of—"

"Stay where you are, Detective! You're not off the hot seat quite yet."

He told the secretary to have him wait, then picked up where he had left off. "Whom do you owe allegiance to, Kitt? Your job? Or Joe?"

"I'm here, aren't I?"

And I feel as if my heart is being torn from my body.

"Let me ask you this, Kitt. What do *you* believe?"

She gazed at her superior officer, considering her answer. What did she believe—with her gut? The part of her that, if she could filter out the static, never let her down?

Problem was, she couldn't filter it out. She couldn't separate her head and her heart. Her heart's call was too loud.

She shook her head. "I can't be objective, Sal."

Sal narrowed his eyes slightly, then looked at Sergeant Haas. "Send Allen and White to pick up Valerie Martin."

The other man got on it without comment, and Sal stood. "Time to visit with Joe."

Tuesday, March 21, 2006
3:35 p.m.

Kitt found Danny in the hallway outside the VCB, pacing. When he saw her, he stopped pacing, expression almost comically relieved.

She drew him away from the door. "What are you doing here, Danny?"

"I had to talk to you face-to-face." He lowered his voice. "Before it was too late."

"Too late for what?"

He shook his head. "Give me another chance. The other night, I blew it. Coming on to you like that, I—"

"I don't have time for this right now." A fellow officer passed, sending them a curious glance. "I told you that earlier."

"Is there somewhere we can talk privately?"

She thought of Sal and Sergeant Haas, reviewing Valerie's re-corded statement, preparing to question Joe, and she shook her head. "No, Danny, there's not."

He stiffened. "I thought we were friends."

"We are. But I'm working and you shouldn't be here."

"You need me." He grabbed her hands. "You need us. I'm wor-ried about—"

"Give it a rest, will you?" She pulled free of his grasp. "I'm fine. You're the one who's acting like he needs help."

And he was. She had always thought of Danny as someone who had learned from his mistakes and then grown up—fast. He'd seemed mature. Steady. Now she wasn't so certain. Now it was almost as if he was two people: the supportive friend and the jealous lover.

He flushed. "Forget about it. I tried to warn you."

She watched him walk away, then called downstairs, to CRU. She told them he was coming down and asked if they would escort him out of the building.

That done, she headed for the interview rooms, checking her messages on the way.

There was one from M.C.

"Kitt, it's M.C. I think we've got him. A clown performed at a party at Rose McGuire's assisted-living community. I'm going to contact the other families, see if they remember a clown. I'll keep in touch."

A clown? If Valerie's accomplice was the clown, Joe *was* innocent.

She dialed M.C. and got her voice mail. "Got your FYI. Any more on the clown angle? I'm at the PSB. Major developments on this end. Call me."

As she ended the call, Sal emerged from the viewing room, nod-ded in her direction, then headed toward room one. They were ready to begin.

She joined Sergeant Haas. He didn't glance her way. He had his eyes fixed on the video monitor. She did the same.

Sal entered the interrogation room. "Hello, Joe," he said. "It's good to see you."

"I wish I could say the same, but considering the circumstances—"

"Understood." He pulled out the chair across the table from Joe and sat. "How've you been?"

"Frankly, Sal, it's been a rough couple of years."

"I know that. I'm sorry." He paused. "I need to ask you some questions."

"Kitt said you would."

"You already know that your fiancée was in this morning."

"My ex-fiancée. Yes."

Sal inclined his head in acknowledgment. "She told Kitt she had lied about you and she being together the night of March 6."

"Actually," he said, voice steady, "she's lying now. We were together all night."

"Can you prove it?"

He thought a moment. "No. But she'll get over this. She's angry. And hurt."

"Because you broke your engagement?"

"Yes."

"Why did you do that?"

"I'm still in love with Kitt."

Joe had told her that himself, but hearing it spoken that way to Sal took her breath away.

"Tell me about Valerie. What she's like?"

"She's patient. A good mother. A real down-to-earth person."

"That doesn't sound like the kind of woman who would be vindictive. Or lie to the police."

"No, it doesn't." Joe glanced down at his hands, then back up at Sal. "For her to do this...I must have really hurt her. I don't know how else to explain it."

"Kitt tells me Valerie's daughter is deaf."

"That's right."

"It must be tough to communicate with her?"

"Not really. She reads lips and signs. The casual observer wouldn't even realize she was deaf."

"What's she like?"

"She's a sweet kid. Shy, though. Because of her handicap, I guess."

"Does she make her mother's life difficult?"

"More than most kids? No. Though, before she could sign, she was wild. Flew into rages. Broke things, would hit Valerie."

"That's rather bizarre."

"The doctors said the behavior was the result of frustration at not being able to communicate. I didn't know either of them then."

Sal sat silently, gaze on Joe, as if weighing what Joe had said. Judging its validity. Kitt knew it was an interrogation technique, used to undermine a suspect's confidence, make them sweat a little.

"Here's the problem, Joe. We link you to one of the victims. We link you to Buddy Brown. Now you have no alibi for the nights of any of the Copycat killings."

Joe frowned. "In a couple of days, Valerie will have a change of heart and tell the truth. I know she will."

"What if she doesn't?"

For the first time, Joe looked uncomfortable.

Sal leaned slightly toward him. "Just tell me, Joe. Was it her plan?"

"What plan? Whose?"

"Valerie's plan to kill the girls to cover up the murder of her own daughter?"

Joe stared at Sal, face the picture of shocked disbelief. Watching, Kitt thought he couldn't feign that.

Or could he?

"That's crazy! Valerie's not a killer! She's a good mother. She loves her daughter. This is— It's outrageous."

"Maybe she set you up, Joe. Have you thought about that? That this was her plan from the start? You taking the rap for her?"

Joe looked directly into the video camera, expression anguished. She could almost hear his thoughts: *Kitt, how could you?*

Kitt stared at him, her life—their life together—flashing before her eyes. Everything they had been in the past—and all that they still could have been.

What had she done?

"Well, Joe? What do you think? You going to take the rap for this?"

Joe looked directly at Sal. "I want my lawyer."

"Of course." He pushed away from the table and stood. "By the way, Joe. You heard about Brian Spillare?" When Joe nodded tersely, he asked, "I wonder, why did he call you last night?"

"He didn't."

Sal flipped open the file folder on the table in front of him and pulled out the call log. He slid it across to Joe. "This says he did."

Joe stared at the log. Kitt saw the exact moment he saw his own number, because he went white. "I want my lawyer," he said again. "I'm not going to say another word until then."

Sal handed him his own cell phone. "You need a phone book?"

"No, I've got it."

Kitt watched as he dialed. He was calling Kurt Petroski, his corporate lawyer and the man who'd supported him during the search warrant. She hoped Kurt had the good sense now to tell him he needed a criminal lawyer. A good one.

She continued to watch after Joe finished the call and Sal left him to wait for the attorney, something plucking at her.

She reviewed Sal's questions and Joe's responses.

Until she learned to sign . . .

She signs quite well. . . .

What had Peanut told her the last time they spoke?

"The victims are talking to you."

"My God," Kitt said.

The sergeant looked at her sharply. "What?"

Kitt stood. "That's it. The victim's hands. They're posed in sign language."

66

Tuesday, March 21, 2006
5:05 p.m.

The department employed only one individual fluent in American Sign Language, or ASL—Jimmy Ye was an officer with the Community Service Unit.

He had agreed to come up to the VCB and take a look at the Copycat crime-scene photos to see if he could interpret them. ID had taken shots from every possible angle of the victims' posed hands; Kitt spread the photos out for him as Sergeant Haas looked on. "What do you think, Jimmy? Could it be sign language?"

He studied the photos. "It could be."

"Presuming it is, what's he saying?"

"That's a little tougher." He picked up one of the close-up shots.

"ASL is a visual-spacial language. Its grammatical system includes facial movements and the use of space surrounding the signer."

"Which means what?"

"Without animation, we're only getting part of the language. It'll be difficult to assess the killer's intent—I can only guess."

"Disclaimer noted. Give it your best shot, then."

He indicated the shot of Julie Entzel. "This girl has her right hand pointing to her chest, the left one outward. Very simply, she could be saying 'I' or 'Me' with her right—"

Kitt cut him off. "*She's* not saying anything, Jimmy. It's the killer who's speaking to us. She was just the vehicle."

He looked taken aback at being corrected. She supposed she could have let it pass, but felt it kept the focus correct—and honored the victim.

"Right. Sorry, Detective. The other hand is pointing outward. This is an example of using space around the signer to describe a person or thing not present."

Kitt wasn't blown away. "Me, you. Me and you."

"Not necessarily. It could also mean 'He,' 'She' or 'It.' You can't apply the rules of English grammatical structure to American Sign Language. ASL has a topic-comment syntax."

"Plain English, please," Sergeant Haas said, sounding irritated.

"As verbal communicators, we express ourselves, our ideas and emotions, in pieces of sentences. In single words spoken with emotion. In phrases and ways that butcher the traditional subject-object-verb structure. And in response to the topic."

Jimmy laid the photo down. "So he may be trying to say me and you. Or she and I. Or I am he. We don't—"

"I am he," Kitt said, trying it out, running it through her head. "He's telling us who he is. The one. The SAK."

The sergeant nodded. "It could be. Let's move on to Marianne Vest."

Jimmy hesitated. "I don't know. I—"

"Best guess."

For long moments, he studied the photos. "Okay, what I think he's signing is individual letters here. A *W* and an *E*. Her right hand is posed with the three middle fingers up and spread and the thumb and pinkie folded across the palm—a *W*. The left is in a loose fist, palm facing out. An *E*."

"Couldn't the right mean three?" Kitt asked. "Like the number?"

"A way of telling us there would be a third victim?" Haas offered.

"It could be. But not if this guy is using ASL. The number three is signed with the thumb and first two fingers, back of the hand out."

He signed both for them and Kitt immediately understood. "I am he," Kitt murmured. "Now 'We.' What about the Webber girl?"

Jimmy Ye seemed to be settling into the task. He selected several of the photographs and looked them over. Each of Catherine Webber's hands had been molded into what appeared to Kitt to be a number one—the index finger straight up, the others folded into the palm, forming a fist.

But the positioning of each in space was very different. The left, back of the hand out, the right positioned centrally, finger near the mouth, palm facing left.

"The left hand is signing the number one, right?" Sergeant Haas said.

"Yes. The right hand's a bit more difficult. It's in the *D* position, but I'm thinking it's the word 'Be.'"

"Why?"

"Watch." Jimmy signed it for them —hand in the *D* position, then he moved his hand straight out, away from his mouth.

"If we're meant to read it from right to left, it's saying what? To be one?" Kitt looked at Jonathan Haas. "With the victim?"

Sal arrived and crossed to them. "Joe's with his lawyer. What've you got so far?"

Kitt explained. When she had finished, Jimmy Ye jumped in. "As I explained, these interpretations are best guesses."

"Noted." He moved his gaze over the photos. "I am he. Or me and you."

"Or read the Vest and Webber scene together," Jimmy said. "We are one."

Sergeant Haas's cell phone buzzed. He excused himself to answer.

Kitt watched him go, then turned to Sal. "That works for me. Jimmy?"

He nodded. "Could be. Of course, I can't prom—"

She cut him off before he could provide another disclaimer. "One last question. Is it logical to assume that since the killer is using ASL, he's either deaf or has a family member who's deaf?"

"Not necessarily. Yes, ASL's the native language of deaf Americans as well as some hearing children born into deaf families. However, courses exist to learn ASL. As do immersion-study programs."

Kitt didn't hide her disappointment. She had liked the scenario as it would dramatically narrow the field of suspects, a field that would include Valerie Martin. "How did you learn?"

"My wife's deaf. She taught me." He paused. "Here's another option. Your guy's not familiar with ASL, but simply looking up English words in an English-ASL dictionary. They have them online. There's one that's actually animated. I could e-mail you the URL, if you want."

"That'd be great, thanks."

Sergeant Haas returned as Jimmy walked away. Kitt saw from his expression that the call hadn't pleased him. "Valerie Martin didn't return to work after lunch. The house was closed up tight, no vehicle in the garage. A neighbor directed them to the daughter's school. There, they learned her mother had checked her out just after lunch."

Sal's expression turned grim. "Let's put out an all-radio bulletin for the woman and her daughter."

"What about Joe?" Kitt asked.

"We keep him until his lawyer starts squealing. Then we'll have to book him or let him go."

"He might have an idea where Valerie headed. I'm worried about Tami. If Valerie is guilty and doesn't suspect we're onto her, the girl could be in danger."

"You want to talk to him?" Sal asked.

"I'll try. I don't think he'll be so happy to talk to me." Her cell rang and she answered. "Lundgren, here."

"It's Sorenstein. Good news. We've got us a match."

67

Tuesday, March 21, 2006
5:40 p.m.

The gun used to kill Brian had also been used to kill a woman in Dekalb, a farming community about an hour southeast of Rockford. Dekalb had two claims to fame—it was the birthplace of supermodel Cindy Crawford and was home to the Northern Illinois University campus. Many locals would add "sweet corn" to the list as a third. In fact, the community sponsored the Cornfest every August, a big street party that hosted an annual two-hundred-thousand visitors who consumed seventy tons of sweet corn.

Kitt peered over Sorenstein's shoulder at the NIBIN monitor. "It's a good match," he said. "Damn near perfect."

Sure enough, the markings on the bullet taken from Brian's body corresponded to those from the bullet of a 1989 murder.

"While I waited for you, I took the liberty of accessing LEDS."

LEDS was the state's Law Enforcement Data System. "So, what's the story?"

"A man named Frank Ballard killed his wife in 1989. He shot her between the eyes. He was arrested, tried and convicted, but the gun was never recovered. It was believed said weapon was the man's service revolver. Same make and model. Standard issue, .45 caliber Smith & Wesson.

"He was law enforcement?"

"That's right. Dekalb County sheriff's office deputy."

Kitt's thoughts raced. Law enforcement. How had that weapon, used in a murder seventeen years ago, shown up here? Now?

And what, if anything, did it have to do with the SAK and Copycat investigations?

"Anything else?" she asked.

"That's about it. Here's a printout. Figured I'd leave the rest of the detecting up to you." He grinned up at her. "Seems to me, I've earned a beer."

"You did, Sorenstein. Thanks."

His grin faded. "Brian was a friend. More than a friend. I want to nail the son of a bitch who did this."

Kitt headed back up to the VCB. She found Sal and filled him in. "I'm going to talk to Joe, see if he has any ideas where Valerie's gone. Then I thought I'd give the Dekalb sheriff's office a call. See if I can get a little more information."

"Keep me informed." He started for his office, then stopped and looked back. "Heard from Riggio?"

"Left her a message an hour or so ago. I'll give her another call, see where she's at."

A moment later, fingers crossed that the clown angle played out, she dialed her partner's cell. M.C. answered on the second ring.

"Hey, stranger," Kitt said. "Long time, no see."

"I was just listening to your message. Major developments?"

Kitt quickly filled her in about Valerie, Joe and the ballistics match. When she didn't comment, Kitt went on, "What about the clown angle?"

"It was a bust. Sorry."

Kitt admitted bitter disappointment. If the clown lead had panned out, Joe would have been a step closer to "free to go." She would have at the very least been able to offer him some reassuring information.

Or was she simply wanting to reassure herself?

"You contacted all the family members who might remember—"

"Yes. Nothing. No clowns. No magic tricks, either."

The last came out of left field. "I didn't know you were looking into that angle as well. If you'd told me, I could have saved you some time and trouble—Joe wasn't even doing magic back then."

"You're not going postal on me, are you?"

"Excuse me?"

"Just trying to go with the flow, take a joke. You know."

"It's been a long day, hasn't it?"

"You have no idea."

"I'm going to follow up on the ballistics match, see if I can get a lead on how that weapon made its way from Dekalb to here. Are you coming in?"

"Thought I'd swing by Mama's, give her my regrets in person."

"Regrets?"

"Tuesday nights are pasta night with my family."

"That's right." Kitt glanced at her watch. "Look, I'm here. Go have dinner with your family. Besides, if I need you, I'll call."

"What if I need you?"

Kitt laughed. "I'll leave my cell on all night, just in case you need saving from Mama Riggio."

"I'm getting another call, Kitt. I've got to go."

She hung up before Kitt could say goodbye. Perplexed, Kitt

COPYCAT   371

drew her eyebrows together. Something about M.C. had seemed off. Brittle. As if she had been working hard to be pleasant.

Was she pissed off about something?

Kitt holstered her phone and shifted her thoughts to Joe. She wished she'd had no part in today. But she had—and she had a job to do. If Joe was innocent, it would be proved so.

She prayed that when that happened, they could salvage what they had and make a fresh start.

She stepped into the interrogation room. Joe, who was now alone in the room, looked at her. She saw how angry he was. How hurt.

"Back for another pint of blood?" he asked.

"I'm sorry you feel that way, Joe."

"How else could I feel? This was an ambush, Kitt."

"I didn't mean it to be."

"Please. I'm not stupid. 'Just trust me,'" he said bitterly, mocking her. "And I did. What a fool."

"When I said that I meant it. Circumstances changed and I had to—"

"You had to do your job." He looked away, then back. "I wish I had a dollar for every time you said those exact words to justify your behavior. I'd be a rich man.

"I suppose what gets me," he went on, "is that even after having known each other most of our lives, after loving—and burying— a daughter, you don't have a clue who I am."

His words cut her to the quick. They hurt because she felt she *did* know him, because she loved him—and because even so, she had suspected him of being a part of this. And would continue to suspect him until evidence cleared him.

It was the nature of her job—and what that job had done to her.

What could she say to him?

She had no defense. She was guilty as charged.

"I love you, Joe. I always have."

He made a sound of pain. "You always put being a cop before me.

That's not going to change, is it? When this is over and it's clear I had nothing to do with this, it'll be something else. Some other case, some other victim."

"That's not true! When this is over and you're cleared, we—"

"There is no 'we.' I love you, Kitt. But I want more than you can give me. I have for a long time."

She held a hand out. "Let's not talk about this. Not now. Please." Her words came out rough, broken.

Broken. The way she felt inside.

She cleared her throat. Refocused. "Valerie's taken off. She didn't show up for work after she left here and she checked Tami out of school. I'm afraid for the girl."

"Of course you are," he said, tone bitter.

"I was hoping you might have some idea where they could have gone."

He made a sound, part anger, part pain. "Check with Valerie's mother. She lives in Rockton. And she has a sister in Barrington."

"You have names?"

"Mother's Rita Martin. Sister is Lori Smith."

Detective White stuck his head into the room. "Lawyer's back, Kitt."

She held a hand up, indicating he should give her a minute.

"Joe, I want you to know that I—"

He cut her off. "Forget about it. Go do your job. Catch your killer, because I'm not him."

She passed his lawyer without looking at him. Her chest hurt so badly she could hardly breathe. She wondered if things could get any worse, then acknowledged she hoped the hell not.

68

Tuesday, March 21, 2006
7:10 p.m.

Kitt hung up the phone. Her call to the Dekalb County sheriff's office had yielded little new information. The evening staff was on duty; the deputy she'd spoken with sounded all of about twelve years old.

Damn, but she was getting old.

The young deputy had promised to ask around, see if anybody on the shift had been around in 1989. In addition, if the night proved slow, he'd pull the files himself and fax them to her. At the very least, he'd leave a message for the sheriff and his chief deputy to call her in the morning.

She hung up, frustrated. In the time it would take someone to get back to her, she could be down there, thumbing through the actual file herself.

She dialed M.C. It went directly to voice mail, indicating the device was turned off. "It's me. I'm going to take a quick run down to Dekalb, to get a firsthand look at the Ballard case files. If you need me, call my cell."

She headed out of the VCB, toward the elevator. She stopped short halfway there.

"You're not going postal on me, are you?"

"Just trying to go with the flow, take a joke. You know."

Dear God. She *did* know. That day the two of them had been joking around, M.C. had said, "If we ever need to signal each other, use you're 'going postal' or 'taking a joke.'"

That's why M.C., who typically kept in constant contact, had been out of touch. Why she had sounded strained.

She was in trouble.

How had she missed it?

The clown, Kitt realized. She had been investigating the grandmother murders, had gotten a lead on the clown.

Could that be what had led her into danger? Had she gotten a name, followed up and then…what?

A sense of urgency pulling at her, Kitt turned and hurried back to her desk. There, she accessed M.C.'s mother's name, then address and phone number.

She dialed the number; it rang a dozen times with no answer. Praying she was wrong, that she'd find M.C. with her family, neck deep in pasta and one of her mother's interrogations, she hurried for the parking garage.

A short time later, she pulled up in front of a rambling, old farmhouse. A couple of cars were parked out front, though she didn't see M.C.'s Explorer.

A young woman with blond hair and blue eyes answered the door, and Kitt thought she had the wrong address.

She smiled and showed the woman her shield. "I'm Detective

Lundgren. I may have the wrong address, but I'm looking for the Riggio home."

The woman returned her smile. "You're at the right place. You're M.C.'s partner."

"That's right." She smiled. "I'm Kitt."

"I'm Melody, M.C.'s sister-in-law."

Kitt shook her hand. "I'm sorry to interrupt the family meal, I was looking for—"

"Mel, who is it?"

A tall, good-looking man appeared at the dining room doorway. That he was one of M.C.'s brothers was unmistakable.

"This is Kitt Lundgren," Melody said. "M.C.'s partner."

He stepped forward, hand out. "I'm Neil. Her respectable brother."

"And my husband," Melody added.

Kitt shook his hand. "I apologize for interrupting your family dinner. But I needed to speak with M.C. Is she here?"

He looked confused. "She's not here." He looked at his wife. "Was Mary Catherine coming by tonight?"

"Not that I know of."

Kitt moved her gaze between the two, a feeling of dread growing. "Isn't tonight pasta night?"

Neil smiled. "That's tomorrow night. We just stopped by to see—"

"Melody, Neil?"

They all turned. Mama Riggio herself stood in the doorway. All five foot one inch of her. From her steel-gray hair to her black orthopedic shoes, Mama Riggio looked like a woman who insisted on being taken seriously.

"Mama," Neil said, "this is M.C.'s partner, Detective Lundgren."

The woman's gaze sharpened. "Just who I want to talk to! Come and eat. Melody, set another place."

The younger woman scurried to do it; Kitt stopped her.

"No, don't, Melody. I really can't sta—"

"I insist!" The woman used a gesture that suggested finality. "I want to hear about this man she's seeing. She's been secretive. I wouldn't have even known if Michael hadn't—"

Lance Castrogiovanni.

The funny man.

"Mama," Neil scolded, "now's not the ti—"

The woman shushed him and went on, though Kitt's thoughts raced. She had no concrete reason to believe Lance Castrogiovanni had anything to do with M.C.'s disappearance, but she couldn't shake the feeling that he did.

"I've got to go," she said, backing toward the door. "Sorry, Mrs. Riggio. But thank you for the invitation."

She turned and hurried out the door and to her Taurus.

Neil followed her. "Detective Lundgren, wait!"

She stopped and turned. He reached her, searched her gaze. "Something's wrong, isn't it?"

She saw his concern. She worked to cover her own. "I don't know that, Neil."

"I'm going to try her cell phone."

"I already did."

Fear tightened his features. "How can I help?"

"What do you know about Lance Castrogiovanni?"

"Who?"

"The man M.C.'s been seeing."

"Clearly, not as much as you do. I know she liked him."

"Any idea how they met? Or where he liv…" Kitt let the words trail off, seeing from his expression that he was clueless.

"If you hear from her, let me know right away."

As she made a move to go, he caught her arm. "I can't just sit and do nothing."

"I'm afraid you're going to have to." She slipped her arm from his grasp. "I'll keep you posted."

After she had climbed into her vehicle and pulled away from the curb, she checked in with the CRU. No word from Riggio. She called Sal at home and after hearing her out, he agreed to an all-radio bulletin for M.C. and her SUV. He also advised her to call in Allen and White, to help track every step M.C. took since that morning.

She did as he suggested. Allen and White were none to happy to hear from her—until they learned the reason.

As she hung up with them, she got another call. Praying it was Riggio, she answered, "Lundgren here."

"This is Deputy Roberts, Dekalb County sheriff's office. I understand you're looking into the Mimi Ballard murder."

Not M.C. But second best. "That's right. One of our officers was shot and killed by an unknown subject on Monday night. We got a ballistics match with the gun used to kill Ballard."

"After all these years? Wow."

"Do you remember the case?"

"I do. I was only fifteen then, but my dad was a deputy. It was a very big deal. As I'm sure you know, this is a rural community. Not a lot of murders around here. And certainly not ones like that."

He went on. "Guy's name was Frank Ballard. Whipped her with a belt, then shot her dead. His prints were all over the belt."

"But the gun wasn't found."

"Until now, apparently. Wonder how it turned up there, seventeen years after the fact?"

"That's precisely what I'm trying to find out. What can you tell me about the murder? The stuff I won't find in the file."

"Ballard was pretty well-thought-of. Not everybody's best friend, but a solid cop. You know what I mean?"

She did. The kind who didn't yuk it up with the guys a lot, just did his job. She told him to go on.

"Everybody was shocked. He claimed his innocence, but was convicted, anyway. As far as I know, he's still serving time.

"Wife was from a local farming family. They owned a big spread, she inherited it all when her father died. Ballard had sold everything but the house and a couple of acres to Green Giant. ConAgra now, I think. But isn't everybody?"

She made an agreeable sort of sound and let him ramble. "Still owned the house until recently. Seems a young couple bought it."

"Anything else about the murder that was unusual?"

"His wife was deaf."

"Say again."

"She was deaf. Which made it all the more horrible. That and the fact the little boy found her. Or was it a girl?"

"They had children? How many?"

"I'm not as clear on that. Two, I think. A boy and a girl."

"Can you remember their names? Their ages?"

"Like I said, it was seventeen years ago. And we lived in Sycamore, a whole different school district, so I'm really fuzzy on this. It might've been just one kid."

The SAK and his Copycat. Brother and sister.

That's how they knew each other. And she would bet one of them had been ten years old.

"Look," she said, hearing the urgency in her own voice, "this is priority. I believe that gun—and its shooter—are also linked to a series of child murders here. I need you to get me those children's names and what happened to them."

"I'll get back to you." He hung up.

CRU rang. "A cruiser located Detective Riggio's vehicle. Corner of North Main and Auburn. They're waiting for further orders."

"Tell them to stay put. I'm on my way."

Tuesday, March 21, 2006
8:40 p.m.

Kitt pulled in behind the cruiser, killed the engine and climbed out. The two officers exited their vehicle and met her at the driver's door of the Explorer.

"Flashlight," Kitt said. The officer closest to her handed over his. She snapped it on and shined it into the SUV. Nothing looked out of order.

"We tried the doors and found them all locked."

She nodded. "Let's open it up."

The second officer jogged to the cruiser, got a shim and jogged back. Within moments, he had the vehicle open.

She checked in the glove box and console, under the seats, in the cargo hold. It was clean.

M.C. had parked the vehicle. She had locked it, taken her phone, jacket and investigation notes.

Kitt snapped off the Maglite and handed it back to the patrolman. She scanned up and down the street. Her gaze settled on the Main Street Diner and its neon Open All Night sign.

M.C. had pointed the diner out to her. She had eaten cream pie there, four slices. With a guy.

Her funny man?

Kitt instructed the two patrolmen to wait at the SUV and darted across the street to the restaurant. They had a decent-size crowd for a Tuesday night. The woman at the register smiled at her.

Kitt returned the smile and crossed to her. Her name tag read Betty.

"Hi, Betty, I'm looking for an acquaintance of mine. He comes here a lot. Name's Lance."

"Oh, sure. Lance Castrogiovanni. He's in all the time."

"Was he in tonight?"

"No. Sorry."

"He live around here?"

The woman's demeanor became less friendly. "Why do you want to know?"

"Because I need to speak with him." Kitt took out her shield and held it up for the woman. "It's urgent."

Betty looked upset. "He's not in any trouble, is he?"

Being even remotely honest would only confuse her. After all, Lance Castrogiovanni could be nose deep in shit, or sitting pretty, smelling like a rose.

"I'm actually looking for a woman he's seeing, a fellow police officer. Mary Catherine Riggio. M.C. for short."

Her smile returned. "That nice policewoman. They were in one night, he introduced us. Come to think of it, I thought I saw her this afternoon."

A minute later, Kitt was on the street, armed with Lance's address. Two doors down, upstairs. An apartment above the head shop. She collected the patrolmen, instructed one to wait downstairs, the other to accompany her up.

She rapped on the door. Then called out. When she got no answer, she tried the door—and found it locked.

M.C.'s SUV and Betty believing she had seen her earlier was enough to convince Kitt she had just cause to enter the apartment uninvited.

She hoped a judge saw it the same way.

"Kick it in," she said.

The lock gave easily and they entered, guns drawn. The apartment appeared empty. Other than what she would call usual household clutter, it was clean.

Just cause to enter did not grant them the rights of a search warrant. They had reason to believe M.C. was there and that she needed their help. If the apartment became a crime scene that scenario changed.

They made their way through. Nothing in the living room. Uneaten turkey sandwich on the kitchen counter. Bathroom empty. Kitt pulled back the shower curtain, found the tub clean. The bed was unmade. She checked under it, then crossed to the closet.

Nothing. She started to close the door when a spot of bright orange caught her eye. Peeking out from a box in the bottom of the closet.

As she stared at the spot of orange, her cell phone vibrated.

She unclipped it. "Lundgren here."

"It's White. I've got a name for you. The clown who performed at the Walton B. Johnson retirement community was Lance—"

"Castrogiovanni," she finished for him.

"That's right. How'd you—"

She handed the phone to the surprised patrolman, then bent and yanked the cardboard box from the closet. She flipped back the flaps, reached in and pulled out a bright orange clown's wig.

70

Tuesday, March 21, 2006
10:10 p.m.

M.C. came to. She hurt all over. She opened her eyes to a deep black. Moving her gaze over the darkness, she searched for a light source and found none.

Her hands were bound behind her back with duct tape. Her feet were also bound with the tape. She lay on her side on a cool, damp floor. A basement, she decided. That explained the damp and the absolute dark.

She maneuvered herself into a sitting position. She tasted blood on her tongue. The blood brought it all rushing back. She'd gotten to Lance's. They'd embraced. He had held her tightly, almost desperately. He loved her, he had said fiercely.

Her funny man had been anything but lighthearted. She remembered thinking it was almost as if he thought it was the end.

The end.

She grimaced. The end of them. Of her.

Good night, Gracie.

She didn't know which tasted more foul against her tongue—the blood or the bitterness of betrayal.

M.C. forced thoughts of betrayal back. That didn't matter now, clearing her head and finding a means of escape did. He'd gone to the kitchen for her sandwich. She'd gotten a call. Wanda, the Walton B. Johnson Center's former director. She had remembered the clown's name. She had been almost giddy about the fact that she had been able to recall it after all these years, and at her age, too.

"Lance Castrogiovanni."

M.C. had been speechless. Phone to her ear, she had stared at Lance, walking toward her with her sandwich. Even as disbelief and betrayal had rushed over her, with her free hand she had gone for her gun.

In the next instant a searing pain had shot through her head and the lights had gone out.

Someone else had been in the apartment.

His accomplice. Together they were the SAK and Copycat? Not adversaries, but working as a team. It had been one of her and Kitt's theories.

M.C. struggled to recall a detail from the moment before she had been knocked out, something that might offer a clue to the accomplice's identity, but came up empty.

When she had come to, she and Lance had been alone. Or so it had seemed. Her hands and feet had been bound. He'd had a gun. A revolver. Looked like a .45 caliber Smith & Wesson.

The .45 Smith & Wesson used to kill Brian?

He'd been crying. His hands shaking as he held the gun to her head. She'd half expected him to pull the trigger by mistake, he'd been so rattled. He'd told her to call Kitt, assure her everything was all right. Tell her that the clown lead had dead-ended.

She had done what he asked to buy time. M.C. had known that when she went missing, Kitt would check every source herself. She had tried to tip off Kitt with their joke about signaling each other with "going postal" and "taking a joke," then with the reference to pasta night.

Nothing had clicked with the other woman—M.C. had been able to tell by her response. But it would—especially when M.C. turned up AWOL.

Of course, by then it might be too late. For her, anyway.

She'd tried to reason with him. Tried to convince him to reconsider. Free her and turn himself in. Turn in his accomplice. Didn't he love her? she'd asked. Didn't he trust her to try to help him?

Lance's demeanor had done a one-eighty. In the blink of an eye, he had transformed from weepy and frightened to enraged. He had struck her with the butt of the gun.

It was the last thing she remembered until now.

M.C. heard a door open and shut, then the sound of footfalls on stairs. Wooden stairs, she realized as one creaked.

She stared into the darkness, waiting. After a moment, Lance emerged from the darkness.

"Hello, Mary Catherine," he said softly.

She didn't respond and he crossed to her. He knelt down and gently cupped her face in his hands. She felt them tremble. "Are you all right?"

She still didn't respond. She didn't trust herself to. She feared she might curse him, or spit in his face. She wasn't certain what had set him off last time, but she didn't want to do it again.

Nor was she convinced her skull could take many more blows. The last had been a doozy.

"It looks like it hurts." He trailed a finger over her temple, over what she was certain was an angry-looking knot. "I'm so, so sorry. I didn't mean for any of this to happen."

"Then make it un-happen, Lance."

He kissed her; she tasted his tears. She wanted to retch. Instead, she played along. "Free my hands. They hurt, Lance. My arms hurt."

"I can't. I'm sorry, M.C."

"I won't try to escape. I promise."

He looked incredibly sad. "I wish I could believe that."

"I love you, Lance. Why would I run away?"

She nearly choked on the words. She *had* thought she loved him. How could he have fooled her so completely?

"I wish I could believe— So many things, M.C. I wish so many things."

He kissed her again. His breath smelled fresh, like peppermint. As if he'd just sucked on a candy.

"He would be so angry," he said. "Angrier than he already is."

"Who, Lance?"

"The Beast." He said it on a whisper, as if afraid of being over-heard.

Her heartbeat quickened. His partner. The one who had struck her the first time. And the one, she suspected, who was calling the shots.

"I'm sorry, for earlier," he said again. "I didn't want to hit you."

"Then why did you?"

"He expected it."

"The Beast?"

"Yes. But I don't want to talk about him."

"What do you want to talk about?"

"My family. I promised to tell you about them. I want you to un-derstand."

"I want to understand, Lance. Tell me about them."

"Not now. Later."

He stood. She saw that he shook.

"What are you afraid of?" she asked. "You know I'll help you. I'll protect you."

He shook his head. "He protects me. He always has. We're one."

"You love him more than me?"

"You don't understand."

"Make me understand. Please, Lance."

"I can't survive without him. I tried."

His voice grew thick. "I'm sorry, Mary Catherine." He turned to go. She called him back.

"You killed those girls, didn't you?"

He looked down at her. Regretfully. "I didn't want to."

"Then why did you do it?"

"He wanted me to."

"And you do everything he asks?"

"I'll be back."

"No, wait!" She struggled against the duct tape, trying to loosen it, getting nowhere. "Are you going to kill me, Lance? Because he wants you to?"

He walked away without responding. She fought the feeling of panic that rose up in her. "You don't have to," she called. "You control your own destiny. Nobody else has that power."

She heard his footfalls, the stairs creak. "Lance, please—"

The door snapped shut and she was once again alone in the dark.

Tuesday, March 21, 2006
10:50 p.m.

From the minute Kitt alerted the RPD of her discovery, things happened fast. A team converged on Lance's apartment. ID, Sal and Sergeant Haas. Half the VCB—awaiting news of M.C. and orders. They didn't care if it took all night; they had come to help Riggio and to catch a monster.

This was the break they had been waiting five years for.

Valerie and Tami had been located at her sister's in Barrington. Valerie had claimed she had run to her sister for help "nursing her broken heart." When confronted, she admitted she had lied about Joe's alibi. She had wanted to hurt him. The way he had hurt her.

She was en route to the PSB for further questioning.

Alibi in place and powerful evidence incriminating Lance, Joe had been released. Sal had delivered that bit of news with a reassuring smile and a gentle squeeze to her shoulder. Kitt had been only partly reassured—Joe was not going to forgive her for this.

In the meantime, Allen and White had made another discovery—weeks before her murder, Marianne Vest had attended a birthday party where a clown performed. In addition, the day of Julie Entzel's party at the Fun Zone, the young man who wore the Sammy Squirrel costume had been sick. They'd hired a substitute— Lance Castrogiovanni.

No doubt more links would be uncovered. That's the way some investigations were—totally mind-boggling until the one piece was uncovered that revealed all the rest.

But had the piece come too late?

M.C. Where could he have taken her?

Kitt paced, frantic. She racked her brain, replaying the facts in her head. Lance had performed for Rose McGuire at her retirement community. He had been at the Fun Zone the day of Julie Entzel's party and had probably been the clown Marianne Vest had seen.

Lance was adopted. A computer search had revealed that information and the names and addresses of his parents. Cruisers had already been dispatched.

They didn't yet have confirmation that he was related to Frank and Mimi Ballard, but Kitt believed they would. She would bet Lance was the little boy who had found his deaf mother shot to death.

Dekalb. The family home.

Kitt rushed over to Sal. "I know where they are, Sal. Dekalb."

Her superior laid a hand over the mouthpiece of his phone. "One minute, Kitt. I'm updating the chief."

The big kahuna, chief of police. She didn't give a shit. "I don't have a minute. I know where he took M.C."

"I'll call you right back." He snapped his phone shut. "Outside. Now."

She followed him out to the front of the building. The area had been cordoned off. A sizable crowd had gathered.

"I know where they are," she repeated.

"Dekalb. How do you figure?"

"The Dekalb deputy I spoke with mentioned a family home. Said that it had only been sold recently, to a young couple."

"I'll call down there, get them to send a unit over."

"Request permission to go myself."

"Denied. I need you here."

"I know I'm right about this, Sal. I need to be the one who—"

"Denied. Discussion over."

"Dammit, Sal!" She caught his arm. "This is my case! M.C.'s my partner! I'm not going to sit here twiddling my thumbs while—"

"You're mistaken, Detective. This is *my* case. Riggio's *my* detective. Back off, right now."

"Yes, sir! Backing off, sir!" She spun on her heel, heading for her car.

"Where the hell do you think you're going, Lundgren?"

"To cool off. Do I need permission for that, too?"

"Five minutes," he said. "Then I want you back upstairs."

Five minutes later, Kitt was heading toward Dekalb. She acknowledged that Deputy Chief of Detectives Salvador Minelli was going to be really pissed off when he realized what she had done. He might even ask for her badge.

He could have it. M.C. was her partner and friend. And this was her case. Peanut had made it hers.

She tried Deputy Roberts. She got him. He was frazzled. "Sorry, Detective, I'll have to call you back. We have an incident here."

"Wait! The Ballard family home, where is it?"

"I've got to go, Detective!"

He hung up. Kitt frowned and glanced at the dash clock. Fifteen minutes. Sal may have realized by now she had decided to disobey direct orders. But maybe not—he was a little busy right now.

She dialed the Dekalb County sheriff's office. "This is Detective Lundgren with the Rockford PD. I believe my chief of detectives called and requested a unit to check out a residence in your jurisdiction?"

When the woman didn't respond, Kitt feared the gig was up. Then the line crackled and she answered. "Yes, Detective. How can I help you?"

"He's instructed me to accompany them."

"They've already been dispatched."

"I'll meet them."

"Do you have the location?"

She said she didn't and the woman rattled off an address, then directions.

"Shall I notify them?" she asked Kitt.

"Yes, thank you."

As she ended the call, another came in. She saw it was Sal.

Sorry, Sal, I seem to have a bad case of selective hearing tonight. I never even heard it ring.

The woman's directions proved easy to follow, which was surprising as the farmhouse was literally in the middle of cornfields.

She took the long gravel drive to the house. She saw the deputy's cruiser sitting out front. Not a light showed from the house or the ramshackle outbuildings situated around it.

She climbed out of her car. The deputy met her. "Detective Kitt Lundgren. Rockford PD."

"Deputy Shanks. I rang the bell. Got no answer, so I did a spin around the property. Doors and windows are all secure. Nothing out of order on the inside. House appears deserted."

"You checked the outbuildings?"

"I did. Nothing."

"A vehicle?"

"Unless you count a broken-down tractor, no."

"Mind if I take a look around myself?"

"Have at it."

She did, taking her time. She checked every door and window on the ground level, shone her flashlight through every window. When she found nothing, she moved on to the various sheds.

She would have come to the same conclusion as Deputy Shanks if not for the prickle at the back of her neck.

They were there.

The SAK. And his Copycat. M.C. was with them.

She swept her gaze over the house's dark facade.

She wanted inside.

The good deputy wasn't going to allow that.

She turned to the young man. "Looks like our lead was a dead end."

"Looks that way. I'm sorry, Detective."

"Thanks for coming all the way out here."

"No problem at all."

They crossed to their vehicles. The deputy opened his door, then looked back at her. "By the way, who're you looking for?"

"Child killer. We think he has my partner."

"Oh, man. Damn."

"Yeah, that," she said. "And worse."

Say you wish you could help.

He made a move to climb into his vehicle, then stopped. "This that Copycat guy?"

"We believe so, yes."

"Sorry. Shit."

Offer to do something more. I'll take you up on it.

Instead, he climbed into his cruiser. She hesitated a moment, then followed his lead. They started their vehicles and headed down the gravel drive. At the end of the drive, he took a right, heading in the opposite direction she had come.

She smiled because he was making it easy for her. *Thank you very much, Deputy Shanks.*

Kitt took the left, drove two and a half miles, then U-turned and headed back. She cut her lights when she reached the gravel drive.

She rolled slowly toward the house, the crunch of the tires on the gravel deafening in the still night.

She eased her Taurus around back, behind the garage. She wouldn't put it past the deputy to ride by again, just to make certain everything was secure.

Before she climbed out, she retrieved her flashlight from the glove box and checked her weapon. She reholstered her cell phone and pocketed her car keys.

The back door lock proved flimsy, and she was standing in the farmhouse kitchen in moments. A big, old-fashioned kitchen, she saw. Looked as if it hadn't been updated since the fifties.

And it was, obviously, empty. She snapped on the pencil light and made her way through the doorway that led into a living room. She moved the beam over the room. Furniture covered in sheets. The stale, airless smell of a place that had been closed up for a long time.

The dining room was completely empty, as was the bedroom on the main floor. Next, Kitt crept up the stairs. Several of them creaked; each time she stopped, held her breath and listened. No one came running. No alarms sounded. Nothing.

If anyone else was in the house they, like her, were trying to be very quiet.

She reached the top landing. The bathroom lay directly across the hall. She crossed to it, eased open the door with her fingertips.

It had recently been used. A roll of toilet paper sat on the floor by the toilet. She stared at the paper, heart pounding.

That meant the water supply to the house had been turned on.

She tiptoed to the sink and put her finger under the faucet—and found it damp.

A moment later, she saw that one of the bedrooms had been slept in. A rumpled sleeping bag lay on the floor under a window. Beside it sat several Coke cans and candy bar wrappers.

She started toward the bag, then froze at the faint sound of voices. Kitt snapped off the flashlight. Where were they coming from? she wondered, straining to locate the source.

The floor vent at her feet.

She knelt beside it to listen. Voices, definitely. So faint she couldn't determine if they were male or female or how many people were speaking.

Where were they? She had searched the entire hou—

The basement, she realized. An old farmhouse like this one would have had a basement, but she hadn't seen a door.

Kitt made her way back down to the first floor. Knowing she wasn't alone, she kept her light off and weapon out, and moved as quietly as she could.

She found the door. Nearly seamless, tucked into the space under the stairs, she had walked right by it earlier. Kitt pressed her ear close.

Nothing.

The silence caused a clammy chill to settle in the small of her back. Voices meant life. A conversation involved more than one person.

She grabbed the knob, gently turned it.

The door was locked.

Kitt nearly cried out in frustration. She laid her ear to the door again. Someone humming. A man. The sound growing louder.

He was coming up the stairs!

She looked frantically around for a place to hide. *The sheet-draped furniture.* She scrambled for the nearest piece, what appeared to be a hulking chair. A key turned in a lock. Crouching behind the chair, she had full view of the doorway. She took aim.

The door swung outward, shielding the man. He left it open. A moment later, she heard the kitchen door open, then swing shut.

Apparently, he hadn't noticed it was unlocked. That had been a stupid mistake on her part. If he did, he would realize she was there, and depending on where he was headed, he could see her car.

She could go after him, but M.C.'s safety was her first priority. Scrambling out from behind the chair, she darted for the open door.

The basement was dark; she snapped on her pencil light and circled the room with it. Typical basement stuff. Metal shelves stacked with all manner of things

M.C. wasn't there. She frowned and moved the beam over the room again, wishing for a more powerful flashlight.

"M.C.," she whispered, as loudly as she felt she could. "Are you here?"

"Here," the other woman called. "I'm here."

Thank God. Kitt hurried in the direction of M.C.'s voice. A wall. Holstering her Glock and holding the pencil light between her teeth, she felt her way across the wall.

"Where are you?" she asked again.

"I don't know."

The sound had definitely come from behind the wall. Another room. A hidden room behind this one.

But where was the door?

From the room above came the sound of footfalls. He was coming back! Quickly, she snapped off her light and ducked behind a group of moving boxes.

A moment later, he trotted down the stairs. Humming again. A tune from *Oklahoma!*

He carried a can of Coke and a straw.

She studied the tall, thin man. She recognized him from his DMV photo she'd called up, though he was better-looking in real life. She saw why M.C. had been attracted to him—he possessed a kind of boyish good looks. Very nonthreatening. Like a redheaded Peter Pan.

Further confirmation her mother had been right—*never judge a book by its cover.*

He crossed to the battered bookcase, crowded with a mishmash of junk. He picked up what appeared to be a television remote control, pushed a button and the bookcase swung open.

A safe room. Shit.

Most safe-room doors were made of reinforced, bulletproof

steel. Once he closed the door behind him, short of dynamite, she wouldn't be able to get inside until he opened it again.

She would not allow him to lock himself inside that room with M.C.

Luckily his back was to her. Kitt eased from her hiding place, weapon out. She took aim, preparing to fire.

Still humming, he tossed the remote back on the shelf and stepped through the doorway.

Kitt let out a relieved breath. Now she knew how to get in. All she had to do was wait for the right moment.

Wednesday, March 22, 2006
12:35 a.m.

At the soft swish of the door opening, M.C. braced herself. Not Kitt, she knew. Not yet. She had heard Lance on the stairs, his humming. Kitt would wait. Until she was certain M.C. was safe. Until she was confident she could take Lance down.

Until she was certain she had no other choice.

"Mary Catherine," he called softly. "I've got your drink."

He came to her and knelt before her. He held the can and straw to her lips. She sipped the sweet, cold drink. It washed away the taste of the blood. She could almost feel the rush of the sugar entering her system.

"I was so thirsty."

"More?"

She nodded and took several more sips, then pulled back. "Thank you."

He sat cross-legged on the floor in front of her. She saw he had the revolver jammed into the waistband of his pants.

"I hope you have the safety on," she said. "If not, you'll have a whole new set of one-liners for your act."

"That's what I loved about you, Mary Catherine. You always got me, you know?"

Loved. Past tense.

Not good.

He looked genuinely regretful. "I wish things could have ended differently between us."

Different than me dying or you going to prison? Gee, Lance, you think?

"We can write our own ending," she said. "Our very own happily-ever-after."

"Happily-ever-after," he repeated, tone wistful. "I believed in those, a long time ago."

"Believe again," she said. "It's not too late."

"It is. It's... You don't understand."

"You keep saying that. Tell me about the Beast. And about your family."

He was quiet a moment, then began. She saw that he trembled. "Mother was special."

"Deaf?"

"Yes. She never heard. Even when we told her. She didn't protect us from him."

"Who?"

"Father."

"He hurt you?"

"Yes."

"I'm sorry. That was wrong. No one should ever hurt a child."

"No. Never."

"You hurt children, Lance. You killed them."

"No. The angels are sleeping."

"Dead," she corrected him.

"Beautiful. Peaceful. No more pain."

"What about Marianne Vest?"

He grimaced. "I don't want to talk about her."

"Who are you, Lance? The Sleeping Angel Killer? His Copycat?"

"We're one. It was always just the two of us."

"You and the Beast."

"Yes. The Other One. He protected me. As best he could."

He. A brother.

"He came up with the plan to save us."

"What was it?"

"We killed her. After."

"After what?"

"After he beat her."

"So, your father hurt her, too?"

He nodded. "We used his gun. He loved his gun."

The Smith & Wesson.

"Then we hid it. Nobody ever suspected us."

"They do now, Lance." She said it softly. "Because of the gun. You used it to kill Brian, didn't you?"

"I killed him because he was bothering you. I tried to talk to him first, explain that you and I were together. He laughed at me. So, I followed him to that motel and I shot him."

"Your brother, was he angry?"

"He doesn't know."

"He's going to know now. They traced the gun."

He sat quietly, face expressionless. She went on, "That call I took, at your apartment. It was a woman from the Walton B. Johnson Center. She remembered your name. They're going to look for me; people knew we had been seeing each other."

"It's over, isn't it?"

His words came out choked. She felt for the little boy whose life had gone so terribly awry. That such evil existed, that it was so often directed toward children, broke her heart.

"It doesn't have to be," she said. "Free me. We'll go to the police. I'll try to help you."

He curled into himself and rocked back and forth, like a small child seeking comfort. "It's my fault, all my fault. I'm stupid. And careless, just like he says."

"You're not stupid, Lance."

"He's all I have. He's going to be angry, so angry."

"I'll protect you."

"You can't." He met her eyes, the expression in his hollow and hopeless. "Only he can."

The hair on the back of her neck prickled. He meant to kill her. He was sweating and shaking.

Lance Castrogiovanni didn't enjoy killing; weirdly, he felt it was his duty.

"Don't do this, Lance!" she cried loudly, to signal Kitt. "We can make it work. I'll go to my chief and—"

Sobbing now, he stood and went for the Smith & Wesson.

The same moment her cop's sixth sense alerted her that Kitt was in the room, she stepped out of the shadows.

"Put your gun on the floor at your feet, Lance," Kitt said softly. "Then turn around slowly, hands in the air."

73

Wednesday, March 22, 2006
12:45 a.m.

Lance did as Kitt asked. Gun at his feet, he turned to face her. She was surprised by his expression—he looked relieved, almost grateful.

Lance Castrogiovanni didn't want to kill anyone else.

"That's good," she said. "Keep your hands up and step away from Detective Riggio." Again, he did as she requested. She motioned him toward the wall. "Hands up. Feet apart."

She frisked him for another weapon, then cuffed him. "You have the right to remain silent, you son of a bitch. You have the right to—"

Her cell phone vibrated. She let it go while she finished reading him his rights, then flipped it open as she crossed to free M.C. "Lundgren here."

"Hello, Kitten."

She had expected to hear Sal's very angry voice. She had expected to be sharing this good news and minimizing the trouble she was in.

She smiled grimly. This was a very satisfying runner-up. "How nice to hear from you now. This very minute."

"And why's that?"

"Because I've won. I know who you are. I have your accomplice, the so-called Copycat here with me. Or should I call him your brother?"

He laughed softly, the sound unconcerned.

"Perhaps you think I'm joking," she said. "I assure you, that's not the ca—"

"Do you have your weapon, Kitten?"

"Of course. And it's aimed at your brother's head."

"What a coincidence. But you'll understand why in a moment. For now, I'd like you to lay down *your* gun. Then turn around with *your* hands in the air."

This time it was she who laughed. "Now, why would I do that?"

"Because, once again, I hold all the cards."

The lights snapped on. Kitt made a sound of surprise. And revulsion.

They were standing in a kind of art gallery. On display were photographs, matted and framed. Very professional.

Of all the little angels.

Photos of them very much alive—at school and at play, shopping with their mothers, exiting church, daydreaming, laughing.

Six beautiful little girls, their whole lives ahead of them.

Tears swamped her. That wasn't all. On the wall were images of them in death. She recognized each girl; this vision of them had been burned onto her brain long before today.

She shifted her gaze. The grandmothers were represented as well. In life—and in their gruesome deaths.

They reminded her of crime scene pho—

"Hello, Lundgren."

He stepped into the room. She heard M.C.'s sharply drawn breath, even as she registered her own shock.

Kitt turned slowly to face him.

Snowe from ID.

She choked back the cry that raced to her lips. *And he had Joe.*

He held a gun to Joe's head. He had sealed Joe's mouth with duct tape and shackled his wrists behind his back. Judging by Joe's bloodied face, he had put up a fight.

"I see by your expression that I am, indeed, the one in charge here." Snowe lowered his voice. "You shouldn't have told me what you cared about, Kitten."

He meant Joe. That night on the phone, she had told him how much she loved him. "Let him go, Snowe. Please, he—"

"Lay the gun on the floor, then kick it my way."

She did, though he didn't make a move to retrieve it. "Do you like my memorial gallery?" he asked, sounding pleased with himself. "Beautiful, aren't they?"

"They're vile."

"Capture the memories," he mused. "Didn't some photographic company use that as a slogan?"

"You're a sick bastard."

"Remove the handcuffs from my brother's wrists."

"Do it yourself."

"Bad idea, Kitten. If I undo the cuffs myself, you and your ex here won't be alive to see it."

She obeyed, thoughts racing, searching for a way out of this. She glanced at M.C. and saw by her intent expression that she was doing the same.

"Back up," Snowe ordered. "I want you where I can see you."

She did. He nodded. "Lance, take her gun. Give it to me."

Lance hurried to do what he asked, flushing at the disgust in his brother's voice.

"Now pick up the Smith & Wesson. Stick it back in your pants, little man. We'll talk about *that* later."

"Why are you talking to him like that?" M.C. demanded. "He's not a child. He's not stupid."

"You," Snowe said, "can shut the fuck up. Or be shot."

Kitt jumped in, not putting it past M.C. to test Snowe's resolve. She knew from their conversations, he would neither hesitate nor show mercy. "Let Joe go," she begged. "He has nothing to do with this. Please, he—"

"Of course he's a part of this. He was my last move, my final bargaining chip. Grow up, Kitten."

M.C. snorted with disgust, struggling to free herself. "You're a police officer. How could you betray your oath this way?"

Kitt held her breath, wondering if Snowe would shoot the other woman; instead he laughed.

"A police officer? Law enforcement? You think I give a shit about our *oath?*" He released Joe with a shove that sent him stumbling forward. He landed face-first with a sickening crack.

Kitt screamed his name and leaped forward. The blast of Snowe's gun discharging ricocheted off the walls, drowning out a second scream—M.C.'s.

It took Kitt a moment of blinding pain to realize that Snowe had shot her. Just like that.

Kitt's legs gave and she sank to her knees. She brought a hand to her chest, near her collarbone. It was wet, sticky. She felt light-headed.

Room spinning, she shifted her gaze to Joe. He lay completely still. Blood leaked from his nose. Not dead, she prayed. Please, not dead.

She'd always vowed she'd solve the Sleeping Angel case, if it was the last thing she ever did.

It looked like it just might be the last thing.

"A nonfatal wound," Snowe said, tone conversational. "Of course, you could bleed to death, if you don't get treatment."

Her stomach rolled, and she fought being sick.

"Our old man was the law. Oh, yeah, carried a gun and wore a badge. He was smarter and stronger than everyone else. Especially me and Lance."

He glanced at his brother. "Isn't that right, Lance? We were stupid and worthless and weak. Isn't that what he told us? He proved it with his fists."

Lance didn't reply. Kitt saw that he was staring at her, a kind of horror in his eyes.

Snowe didn't seem to notice. "Who's stupid now? We outsmarted them all, little bro. You and me."

"But we didn't," Lance whispered. "They know who we are. What we did."

"And whose fault is that?"

"Mine."

"That's right. Stupid little shit. What was the first rule?"

"Never use the gun."

"That's right. But you did. And now we're fucked."

Lance hung his head. Kitt stepped in. If she was going to die, anyway, at least she would die having learned not just who had murdered the angels—but why as well.

"So you killed all those girls…and the three grandmothers, simply to prove you could? That you could outsmart us all with your so-called 'perfect crimes'?"

"Glad to know you were listening."

"Why girls? Why ten-year-olds?"

He shrugged. "Why not?"

"You just picked."

"Yep. That's the key, right? Randomness."

She pressed a hand to her wound in an attempt to stem the flow of blood. "Why me?"

"That's a rather complicated question and I wouldn't want you to get the wrong idea. The Sleeping Angels were mine," he said. "My idea, my perfect crimes. Every aspect of the planning and preparation.

"Lance here got the bright idea to resurrect the Sleeping Angel Killer. So you see, I was being honest, there was a Copycat. My brother and partner."

It had been one of her and M.C.'s theories.

"I don't know why he did, I guess he wanted to prove to me that he could pull it off on his own. That he was his own man." There was no denying the disgust in his tone. He made no secret of the fact he had little respect for his younger brother. "He added his own twist to the murders."

"The hands," she said.

"The hands," he agreed with a sneer. "Felt like he had to express himself. But we both know, when a killer starts expressing himself, it's the beginning of the end."

"Maybe he wanted to be caught," Kitt said. "And be free of you?"

He ignored that. "So I decided to play along. Kick the competition up a notch."

"By calling me."

"Yes. He had nothing to do with that. He had nothing to do with the clues."

"The storage locker and its contents. They were your mother's things, weren't they?"

"Yes."

"And Buddy Brown?"

"That was me. My red herring. I'd busted him years ago, knew he'd gotten out. I paid him a little visit. All care and concern for his future." He smiled. "Mentioned I heard Joe Lundgren hired ex-cons. That Valerie Martin's little girl is deaf was sheer, beautiful serendipity."

Kitt thought of how he had played her—how she had fit the pieces together just as he had expected her to. "And Joe's number on Brian's phone log?"

"Never there. I put the log together, simply added his number. Who was going to check up on *me*?"

She glanced at Joe again, sick with guilt. How could she have suspected him of this?

"Don't feel too bad," Snowe said softly, as if reading her mind. "You got the locker contents belonging to a woman right, that the SAK was a cop. So you scored a few rounds. Which, by the way, brings me to you.

"In our calls, I was honest with you. I chose you because we're two of a kind. We've been hurt by those who should have loved us. We're fighters. Fallen cops. And because, despite being broken, there's so much strength in you."

"You were in my house."

"Several times."

"You read my journal."

It wasn't a question, but he grinned and answered anyway. "Yes. Very enjoyable reading, by the way." He lowered his voice, tone becoming almost tender. "This could have gone either way."

"It went my way. It's over for you."

He shook his head. "I so admire your spunk. You're going to die, Kitten. And so is Riggio and your beloved Joe. I'm sorry."

Lance looked sick. "I don't want us to hurt them, Scott."

"Of course you don't. Because you're weak. I'll take care of them. I'll take care of us. The way I always have. It's you and me, buddy. Like it's always been."

"But Mary Catherine—"

"You don't love her. She used you—"

"That's not true!" M.C. said, sounding desperate. "Don't listen, Lance, he's—"

"You, shut up!"

"She said she'd help me," Lance said. "That she'd help us."

"She's a liar." Snowe all but spat the words. "Did Mother ever help you? Did she ever help us?"

When Lance shook his head, he went on, "Who was the only one who ever helped you?"

"You, Scott. But——" He drew a deep breath, as if screwing up his courage. "We're not going to kill them."

"We're not?"

"We're going to let them go."

Snowe narrowed his eyes. "And why would we do that? Don't be such a pussy, Lance. Jesus, you disgust me."

"Don't let him talk to you that way!" M.C. cried. "You're not stupid! Not worthless! I loved you."

"It's over, Scott. I'm going to free them." He started toward M.C. "You can run if you wa——"

Snowe pulled Kitt's gun from the waistband of his pants, aimed and shot Lance in the back.

His brother stopped dead and looked back at his brother. "Scott?" he said. "Sco——"

Then he went down.

Snowe stared at him a moment, blinking against tears. "You always needed my direction and I respected that. I took care of you. But since you don't need me anymore… Too bad, little bro."

They were next. Kitt looked at M.C. She was struggling against the duct tape. Joe stirred and moaned, and even as her heart leaped with joy that he was alive, she acknowledged the emotion would be short-lived.

Her only hope was that the sheriff's deputy would swing by, realize something was amiss and investigate.

Every moment counted. If she could keep him talking, buy them some time, maybe they would live through this.

It was a slim chance, but it was the only one they had.

"You seem pretty cocky for someone who's going to be arrested for serial murder."

He grinned. "Now you're talking crazy. Nobody besides the people in this room know I had anything to do with this. Lance was neck-deep in it, but not me."

"The Smith & Wesson," she reminded him. "Traced to you. Traced here—"

He cut her off with a laugh. "Traced to Lance. I was sent to a home for kids. I was fourteen, too old to be adopted. As soon as I was old enough, me and a buddy were emancipated. He came to an untimely end, very sad. I took his identity. It was no big deal. A couple of kids with no family to speak of."

"I was wondering how—" she struggled to focus her scrambled thoughts "—how your family history had flown under the RPD...radar. No way they would have hired you if...known your old man was doing life for—"

"Whacking my mother. Exactly."

"So what's your plan?" M.C. asked.

"You all die. Lance takes the rap. It's all sown up nice and neat."

"What ab't th'photos?" Kitt slurred the words and she wondered how much blood she had lost. How long before she lost consciousness.

"What about them?" he asked.

M.C. jumped in. "They have your signature all over them."

"They go with me, of course. I couldn't leave them, they're my masterpieces."

Visual trophies.

"The lock of hair," Kitt asked, "was it from one of the angels?"

Snowe didn't respond and she realized she hadn't actually voiced the thought.

"Disobeying the chief's direct order," Snowe was saying, as if from a great distance. "Now you're all going to die. What were you thinking?"

"I know why Lance did it," M.C. said. "Why he resurrected the SAK."

"That so, genius?"

"To get away from you. He wanted to get caught. Because you're as bad as your father. No, you're worse. Mean. A bully and a brute."

He swung toward her, trembling. "You don't know dick."

"You grew up to be just like him. How does it feel to—"

"I'm not like him," he said, leveling his gun at her. "Time to shut up, Detective Rigg—"

The sound of a gun discharging drowned out his words. Not Snowe's gun. Lance's. He had dragged himself to his knees and shot his brother. The bullet tore into Snowe's chest; he brought his hand to the wound, face blank with shock. He made a move, as if to try to aim; Lance squeezed off another shot. It hit Snowe lower this time, his abdomen. His body jerked and he sank to his knees.

Kitt tried to call out, to beg Lance to free M.C. With horror, she saw him swing toward Joe. He was sobbing. Stumbling. *He meant to kill them.*

She closed her eyes, drifting, flying. She heard voices, an explosion, a scream...

And then nothing at all.

74

Thursday, March 23, 2006
10:50 a.m.

"Hey, partner," M.C. called softly, tapping on the door to Kitt's hospital room. "Can I come in?"

Kitt looked up and smiled. She had awakened in a hospital bed, disoriented and hooked up to all sorts of bells and whistles.

And confused. How had she gone from the Dekalb safe room to OSF St. Anthony Medical Center in Rockford?

Turns out, Lance had freed M.C., then turned the Smith & Wesson on himself. A single shot to the head.

She waved the other woman in. "Please."

"You look good," M.C. said. "Considering."

"Considering" was right. After awakening, she'd learned that due to blood loss, she'd fallen unconscious. Luckily, M.C.'s 911 call had yielded a near immediate ambulance. The EMTs had done their thing, then the doctors. One surgery and a boatload of meds later, there she was.

"What's the latest?" she asked.

M.C. pulled a chair over to the bed and sat. "Sal's ass is so chapped at you. Deep shit, Detective."

"I figured the worst. He hasn't been in."

M.C. grinned. "Actually, you're going to be okay. He's using a medicated ointment that consists mostly of self-aggrandizement and credit-hogging. I expect you'll get a slap on the wrists for disobeying a direct order. More for show than anything else. If not for you, Snowe might have gotten away with it."

"Sal can hog all the credit he wants. I'm just glad that monster won't be hurting any more children."

M.C.'s smile slipped slightly. Kitt wondered if she was thinking of Lance.

M.C. glanced away, then back at Kitt. "Thanks, by the way. I'm very happy to be alive."

"You're welcome, by the way."

"Brought you something."

She handed her a bag from Logli's grocery. Kitt opened it and peered inside. "Snack crackers?"

"And a Diet Coke. Didn't know which kind you liked best, so I bought several."

"Thanks. But I thought I wasn't supposed to be eating this junk?"

"I'm making an exception. Since you got shot."

"Saving your ass."

"Exactly."

They fell silent a moment. M.C. broke the silence first. "Have you spoken to Joe?"

Kitt shook her head. "I got a report from a nurse. He was treated for lacerations and a broken nose, then released."

And he hadn't been by.

It hurt so bad she could hardly breathe.

M.C. squeezed her hand. "I'm sorry."

"I suspected him of murdering children, M.C. How could I have? And how could he ever forgive me?"

"It could be worse. My boyfriend was a serial killer. Actually, I'm thinking of selling my story to the tabloids."

M.C. delivered the comment dryly. Like a big, self-deprecating yuk. Kitt smiled. "I'm sorry."

M.C. shrugged. "I'm over it. Mama's not."

"How'd she find out?"

"One of the Suck-ups. She's starting to think my being a lesbian would be better."

Kitt fought a laugh. "You've still got me."

"You think you can work with a too-ambitious, humorless hard-ass?"

"Sure. If you can trust an over-the-hill screwup to watch your back?"

"I'm willing to give it a try."

"So get out of here," Kitt murmured, leaning her head against the pillow, suddenly tired. "Someone's got to hold up this partnership until the twelve-year-old who's masquerading as my doctor lets me out of here."

M.C. laughed and popped to her feet. "Already carrying you, Lundgren. Jeez."

As she exited the room, a nurse entered carrying a huge spray of flowers. They could be from anyone. The department. Her VCB colleagues. M.C.

She prayed they were from Joe.

With a cheery smile, the nurse set them by the bed. Kitt waited until the woman had exited the room, then reached for the card. But instead of opening it, she held it gingerly in her hands. Heart pounding.

Not yet, she thought. If they weren't from Joe, she didn't want to know. She had lots of time for that. Lots of time.